CORRUPTED HEART

VENOMOUS GODS
BOOK FOUR

JAGGER COLE

PLAYLIST

Shadow - Livingston
THE DEATH OF PEACE OF MIND - Bad Omens
Starburster - Fontaines D.C.
Ballerina - Yehezkel Raz
Trouble - CRMNL
Crawling - Linkin Park
Take Me to Church - Hozier
The Wolf - Manchester Orchestra
Idea 22 - Gibran Alcocer, Anya Nami
X - Welshly Arms
Pain - The War On Drugs
Good Girls - CHVRCHES
Bad Habits - Ed Sheeran, Bring Me The Horizon
i like the way you kiss me - Artemas
Love and War - Fleurie
Way down We Go - KALEO
How Not To Drown - CHVRCHES, Robert Smith
It's a Man's World - James Brown
Beautiful Things - Benson Boone
OWN MY MIND - Måneskin

Devil Side - Foxes
Drown - Bring Me The Horizon
All I Want - Dawn Golden
Some Type Of Skin - AURORA

Listen to the playlist on Spotify!

TRIGGER WARNING

Dear Reader,

This book contains darker themes and graphic depictions of past trauma, trafficking, SA, and CSA. The plot *heavily* revolves around primal/CNC play, impact play, and very rough adult acts of a dubious nature.

Fasten your seatbelts and make sure your tray tables are in the upright position.

While these scenes were written to create a more vivid, in-depth story, they may be triggering to some readers. *Please* know your own triggers, and read with that in mind.

Thanks for reading,

Jagger

1

BIANCA

A CHILLING SENSATION drags up my spine, razor-sharp as the tip of a knife. I can feel my throat constrict, as if an invisible, malicious hand is squeezing. The fine hairs on the back of my neck prickle as my eyes widen.

He's getting closer.

His hand is on the bedroom door now. The knob twists silently, shadows lengthening over the bed like funeral shrouds as he billows into the room, a cloud of black smoke—

"What the *fuck* are you reading?"

It takes everything I have to stifle the scream that rises in my throat. My heart literally stops for a millisecond and pure adrenaline explodes through my system as I whip around, almost dropping my tablet on the dressing room floor in the process.

Alicia's staring down the bridge of her nose at me, wearing her trademark haughty, smug look that would give Regina

George a run for her money. As usual, her number two, Irena, stands next to her and *just* a few deferential inches behind her.

Can't upstage the queen herself, after all.

I glance around the backstage dressing room, realizing I'm the last one here aside from Alicia and Irena. The wall clock, under which Madame Kuzmina has pinned a sign that reads "time is everything", tells me rehearsal ended forty minutes ago. But I left off on a cliffhanger earlier, and I *had* to read the next chapter as soon as rehearsal ended. So I stayed.

"Seriously," Alicia cocks a well-manicured brow, tucking a lock of blonde back into place. "What the fuck is that?"

I can feel my face blush darkly. "Nothing. It's just—"

Before I can finish my sentence, she snatches the tablet out of my hand. Irena crowds closer to her, their eyes fixated on the e-book open on the screen. Immediately, they both make grossed-out faces and then start to laugh.

"Bitch, you *cannot* be serious with this."

My mouth tightens slightly. "It's just this book—"

"About a girl getting hacked to death in her own bed by a psycho?" Alicia raises her eyes from the screen to my face. "Bianca, hon, this is why you're single. FYI. This horror shit is creepy as fuck, and honestly, it's super weird that you read it."

I frown as I snatch the tablet back. "It's not horror. It's true crime."

Alicia and Irena share a look.

"Like, it's not fiction," I try to explain. "It's about a real murder, a girl named Rachel Dawson—"

"Yeah, so, *anyway*..." Alicia says quickly, cutting me off. She arches her brow again as she cocks a hip. "Whatcha doing right now?"

I hate the spark that ignites inside me. I hate that I'm *excited* that it really sounds like she's about to ask me to hang out.

All of us who dance with the Zakharova Ballet are the best of the best. I mean I probably learned first position before I could even walk. I've poured *hundreds of thousands* of hours into honing my craft, and given up so much to be here.

I'm *good*. I'm really good. The Zakharova, under the frosty and merciless direction of Madame Kuzmina, is one of the top ballet companies in the world.

But Alicia Houghton, disproving everything you want to believe about karma, is the best of us. Yes, she's kind of a bitch. She can be mean, catty, and haughty, and is *acutely* aware of her position as the most likely to be the next one promoted to soloist.

Because of that, she's also the reigning queen bee of the corps de ballet, surrounded by her little posse of suck-ups like Irena.

The thing is, Alicia's *just* snooty enough to be annoying. But she's not cruel enough to make you want to avoid her completely. The fact that she's supremely talented, beautiful, and cool makes it even harder to ignore her.

You kinda want to hate her. You also kinda want to *be* her. Which is why despite part of me wanting to have nothing to do with Alicia, the other part of me perks right up when she asks what I'm doing.

That's the allure of cool.

None of us is immune to it.

"Nothing?" I shrug.

It's not a lie, either. I had plans to do something with Milena and Naomi after rehearsal. But Naomi got called in last minute to cover at the bar she works at, and Milena had a family thing she couldn't miss.

…And by "family thing", I assume she means "mafia thing". That kinda goes without saying when your father is Marko Kalishnik, head of the Kalishnik Bratva.

I mean, I get it. *My* dad, Vito, is the don of the Barone family, after all.

But as good as Milena, Naomi, and I are, we're not Alicia-level good. We're also not in her band of mean-girl suck-ups. Actually, if you want to cast this whole thing as a high school movie, my two friends and I would probably be the freaks in black who sit at the weird-kid table in the lunchroom and don't get invited to parties.

"Well, you're doing something now," Alicia grins at me. "C'mon."

She turns on her heel, along with Irena, and starts to waltz out of the dressing room. Like that's the end of the conversation.

"Um, what?"

Alicia sighs heavily, stopping and turning to give me a look that says I've just committed the ultimate social faux pas.

"Are you in or out, Bianca?"

I'm smart enough to know that asking "for what" pretty much guarantees this conversation is over and that I will *not* be going with Queen Alicia on whatever her adventure is. So I shrug as casually as I can and slip my tablet into my bag.

"Oh, in. Totally in."

She grins. "Good. C'mon."

I glance down at my "outfit" nervously before raising my eyes to her. Alicia looks great, of course. She's already showered, her hair is done immaculately. Her makeup is perfect, and her outfit is cute. Irena's the same.

I, on the other hand, am in B-team leggings and a hoodie, with my long hair up in its usual bun, with zero makeup. I also didn't shower after rehearsal, because I don't shower here.

I can't.

"I… Should I go home and change—"

"You're fine. C'mon."

I know Milena would roll her eyes hard enough to sprain something if she saw how quickly I jump to my feet. But she's not here, and you know what, give me a freaking break. I mean I love the friends I have. But it's not like you make a lot of them when you're a mafia don's daughter with three *extremely* overprotective older brothers.

I leave my dance bag in my locker and quickly follow the two of them out of the dressing room. We exit out the back of the Mercury Opera House, which houses the Zakharova Ballet, and then climb into Alicia's Tesla. I manage to hold my tongue for all of three minutes more before I clear my throat.

"So, where…"

Irena grins as she lifts her eyes to the rearview mirror, looking at me in the back seat. "An adventure."

My brows knit as I chew on my lower lip. I glance out the window as Manhattan passes by us. Then I open my damned mouth again. "What, uh... What kind of adventure?"

"The *mayhem* kind," Irena grins.

I'm pretty sure she didn't say that to *calm* my nerves. In which case, bravo. Anxiety gnaws at my stomach as I glance out the window again. Irena is Russian Bratva-adjacent. Her cousin, Grisha Lenkov, besides being a major creep, is an *avtoritet* for the Chernoff Bratva.

He's also Alicia's on-again/off-again boyfriend.

Remind me why I got into this car?

Alicia drives us over the Williamsburg Bridge, then deeper into Brooklyn, until the hipster bars and ironic coffee shops have given way to a truly industrial area. Alicia pulls into a dark parking lot next to a closed-down diner and turns off the car.

I now *fully* regret agreeing to this.

"Um..."

"Don't be such a scaredy cat. It's fine," Alicia sighs as she steps out. Irena shoots me a mean-looking grin before she gets out, too. I slowly follow suit as Alicia hefts a duffle bag out of the trunk.

"Alicia."

She turns to me. "Yes?"

"What are we doing?"

She sucks on her teeth, grinning a little. "Just something for Grisha."

My stomach knots as my eyes drop to the duffel bag.

"Don't..." Her grin fades as she shakes her head. "Don't ask. Seriously. But it's going to be fine. He wouldn't have asked me to do this for him if it was dangerous."

Bullshit.

I've met Grisha once or twice before when he's come to pick Alicia up after rehearsal. Calling him a "creep" is like calling Jeffery Dahmer "a guy with strange eating habits". He's a dick to Alicia, rude to pretty much everyone he sees, and almost definitely arrives early to pick her up just so he can walk into the dressing room while everyone else is still changing.

Alicia closes the trunk and hefts the duffel bag again. "C'mon, let's go."

She starts to walk across the empty parking lot and around the side of the shuttered diner. Irena is right behind her, with me hanging further back.

"Okay, seriously..." I look around nervously as we come around to the back of the diner: an alley with brick walls, a rusted-out dumpster, and only one way in...or out. "Alicia, *what* are we—"

"So, Grisha sends his bitches to do his deliveries for him now?"

My heart lurches into my throat. Whirling, my face goes white when I see the two men now standing behind us at the entrance to the alley. They're both built, with lots of visible tattoos on their necks and hands, and dressed in dark suits with no ties.

7

One of them is a bit taller than the other and seems to be the one in charge. He elbows the second guy and then nods his chin at us with a grin.

"So, you girls come with the coke or what?"

What the fuck.

My eyes rip sideways to stare at the bag in Alicia's hand.

Coke? As in *cocaine*?!

Suddenly, I realize I *vastly* underestimated the bad juju vibes I got earlier when Irena said we were doing "mayhem" tonight.

This isn't an adventure.

We're doing a fucking drug deal for Alicia's scumbag boyfriend.

For a second, I consider just bolting from this scene and not looking back. But even though I've never been at a drug deal before, I do know this world—at least, well enough to realize that running right now would be a very, very bad idea.

Alicia shrugs nonchalantly. "Yep. It's all here. Seven kilos."

Holy shit.

I don't know much about drugs. But I do know seven freaking kilos is a *ton* of cocaine.

"Grisha said you'd have the money—"

"You misunderstand." The taller guy grins salaciously at us. "I didn't mean did the coke physically arrive with you. I meant do you girls *come with* the coke."

His grin widens, and suddenly, my blood turns to ice as he

and his buddy pull guns out of their jackets. Alicia's face turns white. Her lip trembles.

"I...Grisha said—"

"Grisha's a fucking idiot," the shorter of the two guys chuckles. "Put the bag on the ground, sweetheart. And then—all three of you on your fuckin' knees."

Bile rises up my throat as he grins at his friend.

"Looks like Grisha sent us a thank you present for taking the seven kilos off his hands." He turns back, his eyes landing on Alicia. "Dibs on the blonde."

The taller one smiles darkly at me. "Fine by me. I get hard for Italian bitches."

My gaze whips to Alicia and Irena, just as their horrified gazes turn to me, then to each other. The two men begin to approach us, when suddenly, Alicia winds back and hurls the duffle bag right at them.

"RUN!!" she screams.

For a horrible millisecond, I'm frozen where I am, unable to do anything but watch Irina and Alicia shove past the men and go bolting out of the alley. But then, I lurch into action. I whirl, sprinting forward to the mouth of the alley.

"Fucking *bitch*."

My whole world turns to fear and ice as a strong arm wraps around my middle and yanks me back, hard. I scream as I'm thrown roughly to the ground, landing with a wince as gravel and grime bite into my palms and knees.

A weight slams into me, shoving me flat onto the ground as a gun cocks loudly.

"Please!"

The men chuckle. I choke in pain as my knee is torn up even more by the gravel, with the weight of one of the men on my back pinning me down.

"Since you asked so nicely, bitch," one of them snickers. I hear the sound of a belt buckle opening. "You get *both* of us."

Tires squeal on pavement, and my heart drops.

"Looks like your little friends left you, baby," one of them growls darkly. "Guess it's just you and us now."

"Remind me to thank Grisha next time I see him," the other guy chuckles as he starts to kneel down by my head.

Oh my God. Oh my God. Oh my God...

"Please—" I choke. *"Please don't..."*

"Shut the fuck up and open your fucking—"

His words abruptly stop with a sickening, gurgling sound. Wetness splashes the asphalt next to me before the man kneeling in front of me is suddenly yanked away sideways. The weight comes off my back, and I roll away and scramble to my feet.

To *freeze* in horror.

One of the men lies dead in a huge puddle of blood, his neck slit wide open. The other is a few feet up in the air, his eyes staring and terrified, pinned to the wall at his back with a hand wrapped around his neck.

A huge hand, at the end of a huge arm, attached to a *huge* beast of a man.

The guy squirming against the wall tries to raise his gun. Instantly, the huge man pinning him to the wall slashes with a blade. My would-be attacker screams, blood splattering the wall as he drops the gun and his arm goes limp. Deftly, the huge man slashes again.

My eyes go wide and my whole world turns to ice as the giant's blade rips open the other guy's throat. Blood gushes out like a tsunami as the huge hand lets go, letting the second attacker drop to the ground.

Wordlessly, his back to me, the huge, hulking shape dressed in black with a hood up over his head walks over to the duffel bag. He turns it upside down, dumping seven bricks of white powder onto the ground. I'm still frozen and unable to form words or complete thoughts as I watch him slash each plastic-wrapped brick open and dump the contents down a sewer drain.

Slowly, he stands, flexing his shoulders and straightening up tall.

And taller.

And *taller*.

My feet are rooted to the ground as the man slowly cocks his head. He twists around, and suddenly, my hand flies to my mouth.

He's not just huger than huge.

He's *wearing a mask*.

All black, with two glowing white neon X's for eyes, and a wide, demonic, smile, also etched in glowing white neon.

Holy fucking shit.

He turns to face me fully, his head cocking slightly to the side, as if he's studying me wordlessly.

He's still holding a knife in his hand.

It's still dripping blood.

This is it. This is how I go, like one of the unsolved mysteries in my true crime books. Like Rachel Dawson. Another Jane Doe that will wash up a week from now on Brighton Beach without dental records or fingerprints.

He takes a step toward me. My pulse whines like a siren in my ears. My body goes both icy cold and explosively hot in the same instant as he continues to move toward me. My mouth opens and closes. My eyes bulge as the leering, neon mask of pure malice stalks closer and closer.

He doesn't slow. He doesn't stop. And when he's inches away from me, I gasp sharply as his black-gloved hand jerks up and wraps like iron around my throat. I stare up—and I do mean *up*, he's like a foot and a half taller than me—into the neon mania of that mask, with the throbbing pulse of darkness behind it burning into my soul.

"Phone."

The word rasps like metal scraping against metal as it tumbles from his mouth. His voice is deep as thunder, and I can smell a slightly spicy, clean scent on him.

"Wh-what?"

"Your phone," he rasps again, a little more edge in his voice this time. *"Give it to me."*

I nod quickly, shaking all over as I jam my hand into my hoodie pocket and yank out my phone.

"Take it!"

I shudder when his other hand brushes mine when he tears it out of my grip. His head doesn't move, those neon X's just burning right into my eyes as he looms over me.

"Unlock code."

I shiver.

"Code," he snarls again. *"Now."*

Somehow, I manage to remember my numbers, watching as he thumbs them into the phone, opening it. His neon eyes stay locked on me, but I'm sure his real ones—that is, if he's not actually some sort of demon from Hell—are scanning my phone for God-knows-what as he taps away on it.

"I—I have money!" I blurt. "Like, my family does! Please! You can ask for whatever you want—"

"I'm not robbing you."

He suddenly thumbs the phone screen back to black and shoves it back into the pocket of my hoodie. His hand lingers there, and I tremble when I feel the back of it brush against my stomach though the fabric. He does it once more before drawing his hand out of the front pocket. He presses a finger lightly to my sternum, and my breath halts as he slowly drags it up—between my breasts and then higher before he wraps that hand around my throat.

His head tilts slightly to the side, and I can *feel* the psychotic wrath as whatever eyes lurk behind those neon X's eviscerate my soul.

"What did you see here tonight?"

Even though I'm terrified. Even though I'm shaking. Even though my brain is almost numb trying to process this...

I'm not an idiot.

"*Nothing!*" I blurt. "I didn't see anything."

"What happened to those men?"

"Nothing!"

He stays rigid like that, his head still tilted at a slightly deranged angle, saying nothing. Finally, his hand drops from my neck, but not quickly. It's more like a slow, almost sensual stroke of his gloved fingers over my soft skin and throbbing pulse as he releases me.

He steps back from me and his voice rumbles out again, like a boulder grinding a smaller rock to sand.

"Remember what you saw here tonight."

"*I didn't see anything,*" I whisper, shivering.

He's motionless in the gloom of the alley.

"I'll be watching you, *prinkípissa.*"

He steps backward into the shadows, sinking into them like black ink swallowing a white page.

Then he's gone.

2

BIANCA

HANDS REACH for me out of the darkness. Footsteps pound behind—chasing, hunting, drawing closer. I can hear the rasp of his breath and the dark, cold chuckle signaling he already knows the outcome of this.

That I can run, but I can't hide.

Not from him. Not from the nightmare I crave.

The promise of darkness and the fulfilment of sinister, deviant desires. Of the bite of rope and the gag of rubber. Of being used by him in whatever way he wants, with or without my consent…

The promise of utter submission. Of pain.

He draws closer and closer, his footsteps right behind me. His fingertips brush my skin before they suddenly catch and tangle in my hair. They yank. They grasp. I crash to the ground where he roughly pins my hands above my head and growls as he takes his pleasure from me as I writhe and scream—

I wake with a start, a real-world gasp lodged in my throat as I sit bolt upright.

My pulse hammers in my ears. Sweat clings to my skin. I force myself to exhale as I slowly rub my face and push a hand through my long hair.

The dream isn't new. It's not even infrequent.

It happens all the time, as if I need to be reminded while I'm safe in my bed that I'm never safe from the fucked-up darkness that lives in my head. The kinks and desires you can't tell anyone about...as if I even *have* people to tell my kinks to.

And even if I did, as if I ever would.

Fever dreams like these happen all the time. But there was a small difference in the one I just woke up from.

Usually he's faceless, the man who chases me. Who catches me. Who pins me down and has me waking up sweaty, with a racing heart and slick, quivering thighs. I suppose the one last night was technically faceless, too. Except it was a faceless pursuer I know.

One I've met in the real world.

One with a mask.

Just now, in my twisted, fucked-up dreams, I was chased by the huge man in the neon mask. The very same one who melted out of the shadows and killed two men right in front of me in *reality* last night.

I shiver as the vivid red blood on black tarmac and the horrifying gurgling scream echo in my head.

I don't feel bad about what happened to them. Not after what they were clearly about to do to me. But even so, I flinch as I replay the sickening sound of the man's knife slicing their throats open.

My eyes squeeze shut. Even being part of the world I live in, I've never seen death *happen* like that before. I've never watched someone die. And even though I did, that's not what I'm fixating about where last night is concerned.

I'm not thinking about the fact that Alicia dragged me to a massive drug deal. Or that two men tried to attack me last night.

I'm thinking of *him*.

The beast of a man with the gravel voice, the iron touch, and the absence of eyes.

The one who saved me and then melted right back into the darkness, like an apparition or a vengeful spirit.

Exhaling, I flop back across my bed and look up at the ceiling of the room I grew up in. I chew on my lip as my eyes slowly travel the walls of the room, taking in the posters, the achievements, the memories.

It's funny how quickly "normal" feels like kid stuff.

For the last two years, I've had my own modest apartment on the Upper East Side. Money isn't an issue, not when you're from my family. But when I finally told my dad it was time for me to move out, I didn't want to be just another mafia princess in a glass penthouse that Daddy paid for. I mean, yeah, he covers my rent—it's not like ballet dancers earn much. And it's also not like Vito Barone's bank account would notice it even if I *did* live in some palatial penthouse or townhouse.

Still, I wanted to fit in a bit more with the majority of the girls I dance with. So, where I live is just a regular, average apartment. Okay, it's got state-of-the-art security, and a doorman and guards who are on the Barone payroll, because my brothers are all psychotically overprotective of their "baby" sister, even though I'm twenty-one.

But that's not where I've woken up this morning.

After what happened last night in Brooklyn, I came here, to my dad's townhouse in Little Italy. There were pros and cons to showing up at Dad's house in an Uber at midnight, covered in bloody scrapes and dirt, white-faced and freaking the hell out, but honestly, I was too scared to go home after what happened. Scared enough that I was willing to chance him still being up and having to explain the state of myself to him.

Mercifully, though, the house was asleep. And Roberto, the guard on duty at the front door last night, was distracted enough by the football scores on his phone that he seemed to buy my explanation that I'd tripped while out on a walk, and that I was fine.

Part of me wants to stay right here in my childhood bedroom and hide from the world all day. But then another, more adult instinct takes control of mine, and it's one I can't ignore.

The need for *coffee*.

I tie my hair up in it's typical dancer's bun, pull on a hoodie, and pad barefoot downstairs to the huge galley kitchen dad had remodeled a few years ago when he got really into cooking old-school Italian food.

Note I say *into*, not "good at". But hey, it makes him happy.

I can hear his voice as I walk down the hall from the back staircase. As I get closer, I realize this is more of a home-coming than I was expecting.

"Well, well, look what the cat dragged in."

Carmy, the middle of my three older brothers, grins as I shuffle into the kitchen and head directly to the coffee pot. He's sitting at the breakfast table with my youngest older brother, Nico, along with our dad.

"You know, after you move out, especially when you insisted on it, it's usually a bad look to move back in."

I wait until the two gulps of black coffee have worked their magic before I turn to wrinkle my nose and give Nico a stink eye.

"I'm allowed to *visit*, dickhead."

He grins. Dad gives him a lighthearted cuff upside the head. "She's welcome back here anytime. You got that, Bumblebee? *Any* time."

I grin at my favorite nickname of his for me.

"Why thank you, Father."

Technically, Vito isn't my father. At least not biologically. Nor is he Dante's—my oldest brother, who's currently leaning against the kitchen counter with a cup of coffee. I don't really have any memories of our real dad, because I was only two when he and Mom died. But he was a close friend of Vito's—he was his personal tailor, actually. And Dante grew up playing with Carmy and Nico as if they were cousins, or even brothers. Claudia, our older sister, did as well.

So when Mom and Dad passed, Vito immediately took us in as his own and raised us as three other kids in the Barone family.

Dante frowns as his gaze lands on the Band-Aids on both my knees, not to mention the bruises on other parts of my legs. The hoodie's covering the bruises on my arms from last night. But it's not like I knew I was crashing at my dad's house when I left for work yesterday morning, and all I had here were sleep shorts.

"What the hell?" he growls with a mix of accusation and concern. That's pretty much Dante in a nutshell. A little bossy, a little grumpy, and a *lot* overprotective. At least he's mellowed a bit these days since marrying Tempest.

I shrug nonchalantly, trying not to tense when everyone else in the kitchen frowns and studies my bruises.

"Just work. A lift went sideways and I got banged up. It's no big deal."

Actually, it might be. I had a ton of missed calls and texts from Alicia when I got in last night. I didn't feel like talking about what had happened—I'm not sure I *could have* talked about it last night, since I was shaking so hard. But after I cleaned up, I did send her a text that I was home and okay after running away from the two guys who attacked us.

I'll deal with the fact that she and Irena *left me there* later.

That, and the last text she sent me last night that I never replied to:

ALICIA

What about the duffle bag

I have no idea how much money seven bricks of cocaine is worth. But I feel like it might be *a lot*. That's between Alicia and Grisha, though.

"What are you all doing here?"

Carmy shrugs. "I was nearby this morning."

I roll my eyes. "Did you catch her name at any point?"

"Har, har, har," he drawls. "I was nearby on *business*, brat. Besides," he grins. "You know I never actually sleep over."

"Such a gentleman."

Carmy snickers as he turns to Dad. "Back me up here, Pop."

Vito lifts his shoulders. "I mean, sometimes, the ladies… They want you to stay over, you know? A little cuddling, a little pillow talk…"

I make a face and cover my ears. "Oh my God, I am *not* listening to this."

Nico laughs and nods his chin at Dante. "I was with this guy. He wanted to show dad the new online portal for Venom."

Dante is the owner and operator of Club Venom, an ultra-exclusive, members-only club that caters mostly to New York's most dangerous and elite…and, frankly, most deviant. On the surface, it's an ultra-cool club decorated somewhere between the glamor of the roaring twenties and the sultri-ness of *Eyes Wide Shut*.

It also happens to be a place where its members can act out different, usually fairly aggressive kinks. Names are discour-aged, everyone wears these sort of Venetian carnival masks, and members sport different colored wristbands advertising what they're into.

Or...so I've been told. *Obviously*, I've never been. Not because I don't want to go, but because Dante is a tyrant and the world's most over-protective older brother in the universe who still treats me like I'm seven. Which means I'm forbidden from entering Club Venom.

I've heard of this online portal thing before, though. Dante and Tempest had this idea a few months ago to make some kinks available to...*off-site* participation.

My skin tingles as I rake my teeth over my bottom lip.

By "some kinks" I mean "my kink". One of them, anyway. The biggest one.

Primal play.

Being chased and caught. Being forced down and taken, roughly, with or without consent.

There might be more than a few things wrong with me, but I digress.

"Getting your rocks off via the internet," Vito sighs, shaking his head ruefully. "Hell of a time we live in."

Nico shakes his head. "Dad apparently has never heard of Tinder."

"Wanna bet?"

Even my brothers blanch this time, gagging as they laugh. Vito and his wife, Giada Barone, were never exactly a normal couple. They were either at each other's throats, or in bed with each other—or, more frequently, in *other* people's beds. I honestly don't need to know the specifics of their relationship at all.

But given all that, Giada was pretty frequently out of the picture, sometimes for months on end. When I say Vito raised Claudia, Dante, and I alongside his sons, I really do mean that *Vito* did. I loved Giada, and of course I mourned when she died six years ago. But she and I were not nearly as close as I am with my dad.

Vito laughs, waving us all off before patting his chest. "Hey, I'm old, not dead. And if there's still lead in the pencil—"

"Jesus *Christ*, Pop," Nico makes a gagging face. "Let's never mention the fucking lead in your pencil ever again, yeah?"

"Amen to that, *fuck*," Carmy mutters. He runs his hand over the scruff on his jaw before he turns to our dad again. "By the way, I got the updated financials from Ares' team last night for the West Side development."

Vito nods slowly. "We still good there?"

"Golden. Projections changed a little, but not significantly. If you're still sure you want to sell, Ares is still in for the agreed-upon amount."

The development they're talking about is an old, unused, fifteen-story building on the West Side of Manhattan, projecting over the Hudson River. Dad picked it up for a bargain over ten years ago, though he never developed it. But since then, the value has skyrocketed. And when Vito made it known he'd be entertaining offers, they poured in.

For the last few months, there's been a crazy bidding war between the Drakos family, who are Greek mafia, and Davit Kirakosian, the head of an Albanian crime family. But recently, the Drakos family aggressively upped their offer, ending the Albanian's interest.

The Drakos' plans for the property apparently include a luxury boutique hotel, high-end condos, retail, and a restaurant space. So yeah, long term, yeah, the property is going to be worth a fuck of a lot more than it is now. But that's after the upfront costs, the years it's going to take to build, and all those expenses. Not to mention the headache of running the place once it's up. To Dad, taking a gigantic lump sum right now instead of dealing with all that b.s. looked like a better option. Plus, Ares is okay with letting the same local ironworkers union who *was* working on it continue to do so. Which makes dad look like a superhero.

It's a total win win. Which is surprising, given that our dad actually *hates*—

"That fuckin' family," Vito grumps. "I'm telling you, the second that check clears, that's the last time I wanna talk to or even *see* a single one of those fuckin' barbarians." He sighs. "Anyway, I gotta get my ass to the office."

"Same," Dante sighs. He turns to catch my eye. "You sticking around here for a while?"

"Eh, I should head home soon and get some stuff done before heading to the theater."

"You ready now? I can give you a ride if you want."

I grin. "That'd be perfect, thanks."

I say goodbye to my dad, Carmy and Nico, get my stuff, then follow Dante outside to his Range Rover. After I climb into the passenger seat, he frowns as he turns to me.

"What?"

"You wanna tell me why you slept over at Vito's last night?"

It's a weird quirk between us. I call him "Dad" because Vito is the only father I ever really knew. But Dante was fifteen when our parents died. He still loves Vito *like* a father. But he already knew another man way too well as "Dad" ever to call Vito that.

I get it.

I find myself shrinking a little from his question. Putting walls up, as if hiding guilt. Dante and I are close. But I don't think I'm ready to tell him what actually happened last night.

Once again, weirdly, my thoughts don't focus on the danger and the horror of last night. Instead, they settle on the face-less beast with the neon eyes and mouth. The enormous monster who killed two men right in front of me, put his hands around my throat, and sent a spark of something *vicious* deep into my core. A masked man who then proceeded to run rampant through my dreams last night—

"I had a hard day."

I mean, it's not a total lie.

"I guess I was just homesick?"

Dante's brows knit as he slowly nods. "And the bruises?"

"I already told you: happened at work."

"You don't usually get banged up like that, though."

I roll my eyes, huffing loudly to cover the panic in my chest. "Well, I didn't expect I'd be facing the Spanish Inquisition."

"*No one* expects the Spanish Inquisition," he grins, quoting the Monty Python movie we've both seen a gazillion times.

"Actually, common misconception. *Everyone* expected the

Spanish Inquisition. They used to send notices months in advance before someone was questioned."

"Amazing. You do read more than just those creepy true crime books."

"Ha ha ha," I toss back dryly.

Dante turns to grin at me before a shadow crosses his face. "Hey—speaking of which, do me a favor."

My brow arches. "Okayyy?"

"No going out late by yourself right now."

I frown. "I mean, I don't, but why?"

He shrugs. "Just lookin' out for you. I can put some of my guys or some of Vito's men on your detail—"

"Hard pass," I shake my head. "I don't need bodyguards, and I *definitely* don't need any big goons following me around. Not that Madame Kuzmina would even let them into the building during a rehearsal."

Dante's mouth turns up a little at the corners, but his demeanor stays scowly.

"What's going on, Dante?"

His mouth twists. "I just want you to be safe."

"Bullshit. You're keeping something from me." I frown. "You know if you hold out on me, I'll just get Tempest to flip."

My older brother exhales heavily. "*Fine.* There's just been some reports of…" He lifts a shoulder, his eyes firmly on the road. "There might be a new player in town."

I swallow uneasily. "Oh?"

Dante frowns. "Yeah. Someone took out two former enforcers for the Carveli family last night."

My pulse skips. I usually stay out of most things "family"—by which I mean "criminal". But it's been impossible to ignore the political drama affecting the Italian mafia world over the last few months, after the Carveli family was basically wiped off the board.

"Took out?"

"*Killed*, Bianca. Viciously, too. Possibly a drug deal gone bad. But no one in our world typically slashes throats."

My heart tightens for a second, my blood running cold as it all comes rushing back. The violence. The savagery. The raw power lurking behind the creepy neon smile and crossed-out eyes of that inky mask.

"You know what, it's probably just some old beef with the Carveli family. I'm done trying to freak my baby sister out."

I smile weakly. Dante grins at me.

"As if you're not immune to being freaked out by *anything* anymore, after all that creepy horror shit you read."

"True crime."

Dante rolls his eyes as he pulls up outside of my building. "Whatever. Just be safe out there, okay?"

Once again, my mind flashes back to the events of last night. The blood and the violence. The raw power in his huge arms and shoulders. The sinister blackness behind his mask, like ink pooling in water.

…The sinful dreams that chased me all night afterward.

"Bianca—"

"Relax, Dante," I grin as I open the Range Rover's door. "I'll keep my eyes peeled for murderous psychos."

His jaw tightens. "Bianca—"

"I'll be *fine*, Dante. Hi to Tempest for me. *Bye.*"

3

BIANCA

Tragically, no murderous psychos stop me between my apartment and practice.

The fact that I begin that thought with "tragically" is probably grounds for immediately checking myself into a psychiatric ward.

But I can't help it. Mostly because as terrified as I was last night when I looked up into that bleak neon mask of malice, it was a different kind of fear. True fear is awful. I've felt that before. It's what I felt when those two men slammed me to the ground with every indication that they were going to hurt me. It was a numb, eviscerating fear that felt like being stabbed.

But the "fear" I felt looking up into that neon mask was more like terror mixed with...excitement. It was the sort of anticipatory fear you get right before the rollercoaster gives in to gravity and gets yanked down that first drop. The fear that you get watching a great horror movie, waiting for the jump-scare.

That's the sort of fear my masked defender injected into my veins last night. Terror, yes. But a thrilling, exciting, electrifying sort of terror. A...can I say it...*good* kind of terror?

"Quick quick, Bianca!"

I jolt out of my thoughts when I hear the cold, staccato sharpness of the Russian-accented voice.

My creepy masked stranger might be a thrilling sort of fear. But the wrath of Madame Kuzmina when you're this close to being late for class or rehearsal is the true definition of scary.

"*Izvini*, Madame," I blurt.

Her mouth turns up just a hint at the corners. I've also known her long enough to spot the amusement in her eyes.

"Using one of the, what, five words you know in Russian will not make you any less late to being in position at that barre in three minutes, Miss Sartorre."

I flash a weak smile.

"But nice effort," she smirks. "Now get moving. Alicia was an hour early today."

I ignore the obvious barb. Madame Kuzmina is old-school Russian, and she's definitely not above pitting us dancers against each other in the name of "inspiring greatness".

"I'll be right there," I blurt with a smile.

I grab my stuff out of my locker, stripping down and pull on my tights and leotard in record time. I'm sitting on the dressing room bench putting on my ballet shoes when the door bursts open. I startle, ripping my gaze up just in time to see a terrified-looking Alicia come barreling inside.

"Oh my *God*, Bianca!" she gushes, her voice laden with surprisingly genuine concern. "I am *so* fucking sorry—"

"For leaving me?" I snap, bristling a little.

Alicia winces. She might be a bit of a bitch sometimes. But she's not a psychopath.

"Bianca, I'm seriously so fucking sorry. We both thought you were right behind us! And we were so scared when we got into the car, we didn't even notice you weren't in the back seat for like two blocks!"

I flinch as Alicia suddenly hugs me tightly. Okay, her tact could use some work. I'm not sure "we didn't realize we'd fucked you over because we didn't even know you weren't there" is much of an apology. But it's clear she feels terrible about it.

"It's okay. I got away," I mumble, a shiver ripping its way up my spine. "There was a police siren in the distance, and when the two of them bolted, I ran the other way."

She pulls back, her hands on my shoulders and a stricken look on her face. "I seriously can't say sorry enough times. I feel fucking awful!"

I incline my head as nonchalantly as I can. "Well, it's over. And I'm not dead."

She flashes another weak smile. "Thank God."

I nod, looking away as heated flashbacks of my vicious and X-rated dreams from last night tease through my thoughts.

Huge hands. Massive, broad shoulders. Blackness like the mouth of Hell calling to me from behind the leering neon.

"We should get out there."

I pull away from Alicia and turn to head out.

"Bianca…"

Midway through pinning my hair up into a bun, I turn. My brow furrows at the whiteness of her face and the sheer panic in her eyes.

"The duffle bag…"

I swallow, my bottom lip retreating between my teeth. I shake my head.

"I—I'm sorry, Alicia. They got it."

Her face turns ashen and green around the edges, as if she's going to throw up.

"Y-you don't have it?" she croaks in a squeaky, terrified tone.

I shake my head again.

"*Fuck me,*" she blurts, turning as her throat bobs. "Oh *fuck…*"

"TIME!"

The barked word from Comrade Kuzmina outside the dressing room makes us both jump.

"I—I'm really sorry, Alicia," I mumble again. "Look, I'm sure if you talked to Grisha—"

"I am *so fucked,*" she mutters coldly, brushing past me and yanking the door open. She pauses, twisting to catch my frightened eyes with her downright terrified ones. "And so are you."

For a professional dancer, classes and rehearsals take up your whole day. After morning class, the company today breaks into four subgroups, each working on a different piece for our upcoming performance in a few months. After lunch, I join Milena, Naomi, and Miguel, a super-talented new-to-the-company male dancer from Barcelona for an hour of strength and stretch, then it's right back into rehearsing the various pieces until all I know is the count of a metronome, the bark of Madame Kuzmina's voice, and the thud of my pulse as my muscles carry me through the steps.

Yes, it's grueling, and there's never a morning that you wake up and *something* isn't hurting, whether it's an old injury that you tweaked yesterday or something freshly wrenched.

But I fucking *love* this. Always have. And it takes so much concentration and focus that it even manages to take my mind off everything I've seen and every fear I've felt over the last twenty-four hours.

"Hungry?" Milena towels off her long blonde hair next to me, completely unfazed by her post-shower nudity. I mean, I wouldn't be either, if I looked like her. We all have to be in insane shape to be dancing at this level. But my Russian friend was also blessed with runway model legs, and what little body fat she has is in all the right places.

"Naomi and I were talking about going for a bite at that new dumpling place she was talking about."

My stomach gurgles enthusiastically. I'm actually starving.

"I mean, after you shower and change at home."

My two friends are part of the very small group who knows why I don't shower at the theater itself at the end of the day.

I'm torn. I do want to go out with them. But instantly, I start replaying the parts of last night I've forced out of my head. Not the exciting thrilling parts involving the masked giant who smelled like clean spice, whose big hand brushed my stomach through my hoodie and who dragged a thick finger up my sternum before his hand wrapped sensually around my throat.

No, what flickers into the forefront of my head is all the *other* parts of last night. The naked terror of those two men throwing me to the ground. Of them pinning me there and reaching for their belts…

I remember Dante's warning from earlier about not going out at night. It'd be nice to say I'm being ridiculous. But last night *did* happen.

"I can't," I sigh, lying to my friend. "I've got a family thing."

She shrugs. "No prob. I get it."

"Next time, for sure."

Next time, when the memories of last night aren't fresh scars on my psyche...

I change into leggings and a hoodie, hoist my enormous bag over my shoulder, and step out of the back of the theater to go find a taxi.

But the second the stage door shuts behind me, I'm gasping in cold fear as a brutal hand wraps around my wrist and yanks me into the darkness. The breath is slammed out of my body as I'm shoved hard into a brick wall.

"Where the fuck is my money, bitch?!"

The scream dies in my throat as my gaze drags up into the snarling face of Grisha Lenkov.

Alicia's boyfriend and Irina's cousin is a perpetually scowl-ing, built guy with blond hair and a sharp jaw. He'd almost be pretty in a weirdly masculine way if it wasn't for the pure malice always smoldering in his eyes, not to mention the general creepy vibe that emanates from him.

And tonight, it's a lot more than just creepy. Right now, his face is a mask of livid rage.

"*Grisha—*" I choke out.

I don't respect Grisha Lenkov. But I do fear him, despite my family being who they are. Grisha's a lieutenant with the Chernoff Bratva, known for their particularly brutal tactics and involvement in vile activities that most other criminal empires in this city won't touch.

I gasp as he grabs a handful of my hoodie in his fist and leers down into my face with a snarl. "My *money, shlyukha,*" he spits, with all the arrogance of a man who doesn't even care that he's just called Vito Barone's daughter a whore to her face. "Where the fuck is it?"

I whimper, shaking my head. "I—I don't have any money!"

"Then where the fuck is the coke?!" he snarls coldly.

I wither under his glare.

"I—Grisha…"

"You've got three seconds to make me happy, Bianca," he mutters. "Or else you can make me happy with your fucking mouth, on your knees."

I swallow back the bile that rises in my throat.

"Th-the guys…"

"Sp-sp-*spit it out*!" he snaps.

"They took it!" I lie. "Grisha, the men who met us tried to attack us—"

"And I should give a fuck *why?*"

I stare at him. "Alicia was there too, you know. They could have hurt—"

"All I'm hearing is a bunch of bullshit, when all I want to know is where the actual *fuck* my four hundred grand in coke went."

My heart drops through the floor.

What. The. *Fuck*.

Grisha immediately latches onto the horrified look on my face. His lips curl into a sneer as he slams me back against the brick wall.

"You heard me, cunt," he hisses. "Where the fuck is it?!"

"They took it!" I blurt. "They chased me away and took—"

"Bullshit."

"Grisha, I swear to God—"

My words falter. My whole body seizes up as Grisha suddenly grabs me between the legs. His hand cups my sex roughly through my leggings, almost making me vomit as my whole being curls in on itself in shame and terror.

"Grisha, please..."

"Oh, you'll say fucking please, bitch," he hisses darkly. "Because here's how this is going to go down. You either get me back that cocaine, or the money it's worth, *fast*, or I'll take it out of your ass with my dick."

36

Sick rises from my stomach as his hand rubs between my thighs, making me want to shatter into glass shards.

Suddenly, digging deep, I find the strength to fight him off. I grit my teeth, grabbing his wrist and shoving his hand away. In one motion, I manage to slip out from between him and the wall, quickly backing away from him.

"You will *never* fucking touch me like that again," I spit venomously. "When my father—"

"What? Hears what a little whore you are? Hears about you going on drug deals? What then, Bianca?"

I swallow. "When he hears about you putting your hands on me. He'll—"

"He won't do shit," Grisha snarls. "Meanwhile, *my* boss?" He grins. "Mr. Chernoff threw a motherfucker out of a thirty-story window last week just for beating him at poker. And your wop father knows it. He won't do shit to Chernoff, or me." His lips curl dangerously. "But I bet he'll do something when he hears about his little princess muling four hundred thousand in coke."

I stiffen as Grisha flips open a switchblade. His teeth flash maliciously in the darkness.

"Get me that fucking money, Bianca. I mean it."

"Hey!"

Tempest looks up at me in surprise from the kitchen island. She immediately closes the laptop in front of her and slips off her stool to walk over to me.

I make a face. "I should have called first. Sorry."

My sister-in-law grins as she hugs me and then shakes her head. "Dude, never. Our house is your house."

It's happened much less frequently since she and my brother got together. But I do on occasion spend the night here at their place after a long day of rehearsals instead of slogging all the way back to mine. It's a lot closer to the Mercury Opera House, and there's a spare guest room with its own bathroom here, too.

But I'm not stopping by tonight because I'm too worn out to schlep all the way uptown.

I'm stopping by because I'm *scared*.

I hate admitting it, but Grisha's just spooked the living shit out of me with his threats. Not to mention the nauseating way he just put his hands on me. I feel myself shudder again, trying to force away the memory of his hand rubbing me.

The worst part is, he's right. What am I going to do? Tell Vito?

Hi Dad, this guy was a disgusting creep to me after I went on a drug deal for him and lost four hundred thousand dollars' worth of cocaine.

Yeah, no.

I don't know what the hell I'm going to do about any of this. But I do know it's not going to involve telling Vito Barone.

Tempest shrugs. "Are you hungry? I was about to make dinner."

"Really?"

She smirks. "By 'make' I mean *order* dinner from someone who can cook way better than I can. You know how low that bar is."

I grin as my stomach rumbles again. "That sounds great, actually. Mind if I rinse off first?"

"Go ahead! Does sushi work? I'll put in the order."

"Perfect."

Tempest opens her phone and starts placing the delivery order. Meanwhile, I head to their guest room, close the door, and walk into the bathroom. I strip down as the tub fills with bubbles and hot water, then lower my aching body into it. I scrub myself quickly, flinching as I wash my face with a cloth. When I scrub between my legs, I grit my teeth, forcing away the memory of Grisha feeling me up.

After that, I step out and do my usual routine: towel folded under my knees as I kneel next to the tub, the water running as I brace myself and lean forward. I wet my hair, then sit upright again as I shampoo. Then it's back to leaning over to rinse. I repeat the whole thing for the conditioner before turning the water off and wrapping a towel around my hair before I stand up.

Someday, I'll be able to submerge my head in water again without having a total meltdown. But that day is not today.

I dress in the pajamas that I keep at their place, then head out to join Tempest for sushi and trashy reality TV. Dante's working late at Venom tonight, so after she hugs me good-night and disappears into their room, I camp out in the living room for a while, thoroughly creeping myself out reading about Rachel Dawson getting hacked to pieces in her own bed.

Because I'm a freak like that.

Eventually, though, my eyes start to tire. I put my tablet down and sink back into the couch. My eyes drift closed, and I start to replay it all again.

Last night, and *him*.

The massive wall of a man, dripping with power, pulsing with darkness and danger.

The pressure of his strong hand around my throat

The touch of his finger as it dragged up my sternum.

The scent of him.

His size.

And the glow of that creepy mask leering down into my soul.

Goddammit.

The longer I replay it all and think of him, the more turned on I start to get. Black visions and brutal fantasies fill my head. Fantasies I know I shouldn't have leave electrifying throbs sizzling through my core.

The desire to run, and to be chased. The need to be caught and pinned down against my will. To be *taken*, roughly.

What the fuck is wrong with you, Bianca? What sort of messed-up girl wants that? You need fucking help. You're broken.

Words from years ago feel like fresh slaps as they echo in my head, reminding me that what I desire—what I crave sometimes—doesn't "fit" with the world I live in.

That those thoughts don't belong in my head.

Shaking my head, I yawn as the fatigue of the day settles through my limbs.

I should sleep.

In the kitchen, I grab a glass of water to bring with me to bed. Slowly, my gaze wanders and then lands on the laptop sitting on the far end of the kitchen island.

Not Tempest's.

Dante's.

I'm hovering over it before I know what I'm doing. I lift it open, my pulse thudding as my eyes drop to the keyboard.

This is wrong, but I start typing anyway.

"Venom" doesn't work to unlock it. Neither does "Club Venom", "kink", "Kink" with a capital K, or either of our parent's names. I wince when I try "Claudia", Dante's and my older sister who died when she was a teenager.

Nope.

Then, it hits me like the most obvious neon sign in the world.

"Tempest".

Yep, that does it.

Top-notch security, bro.

Breaking into Dante's laptop is a horrible idea. It's not just morally wrong in terms of breaking *his* trust, either. Instantly, I realize I have free access to the members list and member profiles for all of Venom, which could earn some major ransom money in the hands of the wrong people.

But I'm not here to blackmail people or ruin any reputations.

I'm here because a man in a mask last night poured gasoline on the little wicked fire inside of me. Now, it's a raging inferno.

...And Dante's computer has the only water that will douse it.

Obviously, I've thought about acting out my fantasies before. I know now that it would have to be anonymously, or at the very least with a stranger I'll never see again.

People you know can't be trusted with something like this, as ironic as that sounds from a safety perspective. I made the mistake of finally blurting out my dark fantasies to Tim when we were dating.

What the fuck is wrong with you, Bianca? What sort of messed-up girl wants that?

You're broken.

That was the beginning of the end of Tim and me. And then...well, what was *truly* the end. After that, I realized you really *can't* tell some things to just anyone.

Club Venom would obviously be more than ideal for assuaging my curiosity. But there's the small problem that *my brother* runs the place, not to mention its security and an iron-clad vetting process.

You can't fake your way into Venom—trust me, I've tried. Yes, you wear masks. But the wristband each guest wears— the one signifying their kink and whether they're a sub or a Dom—is linked directly to that member. They can even be scanned by security to ID someone. And his entire security team obviously knows who I am.

Even *if* I somehow got around all that, I'd never be able to actually relax enough to explore my fantasy. I'd be too freaked out that I'd be recognized.

But that conversation this morning in Vito's kitchen has the gears whirling in my head.

The club itself is out. But not necessarily its new website portal.

Swallowing and intermittently glancing over my shoulder, I navigate through Dante's private files until I find the dashboard for Club Venom's new "off-site" connection portal, which links like-minded individuals who crave a specific sort of play that at times needs more space—and more realism—than Club Venom can offer.

Primal kink, specifically.

I'm not sure how I feel about the term "rape kink", even though that's basically what it is. The desire to be chased and caught. To be roughly manhandled, and "forced" into things. "Consensual non-consent" is the more polite way of putting it.

Things that Bianca Sartorre, good-girl ballet dancer and mafia princess, shouldn't even know about, let alone want" is yet another way of phrasing it.

But here we are.

My nerves jangling, I find the admin dashboard and navigate to the members list. Guilt and the realization that I'd be *mortified* if someone else was doing this and *I* was on the list suddenly grips me. I quickly resize the window so that I can't see the "names" column of the member list to make myself feel a little better. Then I scroll to the bottom where there's a button labeled "add/import new member."

Heat blooms in my core. My pulse throbs heavily in my veins as I click the button. I'm taken to another screen and instantly my adrenaline jumps.

There are fields to input basic data: name, contact number, email, that sort of thing. Very quickly, my eyes land on the last question at the bottom of the form:

"Individual is existing Club Venom member". Next to it, there's just a simple yes or no toggle.

This is a terrible idea. You shouldn't be doing this.

I do it anyway.

Name: Rachel Dawson.

What? The book about her murder is riveting.

Using my phone, I download a burner phone app and use that to get a new number to put in the phone field. I create a new email account, also via my phone, and use that for the next required field.

Then, my finger drags the cursor to the yes/no toggle, and my breath holds.

"Individual is existing Club Venom member: *yes.*"

Before I lose my nerve, I quickly scroll to the bottom of the page and click the submit button. Part of me suddenly panics, wondering what comes next. Do I have to provide a membership number? Does Dante manually review the list for his new primal kink portal? What happens if he recognizes the name is bullshit? What the fuck was I thinking, using the name of a murdered girl who he *knows* I've been reading about to—

My phone dings. Jolting, I glance down.

Oh shit.

It's an email in my new fake account from Club Venom. Shaking, I tap on it, opening the email as my pulse quickens. An all-black page greets me, with just four words in gold that both terrify and electrify me:

Welcome to the chase.

Beneath it, there's a link to the online login page. Still shaking, I navigate there and fill out the required fields for creating a password and selecting a username.

What the fuck is wrong with you, Bianca? You're broken.

Hmm.

I start to type in "BrokenDancer" as a username, but that hits too close to home. I backspace and go with "BrokenBee" instead.

Then I click submit.

I half expect an explosion to go off. Or an alarm, alerting Dante to my intrusion. But all I get is the quiet ding of another new email.

Thank you for submitting your information, Ms. Dawson. You may use the portal to add in any specific preferences for a potential partner. Or you can choose to be surprised.

I want the surprise. Selecting attributes feels like it takes away from the thrill of a stranger doing...well, what I want them to do.

You will be able to chat with any prospective partners via the portal chat function. We highly encourage members to communicate exclusively through the portal. Exchanging numbers or moving to other chat platforms potentially takes away from the anonymity that we encourage at Club Venom. Please always remember to go over hard and soft limits, desires, and other particulars with your partner before meeting.

We will connect you with a suitable partner as soon as possible.

Heat pools between my thighs.

I'm really doing this. This is really happening.

I exit from the portal dashboard on Dante's computer and make sure to cover any other evidence of my crimes. I slowly close the cover, then bolt to the guest room, brush my teeth, and slip under the covers.

The chase is on.

4

KRATOS

My prey has zero idea they're being watched. Followed. Analyzed.

Hunted.

From the darkness concealing me, I watch my prey's lips pull into a smile, revealing a flash of human emotion and showing me a glimpse of their "person-ness"…I won't call it humanity…that will be extinguished in the next two to three minutes.

The glimmer of a smile doesn't deter me. It doesn't make me feel badly about what I'm about to do in the slightest.

Because actions have consequences. When those actions involve the trafficking of young girls into the hands of monsters to suffer a fate too horrifying to comprehend, the consequences will be appropriately horrific.

Despite my enormous size, I move silently in the shadows. If my prey tonight were to bolt and run, I'd have no trouble chasing them down. I'd enjoy it, too. But tonight, all I have time for is payback.

I'm not sanctimonious or arrogant enough to call this "justice". I'm not "righting any wrongs" here. Yes, I'm guided by my own views on monsters like the one within my sights at this very moment, and he *does* deserve what's about to happen to him, in spades.

But tonight is ultimately about self-indulgence.

It's about letting my monster out.

Feeding the beast, and his need for blood, violence, and mayhem.

Pulling away from the dirty, grime-streaked window looking into the warehouse, I move along the alley at the back of the old brick building. A dumpster I already found gives me access to the old fire escape, which in turn gets me onto the roof.

Once up there, I move even more silently. I keep to the shadows and confine my footsteps to the places I marked yesterday with chalk—to the boards that won't squeak and alert the cockroaches below that the exterminator is coming.

One, I don't want them to freak out and do anything stupid with…or to…the girls they've got down there. But two, I don't want them to scatter. Again, I'd chase them all down one by one if need be. But work smarter, as the saying goes, not harder. It's already taken me a bit longer than I wanted to track down this distribution center of theirs after the change in plans the other night. I'd *meant* to carve the answers to my questions on the two former Carveli enforcers with the tip of a knife.

But they weren't alone. And their company proved...distracting.

Which is putting it very, *very* mildly.

But before my mind can wander again to those big blue eyes and heart-shaped mouth, I yank my consciousness back to the business at hand. She'll come later. First, I have business to attend to.

I left a skylight propped open last night: one, conveniently, in a corner above a hanging light without a bulb. Like a wraith, I slip inside the building, picking my way along one of the rafters. My gaze drops down to the haze of cigarette smoke, the smell of fear and dirt, and I listen to the chuckle of one of my prey as he bangs his gun against the bars of one of the cages. My teeth grind silently when I hear the sobs of the girls shrinking back from the bars and his laughter.

There's evil everywhere in the world. Sometimes, it's so much to think about that it almost overwhelms me. Some-times it sparks a rage inside me that threatens to shatter the mask I've spent so much of my life perfecting for the people I call family and loved ones.

That's what tonight is for. Not saving the world. Not destroying evil once and for all. You can do something, or you can do nothing. And the "something" I'm doing tonight will allow me to vent that rage that inevitably builds inside me.

I double check the knife strapped to my hip. Then I drop down to one of the catwalks just beneath the rafters. I move silently to the far side until I'm above a stack of old wooden shipping crates. Swinging over the edge of the catwalk, I lower myself, shoulders and biceps coiling like thick rope before I drop down behind the crates.

It's a matter of seconds before my beast will be let out. And he knows it. He's salivating for it. I slip the knife from its sheath, fingering the hilt. I slip around the far side of the boxes. My eyes stay shadowed as I keep hidden, taking note of my targets.

There's only three of them. If they knew what was coming for them, they'd have added a fucking zero to that number.

The closest to me will be first, for practical reasons. He's got an M-16 and an obviously inexperienced and twitchy trigger finger. His two buddies are similarly armed—one sitting at a folding table dicking around with playing cards and chain-smoking, the other doing his fuckhead maneuver of clanking the stock of his rifle against the bars while he laughs.

He's apparently quite pleased by his ability to terrify *children* locked in cages.

The three of them have all got guns. I've just brought my knife. But I'm not worried. And it's not as if I didn't think there'd be firearms here.

I prefer the knife.

It's more primal. More savage.

I can *feel it more* when I wipe their existence from the face of the earth.

It's sentiments like that that might possibly indicate something far darker, psychologically speaking, than I care to contemplate most of the time. Does getting excited, maybe even a little hard at the prospect of ripping out the throats of child predators and traffickers make me a psychopath?

Perhaps, at least a little. Because it's not *just* about justice or punishing the wicked to me. It's not *only* about "doing the right thing".

I fucking *enjoy it.*

Ninety-nine percent of the time, I am what I need to be: the strong, silent, gentle giant of a brother. The friendly and helpful grandson. The loyal friend.

But you can't hide your true nature all the time. And it's moments like this where I get to really be who and what I am. When I get to inhale malice and exhale violence and bloodshed.

It's times like this when I feel the most alive.

You know, as in the opposite of what these three fucks are going to be in three, two, one...

Go.

The first never even sees me before my hand clamps over his mouth, wrenching his head to the side and snapping his neck. I drag him into the shadows, my knife cutting his throat anyway, because why the fuck not.

The other two jolt when I slip a shoe off their dead buddy's foot and hurl it at the far wall of the warehouse.

"The fuck was that?!" the one at the table blurts, lurching to his feet and bringing up his M-16.

The dumb fuck still has the safety on when I charge up behind him. He screams, gurgling wetly as my knife punches into his lungs from behind, lifting him off his feet. The third one whirls, his eyes bulging in horror when he sees my size and my mask. Before he can even fire his weapon, I'm hurling cocksucker number two *at* him.

They both slam into the bars behind them. Roughly a quarter second later, I've got them both by the throats. I drag them into the shadows and away from the girls, who've already seen plenty of things they shouldn't have, before slitting their throats as well and spilling their blood onto the ground.

I glance at my watch.

Three minutes and eighteen seconds.

Fuck. I'm getting slow.

"I'M GLAD YOU CALLED, KRATOS."

The man in front of me with the slight Eastern European accent, blonde hair, and haunted blue eyes is my age. And yet Lukas Komarov always comes off as much older. I never actually asked how he knew who I was the first time we crossed paths, because I'd already looked into *him*.

Suffice to say that by the time we finally met, he was more than fully aware of who and what I was.

Lukas' father, Viktor, runs the Kashenko Bratva, which Lukas will one day helm himself. But until then Lukas runs the Free Them Foundation alongside his wife, Lizbet, an organization that focuses on eradicating child trafficking around the world. To the casual observer, they do this by working with local legislators and police forces.

Under the surface, though, they do this by harnessing the power of the Bratva, not to mention Lukas' personal penchant for darkness and violence, to *exterminate* the cockroaches that would harm children.

"Although…" Lukas arches a brow, turning to level his gaze at the three bodies now covered by a tarp in the corner of the warehouse. "When you *did* call, I sort of hoped we might be working together on this one."

"Hey, I *did* call you."

"An hour ago, yeah." He eyes me. "When did *you* get here?"

I lift a heavy shoulder. "An hour and…three minutes ago?"

He smirks darkly before he nods at my face, which is still covered by my mask.

"You know, I do know a thing or two about masked vigilantism myself, Kratos."

Yes. Yes, he does. I've looked into Lukas. His "methods". His savagery. His complete lack of mercy when it comes to the type of men I just killed. Really, you could call me an admirer of his work. A student of it. He might know this.

I might not care if he does.

"Look, Kratos, what you're doing is admirable. You know I have nothing bad to say about anything you do that aligns with our own mission. But we've got *resources*, man. Sure, I used to do it solo, too. But we've got a whole organization now. Teams that can help."

I know where this is going. It goes here every single time he and I cross paths.

He wants me to come work for the Free Them Foundation. Not sitting behind a desk and attending board meetings, either.

He wants me to be a hunter for them.

It's not that I have anything against Lukas, or Lizbet, or their organization. Not at all. But that's just not me.

"Why don't I save you the breath," I growl quietly.

"Kratos—"

"I don't do team sports, Lukas," I shrug. "Sorry."

Behind him, I catch a glimpse of some of his people putting up some temporary cloth backdrops. Past them, a beautiful and powerful-looking woman who I know is his wife, Lizbet, smiles warmly and cautiously as she slowly approaches the now-unlocked cage full of terrified girls.

I don't like calling what I did tonight "rescuing" anyone. I merely curb-stomped evil. Besides, it's hard to sell it as a self-less act when it was at least half about calming my beast.

It's Lukas, Lizbet, and their organization who'll do the "saving" tonight. They'll remove the girls from here, and either find their original homes or make sure they get good, loving new ones. They'll also take care of the therapy and the healing these girls will need.

I'm not the savior. Just the weapon.

Lukas exhales slowly. "The darkness catches up to you, Kratos. The darkness is the house. And you know as well as I do that the house *always* wins." His eyes lock with mine. "You have to know when it's time to take your chips and go home."

I stay silent. Because the thing is, the darkness *is* home to me. This is where I breathe. Where I live. Where I feel alive.

Lukas shakes his head. "Okay, I'm done pitching you."

"Sure, for now," I growl.

He smiles quietly. "Yes." He turns to nod his chin at the bodies. "Let me guess, former Carveli soldiers?"

I nod.

With the Carveli family now leaderless and in shambles, the whole organization is slowly breaking apart. And as that happens, there's been more and more foulness concerning that family emerging from the shadows. Foulness like *this* shit.

The five major Italian mafia families in the States have a sort of "United Nations"-style agreement between them. Not a treaty or anything—more like a code of conduct that allows all ships to rise with the tide without infighting and bickering.

One of the hard and fast rules they set up was a ban on prostitution and trafficking. Say what you will about the Italian Mob, at least they don't pimp girls anymore.

Or rather, they're not *supposed to*.

Except it turns out there were a few little groups of people within the Carveli family who *were*. And I'm damned sure Massimo Carveli himself was getting kickbacks from it. Now that the whole organization is shattering into little fiefdoms, some of those groups are trying to make a go of it on their own. Groups like these dead assholes, or the two fucks I killed the other night.

The ones who tried to attack *her*.

I'll be watching you, prinkípissa.

It wasn't a threat.

It was a promise. And I never, ever break a promise.

I clear my throat and nod at Lukas. "Yep."

"Same as the two assholes who got their throats cut way out in Brooklyn the other night?

I raise an eyebrow at him. He arches one back.

"Not like I don't recognize your handiwork at this point, Kratos."

I sniff. "I'm sure I have no idea what you're referring to."

He shakes his head, looking away. "Look, I know you've got this whole lone wolf thing going on. But if you *ever* change your mind—"

"Something you might not know about me, Lukas," I growl, "is that I'm a stubborn bastard. The day I change my mind, you can go ahead and bring ice skates to hell."

He nods, a small smirk on his lips.

"Your people got this from here?"

He nods.

"Then that's my cue."

I turn and walk back toward the shadows.

"The house always wins, Kratos," Lukas calls after me.

"Then I guess I'll just have to *be* the house, won't I?" I toss over my shoulder before I disappear into the darkness.

I've got somewhere else to be.

Other shadows to stalk.

Someone else to be watching over.

Like I said: a promise is a promise. And I *never* break a promise.

5

BIANCA

"So, what do you think? Pretty good, huh?"

Silence fills the table. I glance to my left, locking eyes with Nico as a slightly distraught emotion creeps across his face. His throat bobs as he valiantly swallows the mouthful of what we've been told is cacio e pepe. Instantly, the pained look on his face deepens.

"Well?"

We all collectively pretend not to hear Vito's hopeful question. I pull my gaze from Nico, turning to glance at Tempest sitting on my other side at the dinner table. She's got an equally revolted look on her face. But after she downs her first bite heroically, she forces a huge smile onto her face.

"Oh, wow, Vito! This is…" Her smile falters a little as she looks past me at Dad. "I've never tasted anything like it…"

"Fuckin' awesome, Pop," Carmy beams, clearly the best actor at the table—or the one with a complete lack of taste buds.

It's been two weeks since that night in the alley, and we're all over at Vito's house for a dinner he's…well, I think "cooked" is an insult to real cooks. Concocted, maybe? Summoned from a demon realm with a blood curse?

Whatever he did, the bite of what can only very loosely be called "food" in my mouth is perilously close to making me gag.

"Yeah?!" Vito beams widely. "Fantastic. Eat your fuckin' heart out, Emeril." He clasps his hands together, rubbing them gleefully as he stands from his seat at the head of the table. "I'm gonna go open that second bottle of Chianti. You guys dig in."

Everyone is all smiles until he leaves the room. Then it's a mad rush to spit the bites of fuck-knows-what out into our napkins followed by large swigs of wine and water.

"That is straight-up poison," Dante mutters from the other side of Tempest. "Fucking hell."

"Oh c'mon," Carmy grins. "It's not…" He lifts a shoulder. "I mean it's got its merits."

Nico rolls his eyes. "A, no it doesn't. And B, how do you fuck up cacio e pepe?? It's literally cheese and black pepper on goddamn *pasta*." He shudders, gulping down more Chianti. "I'm hiring him a chef."

"The fuck you are," Carmine grunts with a sharp glare across the table. "He loves cooking."

"Yeah, but I like visiting without wondering if dinner is going to kill me," Nico mutters back.

Carmy waves him off. "Suck it up already. It makes him happy."

59

"Yeah, so does sunbathing in the nude," Dante snickers. "But that doesn't mean he's allowed to do it in full view of the neighbors anymore."

I make a puking face as Tempest cracks up next to me.

Carmy grins across the table at my brother. "Nah, just at your place, right? Lucky."

This is all true. Vito was very much in the habit of "sunning himself" on the house's rooftop patio. But as New York developed around the building, and more and more new neighbors had the misfortune to look out their window and see a sixty-something Italian man sipping Fernet and letting it *all* hang out, he was forced to change it up.

Now if he wants to sunbathe he has to drive out to Dante and Tempest's Hamptons estate.

And they've now implemented a bathing suits required dress code.

"Anyone need seconds while I'm in here?" Vito yells from the kitchen.

The resulting near-unison "NO" from the table has us all covering our mouths and trying not to laugh.

"I'm good, Pop!" Carmy calls. He braces himself and starts to shove our dad's disturbing attempt at cacio e pepe into his mouth.

Nico turns and dumps the contents of his plate into the container of a house plant behind him.

"You're cleaning that shit up," Dante mutters at him.

"Right, I mean, wouldn't want to kill the begonias."

Vito arrives back in the dining room with the open bottle of Chianti and takes his seat again. He grins at me, nodding his head encouragingly as I take another bite and force a smile to my lips.

Daughter of the fucking year, over here.

Carmine muscles down another bite of pasta like a champ and clears his throat. "Pop, I heard a rumor I wanted ask you about."

Vito nods, shoveling food into his mouth, completely unfazed by the taste. "What rumor?"

"That Ciara Marchetti just got engaged to Giovani Pagano."

My brows fly up. "Wait, seriously? Ciara's engaged?"

Carmy lifts a shoulder, then glances significantly at Dad again. "Well?"

Vito takes a slow, deep breath, followed by a large sip of wine.

"She is, yeah."

Woah. I'm not exactly besties with Ciara. But we kinda grew up together. Her father, Cesare Marchetti, is head of the Marchetti family, one of the main families in The Commission together with our family, the Amatos and the Scaliamis. Up until recently, the Carveli family was also part of that group. Now, of course, there's an empty seat at the table.

Carmy whistles. "Damn, that's a shame."

Vito's brows knit. "Why?"

Dante sighs heavily. "Probably because now your degenerate son has to erase her number from his list of potential booty calls."

Carmy rolls his eyes and flips Dante off. "Give me a little credit, fuck." He takes a sip of wine, then winks. "As if I'd *ever* delete that girl's number."

Nico snickers. Even I crack up a little. Vito looks far less amused.

"Don't even fucking think about it," he says gruffly, jabbing a finger at Carmine. "I mean it. *Yes*, she's engaged to Don Pagano's son, and you know damn well why."

I wince. "Wait, it's an arranged thing?"

Carmy snorts. "As if Ciara Marchetti would ever voluntarily settle down." He frowns at Dad. "Is this about De Luca?"

My chest tightens.

"Yeah," Vito says quietly. "It's about De Luca. It's *always* about fuckin' De Luca these days."

The table gets a little quieter as we're all suddenly thinking about it. The Commission only works if there's five families involved. If there's four or six, votes could end in ties. If there's only three, it's not enough families. And if it's seven, that's too many cooks in the kitchen.

Five is the magic number. But ever since the Carveli empire crumbled, there's been only four. Or there was, until they and a few other auxiliary Commission families decided recently to bring a new fifth family to the high table: the De Lucas, helmed by Nero De Luca himself.

Problem is, no one knew that Luciano Amato and Nero De Luca were distant cousins.

And that means two out of the five families on The Commission might decide to pool their votes and resources into a power bloc.

I can guarantee you, that is why Ciara Marchetti's father is marrying her off to the son of another powerful New York Italian family. They're cementing an alliance to shore up power in case the Amatos and the De Lucas get hungry and greedy.

Carmine frowns. You can see the "cocky playboy" act drop from his face as he switches gears to mafia crown prince mode. It's always interesting to watch the power dynamics between my brothers. Carmy is definitely the looser cannon. But he *is* going to be king one day, when Dad steps down. Meanwhile Nico, despite being younger, ends up acting like a big brother most of the time, like he's helping to coach Carmy into being the man he'll need to be one day.

"How worried should we be about Nero?" Carmine grunts, suddenly all business.

Dad tips his head from side to side, like he's weighing out his answer. "I don't know if we need to be *worried*. But it's always healthy to be prepared. Nero is like a young lion. He's new to being king, and he's got something to prove to The Commission. It could make him a bold asset to the group, or a tyrant."

Nico grins as he turns to me, raising his glass. "Well, Bianca, better go get fitted for that wedding dress."

I glare at him as Carmine laughs. Vito just sighs and smiles, shaking his head. He reaches past Nico to pat my hand comfortingly.

"That's never happening, Bumblebee."

We've discussed this. At length. I mean, I know how the world I live in works, and the role of mafia "princesses" like me. Marriages are how power is planted and grown.

But years ago, when I was fourteen or so, Vito sat me down and told me I didn't *ever* need to worry about that. He told me that no matter what, he'd never force me to marry anyone for political reasons.

"Yeah, we don't do arranged marriages in this house!" Carmy crows dramatically, pounding the table with his fist. "Isn't that right, Dante?"

Dante levels a withering look at Carmy as Tempest groans and hides her face in her hands, blushing furiously.

Yes, they had a forced marriage. In fact, in a weird twist, it was Tempest who forced it. But I think it's safe to say that theirs is one that worked out perfectly for everyone involved.

But as for me, I don't even know if I ever want to get married *period*...let alone because I have to for some stupid and crazy mafia reason.

Vito sighs as he sets his fork down. He frowns a little as he glances around the table. Carmine has managed to choke down his cacio e pepe. Nico's is currently poisoning the begonia plant behind him. I have no idea what Dante and Tempest did to hide the evidence, maybe stashed it in their napkins, but the point is suddenly I realize I'm the only asshole left at the table with a plate full of food.

"You're not having any more?" Vito asks, looking crushed.

"Ugh, love to," I smile back. "But I had a heavy lunch."

"There are starving kids in Africa, Bianca," Carmine grins across the table at me.

"Great, let's send it to them."

Vito slides his chair back.

"Well then, is everyone ready for dessert? I made tiramisù!"

The entire table reflexively puts their hands to their stomachs.

LATER, after I've watched everyone else try not to projectile vomit up Vito's tiramisù, and after Nico's stolen back into the dining room to dispose of the evidence of his crimes against begonia, he and I are in the kitchen loading the dishwasher.

"You know we're both safe, right?"

I turn to my brother. "Huh?"

"We're both future-proofed. Dad promised you that he'd never marry you off. Dante's already wifed up. And I'm the second-born son, so who cares." He grins. "It's just Carmine that eventually will have to get his shit together and be a grownup. I mean, if anyone's going to get forced into a marriage, believe me, it's gonna be that guy."

"Good thing he's had years of practice of forcing his way into *other people's* marriages."

Nico roars with laughter. "Shit, I'm stealing that one."

My phone dings in my pocket. I pull it out, and instantly, my entire body goes rigid as a blush explodes over my face.

"I… I'll be right back."

"Nah, take off if you need to. I'll finish up here."

I grin at Nico. "Thanks."

65

Out of sight and safely alone in my room, I pull my phone out again and click through to the portal for Venom. That was the notification chime I got: a new message.

My hearts skips a beat when I see the single message sitting in my inbox:

ADMIN

You have a match.

My pulse thuds in my ears, my skin tingles, and an achy, needy desire throbs in my core. My thumb hovers the message and my breath catches, as if I'm frozen in place, trying to figure out if I'm going to walk through this door or not.

Yes, I am.

I click on the message, my heart hammering in my chest.

Dear BrokenBee,

A match has been made for you with another Member. You have both been notified. Please use this link to initiate a private chat with your potential partner. Like at the Club itself, we encourage the use of anonymity, as well as open and honest communication. Both parties should discuss hard limits and safe words before meeting. Please enjoy your experience.

For a second, it feels like I'm outside my body, watching myself read the message.

Holy. Shit.

Suddenly, this isn't just fantasy anymore. I'm not just having dirty daydreams about this kink of mine. I'm literally standing at the front door with my finger on the doorbell. Do I push it?

The seconds tick by as I stare at the words "Please use <u>this link</u> to initiate a private chat with your potential partner".

If I click it, this isn't fantasy anymore, and there's no going back. I mean, yes, I could *not* ask to meet up with this person. Or I could just say no, should they ask me first. Still, if I click it, I'll have gone through that door and taken the first step down the rabbit hole.

And I'm not sure you can come back from that the same way you went in.

My thumb taps the link, and a jolt of something electric zaps through my core. Instantly, a chat window is brought up between me and my "potential partner".

RAISEDBYWOLVES

Your safe word is VANISH.

I blink, my heart skipping a beat.

That's the first message. Not "Hello", not "Good evening, BrokenBee". No cheesy pickup line at all. I guess this isn't Tinder.

This is something much, *much* darker, and much more real.

BROKENBEE

Bold to jump right to safe words

RAISEDBYWOLVES

If you're looking for small talk about our favorite books, we can be done now and not waste each other's time.

BROKENBEE

That's not what I'm looking for

RAISEDBYWOLVES

So why don't you be a good girl and tell me what you ARE looking for.

Why don't you be a good girl...

Fuck, that's hot.

BROKENBEE

You know what I'm looking for. It's in my profile

I didn't fill out much of the optional information in the portal, because I didn't want to bring too much attention, or accidentally give out any personal details. But in the "what are you looking for in a partner?" section, I was pretty blunt. And he *must* have read it...which means he wants me to say it anyway.

Fuck, that's hot too.

RAISEDBYWOLVES

Tell me what you're looking for. I'm not into games.

There's a power in his language and the brief, stoic responses. It's *slightly* rude, or at least a little brusque. At the same time, it's also more than a little exciting. It's thrilling, like this person has a real edge of danger to them.

Which, obviously, rings my bell, because I'm insane. Why yes, please, I would *love* a "dangerous" vibe to my internet stranger who I'm chatting with for the sole purpose of acting out a rape fantasy with.

You need psychiatric help, you nutbar.

I take a deep breath. Then my thumbs tap rapidly on the phone screen.

BROKENBEE

I want you to surprise me in the dark. I want to be chased when I'm not ready for it. I want you to catch me

My pulse is roaring in my ears.

RAISEDBYWOLVES

And then?

BROKENBEE

I want you to fuck me. Hard. Rough

RAISEDBYWOLVES

And if you protest? I mean without using the safe word.

Heat pools between my thighs.

BROKENBEE

If I protest, I want you to keep doing it anyway, harder

He's silent for a second. It feels like ten hours.

RAISEDBYWOLVES

What are your hard limits.

BROKENBEE

None

RAISEDBYWOLVES

Try the fuck again. And this time think before you say shit like that to a man like me.

Holy *fuck*. What the hell am I doing?

I think for a second, and then tap out an answer.

> BROKENBEE
>
> No bathroom stuff. No impact play. I mean, slaps are okay. But nothing harder than that.

I hit send, then start typing again.

> BROKENBEE
>
> No water

RAISEDBYWOLVES

Elaborate. I'm not sure dehydration is a kink I have any interest in.

I blush, chewing on my lip.

> BROKENBEE
>
> No, I mean like no going in the water. No boats or anything.

> BROKENBEE
>
> I can't swim.

I add it as an afterthought, like a lame excuse.

RAISEDBYWOLVES

I can agree to all of those. Anything else?

Oh hell yes.

It's stupid. And a little embarrassing. But quickly, I tap it out, because why not.

> BROKENBEE
>
> Can you wear a mask when we do this?
> Hang on

I open a web browser and quickly find what I'm looking for. I copy the link to the image of the black mask with the neon

X's for eyes and the leering, creepy smile. Then I send it to RaisedByWolves via the chat interface.

BROKENBEE

Like this one

There's no response for a second. Then the chat moves on the page as he replies.

RAISEDBYWOLVES

Done.

I take a shaky breath, squirming a little as I shift on the edge of my bed.

BROKENBEE

Any requests for me?

RAISEDBYWOLVES

Just one. Try your hardest to get away from me.

My mouth drops open. *Fucking fuck*, what am I getting myself into?

BROKENBEE

When are you free

I hold my breath. Part of me is hoping my phone suddenly dies, or that he backs out and says never mind.

The seconds tick by.

RAISEDBYWOLVES

2 hours from now. Central Park Driveway and East Drive

A shudder violently rips through me. What the *fuck*. He wants to meet *tonight*? In two hours, so 11:30? In the middle of Central Park? Is he crazy?

71

Are YOU, girl?

My heart pounds as I stare at the chat.

> RAISEDBYWOLVES
>
> If you're not up for the type of games I play, we'll be done right here and now. 3…
>
> RAISEDBYWOLVES
>
> 2…

My pulse spikes.

> BROKENBEE
>
> I'll be there

> RAISEDBYWOLVES
>
> Good girl.

Jesus…

> RAISEDBYWOLVES
>
> Come alone. Remember your safe word.

Vanish.

> RAISEDBYWOLVES
>
> I look forward to hunting you and listening to you squeal as you take my cock in every slutty little hole you have, BrokenBee.

The lit "online" icon next to his username goes dark.

My heart almost stops as I stare at his last message.

Holy. Fucking. *Shit.*

There's no way I can do this. None. This is how you get murdered in the park, idiot.

…Or, conversely, this is how you have the hottest experience of your life.

Maybe wanting to get chased by a stranger through Central Park at night is crazy. Perhaps wanting that stranger to hurt me, and pin me down, and violently fuck me is insane.

Wanting this to be how I lose my virginity is *definitely* lunacy.

But tonight, I want to try on crazy and see how it fits.

Before I know it, I'm blurting out goodbyes to everyone, throwing out some excuse about an early call time tomorrow, and bolting downstairs. I grab a taxi to my place, rip off my clothes, and get through my bizarre bathing routine as fast as I can.

Then I'm frowning at my open closet. I mean, what the fuck do you wear to a rape fantasy chase?

In the end, I go with a not-too-short skirt, moderate heels, and a cute top. I even manage to put my hair up into something other than my usual scraped-back dancer's bun. I ignore one call from Naomi, then another from Milena. I add a touch of makeup. Then, as a last-minute thought, I open a drawer and pull out the blonde wig I got for a costume party last Halloween.

I have no idea who this person is that I'm meeting tonight. But they're obviously a member of Club Venom, which means they may know Dante.

That means there is a very slight chance they'd know who *I* am. And I'd rather be safe than sorry.

I stuff the wig into my bag. Then I'm locking the door to my apartment, feeling like I'm about five seconds away from having a heart attack.

I barrel out the front door of my building, and immediately scream as I slam into a body.

"FUCK!" I choke, almost falling on my ass as I spring back. I'm met with an explosion of laughter. My heart manages to start again, and I realize it's Naomi and Milena standing in front of me.

"Holy shit, jumpy much?" Milena laughs.

I smile weakly, trying to form a sentence. Or even a word.

"Oh, good!" Naomi beams, eying my outfit. "You read my texts!"

I blink. "Um, what?"

"My texts about us going out tonight to celebrate?"

I blink again. "I… No, I don't think—"

Naomi's brow furrows and she exchanges a suspicious look with Milena.

"What are you dressed up for, then?"

Yeah, like I'm going to tell them "Sorry, I can't go out with you. I'm actually dressed up to go get chased and fucked by a stranger from the internet in Central Park".

I laugh weakly. "Kidding! Yeah, let's go! But I totally missed some of those texts. What are we celebrating, again?"

Milena groans. "My dad met with Boris Chernoff this afternoon about me potentially marrying his son, Anton."

My face pales. "Fucking *hell*! Are you serious?! Why are we celebrating that?"

"Because it's all good!" Naomi chips in.

Milena beams. "Yeah, Dad killed that quick."

"Which is great, because this motherfucker definitely lives under a bridge somewhere."

Naomi flashes her phone, revealing a picture of a truly troll-like young Russian man wearing a track suit, with awful facial hair, the world's worst mullet, and...

"Is that..."

"A tattoo of a girl fucking herself with a vodka bottle on his *neck?!*" Milena huffs. "*Sure the fuck is.*"

"*Yikes.*" I make a face.

"So yeah, that's why we're celebrating." Milena flashes a thick black credit card. "On Dad's dime, even."

I start to grin. Then suddenly the reality of my original plans for tonight hits me.

"I—"

"Well?" Naomi turns to hail a taxi. "Where should we go first?"

"Gimme a sec."

I pull up the site again and click on the chat. The icon by the stranger's username is dark, indicating he's offline. I chew nervously on my lip.

BROKENBEE

> Hey, I'm so sorry. Something important just came up, a family thing. I hate to do this to you, but I have to postpone tonight. Apologies again!

I'm about to slip the phone back into my bag when it dings. My pulse skips as I see the new message.

> **RAISEDBYWOLVES**
>
> That's not how this works, babygirl. You've already said yes.

I take a shaky breath.

> **BROKENBEE**
>
> I know, I'm sorry. But something came up

> **RAISEDBYWOLVES**
>
> And I don't care.

I stare at the phone.

"Bianca!"

My head snaps up to see my friends getting into the back seat of a cab. Naomi raises her brows.

"Well? Unless you've got a better offer?"

Not one I can tell you about.

My eyes drop to my phone.

> **RAISEDBYWOLVES**
>
> Either use the safe word, in which case this ends here and now, permanently. Or else you WILL be seeing me tonight.

Shit.

> **BROKENBEE**
>
> I'm sorry. I have to go

I close the chat window and stuff my phone into my bag before I jump into the cab.

6

BIANCA

"Here!"

I groan as Naomi shoves another tequila shot into my hands.

"Naomi, really, I'm good."

"You'll be even better once you drink that!" she grins back at me.

No, I'll be *drunk* once I drink that. I like to have fun as much as the next girl. But I'm not a huge party animal. Mostly it's because of dance. I can say with full authority that the worst hangover in the world is the one with Madame Kuzmina glaring down her nose at you asking why your pirouettes are so off today.

But the other reason is that I just don't enjoy being out of control like that.

Neither Naomi nor Milena is a big drinker either, for the same dance-related reasons. I mean, we all work our *asses* off, day in and day out, to stay at the very top of our game physically. Getting drunk, which is literally ingesting poison, isn't usually on our to-do list.

But it *is* on the docket tonight.

Naomi's already got the rosy cheeks and glassy eyes that come from drinking in loud, energetic clubs with music pounding and people dancing. Milena turns to clink her glass to ours, and she's looking like she's having an even better time.

Hey, I'd probably be as drunk as her right now too if I just found out I wasn't being married off to a troll like Anton Chernoff.

I wince as the tequila burns down my throat, warming my stomach and making my blood pump a little wilder and hotter.

"*Yes!*" Milena crows, slamming her empty glass down on the bar. She turns to survey the crowd of clubbers grinding and gyrating in the pulsing, neon light.

"Okay, first things first, we need to find some cute boys and show them how shitty of dancers these other bitches are."

"Meeeow!" Naomi laughs. "Careful everyone, Milena's got her claws out!"

"Russians and tequila are a fiery combination," Milena giggles, flipping her long blonde ponytail. "Shoulda stuck with vodka if you wanted me docile."

I grin. I'm having fun, and the tequila is melting away the stresses of life. The music throbs and pulses, and the pull of it makes me want to close my eyes and just *dance*.

At the same time, there's the pull of something else. Something dangerous and volatile. Something that feels like a shadow lurking just beyond my peripheral vision, its claws slowly reaching out to me.

I fish out my phone and open the site again. The chat window still shows our last exchange, with the icon by his username still darkened.

RaisedByWolves: Either use the safe word, in which case this ends here and now, permanently. Or else you WILL be seeing me tonight.

BrokenBee: I'm sorry. I have to go

My pulse skips.

I didn't use the safe word.

I just said "I'm sorry, I have to go." I want to tell myself it was just an oversight, a technicality. I mean, I *did* make it clear that I wasn't going to make our rendezvous tonight. But it's not the same thing as using the safe word. And I know why I deliberately didn't use it.

Use the safe word, in which case this ends here and now, permanently.

I didn't use it because I know that when he said "this ends", he meant "forever". Not "for the evening" or "until next time".

Using the safe word with whoever my mystery partner is shuts this whole thing down entirely. And there go my chances of exploring the aching need, however dark and depraved, that I can't stop feeling deep in my core.

It's like staring into the black mouth of a cave and being both terrified of what might be inside but also equally scared to walk away without ever exploring it.

That's why I didn't use the safe word.

"C'mon!" I jolt back to reality, shoving the phone into my bag as Naomi and Milena drag me out into the mass of writhing, dancing bodies. We push our way closer to the DJ booth, creating a little room for ourselves as we start to dance.

I mean, we might be bunheads, but that doesn't mean we can't get down and dirty with some thumping club music.

Soon enough, we're attracting attention from more than a few guys. Three of the bolder ones move into our little dance circle, each of them wordlessly pairing up with one of us. A guy with blonde hair pulls close to Naomi. Another guy with tanned Latin skin and gorgeous long hair starts dancing with Milena.

The one that slips close to me momentarily takes my breath away because of his sheer size.

For a split second, I freeze. My eyes snap up to his face, my pulse thudding as the thought crosses my mind that he's the same man from the alley the other day. The one who's been in my head ever since. The one who inspired me to sneak onto Dante's website and match with the ultra-dominant RaisedByWolves, whom I'm standing up right now.

When the young guy in front of me grins nervously, though, the illusion shatters.

It's not him. The man in the alley might have been wearing a mask, but the raw power, confidence, and darkness that emanated from him like smoke is nothing like the clearly nervous energy this guy has.

"I'm Matt!" he screams in my face.

"Bianca!" I yell back.

"We're celebrating!"

"Yeah?!" I reply.

I'm not focusing on Matt. My mind is still on the leering mask and the hand around my throat. The throb of danger and malice teasing through my core.

"Yeah! We all just got hired at Ironclad Holdings!"

"Oh," I shout without enthusiasm. "That's...cool."

"It's a hedge fund!" he explains in a loud voice over the music.

Ugh. Of course it is.

I glance past him, locking eyes with Naomi. She looks as unimpressed with our new friends as I am. When I catch Milena's eye, she mouths "help me", and I stifle a grin.

"We're gonna go grab drinks!" I scream at Matt. "Nice meeting you!"

"We'll come too!" he yells.

"Nope!" Milena cuts him off, grabbing my hand and Naomi's and dragging us away.

"Oh my God," Milena groans when we're back at the bar. "He was telling me about his stock portfolio."

"At least he was hot," Naomi's face sours. "Mine told me he'd —and I quote—'never been with an Asian before'."

"Oh, fucking *gross*," Milena blanches.

I wrinkle my nose, shaking my head. "Yeah, nope. You wanna get out of here?"

Naomi frowns. "Not yet. I like the vibe here. Let's just put a hard stop on any more finance bros."

"*Deal*," I groan.

"Shots?" Milena grins at us.

I make a face. "I don't know if—"

But she's already flagging down the bartender. Before I know it, the saltshaker is in front of me, another chilled shot of tequila is in my hands, and the fiery alcohol is burning my throat again.

I wince, choking a little as I bite down on the lime afterward.

"*Wow*," I hiss, blinking. "That one…"

"Yeah, we gotta go dance it off," Milena laughs.

"I have to pee, actually."

"Same," Naomi chirps.

In the end, we all end up heading to the bathroom at the back of the club together. The line is, predictably, a menace. But eventually we're at the front. The single bathroom is *tiny*, so there's just room for two people to squeeze in together.

"You go, I can wait," I tell them, since Naomi's been crossing her legs for the last ten minutes.

I'm waiting in line feeling the pressure building in my own bladder when a girl steps out from around the corner of a dark hallway and glances at me. She grins at me and leans close.

"There's actually another bathroom down that hall and around the corner," she whispers conspiratorially. "No line, either."

Oh hell, yes.

I blurt out a thanks and then dash off around the corner and down another hallway. At the end, past an empty coat check and a door that looks like it leads outside, is another ladies' room, just like she said.

And there's not a single other person here.

Perfect.

I step inside to find a much larger bathroom than the tiny one we've all been waiting in line for. This one has four stalls, one of which I quickly occupy.

I'm just finishing up when I hear the bathroom door swing open. It pauses, like someone's holding the door open.

Then I hear heavy footsteps slowly move into the bathroom, and the door closing again. The footsteps move down the line of stalls, until they come to a stop right outside mine.

My eyes drop, and I shiver when I see heavy black motor-cycle boots.

Men's boots.

Something dark twists awake in my gut as I listen to the slow, deep breaths coming from the other side of the stall door. Feel the lurking malice. Smell the danger in the air.

My skin tingles as I stand and pull my underwear back up, the faceless danger lurking barely a foot away on the other side of the stall door.

I could scream. I *should* scream. But would anyone even hear me down here? I pull my phone out of my bag, my hand shaking as I glance down at it.

No service. Of course.

"You tried to dodge me."

I almost shriek when he speaks. My hand flies up, clamping over my mouth as I tell myself that if I'm quiet enough, he won't know I'm here.

Yeah, right.

"You can't hide from me, BrokenBee."

My heart skips a beat. My core clenches, and the color drains from my face.

What the actual *fuck.*

My brain almost can't process it. Because the second he says that name, I know who is on the other side of the door.

It's *him.*

My stranger. The one I blew off tonight. The one I didn't use the safe word with. The man I've planned an anonymous rape fantasy with, who somehow *just fucking found me.*

Alone. In a club bathroom.

My pulse skyrockets. Something raw, exciting, and terrifying explodes through my system as my mouth falls open.

This is real.

This is happening.

Now.

I yank the wig out of my bag. I throw my hair up into a bun and quickly shove the blonde wig on over it, tucking any stray strands under the edge. It's not perfect. And it's probably a stupid idea anyway. But I'm still hanging on to the whole idea of this being at least semi-anonymous.

Not to mention dangerous and insane. What are you thinking?

"Tick-tock, babygirl," he growls, his voice like gravel and whiskey. Like black smoke and the stain of India ink on paper.

I'm pushing one last strand of dark hair under the wig when the stall door suddenly kicks in. My scream lodges in my throat as I look up with wide, terrified eyes at the leering neon mask towering over me.

Holy *fuck*.

He's fucking *huge*. I'm five-foot-four *without* the heels I have on now. And the man still looms over me, easily over a foot taller than me. He's in black jeans and a black leather jacket, left open to reveal a white t-shirt pulled tight across a massive, muscled chest.

A venomous, deviant energy throbs off his very skin as he slowly inclines his head, creepy neon mask and all, to the side.

"You tried to evade me," he growls again, that rough, deep voice sliding over my skin like tentacles tightening around me.

"No...I..."

"That. Was. *Foolish.*"

In a nanosecond, he charges into me. I scream as he grabs me and roughly spins me around, pinning me hard against the metal wall of the bathroom stall. My pulse explodes into orbit, my eyes wide with terror and my ears ringing. He yanks my arms behind my back, and I choke on another scream as a zip tie yanks tight around my wrists.

"Should have used your safe word, babygirl," he hisses darkly into my ear, the spicy clean scent of him mixing with my paralyzing fear. *"Too late now."*

A bag is yanked over my head, plunging me into darkness.

7

BIANCA

IT'S impossible to tell time when you're lying across the back seat of a car with your hands bound and a bag over your head. So it could be either five minutes or an hour before the car comes to a stop, the engine abruptly switching off.

The door by my feet opens and I gasp as huge hands grab me and yank me out of the car. Gravity goes sideways as the man throws me over his huge shoulder. I can feel the rippling muscles rolling against my stomach, and the pulse-quickening tease of air up the back of my skirt.

Wherever we are, it's quiet. Quieter than a city should sound.

He walks, stops, unlocks a heavy lock, and then swings a door open on rusty, creaking hinges. The door clangs shut behind us, the sound echoing as if we're in a big cave or something.

He sets me down on my feet, and I stiffen when I feel the sharp, cold metal against my wrists. But all he does is cut the zip tie.

Then, there's nothing.

The seconds tick by. My breathing is loud in my ears inside the stuffy heat of the bag over my head. Then—

"Take off the bag."

He sounds further away, even though I swear I never heard him take a single step after he cut off the zip tie. My skin tingles as I reach up, grab the velvet of the bag, and slowly pull it off my head.

Woah.

My mouth falls open, my mind a jumble I drag my eyes up and around.

I'm standing in the middle of a huge, old, crumbling gothic church. A myriad of half-melted candles in metal candelabras sitting in groups on the floor cast flickering light and create haunted shadows on the walls. Old pews—some still upright, others knocked over—are in a vague approximation of the rows they were once in. Rickety scaffolding rises almost to the ceiling on one side of the space, and dim city lights pierce cracked stained-glass windows.

"Blonde doesn't suit you."

My eyes suddenly snap to the front of the church, and my pulse jumps.

He's sitting on a huge throne at the front of the nave, where the pulpit would usually be, a few wide steps up from the main floor. But instead of being gilded and ornate, suitable for a king or the Pope, the seat is as decrepit and crumbling as the rest of the church.

The man, still wearing his neon mask, sits sprawled on this throne, an arm slung over the back of it, his other hand meditatively stroking a finger up and down the side of his neck. Thick, powerful muscles strain against the sleeves of his leather jacket and fill out the white t-shirt beneath it. He doesn't look like a king, or the Pope. More like a savage conquering warlord sitting in the ruins of the post-apocalyptic city he's just sacked.

Blonde doesn't suit you.

His words echo in my head. My hand flies up, and I cringe when I realize that the wig has slipped almost halfway off my head.

"Why, exactly, were you trying to disguise yourself?"

I swallow the thick lump that forms in my throat, my eyes blinking rapidly.

"Asks the man wearing a mask."

His head slowly tips to the other side, those neon X's of his eyes piercing into me.

"You *requested* that I wear this, *prinkípissa.*"

I freeze.

Prinkípissa.

I've heard that word before. Someone's *called me* that befo—

Oh God.

The man in the alley.

The huge, built, tall man in the alley that night wearing a neon mask who inspired this whole…

Something clenches in my stomach.

No. There's no way.

"It's you, isn't it?"

My voice sounds so small as I stand there in the middle of the cavernous gothic church, the dark lord sprawling on his antichrist throne, watching me through the dead, neon eyes of his mask.

When he doesn't respond, I swallow and try again.

"The other day. In the alley. Those two men..." My hands clench together in front of me, one finger picking repeatedly at a cuticle. "Was that you? I..."

I'm about to keep going and blather something stupid like "I recognize your voice" or point out that the mask he's wearing isn't *like* the mask I asked him to wear. It's literally the *same* neon mask from that night. I stop when something occurs to me.

I'm alone in an abandoned church with someone who might very well be a violent psychopath, and I'm about to remind him that I was witness to him committing a double murder.

"*Go on*," he purrs, with almost a hint of humor in his deep, dark tone.

I shake my head. "My friends..." I shiver. "There are people who will be looking for me. They'll notice I'm—"

"No, they won't."

He lifts a phone from the arm of the throne, and I recognize the case. It's mine.

"You were feeling sick after that last tequila shot. You thought you might throw up, and just felt *awful*. So you took a cab home. You texted them again when you got home just now, letting them know you're okay and that you'll call them in the morning."

His head tilts to the other side, and I swear that lurid, leering neon smile is curling up at the corners.

"Naomi, by the way, said to feel better, and that the, and I quote, *hot but boring Latin guy* is talking to Milena about his stock portfolio again," he growls quietly before setting my phone back down. "So, no. They will not be looking for you after *all* those shots."

His finger strokes up and down his neck again, between the mask and the collar of his leather jacket.

"You drink too much, *Bianca*."

My blood turns to ice, my heart skipping as my face goes white.

"I—" I shake my head. "That's not my—"

"Well, it's not Rachel Dawson, now is it?"

My stomach drops. My breath starts coming in quick, shallow, staccato bursts.

"Real names are supposed to be hidden on the site," I croak.

"*Nothing* is hidden from me."

He suddenly uncurls his huge frame from his throne and stands. He walks slowly down the wide steps, picking his way carefully through the piles of old bricks, mossy wood, and other debris as he advances toward me down the main aisle between the broken-down pews.

Part of me wants to turn and run. But I'm frozen in place, my throat slowly closing up as he approaches. Besides, there's no way I'd outrun him. He'd catch me, for sure.

And you'd like it, too.

He moves closer and closer until finally he's standing right in front of me, looking down into my eyes from behind his mask.

"Who are you?" I whisper.

"You know exactly who."

I choke, whimpering as his hand jerks up very suddenly. His fingers wrap tight around my throat, squeezing just tightly enough to send alarm bells exploding through my head and adrenaline coursing through my veins. He leans close and that same spicy clean scent of him drifts into my senses as his lips hover less than an inch from my left ear.

"I'm the man you begged to chase you, Bianca," he growls. "The stranger you asked to be surprised by in the dark so that I could *fuck you* until your knees gave out and my cum dripped from every slutty little hole you have."

Sweet Jesus.

My whole core spasms. My fingertips tingle, and my face throbs as his lewd words rake fiercely over my skin.

"Now," he murmurs, his hand still wrapped around my throat and his neon X eyes still stabbing into my soul. "What to *do* with you…"

My knees shake. Adrenaline, fear, anxiety, and desire pulse and throb through my veins like a heady cocktail of drugs.

"I…what we talked about…" I croak.

He tilts his head to the side, leering down at me.

"You want to play that game?"

I tremble, then nod my head.

"I didn't hear you."

"*Yes,*" I whisper.

He's silent. The seconds tick by as his head slowly tips side to side.

"No."

He rasps it out suddenly as his hand drops from my throat. Without another word, he turns and starts to walk back to his throne.

"W-what?" I choke out, shaking.

"I said *no,*" he growls, pausing to turn and level his masked eyes at me.

My lip worries between my teeth. "Why? Because you know who I am?"

"Yes."

My lips curl. "You're scared of my father?"

He barks a sudden, cold, metallic laugh that has me gasping.

"*No, prinkípissa.* I'm not."

My eyes narrow on him. "Why do you keep calling me that?"

"Because I see right fucking through you...princess."

My lips purse. "I'm *not* a princess—"

"You are. You might as well have fucking woodland creatures dancing and singing all around you, with a talking squirrel for a fucking sidekick," he snarls. "You're a princess in the most Disney fucking sense of the word. So go wish upon a star to be anywhere but here with *any* other man but me."

He turns and starts to walk away again.

My hands ball to two fists at my sides as I draw in a shaky breath.

"I'm *here*. You *brought me* here. So are you going to do it or not?"

He audibly snarls as he whirls on me, the neon of his mask looking demonic as he peers down at me.

"Do *what?*" he snaps.

"What… What we came here for."

A low, dark chuckle rumbles from somewhere within the depths of his broad chest.

"And what *did* you come here for?"

My face turns scarlet as my eyes drop to my feet.

"Well?"

"Y-you know," I mumble.

"Maybe I've forgotten. Maybe I want you to be a good girl and just fucking *tell me*."

Heat explodes across my face as I look down at my hands and take a deep breath.

"Are you going to fuck me or not?" I blurt.

The church is silent. Slowly, he turns to face me full on. His neon eyes pierce my very soul, and I shudder when he starts to walk toward me. He circles me like a shark in the water, his gaze never leaving mine as he does so.

He walks all the way around me, then stops right in front of my face.

"*No.*"

I wince. It's like he's just struck me. My spirit cracks, falling to the floor at my feet as he slowly starts to walk around me again.

"Because of who my father is?" I whisper.

I tense as I feel him stop right behind me, and I shudder when I feel him lean down close, his lips near my ear again.

"*No, prinkípissa*," he snarls quietly. "Because I'd *break you* if I fucked you the way I like to fuck. And you'd do well to remember that before you try to cross paths with someone like me again."

He drifts back in front of me, his eyes leering down into my face. Then, without another word, he turns and starts to stroll away, back to his throne.

"Try me."

The words tumble from my mouth before I can shove them back in.

Slowly, the man stops and half turns, the glow of his neon eyes mingling with the flickering of the candlelight in the stone church.

"*What did you say?*" he murmurs darkly.

I swallow, drumming up whatever courage I have inside.

"I said *try me*."

A second ticks by. Then another.

"You've swum out far past your depth, little girl."

He turns his back on me again and calmly walks up the center of the nave back to his throne.

"Maybe you've just lost your nerve."

I can't believe I just said that.

He stops cold, his broad shoulders tensing. His head cocks to the side.

"*What* did you say?"

I swallow nervously.

Just go, I think to myself. *Just drop it and get out while you can.*

Because he's right. I am *way* out of my depth here. There's having fantasies, and daydreaming about things you've seen in dirty videos.

…And then there's *this*. And whatever "this" is, we're a mile past the line of sanity. Honestly, it's a miracle that I haven't been murdered and cut into pieces yet.

But my mouth has never been great at knowing when it's time to call it quits. The tequila shots still coursing through my bloodstream aren't exactly helping, either.

"I said maybe you've lost your nerve. You know, all bark, no bite? Big talk online, but then the whole thing falls apart in real—"

My words choke to a strangled silence when I hear the sharp metallic *shnick* of a switchblade. The knife clenched in his big, veined hand gleams in the candlelight as his head twists toward me a little more, giving me a glimpse of one neon X.

"For the record, babygirl…"

He turns to face me fully in all his dark, malicious wrath. Fear stabs my heart as he tosses the blade casually from one hand to the other, then back again.

"I *did* give you a chance to leave."

One instant, he's standing thirty feet away holding a knife. The next, he's bolting toward me.

I scream, whirling and flinging myself at the huge wooden doors on their rusty hinges behind me. I grab the heavy iron ring and pull...

And pull.

And pull.

Holy fuck.

When it finally registers in my terrified brain that the door is locked, I spin away and bolt to the side. A snarl echoes in my ear, and another scream tears from my throat as I feel his thick fingertips brush my arm.

Pure survival instinct and adrenaline explode like napalm through my veins as I fling myself across the church, hurdling a broken-down pew and dodging around a pile of mossy bricks.

The heavy thud of footsteps behind me propels me forward, sprinting around another splintered pew.

Don't turn around to look behind you.

I feel like I read that in a book once, that turning around slows you down or makes you veer unnecessarily. And if I do either of those, he'll catch me.

And if he catches me?

Well, clearly, he's more than roleplaying the scenario I asked for. Honestly, I don't think he's roleplaying at all.

I think I may have actually invited a *real* psychopath to chase me down and fuck me.

I scream as I dodge right, then left, then jump over another pew. I glance to the left, and my heart leaps when I see a side door. Maybe it's locked just like the others, but I don't have a choice right now.

This is no longer a game.

This is real.

I choke on my breath, my pulse racing as I dodge right again and bolt for the door. I'm so close, I'm almost there...

...And that's when he grabs me.

I scream as his hand snatches a handful of my hair and yanks. Pain explodes through my scalp, and I wince when I get tugged hard backward and spun around. I lose my footing, and as my heart lurches into my throat, I feel the monster behind me shove me face-down onto the dirty, rough ground.

"PLEASE!"

I scream as his knee lands on the small of my back, the sheer weight of him keeping me pinned to the ground. He growls, grabbing my hair again and yanking my head back as he leans down close to my ear.

"You know how to end this..."

Something hot explodes in my core. Something dark, dangerous and deviant.

He's not trying to kill me.

He's just playing the game.

The adrenaline is still roaring through my veins. But the dull stab of fear in my core has turned into something tingling and throbbing.

Something achy. Something needy.

"But until you have the courage to do that," he snarls into my ear, "I'm going to show you what happens to little princesses who think they want to play rough with *me*."

My eyes bulge as he suddenly jams his hand underneath me and yanks on the front of my top, ripping it. I whimper when he roughly pulls my bra down as well. His big hand engulfs my breast, and I cry out a choked, sobbing moan as he roughly twists and pinches my nipple.

"You think you're into primal play, babygirl?" he hisses sharply. *"Let's see how long you fucking last."*

I scream as he mauls my other breast, tugging mercilessly at my nipples until they're sore and aching. Even as my breath comes in choked sobs, a needy heat pulses between my thighs.

The masked psychopath keeps twisting my nipples, his knee and weight still on the small of my back. His other hand drops down, and I jolt when he yanks my skirt up over my ass. He grabs the back of my thong, pulling it tight and causing it to rub against my throbbing center and aching clit. I whimper, biting down hard on my lip as the forbidden pleasure and filthy fucked-up nature of all of this over-whelms me.

The switchblade flicks in his hand. I gasp when I feel the sharp edge of its blade tease first over the curve of my hip and then then the swell of my ass. He pulls my thong tight again, and suddenly, the blade is slicing through it.

He yanks the tattered bits away. I wince as he twists my head around, forcing me to look at him. He brings the sliced thong to his nose through the mask, inhaling as he chuckles a low, dark, psychotic laugh.

"Mmmm, babygirl," he rasps darkly. "Your pussy smells like fear and candy. I'm going to enjoy devouring you."

I could say please. Or stop. Or no. I could use the safe word, and this would all come crashing to a halt.

At least, I think it would.

But using that word is the last thing on my mind.

Because I don't want him to stop.

I haven't gone as far as I can go yet.

"Now, *prinkipissa*," he rasps. "Let's see how messy your little cunt got being chased like a dirty whore."

Without warning, he cups my pussy. I choke on a moan, my breath hitching as he drags a thick finger through my lips. His palm suddenly slaps my ass, hard, making me jolt and squeal. He does it again, then again to the other cheek, then back to the first again. He goes back and forth until my ass is stinging and raw and my whines of pleasure are echoing off the walls of the gothic church.

Suddenly, I feel a finger at my entrance.

No, not *a* finger.

Fingers.

"I—"

My entire body shudders and writhes as he rams two thick fingers *deep* inside me. Deeper than anything I've ever had there. The sheer size of those fingers takes my breath away, and I can feel my feet twisting and scrabbling against the ground as he roughly curls them.

My walls clench around him. My core spasms and quivers as he slides them out and then pounds them right back in.

Wetly.

I'm not just wet, I'm fucking *soaked*.

The mortifyingly slick, squelching sounds of my pussy fill my ears as the masked stranger roughly fingerfucks me. I cry out when he tugs my hair, or pinches my nipples. He slaps my ass again, hard, as he mauls my aching pussy.

Words fail me. My thoughts are a blur of dark need and haunting desire. All I can do is twist and writhe on the ground, moaning and choking on my breath as he manhandles me and roughly shoves me inexorably toward my breaking point.

His thumb flicks back and forth across my throbbing clit. His two fingers ram into me over and over, curling so deep my shoes fall off when my toes curl against the grimy stone floor.

"Such. A needy. Little. *Slut*," he growls, chuckling darkly as he fingers me into oblivion. "Meeting up with a complete stranger and letting him use your slutty little hole on the floor, like the greedy little cum whore you are."

I gasp sharply when I feel his thumb slip between my cheeks and press against my asshole.

"I bet you'd even beg me to fuck your ass right here and now if it'd mean I'd let you come. You'd let me have you right here on the floor like a whore, fucking your ass raw until you'd taken every fucking drop of my cum, wouldn't you...*slut*."

Something explodes in my core. My eyes squeeze shut as my mouth falls open in a silent scream.

"I know you're a virgin, babygirl," he growls low in my ear as the wave builds higher and higher. "Don't insult me by denying it. I can fucking *smell it* on you. You'd like that, wouldn't you? You'd like it if I used my big, fat cock to split this little cunt open right here for the first time. If I were to make you *bleed* on my cock as I took you for the first time. I'd tear you apart, babygirl. I'd fucking *ruin you* for any other man. And you'd fucking thank me for it afterward."

Something snaps inside me. My tether to reality. My attachment to the real world.

My last grip on my sanity.

I've always known I wanted the primal and the brutal. To be chased and caught. To be tied up, or pinned down and used.

But I never knew I had *this* in me until he started talking like this.

The utter submission. The desire to lose all control and hand it over to him, willingly and eagerly. Because right now, he's right. If he were to ask—not even ask, if he were to *tell me*— that he was going to fuck me right here and now, and take my virginity on the dark, grimy floor of this abandoned church?

I'd not just let him.

I'd beg him to.

"Come on. *Thank me*, babygirl."

A moan rips from my throat.

"Thank you!" I sob.

"Now, beg me to let you come," he snarls, roughly fingering my pussy as his thumb presses against my ass. He reaches underneath me and pinches a nipple, his weight sinking onto the small of my back as I start to come undone.

"Fucking *beg me, slut.*"

"*Please!*" I choke. "*Please let me come!*"

"Are you going to be a good little whore for me?"

"YES!"

"My willing, dirty little cock slut?"

"*Please*! Yes!"

My world goes sideways and upside down as he leans down and bites hard on my earlobe.

"*Good girl. Come for me.*"

It's like a bomb going off. It's like reality leaves the building and yanks the rug out after it. My breath chokes in my lungs. Every muscle in my body violently shakes and spasms, and my core turns to molten lava.

And then I'm coming harder and longer than I ever have before in my life.

The waves crash over me again and again and again. I writhe on the ground, choking and sobbing pathetically as the orgasm shatters me.

Suddenly, his fingers slowly start to slip out of me. He lets go of my nipple, and pulls his hand away.

I'm shaking all over as I curl up into a ball, hugging myself and quivering as I start to cry softly.

Jesus Christ, get it together, psycho.

I'm not hurt. I mean, I'm sore as fuck, *everywhere*, and especially between my legs. But that's not why I'm crying. It's also not because I'm scared, or ashamed, or overwhelmed.

It just feels like this huge emotional drop. Like I've tasted this insane high, and now it's fading away.

The man makes a tsking sound with his teeth as he suddenly stands.

"*Fuck*," he growls quietly. "*Fuck*."

He sighs heavily above me as I blink back the tears and bring a hand up to wipe my eyes. I stay on the ground as I slowly lift my gaze to him.

"This was a mistake, babygirl."

I flinch at the words, both physically and emotionally. His head tilts to the side again.

"I warned you, princess," he growls. "I fucking *warned you* that you were way out past your fucking depth."

He exhales again, the neon X's piercing into me.

"Let's call that getting off easy," he mutters. "Now: run home, princess. Go find a nice prince to play grownup with. You don't want me. And this kink you *think* you have is not for you."

Without another word, he turns and walks into the flickering candlelight of the church, then deeper into the shadows before he finally disappears behind the pulpit.

Then I'm alone.

Slowly, painfully, I get to my feet. There's no sign of my panties, as if I could even wear them anyway. Sucking in slow, steadying breaths of air, I cling to the carved stone wall behind me, leaning against it, looking up at the haunted spires and leering gargoyles.

He was right.

He *did* warn me. And I was out past my depth.

But he was also wrong.

This wasn't a mistake. It wasn't too much. And it didn't break me, despite his best efforts.

I'm pretty sure it just freed me. Because I don't want to run scared. I don't want to go home, tail between my legs. And I certainly don't want to go "find a nice prince to play grownup with."

What I *do* want, though, is more of what just happened.

Because I've never felt more alive in my life.

8

KRATOS

THE BEAST inside of me is a fickle one. He's unpredictable at times, and his tastes are...ambiguous. Despite knowing him intimately all my life, there are still times where I'm not quite sure if the desires roaring inside me are clamoring for violence or sex.

Sometimes I worry that it's both. Others, it's precisely the *promise* of both that gives me a rushing high no drug on Earth can mimic.

It makes my reaction to Bianca Sartorre the other night even more curious.

My jaw sets as the gilded elevator slowly rises forty floors above Central Park South.

I'm still trying to figure out my monster's motive for tracking her to that bar, snatching her, and bringing her to my secret sanctuary. Was it to find out why Vito Barone's adopted daughter was running around with bricks of cocaine in back alleys?

Was it a need for violence? A desire to snip off any loose threads, considering what she saw me do in that alley? Maybe it was fueled by a far baser instinct.

Maybe I was curious why the good little princess has been looking for primal play on the website of a fetish club she shouldn't even be a member of. The one she goes on using a fake name.

Like me.

Honestly, that would be the easiest explanation. It's difficult for me to find someone with whom to explore my very specific tastes. Women who say they're into "rough sex" or primal play typically have no fucking *clue* what I mean when I say it.

I don't mean fucking pink fuzzy handcuffs, or a safe word that gets used the second my fingers curl around a throat.

I'm looking to be *savage*. To fuck like it's an extreme sport, or a battle. What I want with sex is a hunt.

A blood-soaked war.

Most women—most people in general, actually—would never guess this side of me. I keep it locked up tight in a safe buried under the fucking floorboards. Very few women get past the facade to see the real me.

And all of them, without exception, run screaming once they do.

Bianca didn't.

I fully expected her to, which is why I came at her with both barrels blazing: barging in on her, masked, in that club bathroom. Binding and blindfolding her before kidnapping her.

The knife.

The chase.

Showing her the true nature of my beast.

I kept waiting for her to break down and scream the safe word, to show me the terrified little mob princess *way* out of her depth that I knew she was. To prove to both of us that she *does not belong* in the shadows.

Except it never happened, until I forced the issue. Until I pushed her a mile past her comfort zone, pinned her to the ground, and savaged that climax from her shuddering body.

That's when she finally broke.

Like I knew she would. Like maybe I *hoped* she would, so I could go on reminding myself why the mask I wear to face the rest of the world is so necessary.

But deep down, I know the reason I walked away the other night wasn't that I'd proved anything to myself. Nor did it have anything to do with who she or her family is.

When I had Bianca on the very bleeding edge between sanity and my own brand of deviant *in*sanity, I saw something curious in her.

Something good.

Something breakable.

Something I used to be, in a previous lifetime.

I blink as the elevator dings. The black thoughts I've been mulling over in the ride up here vanish, and I can't help but grin when the doors slowly glide open, allowing me to step out into the lavish, gilded entryway to the Drakos estate.

Home.

Or at least, home until recently.

"Engonós."

My grin widens as I step out of the elevator into the stunning home on Central Park South—a staggeringly huge neoclassical mansion perched atop a forty-story building across from Central Park. Twelve bedrooms, twice as many bathrooms, *grounds* complete with two pools and a tennis court, and a wine cellar and collection that most aficionados would kill for.

This place was home when I was a kid. Then again after first our father and then our oldest brother Atlas died, when Ares moved the rest of us back to New York from London. But it's not the house, its luxurious views, gilded walls, or even the warm memories that have me smiling.

It's Ya-ya: my grandmother, Dimitra Drakos, who's standing in the lavish entryway beaming at me.

"Geia sou, Ya-ya," I grin, striding across the marble floor and scooping her into my arms. The woman is all of five-foot-nothing and feels like she weighs as much as a bird. But I, and the rest of my siblings, know that to underestimate her due to her diminutive stature would be a mistake.

Ya-ya might be the size of a seagull, but she's as lethal and as cunning as a lioness.

She sighs, clucking her tongue against her teeth as I pull away. "The house misses you, grandson."

I grin. "Miss you, too, Ya-ya."

We all lived here together after we moved back to the States. But slowly and surely, the rest of my siblings have all gone their own ways, with their own "persons": Ares with Neve, Hades with Elsa, Deimos with Dahlia, and Callie with Castle.

A few months ago, it sort of clicked with me that I was A, the last one here, and B, officially a thirty-year-old man living alone with his *grandmother*.

Not that I'm ashamed of that, at all. And, for the record, it was *Dimitra* who not-so-subtly pushed *me* out. I believe her words were something along the lines of me "never finding a good Greek girl to settle down with and have lots of babies with if I insisted on living with my grandmother".

So a few months ago, I moved into an old brownstone I bought deep in the East Village that I've been slowly refurbishing.

"I thought you'd be hungry."

My smile widens and my stomach rumbles as she lifts the plate in her hand and pulls off the napkin covering it with a small flourish: homemade souvlaki wrapped in pita, along with Ya-ya's famous homemade tzatziki sauce. There's even some fries wrapped up in there.

Fuck. *Yes.*

I groan happily as I take the plate and dig in with an enormous bite.

"How did you guess?" I chuckle around a mouthful of juicy souvlaki.

Ya-ya grins, having to stand up on her tiptoes to pat my cheek even though I'm leaning down. "You're my giant, *engonós*," she beams at me. "And all that Spartan blood needs its nourishment."

I bite back a smile. Ya-ya is *convinced* that our family is directly descended from the three hundred Spartans who defended Greece from the Persian hordes at the Battle of Thermopylae. That we're literally related to the dudes with the CGI abs in that *300* movie. Do not ever try to tell her otherwise.

"This is *delicious*," I growl, devouring the pita.

"Well, maybe it'll entice you to come visit more often. You know, my suggestion that you find your own place didn't mean forget you have a grandmother," she chides with a grin.

I chuckle. "Miss me already, Ya-ya?"

She rolls her eyes. "My kitchen certainly does. I don't know what to do with all the food in there anymore."

"I could aways move back in, you know."

"And pigs might fly, Kratos," she smirks with a sternly arched brow. "Which is to say—no, you can't."

I laugh. "That's *cold*, Ya-ya. What, you got a boyfriend coming around these days you don't want me to see?"

"Just one?"

I snort around another bite of souvlaki and gesture past her with my chin. "Am I the last to arrive?"

She nods. "The king is holding court in the library."

"Well, best not keep him waiting."

Ares is a *stickler* for punctuality at these family meetings of his.

The mask has been back on since I stepped off the elevator. And it'll stay there when I greet the rest of them. I've moved mountains to ensure that my family never sees the darker side of me. They know first-hand how cruel our father was. And they all experienced the sadism of our oldest brother, Atlas, before his death a few years ago.

But none of them knows what happened to me. What was done to me. None of them knows what I really am.

"Well, well, look who showed up."

"I had to do a quick thing for Ya-ya," I rumble as I step into the library, rolling my eyes at Ares. "Relax."

Ares, our oldest surviving brother and the official head of the Drakos family, frowns a little, but then he lets it go as he clears his throat. Ares plays the role of protector. The strong shield. The one wearing the heavy crown and making the tough calls. Ironically, he does all this as if he had been born to be king, even though technically he wasn't.

But that's who he is now. And recently becoming a parent with his wife Neve to my nephew, Elias, has only strengthened that.

My gaze pulls around the beautiful old library full of leather-bound books where Ares likes to hold court if we're meeting here at Ya-ya's house. Sprawled on the couch next to Ares' chair is my second-oldest brother, Hades: chaotic, untamed, and impulsive, a physical manifestation of "id".

Or at least, he *was*.

He's still the same maniac brother with whom I share a love of engines and fighting. But now that he's married to Elsa, a stepfather of sorts to her younger sister Nora, *and* expecting a child of his own, his sharper edges have been smoothed a bit.

Deimos, my younger brother, stands by the window. Of any of them, I suppose he's the one I *should* connect the best with, as he's arguably the most like me. Except, while I hide all my dark emotions, urges, and nature deep inside, Deimos wears them on his sleeve. We all *expect* him to be "the scary psycho" of the family, because it's a role he's played ever since we were kids.

I'm fine with him having that role. It took the eyes off me after the horror-show that was my childhood and early teen years. But even Deimos has calmed down a bit in the last year, since marrying Dahlia.

He and I nod to each other before I stride over and slump onto the second couch next to my little sister, Callie. She lived here at Ya-ya's house with me the longest, until she married Castle, the head of the Kildare Irish Mafia family.

Yes, we were all named for Greek gods, muses, and titans. In addition to being a monstrously cruel piece of shit, our father had a bit of a thing for Greek mythology.

And yes, I'm aware that there's another common theme here: all my siblings, even wild-man Hades and crazy Deimos, have moved on. They're creating lives and new directions for themselves with people they love.

Meanwhile, I don't know what I am or what the fuck I'm supposed to be.

Callie turns to smirk at me, her eyes dropping to the remains of the souvlaki in my hands.

"Had to *do a quick thing for Ya-ya*, huh?" She smirks. "Like what, help her empty the fridge?"

I chuckle, offering her the plate. "Wanna bite?"

Callie shakes her head. "What, and take food out of the mouth of the favorite grandchild? Not a chance."

I roll my eyes. "I'm not *the favorite*."

"Dude, *I* didn't get a pita pocket and fucking French fries when I walked in."

"I got French fries," Deimos shrugs, grinning. "But I had to steal them from the kitchen when Ya-ya wasn't looking. You know, because I'm not the favorite either."

My eyes roll as I glance back to Callie and wave the plate in front of her.

"You *suuuure?*"

She sighs heavily and snatches a huge handful of fries, stuffing like four at once in her mouth.

"Ass."

I grin as I watch her scarf them down. "Do I need to have a talk with Castle? Is he not feeding you enough?"

"Oh, don't you worry. He's feeding me plenty. You know, eating for two and all that."

My brows shoot up. "Holy shit," I blurt. "Cals, are you—"

"Kidding," she giggles. "I mean, I'm not *yet*." She smirks at me. "But we're putting in lots of practice."

I make a puke face and wrinkle my nose. "Annnd *there's* that daily dose of way T. M. fucking I. that's been lacking since you moved out."

"Aww," she grins. "You miss it. Admit it."

Ares loudly clears his throat. "So, yeah, if you're done with lunch, Kratos," he grumbles at me. "Could we get this show on the road?"

I grin, offering him my plate of fries, which he takes, because of course he does. No one in their right mind says no to Yaya's food.

"How's my nephew?"

"Loud," my oldest brother sighs, looking about as exhausted as I'd imagine the father of a two-month-old would.

Hades chuckles. "Ares is just fucking pissed that Elias is stealing Neve's tits away from him."

"No, Ares is fucking *tired*," our brother grunts. "Because he hasn't slept more than three fucking hours at a stretch in two months. And he'd like to get this goddamn meeting started so that he can *maybe* sneak in a ten-minute nap before he goes home to diapers and cleaning pump parts. Also, if you could maybe never talk about my wife's breasts again, that'd be *swell*."

Hades chuckles. Callie wags a finger at him.

"Hey, laugh it up while you can, bro. That's gonna be you in three months."

Hades makes a face as Ares clears his throat again.

"*Anyway*. This can be brief, but…" He rolls his shoulders, turning to glance at each of us. "We need to talk about the Italian elephant in the room."

Deimos' brow furrows. "Nero?"

"Nero," Ares grunts, nodding. "We all knew there'd be some upheaval and drama when the Carveli family went down in flames…"

Beside me, Callie shivers a little, hugging herself. I drop a heavy, comforting hand on her shoulder, which she seems to appreciate, turning and smiling at me a little.

I doubt many people ever had a *good* experience with the Carvelis. But Callie especially doesn't look back on them with any fondness. There was a while there when an old blood marker our father made with the Carveli family betrothed our sister to the sleazy, cruel, sixty-year-old father of the late and unlamented Don Massimo Carveli.

"However," Ares continues. "We didn't expect the De Luca family to be the one filling that fifth slot on the Italian Commission. The problem here is—"

"That Nero is a fucking violent, unpredictable lunatic," Deimos grunts from where he's still leaning against the bookshelves near one of the windows.

Hades scowls. "Great. So another fucking Massimo."

Ares wags his head side to side. "Not quite, but he's definitely a wild card. They've been calling him the young lion, both because of his ferocity and the fact that he's got something to prove. To make things even more interesting, apparently Nero has bad blood with Davit."

I wince.

Shit.

"Guess it'd make things too easy if all the criminal scumbags in this city would kiss and make up and stop trying to stab each other in the back, huh?" Callie mutters.

"I'm not sure anyone has ever accused the Albanians of setting aside grudges," I grunt before turning to Ares. "Just how 'bad' is this bad blood?"

Ares looks grim. "Davit and I had a talk this morning, and he promised to turn Little Italy into Kosovo if Nero so much as mispronounces his name."

"*Super*," Callie groans.

Ares is right: this *is* a problem.

Davit Kirakosian is the head of Te Mallkuarit, aka "The Cursed Ones"—an Albanian crime family deeply rooted in mysticism and old-school religion, with a knack for smuggling and a penchant for cutting the heads off their enemies.

I mean that extremely literally.

They've also recently planted roots in New York. Normally, since they haven't made a single move on any of our territory or interests, we'd be leaving people like Davit and his merry band of head-chopping psychos alone. But that was before they made a hard play for the same development site on the west side of Manhattan that we were.

Word that Vito Barone was going to be offloading the building overlooking the Hudson River that he got for a *song* years ago garnered a ton of interest from every developer and investor in the city. Vito's not a huge fan of our family: somewhat because of old Greek-Italian rivalries from way back, but in huge part because of a Deimos.

Before Dahlia, my brother was a member of Club Venom. I don't know, and I'm sure I don't *want* to know the details. But apparently there was an incident of some kind at the club between him and Vito's niece, which resulted in Dante revoking my brother's membership.

Needless to say, Vito hasn't exactly looked kindly in our direction since. But money talks, and we were able to make ours sing and fucking dance when it came to being the top bid for his property.

The Armenians did come in swinging there for a while, with money I genuinely didn't know they had. But pending some last-minute details of the sale, *we'll* be taking that property off Vito's hands, not Davit.

"That reminds me." Ares turns to nod in my direction. "Davit wants to give…well, *lend*…us a token of goodwill. Things got a little tense there during the bidding war for Vito's property. But I think this is his way of settling it between our families. Plus, I'm pretty sure he'd actually like to do some business together sometime. Anyway, I need you to go pick it up."

I frown. "Okayyy…but why me? And what exactly is this token of goodwill?"

"A 12th century statue of the Crucifixion, and I'm asking you because it's *huge* and weighs a fucking ton."

Great. "How heavy are we talking?"

"Davit mentioned bringing a truck."

My brows shoot up. "What's this fucking thing made of, gold?"

Ares smiles, slowly shaking his head.

"Human bones."

"Yeah, no. Fuck that," I shake my head. "I'm out."

"Kratos, I *need* you to do this. It's gotta be someone from the family, or it'll be perceived as an insult. I'd go myself, but I'll be real with you, brother. I'm fucking *tired*. Like, seriously. I'm asking you to do this as a favor for the family."

I sigh heavily.

"Jesus, I'll go with you, ya big pussy," Hades snickers, grinning at me. "Okay?"

"Fine."

Callie frowns. "The Albanians were *aggressive* with wanting that property. The peace offering, however creepy, is a nice gesture. But if they go to war with Nero, and Nero is allied with the Barone family, and we're doing *business* with the Barone family…"

Ares nods slowly. "I've already spoken to Davit about this, as well as Michael Genovisi of the Scaliami family, and Cesare Marchetti. No one *wants* an all-out war. Even Davit is aware how bad that would be for business, and for all his obsession with honor and shit, business comes first." My oldest brother sighs heavily. "But it's a big, flimsy powder keg right now. All it's going to take is one spark, and we're going to have huge problems."

"Well, obviously, the Kildare family stands with this family," Callie says fiercely.

"And I know Castle knows how much we appreciate that," Ares says in a measured tone. "But it's like a bad game of dominos: if we get involved with a war, and then drag the Kildare family into it, that'll drag the Reznikov Bratva into it through *their* alliances. And now we're talking about World War Three in the streets of Manhattan."

"So what's the plan?" I growl.

Ares spreads his hands. "I'm working on one. But in the interim, we need to make sure no one in this family gets into any sort of bullshit or entanglements with the Italians. At all."

My jaw ticks.

Yeah, no. Too late.

It's not just about what happened the other night with Bianca. It's that it was no accident that it was her I matched with on the Club Venom website.

I orchestrated the entire thing.

It all started when I found the two pieces of shit traffickers I'd been hunting trying to attack her in that alley. On the plus side, I stopped those two fucks from brutalizing her that night. But on the bad side?

Well, let's just say she caught my attention.

All of it.

After that night, I did what I always do when something pulls my attention like that. I dug up. I sliced open. I unearthed every secret and hidden place, trying to dissect Bianca Sartorre.

What she was doing in the middle of a drug deal that night is no real mystery. I know now that the two other girls who fled that alley and left her to the wolves are Alicia Houghton and Irina Lenkova, both also dancers in the Zakharova Ballet. It took about four seconds of digging to put together that they're not really friends with Bianca, because she doesn't *have* many friends. It took another two whole seconds to figure out that Alicia's dating Grisha Lenkov, a mid-level Chernoff Bratva wannabe thug who also happens to be Irina's cousin.

That explains the drugs. It also explains why Bianca there, probably seeking approval from two girls who've historically snubbed her, plus why they ditched her as soon as things went bad.

But it *doesn't* explain the way that mix of innocence and darkness in her eyes—of fear and excitement—captivated my attention.

More importantly, captivated my beast's attention.

After that, it was just a matter of time. Especially after I hacked her phone that very first night in the alley.

Since then, I've been in her pocket, next to her bed, and sitting on the bathroom vanity while she showers. I've read her emails and texts. I've enjoyed watching the dirty videos she's viewed in incognito mode.

….And I've watched her log into the Club Venom web portal as "BrokenBee".

I know for a fact Bianca's not really a member of Venom. Dante and I aren't close, but I know him well enough to know there's a snowball's chance in hell he'd ever allow his little sister to become a member of his playground for dangerous deviants.

I'm not a member either. But Xavier, a hacker I frequently work with when hunting down monsters, got me into the Club Venom system. Once inside, armed with a new profile, I could force the match between her profile and mine, as well as make sure no *other* profiles could even see hers.

And the rest, as they say, is history. The sort of history I'm still thinking about, constantly.

The fear and the excitement in her eyes as I chased her like a maniac. The intoxicating scent of inexperience and innocence when I caught her.

The deliciousness of her cries and the heat of her tight little virgin pussy. The willpower it took not to fuck her in every sweet, wet hole she had until she was my perfectly broken little toy.

After Ares wraps up the meeting, when I'm heading down the elevator again, I pull out my phone and bring up the tracking app Xavier helped me install on hers. The willpower I exerted the other night when it comes to Bianca does have its limits, after all.

My lips curl slightly as I watch her phone's location ping like a little blinker, down one Manhattan street and up another, before it moves into a larger building: the Mercury Opera House, home of the Zakharova Ballet.

She's at rehearsal, blissfully unaware that I'm watching her every move.

Hunting her every step.

Still tasting her sweetness on my tongue.

I scowl as my phone buzzes, a text popping up and ripping my attention away from Bianca's location.

TAYLOR

We need to meet. Now. Usual room at The Standard.

My teeth grind.

Fuck.

Ares may want to minimize our "entanglements" with the Italians to make sure things don't get more fucked up than they already are. The problem is that it's not just my hidden darkness and secret nocturnal activities my family doesn't know about.

They also don't know that shit is *already* more fucked up.

Extremely so. Catastrophically.

And something tells me, as I glance at the text from my lawyer, that it's about to get *way* worse.

9

KRATOS

"DID you follow protocol getting into the hotel?"

I nod as Taylor smooths a lock of red hair back into place, glancing out the big window of the hotel suite and down to the Meatpacking District below.

"Yup. Took a cab to the French restaurant down the street, slipped out the back door, stayed out of sight, and entered the hotel via the service entrance."

"You're sure you weren't followed?"

"Positive."

She turns to give me a wary half-smile. "Just checking all the boxes."

No, we're not having a clandestine affair. In fact, I doubt Taylor Crown dates at all, given how married she is to her job.

Taylor's the "Crown" in the hugely prestigious Crown and Black law firm, which my family uses extensively for both our legitimate and not-so-legitimate business needs. She's also my personal attorney. Normally, for pretty much anything else, we'd be meeting at their plush offices in Midtown. But not today.

Not for this.

Taylor glances at her watch as my pulse chugs along like thick oil.

"She'll be here any minute."

Something sharp and barbed twists in my gut. A cold sensation and the need to escape from something unseen overwhelms me.

"Have you talked to your family about any of this?"

I shake my head. Taylor nods.

"Okay. Just curious." She clears her throat, folding her arms over her smart, elegant, all-business charcoal gray skirt suit. "Like we discussed, she's going to try and throw you with all sorts of scary threats. But remember, the CIA cuts deals *all the time*. Now, again, she's almost certain to try and use the history between you to rattle you. So let me do the talking."

I just nod slowly, staring past her out the window.

Yes, Taylor knows Amaya and I have "a history". But she doesn't know what the true nature of that history is.

Nobody does. Nobody alive, that is, aside from Amaya and me.

Jesus. One of these days, all the secrets I keep inside might drag me down...or make me explode. But until that day comes, nothing about the situation is going to change. Not even to my lawyer, who's sworn to attorney-client privilege.

Yeah, Amaya and I have "history" all right.

A dark one.

The sort of history that scars and shapes you, that ends childhoods far too early and molds you into something brutal and twisted.

She helped make me the monster I am today.

But that's not the reason we're meeting her today, in a hotel room of all places, so that no one knows about it.

Back then, when it all happened, Amaya Mircari was working for the FBI. My father wanted a friend in the Bureau. He also wanted to "make a man out of me", since I refused to be his attack dog.

Amaya was gladly able to help with both those things.

That was seventeen years ago. Now, she's moved on and gone up in the world, switching from the FBI to the CIA. That's how our paths have managed to cross again.

Because I fucked up.

Our family has been slowly moving most of our business from the shady and illegal to the legitimate. But there's still a *lot* of money in smuggling weapons and drugs into this country.

If you do it right, it's actually pretty low risk. We only work with people we've known for years. We keep the exchanges under a certain monetary threshold to avoid close scrutiny, and we always meet on *our* terms.

But a few weeks ago, I got sloppy.

Ares had been muttering about a dip in profits from the previous quarter's financial investments. At the same time, I got contacted by a "friend of a friend of a friend"—a merchant who knew someone I'd worked with once, who was friends with someone I deal with regularly. They wanted a huge shipment of weapons.

It was stupid, but they were waving big money around. I got greedy, and it bit me in the ass, *hard*. Because after the lights went down and the curtain went up, it turned out my new "buyer" was the CIA, conducting an anti-terror sting operation.

On the plus side, I did the drop myself, alone, so none of our guys got picked up. And my family doesn't know about any of this shit yet, thank fucking God.

But yours truly is *royally screwed*.

Not just because I'm potentially looking at spending the next thirty years in Federal prison. Even worse, the lead agent on all this is *her*.

As if on cue, there's a knock at the door. Taylor turns, her brow furrowing just a little as we lock eyes.

"Seriously. Let me do the talking. The very fact that we're having this meeting is significant. They want something, and it's not your ass in prison, or you'd *be* there already. Got it?"

I just nod.

Yeah, Amaya fucking wants something all right.

As if she hasn't already taken so much from me.

I'm silent as Taylor straightens her blazer and walks over to the door to the suite. My jaw grinds painfully when she swings it open and a regal-looking woman in her late forties walks in.

Amaya smiles briefly at me. I don't smile back.

"My my, Kratos," she says softly. "All grown up now, aren't we?"

Her hair is dyed blonder than it used to be. Her face has the shiny, tight look that suggests she and Botox are besties now. But those fucking eyes of hers haven't changed at all.

Dark. Cold. Cruel.

She's also still got the brutal-looking scar running up the side of her neck. I don't give a single shit how she got it, but I remember it used to scare me, when I was a kid and we first met.

...Before I found out there were *much* scarier things about her.

"If you'd like to address my client, you can talk to him via me—"

"And you can take that cunty attitude and ten-thousand-dollar Chanel suit and fuck right off," Amaya says with a wide, venomous smile at Taylor.

Taylor's brows arch sharply and her nostrils flare.

"This isn't my first rodeo, Agent Mircari, and I speak fluent bitch. So, we can stand around slinging shit at each other all day, or we can have a productive meeting about—"

"I think it's time you left, Ms. Crown."

Taylor *almost* looks amused. "That's obviously not happening, Agent Mircari. This is a legal meeting, and I'm Mr. Drakos' attorney—"

"And I'm about ten seconds away from waving close to a thousand anti-terror provisions in your face courtesy of the

Patriot Act, Ms. Crown," Amaya spits back, with an almost gleeful expression on her face. "We can start with section C, paragraph twenty-seven. Then we'll move on to provision nine-fifty-two, section D." She smiles icily at Taylor. "Do I need to keep going?"

I can see the wheels turning in Taylor's head. I notice the way her jaw clenches. When she turns to me, I already know where this is going.

"Kratos…"

"It's fine," I growl quietly.

"With the charges being firearms, and given that it was a terror sting op, she *can* actually—"

"It's okay," I mutter.

"*Goodbye*, Ms. Crown," Amaya snaps with a brittle laugh, opening the door for Taylor.

My attorney glances at me once more, her face grim. Then she steps out, the door slamming shut behind her.

The room is quiet as the she-devil from my past slowly turns to me, arms folded over her chest as she leans against the hotel room wall. The seconds tick by in silence as she grins at me, and I glare death right back at her.

"Unbelievable," she finally says quietly. "You got even bigger."

"And I can only assume you've grown another forked tail, some more horns, and scales," I hiss quietly.

Amaya chuckles, slowly shaking her head.

"I've missed—"

"Fuck you," I snap.

She scowls.

"Seems like you've got yourself in a bad spot, Kratos. And it would *also* seem I may be your only way out of this mess. So, maybe we act a little more civil to each other?"

I bark out a cold laugh. "You want me to be civil to a piece of shit like you?"

She rolls her eyes. "Well, in any case," she says, clapping her hands together, "our past—"

"We don't *have* a fucking *past*," I growl darkly at her. "You're not my fucking ex, you miserable bitch."

"Ohhh, I don't know if that's true, do you?"

I look away. "What the fuck do you want, Amaya."

"It's what the CIA wants, actually," she shrugs. "Not me."

"Which is?"

Her smile widens. "Information."

I snort. "You're wasting your time. I'm not a rat."

"No. But you're a Drakos."

My eyes flash with rage, my lips curling.

"You're fucking *high* if you think I'd ever give you a goddamn thing on my family."

"Even if it keeps you out of prison?"

"Like I said," I smile coldly. "Fucking. *High*."

She shakes her head sadly. "Like I said, you're in a rough spot, Kratos. I think you need to face facts. Maybe it's not your family I want. Maybe it's the Irish you're so chummy with."

"No idea what you're talking about...cunt."

Amaya laughs mirthlessly. "Well, I guess we're going to be changing gears, then." She takes a deep breath. "I know you don't care if I threaten you."

I smile, shrugging. "Not at all."

"So, here's what's going to happen, Kratos. You *are* going to rat for me. You're going to get me information on whoever the fuck I want, whenever I want it."

"Whatever you're smoking, I'd suggest laying off it a little—"

"*If you don't,*" Amaya barrels on, reaching into her briefcase and pulling out a stack of manilla file folders. "Then I start going after the people you care about."

She slaps the first one on the table between us, and my jaw tightens.

Ares' name is typed across the front of it.

"Wire fraud, witness intimidation, murder, conspiracy to commit murder, weapons charges, racketeering, drug trafficking, weapons trafficking—"

"If any of this was anything more than conjecture, my brother would already be behind bars."

She shrugs, dropping another file on the table. This one has Hades' name on it.

"More trafficking, more murder, more gun charges, grand theft, grand theft auto, impersonating a federal officer, indecent exposure in a moving vehicle..." She smiles. "Shall I go on?"

"Like I said, if you had anything—"

A third folder drops on the table. My jaw clenches when I see Callie's name.

"You know what all this is, Kratos?" Amaya smiles. "This is a case under the RICO Act. You know, the shit we use to go after mobsters like you and your family. What it means is, we can connect *all of you* to a criminal conspiracy and charge you *all* with *everything.*"

My pulse starts hammering.

"I don't have the hard evidence yet, you're right," Amaya hisses. "But I will soon. And when I do, if you don't do what I ask, I'll put your entire family—your brothers, your sister, even your dear old grandmother—in prison for the rest of their lives. Just think: poor little Elias, growing up without his mommy and daddy, because they're behind bars."

Rage explodes behind my eyes. My lips curl into a dangerous snarl as I glare death at this witch of a woman.

"The walls are closing in, Kratos. So: get me something big. I don't care where you start, or who you throw under the bus. But get me something good, a bigger fish, or I go after the biggest one I have right now, which is you and your family." Her lips draw to a cold smile. "Do we understand each other?"

She makes for the door.

"Do they know what you are?"

Her head turns back to me. "Who?"

"The CIA," I growl. "Do they know you're a fucking predator?"

Amaya holds my gaze with hers. "Really? Is that how you think of me?"

132

"I don't think about you at all, you miserable cunt. I was *thirteen*," I hiss coldly. "I was a fucking *child*."

She rolls her eyes. "As if you didn't enjoy yourself."

She turns to leave again.

"What I think you are, Amaya," I snarl, "is a fucking *monster*."

"Takes one to know one, Kratos," she shoots back. Then she grins. "And I guess that means you *do* still think of me."

"Not if I can help it."

"Seeing anyone?"

My hands curl to fists. "Go to hell."

She snickers quietly as she walks to the door. Right before she opens it, she turns to me again.

"To answer your question, Kratos, they don't give a shit what I am, so long as I put people like you and your family behind bars. Remember that and do what you're told like a good boy." She smirks as she opens the door. "You always were good at that."

10

BIANCA

RETURNING TO REALITY IS HARD, once you've had that first tantalizing peek behind the curtain.

There's an iconic scene in *The Matrix* where Morpheus tells Neo to choose between taking the red pill or the blue pill. The blue pill will erase all memory of the craziness he's just witnessed and ease him back into his fake, comfortable life.

If he takes the red one, though, the veil will be lifted. He'll, as Laurence Fishburne's Morpheus puts it, "see how deep the rabbit hole goes".

In my case, I've taken the red pill, but life keeps trying to convince me I've taken the blue one.

No one in my real world *knows* what I've seen. What I've experienced.

What I've done.

Not my family, because obviously. Not my friends, either.

It's been a week since that night. Since the huge, masked man with the punishing touch and the voice like sin vanished into the ether after chasing me through that church. Since he brought me to heights I've only fantasized about, only to disappear like smoke.

"This was a mistake, princess. I fucking warned you *that you were way out past your fucking depth."*

After the rush and the madness of that chase, and the knife, and him brutalizing the most insane orgasm of my life from my body, I actually waited for him to come back. Seconds ticked by. Then minutes.

Finally I was forced to admit that he really was gone, and that I was alone in a creepy old boarded-up church, fuck-knows-where, without a phone, because he'd taken that, too.

When I'd poked my head outside, though, there was a black car waiting for me, with a driver in sunglasses who never responded to a single thing I said, but freakishly drove me *right to my front door* before handing me my phone.

Milena and Naomi both checked in with me the next morning to see how my "hangover" was. Madame Kuzmina's made a comment here and there over the last week about me being "distracted".

But no one knows the truth. No one knows that I've swallowed that red pill. And now I can't see anything the same way.

I'm early to the theater today, so after changing and stretching a little, I sit in one of the empty seats ten or so rows back from the stage. I frown at the web tab on my phone that's open to my Club Venom account.

No new messages from RaisedByWolves. Not a single peep. I mean it's not like I'd expect an encounter like ours to merit a "hey I had a great time the other night" follow-up. It's not like we went to the movies or shared a milkshake, for crying out loud.

But still. The absence of...anything...makes me feel almost hollow inside. Not quite put back together right. It's not like I feel ditched or discarded—well, maybe a little. No, the thing is that this is the one other person on Earth who knows what I did that night. The one person who could maybe at least *sort of* understand what I'm feeling right now, after diving headfirst into my darkest fantasy.

And he's gone. No messages, I haven't even seen him online at all since that night.

He's disappeared like a half-remembered fever dream. What's even weirder is that I don't have any messages or other chat requests *at all*.

I mean, I know my profile is a little bare bones, but still. I'm on a kink website advertising that I'm into primal play, and I don't have a single response aside from him? I even went back and added to my profile, trying to see if that made a difference. I added my age. I elaborated on my kink. The other day, I even uploaded a picture of my ass in yoga pants.

And not to toot my own horn, but I've been sculpting that butt through brutal ballet classes for like fifteen years.

Not a single response.

I exhale, making a face as I stare at my last few messages to him from the past few days.

BROKENBEE

Hi again

A day after that:

> **BROKENBEE**
>
> Not trying to be weird, I just wanted to thank you for the other night. It was perfect

A few days later, after three glasses of wine:

> **BROKENBEE**
>
> If you didn't have a good time, would you mind giving me feedback? I'm new to this and I'd love to know what I could do better

God. That one in particular makes me cringe when I read it. Hard. But then I glance at the last one, from two days ago:

> **BROKENBEE**
>
> You didn't break me, you know

"Ooo, what's that?"

I almost have a seizure as I all but throw my phone up in the air. I manage to catch it, my breath, and my runaway heart before I turn to look up at Milena with a white, blank expression.

"Um, what?"

She arches a brow, smirking at me.

"Who were you messaging, and what app is that?"

"Tinder," I blurt, shrugging casually.

Milena gives me a look. "Uh, no it's not."

"Sure it is. New interface."

Her grin widens. "Yeah? Prove—"

For once, I'm actually grateful for the cold, barking voice of Madame Kuzmina telling us to get off our lazy asses and to the barre.

MERCIFULLY, Milena has either forgotten about what she saw or has decided to give me a pass on it by the time our day is over. I say goodbye to her and Naomi after they shower and change, then grab my stuff and head out the back door to go find a cab.

To my shame, when the hand clamps over my mouth, and another rough, powerful hand grabs my arm and shoves me against the brick wall, my first emotion isn't fear.

It's *excitement*.

A, because as I've mentioned, I'm a freak with issues. And B, because my first fucked-up thought is that it's *him*. That he's back. That he wants to play again...

"You fucking *bitch*."

It's the voice that takes me from deliciously, dangerously excited to freaked the fuck out.

It's not my masked RaisedByWolves. It's *Grisha*.

I gasp as he spins me around, his mean, slightly-too-skinny face suffused with anger and his cruel eyes boring right into mine. He's flanked by three other youngish Russian guys I've seen him hanging around with. And behind them stands a terrified-looking Alicia.

"I've been fucking patient, you little bitch," Grisha snarls at me. "I've been waiting for you to do the right thing. I *know* you fucking have it!"

My eyes bulge as he shoves me back into the wall again. My gaze rips past him and darts to Alicia, my mouth falling open.

She quickly shakes her head, her face paling. "Grisha, baby, I told you, those guys—"

"Shut the *fuck up*," he snarls at her, his eyes still leveled at me as he leers close. "My idiot girl keeps trying to tell me that you lost the duffle—"

"I—!"

I choke on a scream as the back of his hand smacks hard across my cheek. Stars dot my vision as I hear Alicia shriek, and I taste my coppery blood on my tongue.

"*Grisha!*" I blurt. "I don't—"

"Nobody throws away that much cocaine," he hisses. I shudder as he grabs the front of my hoodie, yanking me close. "Nobody *loses* that much cocaine, either."

"They took it!" I scream. "The men who were going to buy it!" My pulse roars. "They—"

"Do you think I'm fucking stupid?"

I blink. "*What?!*"

"DO YOU THINK I'M FUCKING STUPID!!" Grisha roars in my face, making me tremble.

"No!" I blurt, quivering.

"I fucking *know* you were working with those two, bitch."

It feels like I've been slapped again.

"*What?!*"

"Make a big scene, send my girl and her friend running! Then, you come outta the alley totally fine, but mysteriously without *my fucking drugs*?!"

"Grisha," I plead. "I *swear* to you, I don't know those men! I…"

I want to tell them all about the masked man. About how he killed my two attackers and dumped the coke. But for some insane reason, I don't.

Not just because I sincerely doubt they'd believe me.

You're worried about betraying him.

Yeah, I've officially lost it. I'm actually standing here *not disclosing* this information because…it's what, seriously, a betrayal?…of the masked man who may very well be an actual psychopath, who my only real relationship with—if you can even call it that—is that I let him chase me around an abandoned church with a knife until he caught me and fingered me to orgasm?

What the actual fuck is wrong with me?

I'm about to blurt the whole thing out when suddenly Grisha yanks something metallic and gleaming out of his belt and levels it at my face, and my entire world goes still.

It's a fucking gun.

Alicia slams a hand over her mouth, looking terrified, her wide eyes staring at me past her insane boyfriend.

"*Shut. Up.*" Grisha growls quietly, his voice eerily calm. "Now, I'm going to ask you once more. Do you know the two assholes who took my coke? And I swear to fuck, you'd better not lie."

Tears start to trickle down my cheeks as I shake my head. *"I don't!"* I sob.

Grisha's lips curl.

"No? Well, you're about to prove it, bitch."

Before I can say anything, he grabs me again and starts to yank me toward a black Mercedes. Alicia screams and rushes to him, but he roughly shoves her away before barking something in Russian to one of his buddies. The guy grabs Alicia, holding her back even as she screams my name and Grisha and his two other goons drag me to the car.

My pulse is pounding like a drum in my ears as we drive through the city. I'm in the back seat with Grisha, his gun still aimed right at me as naked fear burns through my veins. We cross the Washington Bridge into the Bronx and drive deeper into the borough until storefronts and apartment buildings give way to old truck depots and derelict buildings. Suddenly, we come to a stop outside an abandoned warehouse.

The car shuts off.

"Get out," Grisha snarls.

He's going to kill me.

We're parked in what may as well be Murder Central: a dark, abandoned street, with nothing around but the boarded-up warehouse and an older-looking Land Rover parked across the street.

I turn to Grisha, pure panic in my eyes as I watch him smile darkly.

"You say you don't know those two fucks?"

I shake my head violently side to side.

"You *sure?*" he hisses.

"Yes!"

Grisha smiles malevolently. "Good. Prove it."

He says something in Russian. One of his buddies passes him a bottle of what I assume is vodka, and a lighter. I frown, peering closer. Then the scent hits my nose.

Oh my God.

He's not holding a bottle of vodka. It's got a rag sticking out the top of it, and it reeks of gasoline.

Holy shit.

He's holding a Molotov cocktail—a glass bottle filled with gas with a rag for a fuse, like they use in urban warzones.

My eyes go wide as Grisha turns to nod at the Land Rover across the street.

"Some of my people saw this car driving away from the scene the other night when you lost my fucking coke."

I swallow a lump in my throat, trembling as he shoves the bottle into my hand.

"You say you don't know those assholes? Prove it." He points to the Land Rover. "I'm gonna light this Molotov, and you're gonna blow up that fuckin' car."

My stomach drops along with my jaw. I twist my head, my stricken face staring at Grisha.

"*W-what?!*" I choke.

"You heard me," he snarls as his buddies start to chuckle. "Blow it the fuck up."

"I—" I shake my head, trembling. "I-I can't—"

His eyes narrow. "Yeah, bitch, you fuckin' can. And you will." I gasp, sobbing out a cry as he grabs my hoodie again and shakes me. "You remember how much cocaine you lost!?"

"I—I can pay you back!"

I have no idea how, but if it gets me out of whatever the hell this is, I'll figure out a way—

"You think I'm slinging 8-balls, you dumb bitch?" he snaps. "Those were *bricks* you decided to just run away from. You got four hundred grand on you? Because rest assured, I fucking *will* be collecting on that. But for now…"

I jolt, gasping, tears springing to my eyes as Grisha jams the gun against my neck.

"Light it."

A hand reaches past me. The lighter flickers. Instantly, the rag stuffed into the bottle catches into a hungry blaze. Grisha and his buddies giggle and snort, springing away before Grisha points the gun at me again.

"Better throw that quick!" he snarls. "Else it's gonna blow your fuckin' head off."

I turn to stare at the old Land Rover. My hand trembles as the heat of the flames ripples up my arm.

"And if you miss…" Grisha growls from behind me.

The cocking of the gun hammer tells me how that sentence ends.

"Do it," he snaps. "Fucking *throw it!*"

My arm winds back. The flickering flames gleam and dance in the windshield of the car.

No one's in it. It's just a shitty old truck.

Also, I don't want to die.

With a deep breath, I wind up and hurl the flaming bottle at the vehicle. The glass shatters on impact. Instantly, liquid flames engulf the hood, the windshield, and the passenger side door. The fire roars like an angry dragon, licking over the roof, down the side, and then dripping to the ground around the wheels. One of the tires pops with a bang, making me scream and sending Grisha and his friends into convulsions of laughter.

The windshield and one of the rear windows burst. Metal begins to whine and shriek. The heat of the pyre scorches my face as I stare in horror at what I've done. Slowly, I pull my eyes away, turning and walking back to Grisha.

"Okay, I did it," I mumble, shaking as I hug myself. "Can I please go—"

The explosion is deafening. The force of it knocks the wind right out of me and hurls me to the ground alongside the three Russians. The pavement bites into my palms and my chin, making me wince in pain. Grisha and his buddies hoot with glee as something roars like a hurricane behind me.

Sucking in air, I roll over. My eyes go wide, my mouth falling open as I stare at the mangled twist of metal billowing with flames where the car used to be.

What the *fuck* have I done?

An hour later I'm home, at my apartment.

I can't. Stop. Shaking.

I have a million missed calls from Alicia and a hundred panicky, apologetic texts. I ignore them all as I crawl into the hottest bath I can stand and start to scrub the grime and gasoline-scented soot from my skin. I wince when I clean the cuts on my hands and my chin, then get out and quickly kneel next to the tub to try to wash the smoke from my hair.

Back in the kitchen, I reach over and mute my phone, since it just keeps blowing up with Alicia's texts. I pour myself a huge glass of red wine, downing half of it in one go.

I still can't stop shaking.

Suddenly, I frown, thinking. I lurch from the stool in my kitchen and bolt to the front door of the apartment.

No.

It's not hanging by the door.

Oh fuck.

It's not in my dance bag, either. Or on the couch, or anywhere in my room. As I turn my apartment upside down, I start to realize that my purse isn't here at all.

And I *know* I had it when I left the theater.

The pounding of fists on my front door almost stops my heart. My throat strangles the scream as I whirl, white-faced, and stare at it with horror.

"BIANCA!"

The air leaves my lungs in a whoosh.

It's Dante.

When I open the door, I gasp as he storms in, his face grim. He glances around, and it's only then that I realize he's holding a fucking gun.

"Dante—"

"Why the fuck weren't you answering your phone!?" he barks, concern in his voice and all over his face.

I swallow. "I—I was in the bath? What the hell is—"

"Shit's going down, that's what. A war might've just started, and I wanted to make sure you were home and safe."

Something cold settles in the pit of my stomach.

"A…a war?" I croak.

He nods, marching over to my windows and checking that they're all locked, even though we're ten floors up.

"Someone raided one of Nero De Luca's warehouses in Brooklyn."

I exhale.

Thank God.

"And… You think that means war?"

"On it's own, it could just be a regular gangland bullshit," he growls, turning back to me and holstering the gun. "But barely an hour later, someone torched Kratos Drakos' car in the Bronx."

The cold knot rips through my stomach again with a

vengeance. My throat tightens, a whining sound ringing in my ears.

Dante frowns and sniffs the air, his brow furrowing. "What the..."

Oh God.

He sniffs again, glancing around the apartment.

"Bianca, why does it smell like..."

He freezes as he suddenly turns toward me. I gasp as he storms over to me, grabbing a handful of my still-damp hair and yanking it to his nose.

"*Holy fucking shit,*" he whispers in a haggard voice. He backs away from me, slowly shaking his head. "Bianca—"

"I... I can explain—"

"What the *fuck* did you do? What THE FUCK did you do?!" he roars.

I cringe, shaking as my brother whirls away. He grabs his phone out of his pocket and hits a number. Seconds later, I can hear him yelling to someone I assume is Carmine things like "security measures" "lockdown" and "prepare for the worst".

I want to cry. I want to break down and scream. I want to tell him everything.

Just then, out of the corner of my eye, I see my phone silently light up on the kitchen counter. I shudder as I walk over and pick it up.

ADMIN

You have one new message.

It's from the Venom site.

My hands shake as I unlock my phone and scroll to the page. Sure enough, my chat box is blinking with a new message from *him*.

RAISEDBYWOLVES

You shouldn't have done that

Instantly, another message comes through: a picture. It takes a second to load, but when it does, my heart drops through the floor.

Someone torched Kratos Drakos' car in the Bronx.

I only know the giant, stoic Drakos brother by reputation. Or at least, I *thought* so.

But as the image of the flaming wreckage of a Land Rover appears in my chat window, I realize I know Kratos *much more* than by reputation.

…Because the other day, he fingered me to oblivion on the dirty floor of an abandoned church, after chasing me down with a fucking knife, wearing a psycho mask.

That's who my masked stranger is. *That's* who I've been chatting with, who I begged to fuck me. Who I chose to act out disturbing, fucked-up fantasies with.

Not just some Club Venom rando.

I goaded a lethally dangerous mafia prince. I told him my darkest fantasies. He knows who I am.

…And tonight, I burned his car to the ground.

Holy shit…

My phone dings again.

RAISEDBYWOLVES

You crossed a line, babygirl.

RAISEDBYWOLVES

So now I'm going to eradicate yours.

Then the icon next to his name goes dark.

I think I'm going to be sick.

What the fuck have I done?

11

BIANCA

Iᴛ's the waiting that's the worst.

Not the web of lies I have to create to explain to Dante why I torched a car in the middle of nowhere in the Bronx. I can't, I simply *won't*, tell him about the drug deal I was drawn into, even if it was completely inadvertent on my part.

Drugs are a hard line for my brother, mainly I think because of what happened to our older sister, Claudia. I was really young when it happened, but I can still remember the anguish of learning she'd been drugged and killed by those monsters when she was out one night.

The only comfort I have there is knowing the men responsible have been completely destroyed. Dante's gone to great lengths to hide all that from me, but I know that he hunted those men down and meted out his own brand of justice.

But it's not just Claudia. Tempest has her own family tragedy involving drugs. *Her* older sister, Layla, ended up dying in college from a heroin overdose.

So, no. I can't, in any way, tell Dante that all of this stemmed from me being dragged into a drug deal that went wrong. I also can't...or won't...tell him about my mystery masked man.

...Who isn't so much a mystery anymore.

A few days ago, I only knew Kratos by reputation. Since then, thanks to the internet, I've become an expert on him.

It's done less than nothing to quiet my shaking nerves.

Through random searches online, and by stalking the social media of some of his siblings, I've learned more about him. Like how he's into boxing and underground fights. How the car I destroyed wasn't just some shitty old truck. It was a 1980 Land Rover Defender 110 with "European specs", whatever the hell that means.

It also had a price tag north of three hundred grand, after all the retro mods, vintage parts, and work done on it. Which brings my total bill for destruction so far to—checks notes— seven hundred thousand dollars, between the car I didn't want to torch and the cocaine I neither lost nor sold.

I've learned that he's close—*really* close—with his family: three brothers, and a sister who's only a few years older than me. I've discovered how the Drakos family is now closely connected to the Kildare Irish Mafia family, both via Ares Drakos' marriage to Neve Kildare, and through Calliope aka 'Callie' Drakos being married to Castle Kildare himself, the head of the whole Irish family.

I know he likes to cook, through a bunch of gushy posts on Callie's Instagram, and that he's pretty good at it. I know he's gotta be smart, since he went to Lord's College in London. That's no small thing.

Lastly, I know the man is built like a Greek *god*, also courtesy of Thirst-gram. I mean Instagram.

And I do mean a *god*.

He's over six and a half feet tall, and all muscle. Callie posted some random photos from a trip to Greece she and some of her brothers took a little while ago, and there were pics of Kratos in a bathing suit lounging on the beach.

And sweet fucking *Jesus*.

The shoulders and arms of a Marvel superhero—Thor, specifically. A rock-solid, chiseled chest and abs, even those stupid V-lines that you *cannot* ignore that drive down from his hips into the waist of his *very* well-fitting bathing suit.

Tattoos all over. Eyes like blue icebergs. And a look on his face that somehow straddles charmingly friendly and captivatingly intense.

And the longer I look at pictures of the man who told me the other day he was going to "eradicate" my lines, the more I realize something: not a single one of the photos I've found of him online is *really* him.

It's like I'm looking at photos of a fake Kratos. A fraud, who's doing his best to look like the middle Drakos sibling.

Someone behind a façade.

Because I've seen into those eyes in the real world, through the neon X's of his mask. I've seen them glint and surge with energy. And none of those first-hand glimpses I've caught of him looked anything like this smiling, charming, nonchalant man on a beach vacation.

Which is curious, to say the least.

But again, it's the waiting that's the worst. Not lying to Dante, or Dad, or Carmy and Nico about what happened. There was no denying that I had something to do with the car—I mean the guilt was all over my face, and Dante could smell the gas and smoke on me, even after my attempts at washing it off. But I white-lied it, and told them I'd gotten caught up with some girls from ballet I shouldn't have, and was pulled along for the ride. Well, I mean, that's kinda true.

Let's be real: Carmy and Nico, and even Dante, used that "I just happened to be there, Pop" bullshit with Vito throughout their entire adolescence and young adult years. I don't know if my dad ever totally bought it, or is buying it from me now. But I think he recognizes that I didn't do anything maliciously. Plus, I think he remembers giving his sons leeway whenever they used that excuse, and realizes I deserve the same courtesy.

Just the same, it's not good. There's been no word *at all* from the Drakos family, which is...unsettling.

There's also been no word at all from *him*, via the Club Venom site.

And the waiting is driving me insane: the constant, needling feeling up the back of my spine. Like waiting for the pop of a balloon as it blows up bigger and bigger, or constantly expecting that a hand will reach out of the darkness to grab me.

Part of me even wants to walk out into Central Park alone one night and just scream for him to come get it over with, whatever he's going to do to me. But a week after the car incident, I haven't, and there's still nothing.

"Bianca..."

I flinch when I hear Alicia's voice behind me in the dressing room. I thought I was the last one here, but apparently that's not the case.

Turning, my chest tightens as I meet Alicia's scared-looking gaze.

"What," I mutter quietly.

She's tried to get me alone almost every day this week, with the same petrified, scared, contrite look on her face that she has on now. I mean, I get it: bitch or not, I think seeing her boyfriend stick a gun in my face and drag me into a car probably has her seriously shaken up.

Still, *I'm* the one who had the gun in my face, all because *she* dragged me out to a fucking drug deal I never wanted any part of. So I'm fresh out of fucks to give about how bad she's feeling, or how sorry she is.

"I…" She swallows thickly. "I just wanted to say…"

"Yes?" I snap coldly.

Her lip quivers. "I'm *so* sorry, Bianca," she croaks. "Please, I had no idea—"

"Stay the hell away from me, Alicia," I blurt, yanking my hoodie on.

Her face droops a little, but she nods. "I…I just wanted you to know how sorry I am."

"Duly. Noted," I mutter, looking away.

"And that I'm not with Grisha anymore."

I pause, turning to glance at her over my shoulder. To be fair, she looks truly broken and seriously shaken up. There's bags under her eyes and a haggard, weary look on her face.

"Am I supposed to feel sorry for you?"

Her throat bobs, and she shakes her head. "N-no. I just..." She looks away. "*I* left *him*. I..." She shakes her head helplessly. "I always knew he was dangerous. I guess that's probably why I went out with him. But that?" She shakes her head again. "I know when I'm in over my head. What he did was really fucked up, Bianca."

Yeah, I know, Alicia. I was THERE.

"Anyway, I just wanted you to know," she says quietly. "And I'm truly sorry for what happened, and for dragging you into it. You didn't deserve any of that."

I give her a curt nod. "Thanks."

After Alicia leaves, I finish packing up my stuff, swing my bag onto my shoulder, and turn off the lights on my way out. The back door creaks as I swing it open, and the shadows in the alley behind the theater claw and creep their way up the brick walls as I step out into the night.

I yank my hood up over my head and grip my bag a little tighter. For a minute, I flash back to how I felt with him in the church: raw, primal danger coupled with a needy, aching desire to be caught.

Fear and lust. Panic and excitement.

A push-pull sensation I *cannot* get out of my head.

I make sure the theater door is shut and securely locked behind me. I take a shaky breath, side-eying the creepy shadows reaching for me with their imaginary claws as a shiver ripples up my spine. Then I shake it away, shoulder my bag, and head toward the mouth of the alley to find a cab.

This time, the shadows really do grab me.

A hand slams over my mouth. A bag is yanked over my head.

My heart lurches into my throat, and I'm dragged into the darkness.

MY BREATH CATCHES as the bag is yanked off my head.

I'm back in the church. This time, things are…different.

Darker.

More terrifying, and more real.

The candles aren't lit. And even though there's some light creeping through the cracks in the stained-glass windows, the crumbling old church is largely bathed in darkness and gloom. Haunting shadows pulse and ooze in the corners and the arched stone rafters.

And I'm alone.

Someone pulled the bag off my head. But when I glance around behind me, all I see are more shadows, darkness, and silence.

A small noise near the front of the nave whips my gaze back forward. My pulse races, and my skin tingles with fear and forbidden excitement, remembering last time. I frown, peering into the gloom, trying to figure out if the shadows up there really *are* moving, or if I'm imagining things.

Is it him? Or is it actually a ghost or an apparition that's pulled me back into this place—

Suddenly, as if my question had been asked out loud, I get my response in the form of two glowing X's and a leering, neon smile illuminating the darkness up where the throne was before.

My pulse skips. My throat tightens around my windpipe as a spike of something vicious and heated stabs through my chest.

The church is still utterly silent. But slowly, the glowing mask tilts eerily to the side. Something glints; a second later, I realize it's a blade. A huge hunting knife, twisting slowly in his hand with the neon of his mask bouncing off its lethal edge.

You crossed a line, babygirl. So now I'm going to eradicate yours.

My entire chest constricts. My face caves, and whatever deranged excitement I felt before shatters like glass into pure fear.

"What the fuck is this?" I whisper in a choked, hoarse voice.

The mask tilts to the other side, leering at a creepy angle.

"This is what you signed up for...*Bianca*," Kratos growls quietly. The rough, whiskey-and-leather timbre of his voice rumbles through the echoing old space. In here, it almost sounds like stone grating against stone.

"I'd say this is your last chance to walk away..."

He utters a rough, rasping, mirthless chuckle.

"...But we're well past that now, aren't we?"

I swallow the lump in my throat. My heart flip-flops as the mask rises when he stands from his throne hidden in the dark. The mask moves nearer to me, like he's stepping over the rubble and the broken old pews, coming closer. And closer.

"The time to run away from this is long past, princess."

My chest tightens, a cold shiver jerking my spine upright as he leers down into my face.

"But the time to run from *me* is right the fuck now."

"I—" My eyes are wide as I stare up into the twin neon X's. "It was an accident. The car…"

"I'm sure," he growls.

Another cold shiver ripples through me as the knife glints in his hands. For a second, I consider that I might be *even further* past my depth with all of this. The last time I was here, I knew it was a game. A terrifying, demented, twisted game, but a game nonetheless.

This time, I'm not so sure we're playing anymore. And I don't know if this is meant to be something sexual at all, even if I *am*, shamefully, excited.

This time, he might not want to chase me so that he can rip my clothes and fuck me.

It might simply be that he wants to rip my *throat*.

"Do you know what you destroyed?"

My lip retreats between my teeth.

"I—I'm sorry."

"Not yet, you're not. But you will be."

I swallow again. "The car—"

"It wasn't *just* the car, princess," he hisses.

"I…" I tremble as he raises the knife again, twirling it thoughtfully in front of his face. "I'll pay—"

"Fucking right you will."

I gasp sharply as he brings the blade down to the front of my hoodie. He uses the razor-sharp tip to pull the neck down a bit, before running the knife down my sternum, letting it tease down between my breasts before he drags it to the side. My breath catches and a low pulse throbs in my core as the jagged tip of the blade drags over the hoodie, across my left breast, dancing right across my nipple.

I'll pay.

Fucking right you will.

And suddenly, it clicks, even as a horrifyingly exciting shiver ripples heatedly between my thighs.

I'll pay for what I've done. But it won't be with money, or even my life.

It'll be with something else.

When I drag my wide eyes from the blade teasing my nipple through my hoodie, up to those soulless, chilling neon X's of his eyes, I know I'm right.

"If…" I breathe. "If we do this…"

I can *feel* him smirk behind the mask.

"Yes, princess?" he growls quietly.

I don't have to finish the question, because I already know I'm right. *This* is the payment. *I'm* the payment for what I did. I fucked up. I destroyed what was his. And now, he'll destroy me. It should feel barbaric and horrifying. I should hate this. Or at the very least, fear it.

I shouldn't be so excited.

I shouldn't be so *wet*.

My teeth drag over my bottom lip as I peer into his face.

"Why are you still wearing a mask?" I breathe.

I mean, we both know who the other is now. This isn't an anonymous "meetup" via the Venom site anymore.

Kratos tilts his head to the side, letting that leering neon smile and the real one faintly glowing behind it pierce my soul.

"Because you wanted me to," he murmurs.

The knife's tip slides over my nipple again. I gasp sharply, feeling the pressure of it through my hoodie as he starts to walk around behind me. The knife drags across my chest, teasing across one breast and then the other, the tip passing directly across that nipple too.

My breath stutters as I feel him stop right behind me, the sheer size and mass of him looming over me from behind as he lowers his mouth to my ear.

"Because, princess…" he purrs softly. *"You asked for it."*

My pulse spikes as the blade drags up my breast, the lethal tip dancing a fraction of an inch from my skin as it slides up my jugular.

"Now…" Kratos growls into my ear.

The heat, the scent, and the sheer power of him vibrates against my pebbled skin.

"Run."

12

BIANCA

EVER SINCE HE grabbed me behind the theater, the adrenaline has been coursing through my veins like diesel. And the second he says it, it's like lighting it on fire, like another Molotov cocktail.

Blood roars in my ears as I explode away from him, flinging myself into the near-total darkness of the old church. My eyes have adjusted a little bit to the gloom, and I'm not completely blind, but it's still a beyond harrowing rush as I bolt into the blackness.

"Runnnn, prinkipissa...."

The voice snarls and growls all around me. He's everywhere and nowhere. It's like I'm drowning in a pool of inky black paint, slowly choking me and turning my entire existence opaque.

I zigzag to the left, then to the right, my legs pumping hard as I gasp for air. One second, I swear he's right in front of me. The next, behind me.

Beside me. All around.

Inside my fucking head.

I fling myself in another direction, my breath heaving as I charge half blindly into the darkness. A split second later, I'm screaming as my shin bangs into what feels like stone, or maybe one of the splintered pews.

I cry out and go sprawling onto the grimy floor. I plant a palm and a knee, ready to spring back up.

Too late.

The scream is torn from my throat as his enormous size and weight slam into me from behind.

"*Gotcha,*" his stony voice rasps.

The pain receptors in my scalp explode as he grabs a huge fistful of my long hair and yanks. I cry out again, my head snapping back as his knee plants between my shoulder blades, pinning my chest firmly to the ground.

Kratos growls when his huge hand suddenly grabs the back of my yoga pants. He pulls, making me whimper as he roughly hauls my ass into the air, forcing me to my knees with my torso still pinned to the ground.

Suddenly, the fist holding the back of my pants yanks them down to my knees. The wind rushes out of me, my veins throbbing with heat as his huge palm spanks my bare ass, hard. The sharp, cracking sound of skin on skin makes me yelp, the sound of it echoing through the church.

He spanks me again, then again, roughly and repeatedly spanking first one cheek and then the other as I writhe and sob and moan under his rough touch. Suddenly, his fingers slip under the edge of my thong. He pulls it tight like he did last time, creating a delicious friction as the lace rubs tight against my clit.

"You wrecked something important to me, *prinkípissa*," he snarls into my ear. "I think it's only fair I wreck something that's important to you."

He yanks harder and the thong digs into my skin before shredding away entirely.

"And I'm going to start with this pretty little virgin pussy."

I choke on my breath as his huge hand suddenly cups my sex from behind. He drags a massively thick finger up through my lips. He roughly plunges the finger inside, driving into me hard as I squeal and writhe under his touch.

"So fucking *tight*," he snarls darkly. "So fucking *small*." I shudder as he drags the blade of his knife down my spine. "You've never had a man before, have you, *prinkípissa*? No one's ever stretched this tight little pussy out, have they?"

I whimper, shaking my head as best as I can with my cheek flat on the ground.

"A shame," he murmurs savagely. He spanks my ass again, making me yelp before his thick finger drives right back into me, knocking the breath from my lungs and making my toes curl. I shudder as I feel him lean down close to my ear again. "Because my cock is going to split you in fucking two when I take your tight little hole."

His finger roughly rams into me, and the lewd, loud, wet squelching sounds of arousal as he roughly manhandles me give away exactly how much I want and crave this.

How much I've been waiting for this.

And he fucking knows it.

Kratos chuckles a dark, devilish laugh in the darkness.

"What a greedy, *eager* little slut I've found," he growls, fingering me even harder. "I bet this slutty little cunt's been making a fucking mess of your panties ever since you destroyed what was mine, just *aching* for me to find you."

His finger rams into me, and I cry out.

"And chase you."

I shudder when I hear the jangle of his belt buckle and the sound of his zipper being tugged down.

"And catch you."

I shriek again as he reaches beneath me and yanks my hoodie, top, and bra right up to my chin. He roughly cups one of my breasts, pinching and twisting the nipple as I writhe in a mix of pleasure and pain.

"And ruin you."

His finger curls deep into me, making my eyes roll back and my feet curl and claw at the dirty ground. Then he slides his hand away with one last hard spank on my upturned ass.

He moves in front of me, sinking to his knees. His hand tangles in my hair, lifting my head and locking his eyes with mine.

Holy fuck.

He's still wearing the mask, but he's shirtless now, the hard grooves and veins of his arms and torso standing out sharply in the gloomy darkness and the veiled light coming through the broken windows. His tattoo ink dances like black magic on his tanned skin. His massive chest bulges when he moves, and the thick, corded muscles of his veined forearms ripple as he grabs a fistful of my hair.

Kratos drops his other hand to his unbuckled, unzipped black jeans. He reaches inside, and I moan quietly, my gaze riveted on his movements as he starts to stroke himself in his pants.

"Are you going to be a fucking good girl for me?"

Sweet Jesus.

I whimper, nodding. My thighs clamp together, squeezing in an embarrassingly needy way as the throb between my legs screams for more.

Kratos raises his other hand, letting the dim light glimmer on the big hunting knife in his hand.

"Let's fucking hope so."

Without warning, he shoves his jeans and boxers down together. Suddenly, his cock springs free, slapping heavily against his abs before bobbing right in front of my face.

Holy. Fucking. Shit.

I understand that porn amplifies sexuality. Everyone moans a little louder than they would in real life. Every position is orgasmic. Every blemish and fault airbrushed away or fixed with makeup.

Every ass is perfectly sculpted. Every breast perfectly round and perky. And every cock huge and throbbing.

But I can say without a second's hesitation that not a single dick I've ever seen in any porn online comes even close to what I'm looking at right now.

It's not just Kratos' height or muscles that are huge. I'm staring at what has to be the biggest cock on the fucking planet.

Not a dick. Not a *penis*.

"Cock" is literally the only word you could use to describe the fat, swollen, almost monstrously huge appendage that he wraps his hand around and begins to stroke, right in front of me.

How the fuck is that going to fit inside me.

Just as I'm thinking that, his fist tightens in my hair. He growls deeply, pulling my face close to his cock as his mask tilts to the side. A low chuckle rumbles from his throat.

"Oh, I'm not going to fuck you."

I shiver.

"Not *yet*. And not because I'm worried about breaking you in half, either," he rasps darkly. "But because you haven't *earned it* yet."

My breath comes haltingly as he pulls me closer, stroking his massive cock inches from my face.

"So open your fucking mouth," he growls. "And show me how a good little slut *earns it*."

He barely waits for my mouth to open. The thick, swollen head of his cock smears precum over my lips, making me gasp quietly before they part. Roughly, gripping my hair, he sinks himself between my lips, pushing his head over my tongue as I swallow back a moan.

"Bad sluts who torch my car don't get fucked, babygirl," Kratos hisses. "They get treated like cheap whores."

Everything about this should be ringing alarm bells in my brain. The fact that he brought me here against my will. That he just *chased me* through the dark with a fucking knife before pinning me to the ground on my hands and knees and forcing his cock into my mouth.

All of it should be a huge red flag.

But it's not. Not to someone broken and flawed and demented like me. It's not that this isn't scary or a little too much. It *is* one hundred percent those things.

And it's precisely all that that's making me wetter than I've ever been in my life. It's that fear factor, and the roughness, and the dubious level of consent that's pushing every single one of my buttons.

It's knowing that even if I told him to stop, *begged* him to, he wouldn't. In fact, he'd just go harder, and rougher. *That's* what has my pulse roaring in my veins, and my core quivering and aching for more.

"No" wouldn't stop this. "Stop" wouldn't, either. There's only one word that would end all this right here and right now.

Vanish.

That's what's lurking in the depths, under all of this: knowing that I *could* stop this, with just one single word. That I have that ace in my back pocket that I could use at any time.

But stopping this *stops it*. Permanently. The dream ends. I wake up to reality. And I never get to see how deep or how dark the rabbit hole can go.

So I don't say a thing. All I do is moan as Kratos grabs a fist of my hair and pushes his huge dick into the back of my throat.

I can feel myself sputter and choke a little. Spit and precum drip from the corners of my lips and trickle down my chin. He groans deeply, his v-lines and abs flexing and rippling as he grabs my hair and takes his pleasure from my mouth.

"*There's* a good little whore," he grunts. "Now use your tongue, like a good little fuck-toy."

I whimper as he pulls my mouth off his slick, glistening head. He brings my mouth down to the underside of his swollen shaft. I tongue and lick it, dragging my mouth up and down the sheer size of him as he hisses in pleasure.

Kratos bends over me, reaching down. I cry out, moaning around his thick dick as he spanks my ass. He does it again, using his grip on my hair to pull my mouth down to his big, heavy balls.

"*Suck*," he commands. "Like the greedy little cum slut you are, babygirl."

I moan, doing exactly as he says. My lips open wide, sucking one heavy orb into my mouth. My tongue drags over its silky skin, and when he groans deeply, something powerful explodes through me.

Another moan tumbles from my mouth as his thick finger drags up my slit from behind. He plunges it inside, fingering me hard and fast, filling the church again with the lewd sounds of my sopping wet pussy. His finger pushes lower between my legs, rubbing my clit as I gasp for air and tongue his heavy balls.

Kratos' hand pulls away, clearly reaching for something. My eyes flare, my breath catching as I feel the cold, naked edge of his knife drag down my spine. He's not cutting me, but I can feel the lethality of that point as it hums a hair's breadth from my skin, delving lower and lower toward my ass.

"Open your mouth, my little slut."

When I do, he pushes his swollen head back inside.

"Spread your fucking legs."

He slaps my inner thigh, making me yelp and whimper before I scramble to do as he says. Then my eyes bulge wide when I feel the cold steel drag down the back of my thigh. I start to pull away, but Kratos holds my hair firmly in his fist, keeping me right where I am.

The blade dances over my skin, teasing inward and then slowly, achingly, teasingly dragging up my inner thigh, closer and closer and closer…

For one brief, horrifying second, I think I've misjudged all of this, and him. For a split-second, as the blade edges toward my pussy, I wonder if maybe I've *vastly* underestimated exactly how crazy Kratos is.

But just before the tip of the blade touches my most intimate area, he suddenly flicks his wrist, spinning the knife in his fingers. Suddenly, something hard with a rounded end presses between my pussy lips, just as he thrusts his cock into my mouth.

Holy fucking hell.

He might not be *completely* sadistic. But instantly, it's clear I have underestimated how psycho this man is.

He's just shoved the handle of his knife into my pussy.

The thing is, though, I might be just as fucking crazy. Because as he starts to fuck me with that smooth, bulbous hilt, I can already feel myself start to melt around it. And when I whimper a sloppy, muffled moan around his giant cock, he knows it, too.

Kratos chuckles darkly, groaning as he starts to fuck my mouth with shallow thrusts that gradually grow faster and deeper.

"What a fucking *greedy* little slut I've found," he groans.

My eyes roll back, and my pulse turns to napalm in my veins as he starts to fuck me roughly with the handle of his blade. He thrusts into my mouth again, keeping it in tempo with the hilt thrusting in and out of my slick, eager pussy.

I moan louder and louder as I start to lose myself.

My control.

My connection to reality.

All I know is the captivating, intense, insane sensation of this *huge*, savage, possibly criminally insane man fucking me in both ends with his cock and his fucking *knife*.

The bulbous top of the hilt hits *just* right, rubbing against my g-spot as he grunts and roughly fucks my mouth. The sounds of his groans mingle with the wet, sloppy sounds of his knife handle fucking my dripping wet pussy and the loud, eager moans from my own throat.

Every muscle in my body begins to tense up. My arms quiver. My legs shake. My entire fucking body starts to tremble from head to toe as a forbidden, fucked-up, vile sort of pleasure threatens to engulf me from the inside out.

"*I wonder*," he growls, chuckling darkly to himself as he fucks my mouth and keeps thrusting the handle into my pussy. "I wonder what all those prim and proper little ballerina friends of yours would think, seeing you behave like *such a fucking whore* for me."

My eyes roll back in my head. A low, desperately eager moan begins to build in my chest. My core tightens, my muscles quaking, beginning to give way completely as the wave starts to crest over me.

"This is just the beginning, you know," Kratos rasps. "Don't you for one *second* think we'll be done with all this after I come down this pretty throat."

I whimper.

"No no, *prinkípissa*," he growls. "No. Tonight, I'll take your mouth. But soon, I'll take this messy little pussy, too. I'll watch you scream and moan like a cum whore when you take every inch of my big cock deep in your slutty hole."

He starts to fuck me with the handle even harder, in and out, twisting it sometimes, until I know there's no going back.

"And then, after I've ruined your mouth and your cunt for any other man, know that I still won't be done with you."

He leans down, grunting as he starts to fuck his cock into my drooling mouth even harder and faster.

"*I'll take your ass, too, babygirl.* I'll have my cum pouring out of every fucking hole you have. Now be a good girl and *make me fucking cum.*"

It's all of it: the rough, brutal way he's manhandling me. The filthiness of his words. The sheer size of him. The dark, grimy gloom of the church, and the lunacy that I'm about to come on a fucking *knife*.

It all hits at the same time. And when it does, my whole world turns inside out.

I scream around his cock, my legs buckling and kicking at the ground as I spasm and explode. The orgasm thunders through me, turning my vision black and red as I writhe and moan.

Kratos grunts deeply. He rams his cock into the back of my throat, his fist tight in my hair. Suddenly, his huge cock swells in my mouth. It jumps and twitches, and I whimper when hot, thick ropes of his cum explode across my tongue.

I gulp it down greedily, feeling drunk and high and insane as I keep coming for him. His cock twitches again and again, spilling more and more cum against the back of my throat. He groans as he pulls his cock from my swollen lips, stroking himself against them. His hot cum drips onto my cheeks, down my chin, over the bridge of my nose, and all over my lips as his knife hilt wrings another shaking orgasm from my body.

When he pulls away from me, my arms and legs give out. With a dull whimper, I collapse to the ground, shaking and trembling. Just as I do, I suddenly cry out as a sharp pain cuts into me, right next to my pussy.

"Don't move."

It's only when he carefully slides it from me that I realize I've dropped to the ground *with the fucking knife still inside me.*

Kratos, with a gentleness that confuses me, flips me onto my back. Before I can say or do anything, he's pushing my knees apart and lowering himself between my legs. He grabs the bottom of his mask, pulling it up over his mouth before he suddenly drops between my thighs.

Holy mother of God.

His mouth fastens over the small cut the knife's just given me, sucking on the delicate spot right where my thigh meets my bikini area. There's a mix of pain, pleasure, and insanity that throbs in my core as he nurses the cut right next to my sex. Slowly, his neon X eyes locked on mine, his mouth slides over.

Holy fuck...

His tongue drags through my lips and swirls over my clit. He groans deeply, shoving his tongue deep into me like he's trying to devour me from the inside out. His huge, muscled hands keep my thighs pinned wide apart.

His tongue alternates between plunging into me and swirling aggressively over my clit.

My legs shake. My stomach clenches tight as my core quivers. Kratos' lips fasten around my clit, and when he suckles it, it's like pulling a trigger.

I scream into the darkness as I come again, my back arching off the ground and my hips rocking against his face.

I'm still shaking and gasping for air when he turns his mouth, smirks, and then suddenly clamps down on my cut again. A zap of something electric explodes through me as he sucks hard on the wound before moving away.

My entire reality is a dim, sultry haze as I look down at the psychopath between my legs looking up at me, my cum and blood glistening on his lips as they curl into a demonic grin.

"I'll need to taste that combination again soon, babygirl," he growls quietly, licking his lips.

Without any warning, he stands, tucking his still hard, ludicrously huge cock into his pants. He turns away, pulling on a shirt before tugging the mask back into place. Then he twists to look down at me with his head tilted in that slightly maniacal way.

"A change of clothes, and your phone, are up there."

He points past me to the crumbling throne where the pulpit would be.

"And there's a car outside to take you home."

Without another word, he turns away, and walks into the darkness.

"Wait…"

The word tumbles from my bruised, panting, parched lips.

His dark, hulking shape stops, but he doesn't turn around.

"Yes?"

I shiver, trembling and quivering everywhere.

"When…" I chew on my lip. "You said we weren't done…"

"We're not," he growls. "Not by a mile."

Eager heat pools between my thighs.

I need psychiatric help.

"So, when…"

Kratos' voice chuckles in the darkness.

"*Greedy little thing,*" he purrs. "You want to know when we'll be doing this again?"

I can feel the heat rising in my cheeks.

"*Yes,*" I whisper.

My heart skips as he suddenly twists his head, letting the neon X's gleam at me.

"That's easy," he murmurs. His head tilts to the side. "When you least expect it."

Then, like smoke, he's gone, drifting silently out the side door.

I stay on the ground, breathing deeply and trying to wrangle some sense of reality back into my head. Slowly, I roll onto my hands and knees, wincing with every move. I wince again as I drag myself to my feet, sore *everywhere*. But it's a delicious soreness.

At the throne, I find a fresh set of clothes—my *own* clothes. Something terrifying surges inside of me briefly as I wonder how Kratos even *has* a change of my clothes ready for me. But I'm too worn out and too near collapse to think about that right now.

I dress quickly and walk out through the front door. Sure enough, same as last time, the black car with the driver wearing dark shades is waiting for me, the back door already open.

I wince and hobble gingerly toward it, pulling my phone out of my pocket as I do.

Fuck.

I have tons of missed calls from Dante, and Carmine, and Nico. From Milena and Naomi, too. There's more unread texts than I know what to do with. But it's the newest notification that just dinged, from Nico, that rips into my mind like a blade.

NICO

EMERGENCY. WHERE THE ACTUAL FUCK ARE YOU

Oh God.

13

BIANCA

"SERIOUSLY. WHERE THE *FUCK* WERE YOU?"

There's a shocked numbness in the car as Nico roars through the city toward Mt. Sinai Hospital. I still don't know where Kratos' gothic church is, because the car that's taken me away both times I've been there has blacked-out rear windows. This time, when I jumped in, I told the silent driver to take me to Nico's address.

He refused with a shake of his head, and would *only* drop me off back at my house. So that's where Nico's just picked me up, to bring me to the hospital.

"Bianca!"

I flinch, my face burning as I turn to him.

"I stayed late at work," I lie, feeling like shit.

"With your fucking phone off?"

"I'm sorry," I mumble as I turn and stare out the window. "I..."

Nico exhales. His hand reaches across the center console of the car, taking mine.

"Sorry," he mutters. "I'm just..."

I twist to look at him, watching his eyes grimly staring at the road as his jaw grinds.

"This is all my fault, isn't it?"

His eyes soften as he glances at me.

"Stop it."

I blink back tears. "No. It is. This is because of *what I did*."

"Bianca, this is the world we live in, okay?" he hisses. "This is the mafia. Shit like this happens—"

"I torched Kratos Drakos' fucking car, Nico!" I yell, my face paling.

I swallow down the lump that's formed in my throat as I glance at the streets of Manhattan speeding past us as we roar toward the hospital where Dad is being taken care of.

And here I thought the punishment for my sins had just been doled out, back in the church, by Kratos' own hands.

And mouth.

And cock.

Oh, God.

As it turns out, I was wrong.

Dad was in the basement of one of the restaurants our family owns, hosting one of his monthly poker games, until a home-made firebomb was tossed through the window, blowing the place all to hell.

The bomb was thrown by men wearing masks who drove off in a very specific vintage car: a '67 Camaro Z28, black with white racing stripes. There's all of *one* of them registered in the state of New York.

It's owned by Hades fucking Drakos.

"WHERE THE *FUCK* WERE YOU?!"

I flinch as Dante grabs me by the shoulders, shaking me hard. His face is livid and haggard, his mouth lined around the edges. His eyes look wild in the overhead fluorescent hospital lights.

"I—"

"Jesus, Dante…"

Tempest's face is as worried as my brother's. But she puts a restraining hand on his arm and shakes her head at him.

"Take. A fucking. Breath," she says quietly, looking straight at him.

Dante closes his eyes, his chest rising and falling heavily before he opens them. This time, there's a softer look in them. In seconds, he's hugging me tight, pulling me into his chest.

"I'm sorry," he growls quietly. "I was just fucking terrified after it happened and we couldn't get hold of you."

"I…"

Fuck, I hate lying to my own family. But if I wasn't going to tell them I was, oh, you know, indulging in some fucked-up primal fetish sex stuff with Kratos Drakos *before* all of this, I sure as hell am not now.

"I stayed late to get in some conditioning before going home," I mumble. "My phone was off—"

"It's okay," Dante breathes, pulling away and smiling wanly at me. "I'm just glad you're safe."

Tempest hugs me next, wrapping her arms around me tightly. I meet Dante's eyes over her shoulder. When he sees the look in my eyes, he shakes his head.

"Don't."

"Dante," I choke, pulling away from Tempest.

"This *wasn't* because of you."

"Of course it was! I blew up his car, and this is their response!" I hiss quietly, feeling the panic clawing at my chest. "This is—"

"Look at me."

I shiver as Dante grabs my shoulders and peers hard into my eyes.

"This is *not* your fucking fault. Do you understand me?"

I swallow, looking away.

"How is Dad?"

My brother nods slowly. "He's…okay, surprisingly enough. There was a lot of blood when they pulled him out of the building."

I tense again, my eyes flying wide. Dante shakes his head.

"It wasn't his," he reassures me.

"It was Tony Pagano's," another voice says.

I pull away from Tempest, smiling weakly as an older man in a black coat and an old-school fedora comes over.

"*Piccola piuma*," Aldo says somberly, pulling me into a hug.

Aldo Bernardi has been one of Vito's closest *consiglieres* since...well...forever. He's been like an uncle to Carmy, Nico, Dante and me our whole lives. "Little feather" is his favorite nickname for me, from when I was first discovering ballet, and used to flit around the room.

"You're okay?"

"She was at practice," Dante sighs with an edged tone.

Aldo smiles fondly and pats my hand. "But of course you were."

Nico frowns. "How's Don Pagano?"

Aldo grimaces. "Missing his eyebrows and pissed the fuck off. He took a piece of the poker table itself through his leg. But he's going to be okay."

I turn to Dante. "Where's Dad?"

"In there." He points toward a closed hospital room door, with two big guys I know as Barone muscle—Leo and Rocco—and about ten other obviously made men standing guard.

I pull away from Aldo and start to march over, but Dante puts out an arm to stop me. I glare at him with fury in my eyes.

"What the fuck, Dante!"

My older brother frowns. "Easy, Bianca. He's—"

The door to the hospital room suddenly opens, and Carmine steps out. When he sees me, he visibly relaxes as he storms over to hug me.

"Fucking hell, Bee. Keep your goddamn phone on."

"I need to see—"

"Soon. There's an emergency Commission meeting going on in there right now. Sit tight, Pop's okay."

I nod meekly. When I suddenly notice the bandages on Carmy's hands, my eyes go wide.

"Oh my God, Carm!"

"It's fine," he shrugs. "Just burns."

"Carmy was at the game with dad," Nico explains. "Pulled him out, too," he adds, clapping our brother on the back.

"Dad's really going to be okay?" I ask quietly, eyeing Carmine.

He nods. "Totally. He's mostly just pissed about one of his favorite suits getting fucked up, and that he was on a serious heater when the bomb went off." He frowns as my face twists miserably. "C'mon, don't, Bianca."

"It... It all got out of hand," I blurt hoarsely. "I *never* meant—"

"What you did was fucking stupid," Carmy growls. "There, you happy? It was fucking reckless *and* fucking stupid. No one's saying otherwise, Bee."

My shoulders slump.

"But it *wasn't* an act of war," he hisses. "And it sure as fuck didn't merit a response that was as good as a goddamn assassination attempt," he spits angrily. He gives me a wry look before pulling me into a tight hug. "The important thing is, everyone's okay. Yeah?"

I nod miserably into his chest.

I don't feel okay. At all.

I feel used.

Aldo's phone dings. He pulls it out of his coat pocket and turns away as he answers it quietly. We all watch as he nods somberly, then slips the phone back into his pocket and turns back to us.

"Your father is about to be discharged. He wants to meet with all of you."

I grin, turning toward the door to my dad's hospital room.

"Not here," Aldo adds. "Back at the house."

"Easy, easy, Bumblebee," Vito chuckles as I all but vault into his arms the second he walks in the door to the study, where we've all been waiting.

He hugs me just as fiercely as I'm hugging him before he slowly pulls back. When he does, I can't help but notice that he won't meet my gaze.

"Dad—"

"This isn't your fault, Bianca," Vito says quietly, smiling softly as he pats my hand. "But…" His mouth thins. "There's a lot we need to discuss right now." He turns and clears his throat, nodding to Leo and Rocco and a few other Barone men present. "I need to speak to just family. Aldo, that includes you."

The men nod solemnly before turning and filing out. When they're gone, Carmy closes the door behind them, then joins the rest of us on the chairs and couches near the fireplace. With the Barone muscle gone, it's just Dante, Tempest, Nico, Carmine, Aldo, Dad, and me.

Dad exhales slowly as he sinks into his favorite chair. I plop down on the end of a couch right next to him, and he pats my hand before turning to Aldo, who's standing by the window.

"I could use a drink, Aldo."

Wordlessly, Aldo pours two Fernet-Brancas, handing one to Dad, and tapping the side of the glass he's kept for himself against it. They both drink deeply before Dad exhales again. He turns to me, a strange, dark look in his eyes.

"I want to be clear. *This isn't Bianca's fault,*" Dad growls quietly, dragging his eyes around the room. "She's not to be blamed, and none of you gets to hold this over her head. Ever." He arches a brow at Carmine. "You've all pulled way worse than torching a car. Is that understood?"

Carmy nods. "Of course, Pop."

"Good." Vito clears his throat. "I've been in contact with Ares Drakos."

Carmine's lips instantly curl. "*Fuck* those fucking Greeks—"

"Carmine."

Vito's tone quiets my brother.

"Please, allow me to finish uninterrupted. As I was saying, I've spoken with Ares. He's not a rash or reckless man, and firstly he wanted us all to understand that the restaurant tonight was selected because they believed it was empty. The restaurant itself was closed, and the apartments upstairs are very obviously being gut-renovated. The game in the basement isn't exactly publicized, either. After talking with Ares, I don't see any reason to suspect that the Drakos family was intending for anyone to get hurt."

"So those fucking pricks decide to bomb a goddamn *building* just because an old car got burned?" Nico hisses. "How the fuck is that an appropriate response?"

"The issue isn't so much the car itself," Dad mutters. "It's what was *in* the car." He grimaces and takes a heavy swig of his Fernet. "Though they were bidding rivals for the West Side building, the Drakos family have recently been in alliance talks with Davit Kirakosian."

Sitting on the couch across from me, Dante scowls deeply. Aside from running Club Venom, my brother trades in whispers, secrets, and information. But it's clear this proposed alliance is news to him, and I can tell that's pissing him off.

"Te Mallkuarit loaned an artifact that's been in their family for generations to the Drakoses, as a show of goodwill. A 12th century crucifix made from human bones."

Nico makes a face. "What the fuck?"

"That's Te Mallkuarit for you," Dante mutters. "Deeply religious Albanian crime weirdos with serious roots in Eastern European mysticism."

Carmine shifts uncomfortably. "Please don't tell me this fucking thing was *in* the car."

Vito's expression says it all.

"*Shit*," Carmy mutters.

Dad sighs, taking another sip of his drink. He's still avoiding looking at me. "The Greeks had no choice but to retaliate, or face trying to explain to Davit that his creepy-ass relic got torched without payback. The problem is, Kirakosian isn't satisfied. That fucked-up bone statue held a *lot* of meaning for his family. They don't know it was Bianca, but they do know it was someone at least connected to our family." His face darkens. "And now Davit's calling for war."

I shudder, my face paling as I desperately try to meet Dad's gaze. He *still* won't look at me.

"So that's one problem," Dad continues. "But there's more. Davit isn't the only one banging his spear on his shield."

"Don Pagano," Dante mutters.

Dad nods slowly. "Yeah. Tony's got a hot temper, and he wasn't backing down after the attack. The problem is, as you know, his son Gio just got engaged to Ciara Marchetti. So now Don Marchetti's obliged to side with the Paganos if they were to go to war with the Greeks over the restaurant fire. My guess is, when any shooting started, Nero De Luca would have joined in, because he's got too much to prove, being new to the table. And if he jumped in, you could bet Don Amato would have, too."

There's something about his wording that suddenly makes me frown.

"You just used *were* and *would have* a lot." My brow furrows. "So is this war officially *not* happening now?"

My dad doesn't meet my eye. Instead, he turns to Aldo again.

"Got a smoke, Aldo?"

Wordlessly, Aldo pulls a silver cigarette case out of his jacket pocket, pops it, and offers one to Vito. He lights it and my dad takes a deep puff as he nods a thanks.

"I've struck a deal."

The words come out sounding rough, like he's having a hard time forcing them over his lips.

Carmine frowns. "What sort of 'deal'?"

"One that the other Commission families are in complete agreement with, and one that will smooth things over with both the Greeks and the Albanians."

"Pop," Carmy growls quietly. "*What's the deal.*"

Dad turns his head slowly, leveling a sad, deeply remorseful look at me. "Bianca…"

There's a knock at the study door. It opens, and Leo pokes his head in.

"They're here, Don Barone," he grunts.

Dad nods slowly. "Send them in, Leo."

Nico frowns. "Send *who*—"

Instantly, he, Carmine, and Dante spring to their feet, reaching for guns tucked into waistbands and inside jackets as Ares Drakos strides into the room.

"Put them down!" Vito barks with the full authority of his crown. "*All* of you," he growls, shooting dark looks at my brothers as Hades Drakos walks into the room behind Ares, followed by Deimos, and then Callie. "They're our guests here," Dad mutters, standing.

For a brief second, I almost visibly exhale in relief. When Ares stepped in just now, especially when his siblings began to follow him in, obviously, my thoughts went to one place.

One *man*.

Kratos.

So far, my…"interactions" with him have been happening in almost a dream state. We meet in the darkness of his crumbling church. He wears a *mask*, for God's sake. The point being, what we've done and where we've met up is in the shadows, away from the light.

Like a dirty little secret.

For a second, I was terrified to think that he was going to be here too, forcing me to confront those dark, dirty parts of my psyche right here in the open, in front of my family. But it seems only his four siblings have—

I freeze as a massive shape fills the doorway. My heart clenches as my eyes lock with his icy blue ones. A small, almost invisible smile curls the corners of his mouth.

Hungrily.

Dangerously.

The man literally has to duck his head a little as he steps through the door into the study. His eyes lock on mine, and even though his face is blank and emotionless, when he tilts his head to the side slightly, I can feel the tingles rippling over my skin.

Mask or not, I know that look.

And it *does* something to me.

As the room goes quiet and still, I realize something. I see it in the way his siblings interact with him—the way Callie reaches over to him and squeezes his hand. The way Hades good-naturedly pats his shoulder.

They don't see him the way I do.

And when Kratos smiles downright *warmly* at something Ares says to him, it really does click for me:

I don't think his family knows him at all.

Not the way I do. They don't realize the kind of savagery that lurks under that smiling, friendly-giant surface.

They don't see the monster, or the beast he is.

But I do.

Ares and my dad meet halfway and shake hands firmly.

"Bianca," Vito says gently, turning to me.

I clear my throat, looking at Ares, heat creeping up my neck and into my cheeks.

"I…" I swallow. "I'm truly sorry about the car," I murmur quietly. "I was pressured into it, and I know that's no excuse, but I—"

"What's done is done," Ares says in a cool, even tone. "We appreciate the apology. But our options now are limited. You've got the other Commission families to consider. Meanwhile, we've got our own allies to think about. Not to mention, what you inadvertently destroyed in that car meant a lot to, frankly, a very crazy Albanian."

He turns to my dad.

"How are you feeling, Don Barone?"

Dad smirks. "Like I've been barbecued. But I'll survive."

Ares dips his head. "My apologies again. As I mentioned earlier when we spoke, we didn't know your poker game was going on in the basement."

"Thank you for being the level-headed man and strong leader I've always been told you are, Mr. Drakos," Dad replies with a nod.

Ares draws in a breath as his eyes slide to me. So do those of his siblings. I shift uncomfortably as they all openly size me up.

All except *him*.

Kratos isn't looking at me like he's sizing me up, or even like he's angry.

He looks unreadable.

And it's throwing me off.

"Have you told her yet?" Ares growls quietly.

I frown. "Huh?" My head snaps around as I look quizzically at my dad. "Have you told me *what* yet?"

Vito's mouth is tight and unhappy. He clears his throat as he steps closer to me.

"That...thing...we agreed wouldn't ever happen..."

Oh God.

Instantly, whatever color was left in my face drains away. My head starts to shake slowly, my eyes staring into the middle distance as my breath chokes off.

"*No—*"

"I have no choice. It breaks my heart, but I gotta break that promise, Bumblebee," Vito says quietly, his face twisting with emotion.

"I—" I stammer, my head swimming as the room spins. "I—what does that *mean?*"

"It means, *dear…*"

I shiver, my core clenching and my skin tingling all over as I turn to the sound of his baritone voice rumbling from across the room.

Kratos smiles a wry, cold, slightly unhinged smile at me.

"That you and I are getting married."

14

BIANCA

AT FIRST, it's sheer chaos. Dante is lunging out of his seat to get in Vito's face. Nico pounds his fist into his palm, demanding a recess so we can all talk this over. Carmy and Hades roar at each other from across the room, which escalates into a shoving match before Dante and Ares yank them apart.

Strangely, eerily, throughout the whole thing, despite his size and strength, Kratos just stands to one side. Leaning against the bookshelves.

Looking right at me, his mouth curled slightly at the corners, sending shivers through me.

We might be out in the light now. And without a mask between us, and standing here in the chaos of our families going at each other's throats. But all I can see is that same dark, predatory monster from the church, smiling savagely at me with my cum and blood dripping from his lips.

Suddenly, his eyes leave mine. He stops leaning against the

bookshelves, and rolls his neck before he opens his mouth and roars.

"*ENOUGH!*"

Kratos' thunderous, deep baritone quiets and stills the room instantly and all heads swivel toward him.

He clears his throat. "If it's all right with you, Don Barone," he bows toward my father. "Respectfully... I'd like the chance to speak with my fiancée alone."

Respectfully.

God, he's good at this—wearing a mask, I mean. Because it's clear now that the dark one with the neon X's for eyes isn't the only mask Kratos wears. There's this one, too: the one he dons for the rest of the world, when he goes out in public. When he's talking with his family. When he wants to hide what he is.

But I know the truth. This isn't the "real" Kratos, schmoozing my father, bowing, asking permission, and being *respectful*.

The real Kratos is the vicious beast who chases me through the dark, rips my clothes off, and brutalizes me until I'm gasping for more.

My dad takes a deep breath, glancing at my brothers and nodding his head.

"Yes, Mr. Drakos," he growls, turning to face Kratos. "That would be fine with me. If it's fine with my daughter, that is."

All eyes turn to me.

Is it fine with me? I'm genuinely unsure if the idea of being alone with this man right now is terrifying, or thrilling.

Or both.

"S-sure," I stammer awkwardly.

It's clear they don't want to leave, but Vito manages to shepherd my brothers from the room after the Drakos family leaves. Carmy stops right next to Kratos, not even looking at him.

"*Watch yourself, Greek,*" he growls quietly. "You so much as make her nervous and I'll rip you in half."

"I somehow doubt that."

Carmine's jaw clenches as he turns toward Kratos. "Do we have a problem—"

"Carmy," I say quietly. He glances at me, then glares at Kratos.

"Mind your fucking manners, is all," he mutters to Kratos before striding out the door and slamming it shut behind him.

Then we're alone.

The seconds tick by. I squirm under Kratos' gaze, and all I can think about is earlier tonight. All I see when I look at him are my own sins, my own twisted, fucked-up desires.

"*Dirty girl,*" he growls under his breath.

I tremble as he starts to walk toward me.

"Don't—

"Don't *what,*" he rumbles, prowling closer.

"Don't touch me," I whisper, quivering as he comes to a stop, looming over me, smirking darkly down into my face.

"The rest of them aren't here anymore, babygirl," he

194

murmurs. "And you didn't seem to mind me...*touching you*...earlier."

My face throbs with heat. I squirm under his piercing eyes.

"That... That was different."

"Oh, I agree."

I shiver as he leans down, his lips brushing my ear.

"I had *much* more room to chase you earlier," he murmurs. "More room to get your pulse quivering under your skin, to get the sweet scent of your fear and excitement going, and to make your tight little cunt *nice and wet for me*."

Jesus.

My thighs, clearly having a mind of their own, clamp together. My pulse sizzles through my veins as I swallow miserably.

"Why are you doing this?" I ask. "Punishment?"

He tilts his head slightly to the side in that way I already know so well, his eyes eviscerating me.

"Maybe."

I tremble. "I thought you already did that."

He smiles wickedly. "If you think 'punishment' is me making your little pussy cream all over my fingers and my tongue, than we have *wildly* different opinions on the definition."

My face throbs with heat.

"So chasing me wasn't enough?"

His lips curl. "Not so far."

"And, and..."

"And *what*, babygirl," he rumbles lowly.

"And...the other stuff."

Kratos smirks. "*Other stuff*? Would you care to elaborate?"

My cheeks simmer. "*No.*"

"Oh, you mean when I pinned you down, shredded your fucking *soaked* panties off you, and then fucked you with the hilt of my knife while you inhaled my cock like a greedy little slut."

Holy fucking hell.

"Or perhaps you mean when you swallowed my cum and then came all over my chin."

Every inch of my skin pulses with wicked heat.

"For the record, babygirl, *I'm* not doing this at all. This was Ares' call."

"You're just going along with it?"

"You're asking if I'm loyal to my family. The answer is 'yes, unequivocally.'"

I tremble as he reaches up, the knuckle of one of his huge fingers brushing my chin, tilting my face up to his. A quiver ripples through my body as our eyes lock.

"This is happening, Bianca," he rumbles. His mouth curls in a slightly unsettling but also horribly enticing psychotic way. "You're *mine* now."

A chill ripples up my spine.

"*Please—*"

"You'll always have your safe word."

I go still. The whole room does.

"And you may use it anytime."

By throat bobs.

"And *yet*, you never have. I don't think you will right now, either," he muses. I gasp quietly as the hand at my chin up twists to cup my jaw. "Because you *want this*."

I blanch. "I don't—"

"Maybe you don't want *me*, specifically. But you want what I can offer you."

My throat tightens when he leans down and brushes his lips over my earlobe.

"*Escape*," he growls. "A release from that awful ache inside of you."

An electric pulse jangles through me as he runs his knuckles down my jugular.

"Cold, brutal mercy."

His hand drops. My jaw does too, when he boldly cups my pussy through my yoga pants and panties.

Slowly, he starts to rub.

My eyes bulge, my head whipping around to the door that my fucking family is *just on the other side of*.

"*Kratos—*"

"*Say it, babygirl*," he snarls in my ear. "You know the word. Say it, and this all stops. Me haunting your shadows. My control over you..."

I bite back a whimper as he starts to rub a little harder. The friction of my panties against my throbbing, swollen clit has them soaked instantly, my pussy leaking into the lace. My face flushes deeply as my teeth sink into my lip.

"Say the word, Bianca," Kratos growls darkly. "It all stops."

He starts to rub my pussy harder, adding pressure to my eager clit. I know he can feel how embarrassingly soaked I am—how desperately needy I am for this, even now, with everything happening.

I shudder. Kratos chuckles darkly.

"*Yes*, even that. You say your word right now, and it *all* stops. Even this marriage deal."

The wide, thick pad of his finger keeps rolling over my clit, making my legs shake as I bite back a moan.

"But we both know you won't," he murmurs into my ear. "*You can't*, can you?" His teeth bite my earlobe sharply, making me wince as my pussy clenches and quivers. "*You're just too greedy a little slut to shut the whole thing down...aren't you.*"

My whole body begins to shake. My pulse roars in my ears. My breath chokes off as my eyes roll back.

"Say it, babygirl."

The filthy, squelching sounds of my messy, wet pussy rubbing against my slick panties is so loud I can feel my face burn. But he's right.

I'm not going to say it.

I can't.

I need this darkness.

"Say it."

Kratos rubs harder and faster, groaning deeply into my ear as my legs begin to give out. The thickness of his finger rolls perfectly over my swollen clit, until suddenly, I can't hold back any longer.

When I come, he clamps a hand tightly over my mouth. I know it's to muffle my cries, but the sudden lack of oxygen sends me into orbit. I scream into his hand, my entire body shuddering as I slump against him. Kratos keeps me pinned to his massive body, his finger still rubbing my aching pussy through my pants until I swear I'm about to faint.

It's only then that he pulls away, a dark, satisfied smirk on his lips.

"Well," he growls quietly. "I guess that's your final answer... *fiancée.*"

15

KRATOS

"Mr. Drakos?" The man in the dark suit bows. "Mr. Kirakosian will see you now."

I nod back, standing stiffly and grimacing as I flex my shoulders in my tuxedo.

I hate getting dressed up. That's not to say I don't like looking good or dressing sharp. But when you're my size, "fancy" clothes are usually a major pain in the ass. People shit on NFL players for showing up to prestigious award banquets in track pants. But for real? I get it.

I haven't donned a tux specifically to meet with Davit. But Bianca's and my engagement "party"—if you want to call it that, which I don't—is starting soon, and I needed to see Davit quickly before it begins. Obviously, he was invited to this shitshow, as were *many* heads of criminal organizations here in New York: the Kildares, the Reznikov Bratva, Jayden Robinson—who helms the Jamaican Cartel here in the city and is a close family friend—and more.

Oddly enough, Davit sent word just last night that that he'd be unable to attend. So I've opted to stop by before the party starts, to see if I can suss out *why*.

I follow a guard through Davit's stunning Gilded Age mansion on the Upper West Side. They may be new to New York, but the Kirakosian family and Te Mallkuarit have done extremely well for themselves over the years. Spoiler: it shows.

The man opens a set of double doors, and I step into what appears to be Davit's personal study—a huge, light-filled room with ornate furnishings and floor-to-ceiling shelves of books. What stops me cold isn't the elegant room, though.

It's the fact that Davit nods his head in greeting from the hospital bed he's lying in.

My brow furrows. "Mr. Kirakosian, I—"

"Didn't know?" He smirks. "Well, that would be because I'm keeping this a secret."

"And it's going to *stay* a secret," a stern voice growls from behind me.

I half turn and nod my head at the younger man around my age striding into the room. Arian Kirakosian, Davit's only son and next in line for his father's position as head of Te Mallkuarit, gives me a dark, lingering glare.

"Is that clear?" he mutters, eying me. "Or is that secrecy something *else* you and your family will carelessly destroy?"

I could take the bait, but I choose not to—just as I choose not to drive my fist into his face right now. Because I can see more than five minutes into the future, and I'm smart enough to know that settling any animosity between the Albanians and my family is ultimately a good thing.

So I just nod, smiling politely at him.

"It won't be shared," I say evenly. "You have my word on that," I add, turning to Davit.

He smiles and nods back. "Forgive my son's zeal. He's merely trying to protect me and the family. You'll understand why my...*condition* has been kept quiet, especially while your family and I were engaged in a bidding war."

"May I ask..."

"No," Arian says flatly.

His father sighs. "A temporary issue with my liver, it would appear. Nothing serious."

Says the man in a hospital bed, in his own home.

He smiles wryly. "I suppose now you see why I turned down your gracious invitation to the festivities today."

I clear my throat. "Once again, I want to apologize for what happened involving your family's heirloom—"

Arian mutters something in Albanian. His father shoots him a warning look, responding in the same language, before he turns back to me.

"I'm told the responsible party was the Italians."

I nod.

"Specifically, your *fiancée*," Arian adds, smirking.

His father chuckles. "What did you do, Mr. Drakos? Fuck her friends?"

No, but I did chase her through an abandoned church, cut her panties off, and fuck her mouth afterward.

I smile quietly. "It was a very unfortunate misunderstanding. However, my family has prepared this as a token of our esteem, together with the hope that we can continue to build a mutually beneficial relationship and peace between our families."

I slip the envelope containing a check out of my tuxedo pocket and walk over to hand it to Davit.

Arian barks a cold laugh. "*Money?* You destroy a priceless heirloom that's been in my family for nearly a *millennium*, and you think your fucking *money* will fix the problem?!"

"Arian!" Davit snaps. "Be civil."

"*Babai—!*"

"Enough!!"

Davit exhales slowly, his face pinched and tired. Then he composes himself.

"Arian," he says, more quietly now. "Mr. Drakos is our guest. And what occurred was beyond his control."

"Perhaps Mr. Drakos should have better control over *his own fucking fiancée*," Arian hisses, shooting me a cold look.

I resist the urge to respond with "Way ahead of you", and just smile as I dip my chin.

"I understand what was destroyed is beyond monetary value. And I can't put a price on sentimentality. But I do hope the check for twenty million dollars in that envelope can ease at least a little of the suffering we've caused."

I get that this thing was important to their family, and old as fuck. But let's be real: it's not gold, or bejeweled. It's fucking old bones. We looked up similar pieces for appraisal comparisons, and the thing was *maybe* worth a tenth of twenty mil.

Davit eyes the envelope. Then he raises his head and smiles. "Mr. Drakos, I appreciate the gesture. Please, consider any issues between our families settled, and the matter closed."

Arian's face goes livid.

"*Father—*"

"I said *closed*, Arian."

His son's mouth twists. But when he turns back to me, he nods stiffly. "It is as my father says," he growls. "Now, if you'll excuse me…"

He turns and strides out of the room.

When we're alone again, Davit sighs. "My apologies."

"None necessary, Mr. Kirakosian."

He smiles and grasps my extended hand, albeit with not much strength. My brow furrows.

"I *do* hope you're feeling better soon, sir."

"Oh, I'll be up in no time," he smiles back. "And I appreciate the visit. *Pergezime* on your wedding, Mr. Drakos."

———

"All good with Davit?"

I accept the tumbler of whiskey Ares offers me and take a large sip before I nod.

"All good."

My eyes scan the event as I take a second, more moderate sip. Yes, this entire thing is fake: we're obviously just doing this to stop World War Three from erupting in the streets of New York. Yes, Davit came across as gracious and understanding just now, but I know for a fact that all would have gone in a whole other direction if I *weren't* about to marry Bianca.

In our world, especially for the older generation, these "marriages of convenience" matter. A lot. No one, including Davit, is under any delusions that Bianca and I are two love-struck kids tying the knot. They all know what this is. But in matters like this, the end does justify the means.

I'm about to say something to my brother, when suddenly, something catches my eye, and I freeze. My pulse skips, and my jaw tightens as my eyes zero in on a figure who's just floated her way into my field of vision through a gap in the milling guests.

My cock stirs in my tux pants, and the beast within me stretches awake.

There's no denying that Bianca is beautiful. It might not be overt or flaunted, and she *is* usually in some combination of hoodie and yoga pants, no makeup, her long hair scraped back in a severe dancer's bun. But she's still obviously attractive.

When she slips into view now, I realize this is a side of her I've never seen before.

It floors me.

She looks like a fucking *goddess*.

She's in a stunning sage-green sleeveless, off-the-shoulder gown that falls to the floor in sleek, silky lines that accent her every delicate curve and the athleticism of her dancer's body. A slit up one side to mid-thigh reveals a glimpse of one of her long, toned legs. Her long hair is actually down for a change, braided and slightly curled into this long, Rapunzel-esque twist that hangs forward over her bare shoulder and one of her breasts.

She looks gorgeous. She looks elegant. She looks fucking amazing.

But mostly, she looks like someone I want to drag into an alley, gag with her panties and rip that dress from before I smear my cum across her face and fuck her like an animal until her tight little virgin pussy quivers and comes and bleeds all over my fucking cock.

Yes, I've tried therapy.

I suppose you could say it's never worked.

My brow furrows as my gaze follows her across the lavish River Café, the Michelin-starred restaurant right on the East River that we've booked out for the evening. I watch the way the sage dress clings to her every curve, how it brings out the tan of her Mediterranean skin and the soft blue of her eyes.

But curiously, what really catches my eye, beyond her body and all the things I'd like to do to it, is the way she carries herself. The way the slightly mouthy, impulsive, magnet-for-trouble Bianca Sartorre, who I've usually seen when she's completely out of her element, is very much *in* her element right now.

I watch as she smiles gracefully, even bowing a little when she greets Konstantin Reznikov, Gavan Tsarenko's brother and co-helm of the Reznikov Bratva, who's here with his wife, Mara, and their twin girls, Talia and Mila—toddlers in matching maroon velvet dresses who are stealing the show. I watch curiously as Gavan, his wife Eilish, and Callie roar with laughter at something Bianca's just told them.

This is...*strange*.

I'd have expected Bianca to be graceful on stage, dancing. But everything I've seen from her, which is a lot, would have suggested the opposite in any other scenario.

As if reading my mind, Callie turns and catches my eye. She smirks a little, excusing herself from the group before she walks over to Ares and me.

"Hmm, interesting," Ares muses.

Callie frowns. "What?"

"You just walked past two different waiters with trays full of Dom Perignon, and you didn't take a glass from either of them."

"Careful, Ares."

He arches a brow. "Of?"

"Of the fact that you're dangerously close to getting a lesson in fertility cycles, ovulation—"

"Yeah, thanks, I could go ahead and live the rest of my days without hearing my sister say the word 'ovulation' ever again," Ares mutters.

I chuckle deeply, clapping him on the back. "You sort of asked for that."

"Well, color me regretful," he grumbles.

Callie sticks her tongue out at him before turning to me. "For the record?" She turns and nods her chin at Bianca, who's now moved on to talking to the King and Queen of the Damned themselves, Cillian and Una Kildare. "I like her. A lot, actually."

"Because she's impulsive, difficult, and doesn't know when to keep her mouth shut?" I mutter.

Callie snorts. "See, I get that that's supposed to be a jab at me. But what's *actually* funny is that I distinctly remember this one"—she pokes a finger into Ares' chest—"saying the exact same thing a few years ago about the now mother of his child."

My brother snickers. Just then, we're joined by another figure.

"I hate to interrupt a sibling moment," Drazen growls quietly in his deep voice, "but I was hoping to have a word with the two of you," he says, eyeing Ares and me.

Callie sighs. "And I suppose this is an A-B conversation, and I should C my way out of it?"

Drazen smiles, at least, as much as I imagine he's capable of smiling.

"That is a funny joke," he grunts in his thick Serbian-Russian accent. "I think I will keep that one."

"It's all yours," Callie shrugs. "Now, if you'll excuse me, I'm ovulating and I need to go find my husband."

Ares and I make pained faces as she grins at us and then sashays off through the crowd.

"Is this also a joke?" Drazen rumbles curiously.

"*No*, that's just Callie being fucking gross," Ares mutters. "What did you want to talk about?"

Drazen Krylov is an interesting character in the New York scene. A few years ago, he was basically a ghost—the boogeyman of the Bratva world who scared the shit out of even the most hardened *pakhan*.

As far as I can tell, no one knows much of anything about the background of the half-Serbian, half-Russian kingpin of the newly resurrected Krylov Bratva. I've heard he's got a military background; other rumors say he was a child soldier in the Kosovo conflict of the 90s. Beyond that, the man is a mystery.

A very, very wealthy, extremely *powerful* mystery. I wouldn't say Drazen and my family are allies, per se. Or even friends. But I know we're not enemies, because I'm *positive* if we were...we'd know.

I do like him, though. And I'm pretty sure it's because I can sense a blackness inside of him that mirrors my own. There's a monster like mine lurking deep in his soul.

Mine can smell it.

Drazen clears his throat as he turns to me. "I hear you just met with Davit Kirakosian."

"I did. He wasn't able to come tonight, so I wanted to be sure we'd smoothed things over."

Drazen nods. "I've heard..." He shrugs. "*Rumors* about Mr. Kirakosian. About his health."

Ares glances at me curiously. "Actually, I was going to ask you about those same rumors."

Okay, I did promise Davit and his son that I wouldn't say anything. But Ares doesn't count. And even if I don't know Drazen *that* well, it's clear that he's the sort of man to value silence and discretion.

"He's...laid up," I say in a slow, measured tone. "Hospital bed, in his home office." I eye them both. "I'd appreciate you keeping that strictly to yourselves."

Ares gets that I'm saying this more to Drazen, but nods anyway.

"Of course."

"Not a word," Drazen adds.

"Davit said it was a temporary liver thing, but I don't know. I tried to dig a little, but his son..."

Drazen's mouth twists. "Arian was there?"

I glance at my brother, then back to Drazen. "You know him?"

Drazen doesn't say a word, move a single muscle, or even *blink*. I take that as a "next question" sort of statement and move on.

"Arian is..."

"Tempestuous," Drazen finishes quietly. "You said Davit said it had been smoothed over?"

I nod.

"Then you'd better hope his illness really is temporary. If Arian were sitting on the throne, you can bet he'd have a different idea about things being 'smoothed over'."

I share another quick look with my brother.

Interesting.

My phone rings. Frowning, I take it out and glance at the screen. Taylor's name and face pop up, but I let it go to voicemail. I can check in with her later about whatever it is.

"You're friends with Ms. Crown?"

I raise my eyes to Drazen, who's looking at my phone with a strange expression on his face.

"She's my lawyer."

Drazen nods, still looking at my phone. When I slide it back into my pocket, the odd spell over him lifts.

"How do you find her...legal expertise," he growls quietly.

"Uh, great?" I shrug. "If you're looking for representation, Crown and Black are fantastic. Seriously, she's a phenomenal lawyer."

"Indeed," the mysterious Serbian murmurs, almost to himself. He clears his throat, pulling his lips into what I guess passes for Drazen's version of a smile. "If you will excuse me, I need to see to a piece of business before I indulge in any more of your excellent champagne, Mr. Drakos." He nods as he clinks his empty glass to mine. "*Čestitiam* on your engagement, Kratos."

Ares shakes his head, eyeing Drazen as he disappears into the crowd. "That dude scares the shit out of me."

I chuckle, patting Ares on the shoulder. "Ten bucks says it's all bullshit and scary bedtime stories the Bratva told their kids growing up."

"What, like the one where they call him *the headsman* back in Serbia?" Ares snorts, running his fingers over the stubble on his chin. "I'm just saying, if the fucking *Bratva* tell their kids scary bedtime stories about him, I'm just glad he seems to like us. He's like your size with Deimos'...well, *Deimos-ness*."

I know he means "psycho-ness".

Oh, if only you knew, brother.

You don't need to inject crazy into me to make me Drazen. It's why he and I get along, without ever having had a single conversation about it.

Because in an alternate universe, where I'm unlucky enough to be born into war-torn Yugoslavia, and go through whatever shit Drazen did?

He and I are the same fucking guy.

"I'm going to mingle," Ares mutters. "Wish me luck."

When he's gone, I turn to survey the crowd of guests again. In some ways, it makes my chest swell to spot my siblings and see each of them so happy and fulfilled with their own new lives and families: Callie, throwing her head back and laughing as she dances near the band with Castle. I grin as the Captain America-looking motherfucker dips my sister extravagantly and then leans in to kiss her softly.

Callie deserves that. She *earned* that.

Near them, Deimos, unbelievably, doesn't suck at dancing—at least, not too badly—as he twirls a beaming, orange-clad Dahlia. Hades stands near the back of the crowd behind Elsa, one arm slung possessively across her collarbone as he rests his chin on top of her head. The other hand snakes around to her stomach, his hand splayed across her third-trimester belly.

I grin when I see Ya-ya cut in on Callie and Castle, stealing the latter away with a big belly laugh so she can go dance with "her Adonis" as she loves to call her son-in-law.

Turning, I chuckle to myself and shake my head when I spot Ares "mingling"—that is to say, sitting in a quiet corner near the windows overlooking the Manhattan Bridge and the East River, bouncing my nephew Elias on his knee with Neve curled up next to him.

And then there's you.

Yeah, then there's me.

It's not a pity party. I'm not lamenting that I've never found anyone—which I get is either gallows humor or just plain rude to say at your own engagement party.

But it's true.

Some of us are meant to be alone.

I take a sip of my drink, my eyes scanning the room again. This time, it's not my family my gaze settles on.

It's Bianca.

She's with her own family off to one side of the dance floor. Dante and Tempest are having a great time dancing. Nico looks bored and is playing on his phone, while Carmine seems to be visually checking over every unaccompanied female in the room. Don Barone himself looks to be *very much* enjoying the open bar. The band swings into some Sinatra, and Bianca's adoptive father hops out of his chair with a whoop, cigar in hand, as he starts to cut a rug enthusiastically on the dance floor.

My gaze drags back to Bianca. Something dark and swirling surges in my chest as my beast prowls behind his locked bars.

This...*whatever-it-was* between us was one thing. But now it's something else, something I didn't plan for.

Marriage changes the dynamic.

Before, this was a game. Before was about her dipping her toes into her own darkness, and me being all too happy to oblige.

Or at least, that's the bullshit I've told myself.

Because as I watch Bianca smile at something Nico says to her, I know there's a truth I've been trying not to admit.

It's not only that finding a willing partner for my fucked-up tastes is hard, and Bianca *being* such a willing partner, and a repeat one at that, is a new thing for me.

It's that the little ballerina *does something* to me. She...quiets something inside of me.

And I'm not quite sure what to do with that, considering that I'm now *miles* past wherever I expected this to end when I set these wheels in motion.

A finger taps my shoulder. Frowning at the distraction, I pull away to fake a smile at whichever mafia world player has decided that *now* is the opportune time to come interrupt my thoughts with their bullshit congratulations.

When I turn, and my eyes latch onto overly-dyed blonde and too much Botox in a dark blue Chanel gown, my jaw tightens.

"I'm positive you weren't invited," I growl.

Amaya smiles. "Funny, mine must have been lost in the—"

"You have five seconds to—"

"Oh, *no*, Kratos," CIA Special Agent Amaya Mircari smiles at me. "*You* have five seconds to come outside and talk to *me*. Or, I promise, you'll regret it."

16

KRATOS

THERE'S a kind of whispered white noise constantly running in the background in my mind. It's always there, like the distant clatter of a train, or the low growl of a truck engine on the highway.

But being this physically close to the woman who stole my childhood turns that whisper into a fucking scream.

I was thirteen when my father dragged me to the hotel suite in midtown. By that point, I was already the size of a college sophomore, and Dad had already spent years trying to mold me into some sort of monster.

Aeneas didn't just name us all after Greek gods and titans because he had a thing for mythology. He truly *wanted* us to be the bloodthirsty, conquering gods and demigods of those stories. He didn't want sons. He wanted soldiers. *Killers.*

He succeeded with Atlas, our cruel, oldest brother. The divine comedy...or is it Greek tragedy...there is that it was Atlas himself who ended up killing our father in a greedy attempt to seize a throne he was never going to be smart or level-headed enough to actually sit on. Atlas' reign of terror lasted all of a *week* before a fight he picked with a powerful man over a woman Atlas thought belonged to him ended with our brother dead and Ares taking over the throne.

We never mourned the death of our tyrant father. Nor that of our cruel, sadistic brother. But while the rest of my siblings celebrate my father's failure in turning any of us into the twisted, cold monsters he'd hoped to create, deep down, I know he didn't really fail.

Not entirely.

Not with me.

For years, I ignored the constant verbal assaults as best as I could; the attempts to warp me into his cold, ruthless weapon. He wanted me to be his Goliath: the huge, tough son he could parade in front of allies and enemies alike, to frighten them into either allegiance or submission. I resisted those attempts for *so long.*

But in that midtown hotel suite, he won.

That's the night he sat me down and told me I needed to "do something for the family". For him. For my siblings, because didn't I want to protect and safeguard my siblings?

There was an FBI agent looking to make "connections" with families like ours. An agent with an eye on a much higher position.

An agent who also had an eye for much, much younger... well, to say *men* feels like a crime.

I wasn't a man. I was fucking thirteen. And she was thirty.

Aeneas wasn't subtle. Before he left me alone with her, he told me exactly what he expected of me.

"Time to grow a pair of balls and be a man. For the family. Be a good boy, Kratos, and do as she says." He'd chuckled then. *"And don't look so fucking glum, you fucking pussy. You should be thanking me for this."*

After that, he left, and *she* walked in.

That was the first time I ever met the witch now standing in front of me at my own engagement party.

That was the first time I went to the place where my mind shuts down, and I block it all out. But it wasn't the last. Not by a goddamn mile.

The roaring in my head only gets louder as I step out of the main ballroom and into a side room, alone with Amaya.

"I'm *hurt*, Kratos," she purrs, smirking at me with smug arrogance that makes me want to rip her in half. "I'd think with our history, I'd at least merit an invitation—"

She gasps, her breath hitching as I surge into her. My hand darts out, eager to wrap around her fucking scarred neck and squeeze until I hear the satisfying snap of her spine. But I stop myself short, my hand an inch from her throat.

My jaw grinding. My fury near nuclear in my chest.

Amaya swallows. Then she composes herself, her lips curling snidely.

"You can't do it, can you?" she hisses quietly.

I suck in air, my blood burning like liquid fire in my veins.

"I wonder...is it the fear of repercussions, given who I work for?"

Yeah... Given her fairly high-level anti-terrorism position within the CIA, she's powerful, and she knows it.

"Or…"

I stiffen, my mind going a little blank when her fingers brush my arm. Flinching, I yank my hand away. Amaya grins.

"No, you're not scared of repercussions. Not my Kratos. He's not scared of *anything*."

Nausea and a pain I can't identify wash over me.

My Kratos.

The words are like chains that never left my wrists and ankles.

Amaya's eyebrows lift. "No, it's not fear that keeps you from hurting me."

My reality bends, like watching heat pulse off a parking lot in July.

"I think it's that you still care too much," she purrs. "That's it, isn't it—"

With a loud snarl, I wrench myself away, taking a step back as I glare pure hate at her.

It's not fear of repercussions. And it's *not* that I give a single fuck about her.

The only thing stopping me from snapping Amaya's neck with my bare hands is that I'm fairly sure touching her at all will shove me into a hole so deep I'll never climb back out again.

"Kratos—"

"Why are you fucking here?" I snarl savagely—so much so that she flinches a little. But she recovers again, smirking haughtily at me.

"You've been ignoring my calls."

"And I'll continue to do so," I snap. "We have *nothing* to discuss. Stay the fuck away from me."

She smiles. "We both know that's not an option for you. Not when you were such a naughty boy." She wags her finger at me. "Need I remind you that you sold guns to a United States CIA officer, Kratos? Being naughty like that has its consequences."

Amaya grins.

"Luckily for you, because of our"...she smirks up at me... "*history...*"

My head swims again.

Be a good boy for me, Kratos...

We're not done yet...

You'll never find anyone like me. No one will love you like me...

My thoughts glitch as I rip myself back into the present.

"I have a way out for you, Kratos."

I don't respond. Amaya eyes me steadily.

"It involves your engagement to that silly little mafia ballerina princess."

Alarm bells whine in my head.

"Tell me, Kratos," Amaya murmurs quietly. "Does she know what you are? Would you *dare* show her the darkness I know you've still got inside—"

"*Careful*, witch," I snarl with a venom that catches even me a little off-guard.

Amaya's mouth curls.

"I found that bigger fish I was telling you about, Kratos."

"Excuse me?"

"Your bride-to-be is a direct line to Vito Barone. And through him, all five families of The Commission."

I bark a cold laugh.

"You're fucking insane, you miserable cunt," I snap. "Not in a million years. And as you yourself said…" I snarl into her face. "Your invitation seems to have been lost. So I'd suggest *fucking off*."

I turn to leave, but her voice stops me.

"Walk away and this deal expires. Immediately. And you won't have to worry about marrying that girl you clearly don't give a shit about, because you'll be in prison, along with the rest of your family."

Pure rage consumes me. In a flash, I'm whirling, storming over to Amaya, grabbing her by the high neck of her gown, and slamming her back into the wall.

I relish the flicker of real fear that burns in her eyes as I snarl down into her face with my teeth bared.

"Listen to me *very fucking carefully*, you miserable piece of shit," I spit. "I do *not* take threats against my family lightly."

"Then perhaps it's time you take what *I'm* saying a bit more fucking seriously," she snaps back. "You're going to do this for me, Kratos. Use the girl to get to her father, and get me access—a bug, a mole, anything—to the Barone family and The Commission. If you make me happy, maybe I can forget about those pesky gun charges."

I go cold as her hand wraps around my wrist, her eyes locking with mine.

"And you remember how good you were at making me happy, don't you, Kratos...?" she breathes.

My mind goes numb. My vision turns white as the oxygen leaves my body.

"Am I interrupting something?"

Her tone is sharp and icy. But even so, Bianca's voice behind me pulls me out of the black abyss I'm drowning in, a lifeline thrown in a storm. I cling to it, sucking in air as I drop my hand from Amaya's gown, yanking away from her touch with a nauseous feeling.

Swallowing my revulsion, I turn. Bianca's standing in the doorway behind us, her mouth small, her hands balled at her sides, a cold glare leveled at me.

Instantly, I understand how bad this looks.

"Bianca," I growl, cracking my neck. "This is..."

"Amaya, *hi*," Amaya sneers with all the friendliness of a wolf with bared teeth.

"Bianca, *hi*," Bianca hurls back in the same cold tone. "His fiancée. And you are...?"

"Amaya is an *old* family friend," I say icily, emphasizing "old" in a way I hope grinds Amaya's gears.

"Well, thank you *so* much for coming," Bianca says in an unsmiling tone.

Amaya grins like a shark. "Of course. Kratos and I go *way* back, after all." She levels a smug look at Bianca. "*Lots* of history." She turns to me. "Isn't that right, Kratos?"

I say nothing.

"Think about what we discussed, won't you?"

She pats my chest. I flinch. Then she strolls past Bianca, barely breaking her stride as she mutters "Happy engagement".

When she's gone, Bianca levels a withering look at me.

"*Old family friend?*" she says icily.

My eyes narrow. "Jealous, *prinkipissa?*"

"Stop calling me that."

"Start answering my questions when I ask them."

Her lip curls.

"*No.*"

My brow lifts in amusement. "No, you're choosing to defy me? Or no, you're not jealous? Because that's obviously a fucking lie."

Bianca glares at me, gritting her teeth. "No, I'm not *jealous*. I just think maybe it's bad form to have your *ex* or your fuck buddy or whatever the hell she is at your engagement celebration." Bianca purses her lips. "I mean, have a little fucking class."

She whirls to walk away, then fires a parting shot over her shoulder.

"Or at the very least, a little respect—"

Bianca gasps as I grab her arm, yanking her around and then to my chest.

Time stops for a millisecond. The roaring quiets in my head. I feel her pulse under the silky skin of her arm. I feel the muscles of her dancer's body ripple against mine as she presses flat against my body.

I made damn sure my skin never touched Amaya's just now. The very thought of that happening makes me want to explode, screaming, into ash.

With Bianca, *all* I want is to touch her.

To feel her squirm against me. To feel the heat of her skin and the shiver of her fear and excitement under my fingers.

A different roar fills my head. One I don't want to push away, one I don't want to escape from. It thrums louder as I pull her tighter to me, relishing the hitch of her breath and the roundness of her big blue eyes. The heat in her cheeks, and the feel of her nipples hardening to points against my chest.

Bianca trembles as I cup her jaw, lifting her chin. Our eyes lock.

A camera goes off in our faces, blinding me for a second. When I blink away the stars, I glare, snarling, at the photographer I'm guessing Ya-ya hired for the event.

"Now *that* is a keeper!" he gushes. "The happy couple, lost in their own—"

Bianca pulls away. Her eyes snap to mine, full of some emotion I can't pinpoint. Then, without another word, she's whirling and bolting away back to the main ballroom. I turn to level a savage look at the photographer.

"*Get out.*"

I storm after Bianca. But by the time I get back to the ballroom, she's disappeared into the crowd. I get stuck talking to

Ezio Adamos, the head of one of our tributary families who's *deep* in his drinks tonight, for a good ten minutes or so before I can extricate myself.

By then, there's no sign of Bianca anywhere.

Why are you even looking for her?

I know why.

She never should have been in that alley. But she was. And like it or not, she caught the attention of my monster.

His *full* attention, in a way no woman ever has before.

I don't know how I feel about our game turning into a *marriage*, and what that means for us and our dark play.

I don't even know how I feel about the fact that Bianca is clearly a virgin, given my own fucked-up history involving sex and "first times".

But I do know that once my beast's attention has been caught, there's no evading it. No escaping it, like the jaws of a crocodile.

Come what may, Bianca is *mine* now.

So where the fuck is she.

She's not with her family. She's not in the restrooms, or at the bar. She's vanished.

Until I step outside onto the deck overlooking the East River, that is, and hear her voice coming from around the corner, in the shadows of the restaurant.

"Stop it, Grisha."

Scowling, my jaw set, I prowl toward the corner of the deck, pausing behind a wall of climbing ivy to listen.

"Ah, but we have history, beautiful."

Something venomous and toxic spills like black ink inside my chest.

Rage explodes through my veins.

What fucking history does she have with fucking Grisha Lenkov?

"Please, get away from—"

"But the thing is, *shlyukha*," Grisha mutters, "you *owe me*. And you owe me *a lot*. Now, you can go ask your new fiancé for the money and tell him *why* his little wifey needs four hundred grand. Or you can be a good little whore and get on your knees, and start paying me back *right now*—"

I think he actually pisses himself when I storm around the corner at full speed, my face a mask of rage. Grisha sputters, dropping his grip on Bianca's wrist as she backs away.

"Now listen, Kr—"

"*No.*"

My fist smashes into his face, hard. He screams as his nose breaks, blood exploding across his face and streaming down his chin as he stumbles backward.

I turn to Bianca. Our eyes lock—mine full of fury and wrath, hers wide with fear.

And something else.

Danger-lust.

Sin and temptation.

Excitement.

"Kratos, I…"

"Wait here."

I turn just as Grisha starts to reach inside his jacket. I punch him again, relishing the sound of his orbital cracking as he drops to the ground, squealing. The gun tucked into his waistband clatters to the ground, and I immediately kick it off the deck into the river.

"Do you know who my uncle is?!" he screeches from the decking.

I do. But I also don't give a single fuck that Artem Lenkov is high up in the Chernoff Bratva. Or that Grisha himself has a the title of *avtoritet*. This little fuckstick just laid his hands on what's *mine*.

That will not go unpunished.

My eyes go to his hand—the one that was grabbing Bianca's wrist.

Grisha *screams* as I stomp down hard on it, breaking a few of the bones. He's sucking in ragged breaths when I stoop down to yank him up by his collar into my face.

"I don't give a fuck if your uncle is Jesus fucking Christ himself," I snarl. "If you ever come *near* her again, I'll cut your balls off and enjoy watching you choke on them when I ram them down your fucking throat."

I hurl him down to the deck and turn to grab Bianca's hand, but the little fucker springs up behind me. I whirl as his blade flashes, hissing when it gets me on the arm. Bianca screams as I wrestle the knife out of Grisha's hand and toss it into the river to join the gun before I start to beat the ever-living fuck out of him, roaring.

Footsteps and shouting thunder behind me. Arms grab me, yanking me away.

"ENOUGH!" Ares hisses in my ear. Hades is suddenly standing in front of me, too, shaking his head as he plants a hand on my chest.

"We'll get rid of him, brother," he growls. "But no matter what he did, I can't let you kill him."

Deimos and some of our men are dragging the whimpering, bleeding Grisha away. I shake off my brothers, nodding curtly before I spin.

I grab Bianca's hand and storm away, pulling her behind me.

We head around the corner and toward a side exit before she suddenly yanks her hand free of mine.

"Let *go* of me!"

I turn to her. Bianca's mouth is a tight line.

"I can handle my battles myself!"

I take her wrist again. "Clearly. Let's go—"

She yanks her hand back, shaking her head. "I said can take care of myself, Kratos! And you had no right—"

"I had *every* right!" I roar.

"Why?!" she hurls back. "Because you *own me* now, since we're getting married? Or because—"

She gasps as I yank her against my chest again, grab her chin, tilt her face up to mine, and let my gaze eviscerate her on the spot.

"Because you're going to be my fucking *wife*! And no one..." I hiss through clenched teeth. "*No one* touches you but me."

In a heartbeat, I eradicate the distance between her mouth and mine. And suddenly, for the very first time, I'm kissing her.

Not just *our* first kiss.

My first kiss.

Ever.

And when I taste the soft sweetness of Bianca's lips, I'm not sure I'll ever come up again for air.

17

BIANCA

"*WHAT?*"

Milena and Naomi stare at me, mouths open in shock. We're the last ones left in the dressing room. I asked them to stay after rehearsal because I "had to tell them something".

Namely, that I'm getting married.

Naomi blinks. "This is, like, a mafia thing, right?"

Milena turns to shoot her a look. "You know she can't answer that." Her gaze switches to me. "It's a mafia thing, isn't it."

I sigh. "It's...an arrangement between our families."

Naomi shakes her head, whistling. "It's crazy to me that in your world, you guys can just...like...*get married*. No dating. You just go and—poof—get hitched to guarantee an heir or stop a war or something, right?"

Milena shrugs. "Pretty much. It's medieval as fuck. Luckily, my dad's already promised me that he's never doing that with me."

I smile bitterly. "Funny, my dad promised me the same thing!"

Milena makes a face.

"W-what does this mean for you?" Naomi asks uncertainly. "Like, with dancing, with...your whole life?"

I sigh. "I don't *think* anything changes. I mean, it's not like I'm going to stop dancing or anything."

"What if he makes you?"

"Then she stabs him in the nuts while he sleeps," Milena mutters. "C'mon, the arranged marriage thing is ass-backward. But it's usually not *that* hardcore. I mean, no one's being chained to a bed until they pop out an heir or anything." She shoots me a quick, furtive look. "You're not, right?"

I roll my eyes, blushing. "*No.*"

"Okay, but with these arranged things..." Naomi's cheeks redden. "I mean, do you *have to...*"

Milena snickers. Naomi blushes even harder.

"C'mon! I don't *know* these things! Is it assumed that you'll have sex? Can you say no?"

"It depends on the families, the arrangement, all that," I sigh. "But no, nothing's implied or expected with *my* situation, okay?" I glare at Milena. "No one's being chained to a bed to be a baby-maker."

"So..." Milena eyes me as we grab our stuff and walk out of the dressing room. "Is he hot?"

My cheeks sizzle, and they giggle.

"That's totally a yes," Naomi snickers.

"Which means you're totally fucking him," Milena grins.

My face burns hotly. "I am *not!*"

Not yet, anyway.

We walk down the little hallway and onto the dimly lit, empty stage.

"Is he old?" Naomi asks.

"He's...old*er*?"

She grins. "Well, whether you're screwing him or not, we definitely need to meet this fiancé of yours."

"That could be arranged."

Naomi shrieks and the three of us jump, whirling at the sound of the deep, rough, baritone voice. Kratos materializes like smoke out of the darkness of the wings as he steps onto the dimly lit stage. My pulse roars as his eyes lock onto mine, that same animalistic, feral look in them that I saw the other night at the engagement dinner.

When he beat the shit out of Grisha.

And then kissed me for the first time.

It's not like I hadn't *noticed* that Kratos hadn't ever kissed me before. But in my head, I guess I'd just assumed kissing wasn't something he did. At least, not as part of the dark games we'd been playing.

Kissing isn't necessarily a given when you're being chased around an abandoned church, pinned down, and made to scream in vicious pleasure.

But I never realized how much I *wanted* Kratos to kiss me until he did, the same way he does everything when it comes to me: violently. All-consumingly. Like a conqueror.

It was *everything*. It was madness and bliss. Heaven and damnation.

It was the hottest kiss of my life, with a man who scares me as much as he turns me on.

Out of the corner of my eye, I watch my friends' shocked faces as Kratos strides across the stage toward us. I mean, he's already an enormous human…

Everywhere, I think with a fierce blush.

But with the footlights from the edge of the stage shining up his back, Kratos looks even larger than life as he comes to a stop right in front of us.

"Uh…hi?" I blurt, swallowing nervously. I realize I'm staring up into his stupidly handsome face, and that he's staring right down into mine. One of his big hands comes up, and one of his thick fingers brushes a wayward lock of hair back behind my ear.

"What…" I shiver. "What are you doing here?"

"My grandmother wanted us to come see her."

"Oh…okay," I say. I clear my throat. "Uh, these are my friends, Naomi and Milena."

Kratos' brow furrows. "Milena Kalishnik, if I'm not mistaken?"

Her face turns beet red as she smiles bashfully, staring at him with wide, starry eyes. "Uh-huh," she whispers.

"I've done business with your father."

"That's so awesome," Milena breathes, still moony-eyed.

"I'mNotInTheMafia," Naomi blurts rapidly.

"That's probably a good thing," Kratos rumbles.

Naomi and Milena both laugh like it's the funniest joke in the world. Oh my God.

"*Anyway*," I mutter, clearing my throat. "We should go, yeah?"

Kratos nods. "Indeed. Best never to keep Dimitra Drakos waiting." He turns and bows a little bit to my two blushing friends. "Lovely to meet you, ladies."

"Totally," Milena gushes.

"Any time!" Naomi squeaks.

Kratos walks to the front of the stage. I turn to glare at my friends.

"*What the fuck is wrong with you two?*" I hiss under my breath.

"*Sorry!*" Naomi mouths, looking panicky. "*He's just SO fucking hot.*" She swoons, fanning herself.

I roll my eyes. "Thirsty much?"

"For *that?*" Milena grins. "*Parched.*"

I poke them both in the ribs, rolling my eyes again before I walk over to the edge of the stage to jump off it and into the house. Just before I do, huge hands swoop out of the darkness. My pulse jumps as Kratos gently lifts me by the hips, easing me off the stage and down to the ground as if I weigh nothing.

Then, without another word, he takes my hand and walks me up the aisle and into the foyer.

Once outside, he opens the door to a matte black Mercedes G-wagon. It's funny, in my stalking of Kratos via his siblings' social media, I've seen how he, like his brother Hades, is into cars. But I'm starting to realize that his taste in vehicles probably leans more toward big SUVs, like this G-wagon or the Defender I...cringe...burned. It's not like someone his size is going to be cramming himself into a two-seater sports car.

We drive in silence for a few blocks before I clear my throat.

"Sorry about my friends. They're...weird."

He doesn't say anything. But when I glance at him out of the corner of my eye, I see him grinning to himself.

"Why does your grandmother want to see us?"

I've met Dimitra twice now: once at a sit-down meeting involving the Drakos family and mine, and then again briefly at the engagement party. Both times, she's been fairly cool to me.

Honestly? I'm not sure she likes me much. Which is fair, given my reckless actions made it so her grandson *has* to marry me.

"Not us. Just you."

I stiffen, whipping my gaze to him.

"Wait, what?"

Kratos keeps his eyes on the road. "The Lord, and Dimitra Drakos, work in mysterious ways. You don't have to worry, though. She's harmless." He turns to smirk at me. "Unless you make an enemy of her."

I sink into my seat, apprehension washing over me as we make our way down Central Park West.

"Are we going to my place so I can change clothes?"

He shakes his head. "Nope. Ya-ya is expecting us."

My eyes widen. "Like, right *now*?" I glance down helplessly at my attire: I mean, I'm in leggings and a long-sleeved warmup top.

"Don't worry. She really won't care what you're wearing." He lifts a shoulder, his eyes still on the road. "Besides, you look good."

I can feel my cheeks simmer. My phone buzzes, and I open it to see some new texts on my "Ballet Bitches" chain with Naomi and Milena.

> NAOMI
>
> You neglected to mention that he's a freaking GIANT! :o
>
> MILENA
>
> Seriously
>
> MILENA
>
> Is he…"proportional"?

My face burns as I scrunch down lower in my seat, twisting the phone away in case Kratos looks over.

> NAOMI
>
> OMG MILENA
>
> MILENA
>
> Fuck you! We're both thinking it! ANSWERS, B! We need answers!
>
> MILENA
>
> 8===============D
>
> NAOMI
>
> LMAOOOOO

ME

They're called BOUNDARIES

NAOMI

lol

Milena sends a gif of a baby hamster nibbling on the end of a banana. My face explodes with heat.

Oh my fucking God...

I close the chat and flip my phone face down on my lap. Just as I do, we come to a stop on Central Park South, right across the street from Central Park. Kratos steps out, and I blink in surprise when he hands his keys to a man in dark suit who looks somewhere between a mafioso and a valet. I step out of the car onto the sidewalk and look up at the forty-story building towering over us.

"Uh, where are we?"

Kratos smirks. "Home."

———

HOLY. Fucking. *Shit.*

I've known luxury for most of my life. Well, from the little I remember, we lived modestly but comfortably with our birth parents. But after Vito took Dante, Claudia, and me in, it went up about a hundred notches: enormous brownstone townhouse, nice cars, not wanting for anything. That's the mafia world.

But *this?*

My mouth falls open as I step out of the elevator and stare up at the gilded splendor of the Drakos estate.

I mean, it's a freaking *palace*.

Marble floors, gold chandeliers, framed classical art on the walls. I'm so stunned that I barely notice when Kratos takes my hand and leads me through the sprawling mansion. My eyes bulge as I stare out through a wall of elegant French doors that lead out to a huge, manicured patio and garden. Beyond it, the grounds—and yes, I'm calling those grounds, which is *insane* given that we're on top of a forty-story building—stretch out, complete with white Grecian statues, rose gardens, a fountain, what looks like a tennis court, and —holy shit—*two* pools.

"It...leaves an impression," Kratos rumbles next to me.

I twist my head, craning my neck to look up at him. "This place is *huge*. Do you all live here?"

He shakes his head. "Not anymore. Ares and Neve are over on the West Side. Hades and Elsa are in Brooklyn Heights. Deimos and Dahlia keep a place on the Upper West Side, but they're mostly at their estate out in Connecticut. And Callie lives with Castle at the Kildare home on the Upper East Side."

My brow creases at a thought I actually hadn't considered yet: my new living situation.

"When we...you know," I mumble. "Will I—"

"I don't live here anymore either," Kratos says. "You'll be moving into my brownstone in the East Village."

There's something about the decisive way he states it, like this isn't up for discussion at all, that both flusters me and turns me on a little.

Dear world: send professional help. Pretty sure I need it.

Kratos takes my hand again, which isn't necessary—it's not like I'm a child and we're crossing a busy street. At the same time, it feels weirdly normal. As if my small hand was meant to fit into his gargantuan one.

"Is that, like, set in stone?"

He looks at me, half-amused, out of the corner of his eyes. "Us moving in together once we're married? Yes."

"I already have my own apartment, though."

"That's wonderful. Married people live together."

"Well, *yeah*, but this isn't a real—"

One second, I'm walking through the nicest, most elegant home I've ever seen. The next, the gorgeous, dark giant next to me is whirling, pinning me against the wall, grabbing my whole jaw in one hand, and crushing his mouth to mine.

I *melt*.

My skin ignites like there's liquid fire rippling across the surface. My core clenches, my legs trembling as his tongue teases over my lips and then breaks through my defenses. My body goes numb and weightless as he kisses me slowly, deeply, and possessively.

He starts to pull back when suddenly I jolt, a muffled squeal catching in my throat as I feel his teeth nip sharply at my bottom lip. I shudder and taste warm copper. At the same time, Kratos growls low, sucking on my bottom lip.

On the bite he's just given me.

Tasting my blood, and my whimper.

Why the *hell* is that so fucking hot?

When he finally pulls away, I'm in a state of shock, my eyes wide as I stare up at him. My core ripples, and my thighs are clenching together tightly.

"Hmph," he grunts. "Tastes real to me."

No words. Before I can even attempt to find any, Kratos turns and knocks on the closed double doors we've arrived at.

"Oh, and one more thing," he growls quietly, turning to me. "Later tonight, you're meeting me at the church."

I know what that means. Every fiery inch of my body knows what that means. But I ask anyway.

"Why is that?"

Something lethal and exhilarating flickers behind his piercing blue eyes.

"Because I have no intention of fucking a virgin on my wedding night."

Holy fuck.

My core spasms, my pulse skipping as Kratos turns to the door in front of us as footsteps approach on the other side.

"Tonight, we'll be taking care of that."

"Do you like baklava?"

I'm sitting alone with Dimitra Drakos, or "Ya-ya", as her grandchildren call her, on the terrace of her private office. Before us lie the sweeping, gorgeously manicured grounds of the Drakos estate. They extend out to every edge of the building, where the rose bushes, manicured lawns, and stone walkways suddenly drop away like cliffs to Central Park below.

It's just Dimitra and me: Kratos left as soon as she welcomed me into her office. The woman is *petite*—like not even five feet, and probably ninety pounds after a swim. But there's still an unquestionable power that radiates from her.

Obviously, Ares is the head of the Drakos family. But at the same time, I get the sense that Dimitra would get the final word on most issues if she put her foot down.

My stomach grumbles at the word "baklava".

"I *love* baklava," I enthuse. "There's this little Greek pastry shop on 26th and Lexington—"

"Yiorgos' Café, yes," she finishes. "I know it. Good baklava..." She lifts a bird-like shoulder. "But if that's your favorite, we need to expand your horizons."

I grin. "Any recommendations?"

"Yes. My own."

I blink as she puts down her cup of tea and stands. "Come with me." She winks. "We're making baklava."

Okayyy? I follow Dimitra through the gorgeous home until we step into a *jaw-droppingly* beautiful kitchen.

"It's easier than you think. Plus, it's Kratos' favorite."

For some reason, that hits weirdly. I stiffen as she bustles around the kitchen, pulling various ingredients from shelves.

"You're teaching me because I have to make my husband happy?"

Shit.

It comes out with way more attitude than I intended. I wince, bracing myself for Dimitra's wrath, or a stern talk about how it's a mafia wife's duty to make her husband's life comfortable and bear his children.

But instead of a scowl, it's a grin I see on her face when she turns toward me, shaking her head. "No matter how many times I hear that said, especially by older generations like mine who should know better, it never ceases to make me angry." She frowns. "A wife should make her husband happy by her mere presence. Because she's who she is, and *that's* what he enjoys about her. Not because she's cleaning up after him or making him the 'right' meals." Her silvered brows knit as she shakes her head again. "That's not marriage. That's indentured servitude."

I grin.

I think I'm going to like this woman a lot.

"Our world, Bianca, is full of marriages of convenience, or of inconvenience, or marriages to keep the peace. That's simply the way it is. But no matter the reasons for two people getting married, it's still a promise. And a promise goes both ways. Yes, I hope that you make my grandson happy, just as I hope *he* makes *you* happy. But not because you break your back doing things for him."

She starts to line her ingredients up on the kitchen island between us.

"Bianca, I don't want to teach you how to make my baklava today so you can satisfy Kratos. He's a grown man, and a very fine cook himself, and he can make his own damn baklava if he wants some." She winks at me again. "I'm teaching you because you're going to be part of our family, and I've always taught all the women in our family how to make it so that they can make it for *themselves* should they choose to. Okay?"

A wide smile threatens to split my face as I nod. "Okay."

Dimitra nods. "Good. Let's bake."

18

BIANCA

THE CREAKY OLD doors groan as I open them. Stepping inside, a cold shiver finger-walks up my spine as I step back into this place.

The scene of the crime.

The place where I can let go of reality and submerge myself in the fucked-up and deliciously deviant.

The doors close with a whine behind me, and I tremble.

It feels different this time. The church is even darker, like the lights outside have been turned out.

I don't mean that metaphorically. It's *literally* almost pitch black in here, as if he really did cover the windows. There's no trace of the faint glow of stained glass like the last two times I've been here.

Only a throbbing, magnetic, slightly unsettling black promise. Only darkness, with a single candle flickering in the middle of the floor.

No sign of Kratos.

My skin tingles with nervous energy, the mix of fear and excitement the strongest drug in the world as it courses through my veins.

A needy, achy heat pools slickly between my thighs. And that's how I know it's not just that I've "agreed" to this.

I *want* it.

I crave it.

And the truly fucked up part is, I might need it, too.

"Kratos?"

My voice echoes in the stuffy stillness of the old church. But there's no response. Not a sound.

My lower lip disappears between the safety of my teeth. My core tightens as cold shivers prickle my skin.

"Kratos?"

More silence. Eerily so. It's the sort of quiet that comes before a storm, when even the birds have fled, sensing the coming fury and wrath.

Yet you're dumb enough to stay.

Willingly.

And...shamefully...*eagerly*.

"Hello?" My voice breaks. My anxiety climbs. Just then, I hear the shuffle of something. The crumble of stone, as if underfoot.

I whirl, my eyes scanning the darkness, peering into the

unknown, trying to see him. To see *anything* at all. But there's nothing.

Only shadows, reaching out and clawing their way into my imagination. Only the dark, dangerous promise of something lurking, waiting for me.

I take a few more timid steps into the utter blackness of the church.

This isn't me, at least not on the outside. I don't do "dirty" things like seeking danger and chasing fucked-up kinks in the dark.

I don't go actively looking to lose my virginity like *this*: being chased by a monster until he takes it from me.

Roughly. Without mercy.

I'm a good girl. Or at least, I've always thought so. But now that I'm here, back for more, and desperate for him to take it all, I start to wonder if maybe *that* is my mask, and not the opposite.

Maybe the girl who strives to keep the peace when her brothers bicker, and does what she can to make her dad proud, and works her ass off to be the most delicate, elegant dancer ever to float across a stage is the façade. And maybe this fucked up, deranged fantasy is my truth.

The real me.

I flinch, my body clenching tight at the soft crunch of footsteps behind me. I whirl, my breath clawing its way into my throat and my heart thumping against my breastbone.

There's nothing there.

Only shadows.

Only ghosts.

Only a lurking presence, and the undeniable sensation that I'm being watched.

"Kratos?" I croak. "I—"

The single candle in the middle of the church snuffs out, plunging the church into pure darkness. My pulse slams through my veins, my breathing becoming ragged as I whirl wildly.

More crunching footsteps behind me. My mouth goes dry, and my hands ball into anxious fists as I spin around again.

Still nothing.

Only shadows.

The crunch comes again, back on the other side of me now. I whirl again, feeling like my head is spinning. A low rasping sound whips my attention to yet another random point on the insane imaginary compass I'm standing on, and my chest constricts as I peer vainly into the blackness.

Time stops.

The only sound is my own ragged breathing.

My thighs quiver, and my nipples tighten to hard, anxious points as the tension builds to near madness.

A crunch behind me has me whirling with a choked scream to find…nothing at all.

"Where—"

That's when he strikes.

Pain explodes through my scalp as my hair is grabbed from behind. A hand clamps over my mouth, and I scream into it as I'm lifted into the air and pulled hard against a firm chest.

I flail and writhe, kicking and squirming helplessly in his powerful grip. I choke on another gasp as I'm flung roughly to the ground. I try to scramble up from the dirty stone floor.

He's on me in milliseconds.

"Where the *fuck* do you think you're going, my little fuck toy?"

Jesus Christ.

Kratos' voice is always low, and deep, and growling. But right now, it sounds legit *possessed*. Like there's an actual demon here in the darkness, ready to destroy me.

He yanks me up to my knees by a fistful of my hair. He tugs back hard, making me cry out as my gaze is ripped upward.

And suddenly, there it is, flicking on and blinding me in the sudden light.

The mask.

Two X's for eyes, and a leering, psycho smile, illuminating the tight black of his t-shirt over his bulging chest, illuminating the corded muscles of his arm as it grips my hair...

...and illuminating his *cock*.

His thick, swollen, massive cock, hanging heavily out of his unbuttoned, unzipped black jeans and pulsing as it bobs right above my face.

I whimper as his hand tightens in my hair, dragging me back until I'm sprawled on my knees at his feet with my back pressed hard against a wall or a pillar of some kind.

The mask tips to one side at a deranged angle, those X's peering down into my face.

"*Open fucking wide*," demon-Kratos rasps in a devil's voice. "Suck my cock like a good little whore and get it nice and fucking wet with your spit." The mask slowly tilts to the other side. "You'll need it wet when I tear into you."

I choke on a whimper, true fear and explosive need roaring through my system like a drug. He leans down, reaching out to roughly grab my jaw.

"When I shove every fat inch of this cock deep into your virgin pussy."

He wraps his other hand around the base of his cock, fisting and pumping it slowly, lewdly, right above my face. Precum beads at the tip. His grip tightens in my hair, making me mewl in pain and excitement as he yanks my head back.

He pushes his hips forward. Without hesitating, I open my mouth wide. But even still, when the swollen head slips past my lips, I feel my jaw straining to the limit as he grunts and pushes into my small mouth.

"*Fuck*," he growls. "Your lips are so tight, babygirl. Your slutty little mouth is trying so hard to take my big cock." He chuckles darkly. "Imagine how fucking tight it's going to feel when it's your pretty pussy wrapped snug around me. When I split you in half with my cock."

Fuck *me*.

The crude, fucked-up dirty talk is *exactly* what I want to hear. It's ticking every twisted box and pushing every deranged button in my head.

It's exactly what I crave.

Utter submission. To be used, on my knees. To be forced.

To be taken, whether I want it or not.

Kratos growls deeply, throwing his head back as he takes his pleasure from my mouth. His hips roll as he fucks my mouth, hitting the back of my throat. He thrusts his thick cock over my tongue, the filthy, wet *glucking* sounds filling the cavernous church. I whimper and moan around him, drooling precum and spit down my chin and onto my shirt.

I raise my hands to put them on his hips to steady myself, but he slaps them away.

"Don't even think about it, slut."

He grabs my hands and pins them over my head, holding them there as his cock glides roughly over my tongue.

Without warning, something flashes in the gleam of his mask. I moan around his dick when I realize it's his knife. In one motion, he brings it down and slides the tip down into the neck of my shirt. His arm jerks, and I whimper in true fear as the razor-sharp edge slices my shirt open. He jerks his arm again, slicing the shirt all the way open before slitting the front clasp of my bra as well, spilling my breasts free.

The knife disappears behind his back. When his hand reappears, he reaches down and roughly pinches and rolls my nipples, eliciting a whining moan of pain and pleasure as I choke on his cock. He's merciless, twisting and pulling, sending pulses of electricity coursing through me to land at my core.

Suddenly, his hand grabs a fistful of my hair again. I gasp for air as he pulls me away from his cock, a thin strand of drool suspended between my bottom lip and his swollen head. He spins me roughly, pushing me down to my knees with my top half pressed to the ground.

Oh fuck. Oh fuck. Oh my fucking FUCK.

I can hear him opening his pants the rest of the way and shoving them down. The metallic jangle of his belt. A low groan of pleasure as he strokes himself.

I know what comes next, and the nervous energy and eager anticipation are turning me inside out.

"Did sucking that big dick get your greedy little pussy nice and messy for me?"

I whimper as he slaps my ass, hard.

"You'd better fucking hope so, babygirl," he hisses darkly.

Kratos grabs the back of my leggings and yanks them down to mid-thigh. Then I'm gasping at the sensation of cold steel on my skin as he half-yanks, half-rips my panties away before completely slicing them off with the blade.

He takes my hair in his fist, keeping my cheek and breasts pinned to the ground. He bends over me from behind, his swollen dick pressed to my slick, swollen lips.

Spreading them. Adding a little pressure.

"…Because I'm *not* going to be gentle."

I choke out a low, whining moan as his palm slaps my ass.

"And I won't go easy. I'm going to fuck you like the greedy little cum slut you are, babygirl."

I jolt, crying out as he slaps the inside of my thighs.

"Spread your legs."

This is so fucked up. *This* is how I'm going to lose my virginity.

On my knees.

On a grimy floor.

Covered in drool and precum.

I cry out as Kratos sinks two fingers into me. I shiver, moaning as he starts to roughly stroke in and out, pressing against my g-spot as his thumb rubs my clit in hard, deliberate circles.

"*Moan* for me," he rasps. "Because that's just my fingers, babygirl. Just imagine how fucking much you're going to stretch when I fuck my thick cock into this tight little cunt."

He fingers me harder, the sloppy wet sounds filling my ears as he leans over me. His teeth find the soft skin of my neck, and I scream when he bites down hard. He does it again, biting and nipping my throat before his mouth drags hotly to my ear.

"*Beg me*," he growls darkly. "*Beg me for my fucking cock.*"

His hand tightens around my throat.

"*Please!*" I whimper.

Kratos chuckles a cold laugh behind me. "Please *what.*"

"*Please fuck me!*"

"How."

"*Hard,*" I sob, shaking as his fingers stroke my g-spot over and over.

"I didn't hear you. Fuck you *how.*"

I choke out a cry of pleasure.

"Fuck me hard like the filthy whore I am!"

"Good girl."

And then, he thrusts.

Sweet. Fucking. GOD.

Kratos' huge, thick cock rams into me all at once.

No teasing. No easing it in slowly.

No mercy.

I scream as his massive size invades my body, a burning, pinching pain rippling through my core as he buries himself in me to the hilt.

It fucking hurts.

But fucking *hell*, it also feels so good in a way I don't even know how to describe. It's the violence and sheer size of him; the utter domination and the heaping dose of sadism. It all has me moaning for more as he grinds himself deep.

He's so fucking big, it feels like he's rearranging my insides, pushing my organs into new positions. The sheer girth of him stretches me to my absolute limit, and I wince as I bite down on my lip. My fingernails drag over the dirty floor, one of them breaking as I whine in pleasure.

Slowly, the feeling of being filled past my breaking point melts into something else. The burning turns to an achy need. The pinch deep inside dissolves into something primal and desperate.

I need more.

"More..."

The moan tumbles from my lips. Kratos groans deeply behind me.

"What was that, babygirl?" he rasps.

"*More,*" I choke.

"More *what.*"

More everything. More of your cock.

More you.

"*Fuck me harder…*"

I cry out sharply when he suddenly slaps my ass. His massive hands wrap around my waist, his fingers almost touching as he rolls his hips back, sliding his huge dick out of my soaking pussy. When just the head is inside, he buries himself again, ramming in and knocking the wind out of me as my knees scrape the ground.

Holy fucking shit.

He does it again, and again. He starts to fuck me a little harder, then harder still. Then brutally, his hips pounding and slapping against my ass with each demonic thrust.

My choked, sobbing moans fill the blackness as his huge cock dominates me.

Consumes me.

Breaks me in two.

I can feel pressure building inside me, my back arching and my fingers clawing at the dirty ground. My pebbled, hard nipples drag across the stone floor with each thrust. The aching throb grows hotter and more needy with my screaming desperation for release. My toes curl as he slaps my ass, pulling my hair as he roughly fucks me into oblivion.

"*Squeeze* that dick, babygirl," he growls. "Let me feel your little pussy choking my fucking cock."

His hand twists in my hair, roughly pinning my cheek to the ground as he leans over me, fucking me into the floor.

"Is it the pain that turns your slutty little pussy into a fucking *mess* for me?" he snarls into my ear. "The way my dick stretches you wide and fills you past your breaking point?"

My back arches, a sob of pleasure wrenching from my throat as he fucks into me.

"Or is it the *fear*. The wondering if I've barely cracked the surface with you. If I might cross a line…"

My eyes stare, my breath choking as his blade lightly dances across my throat. I whimper as he bends over me again, his hips fucking into me as his teeth bite my earlobe sharply.

"Do you wonder if maybe you'll hit your breaking point and scream your safe word…and I'll fucking *ignore it*."

That's when I shatter, looking down and realizing there is no safety net.

Nothing to catch me.

Just a free-fall into oblivion, or Kratos' madness.

Either way, when he says that, my core clenches, and I fucking *explode.*

I scream into the floor as my entire body spasms and jerks. My back ripples and arches, my toes and fingers scraping and clawing at the ground as the orgasm thunders through my core.

He's everywhere and all around. Over me, on me, *in me*, consuming me.

Swallowing me fucking whole, and I'm begging for more.

With a low groan, while I'm still quivering and shaking uncontrollably, Kratos roughly flips me onto my back. I whimper as he cuts through my leggings with one flick of his knife, spreading my legs wide. He slaps my inner thighs, making my nerves scream with sweet, desperate agony.

Suddenly, he's looming over me, the blade at my throat. His mouth crushes roughly to mine just as he sinks his swollen cock into my tender, still pulsing pussy.

The darkness fills with the wet, slick sounds of my pussy wrapped around his massive dick. The slap of flesh on flesh. My cries of pain and pleasure mixing into pure heaven as he fucks me like a demon.

He bites my neck, mauling and bruising my skin as his lips find my ear.

"Now be my good little cock slut and come for me again. I want to feel this little pussy milk the cum right out of my fucking balls."

I go off like I've been struck by lightning. Like I've touched the third rail. I scream as my back arches violently off the floor, my body spasming and wrenching as my pussy clamps like a vice around his thick cock.

Then his hand wraps around my throat.

And squeezes.

Oh fuck...

Kratos roars, and when I feel his swollen cock begin to throb and pulse deep in me, my orgasm goes thermonuclear. My vision turns white and my breath leaves my body in a whoosh. My eyes roll back as every muscle in my body clenches at the same time and then detonates. His teeth sink into my neck as his hot cum floods into me, filling me as I shake and cling to him.

I'm still trembling all over as he eases his fat cock out of my swollen, brutalized pussy. I can feel a huge amount of his cum dripping out of me as I collapse onto the ground. His teeth nibble at my neck, his mouth sliding lower as his lips wrap around a nipple.

Then he moves lower.

And lower.

My eyes bulge.

"Kratos…"

His big hands keep my thighs apart as he delves between them. My breath catches as his mouth centers on my throbbing pussy, his tongue tenderly dragging through my lips.

Oh shit...

My back arches again, slower and gently this time as he licks away all the pain and soreness, his tongue exploring and cleaning and lapping until there's nothing but a throbbing tingle of bliss between my legs.

I whimper when he lifts his head up, blood and cum on his lips as he licks them. He sits up, and suddenly he's taking me by the hips and pulling me into his lap. I gasp quietly as I sit astride him, my nipples dragging against his muscled chest and his still-hard cock pulsing and leaking cum against my stomach.

His hand tangles in my hair and pulls. My eyes go wide when I realize what he's doing, and I shiver as his lips press hotly to mine in a deep, slow kiss.

Copper and salt.

Lust and need.

Danger and excitement.

Heaven and hell.

That's what we taste like together.

19

KRATOS

"This is ground control to Major Drakos. Can you hear me, Major Drakos."

I blink before I pull my gaze back to Ares.

Yes, I was zoning the fuck out. And no, it's not because I'm disinterested in going over the quarterly financials of our legitimate investments with my brother.

It's because somewhere along the line, the game became real. Somewhere, Bianca went from my toy to my *wife*.

My plaything to something more.

Much more.

Someone who doesn't flee or try to hide from my darkness. She complements it. Encourages it. And yet also soothes it, like a cool drink of water my parched mouth never knew it needed.

The other night at the engagement party, I should have spiraled. Being cooped up in a room with Amaya, being threatened by her and backed into a corner, should have shoved me down into a black pit for the next *month*.

Instead, I kissed Bianca.

Our first kiss. *My* first kiss at all.

Bitterness clouds my thoughts. That's another aspect of my fucked-up brokenness that the she-devil is to be thanked for. I've put this all out on the table enough times to enough "expert therapists" to know that my need for darkness, dominance, and yes, some violence in my sexual encounters stems from that time when *I* was the one without the power.

Are you going to be my good boy today?

A viscous, inky blackness bleeds though my brain, then I force it back into the shadows.

Yes, kissing is another of my hangups. Because it was the one thing Amaya wouldn't do with me.

Assaulting me for years when I was barely a teenager was fine in her books. But kissing, allowing a modicum of human intimacy, was strictly off the table.

And that's precisely why I'm the way I am. Because it was hammered into me, far too young, that sex equals power, not love. Sex is a war. A battle to be won. And battles and war necessitate strength, brutality, and ruthlessness.

Needless to say, there's a reason I'm the last of my siblings to have found someone. Why I don't date. Why I seek women for temporary arrangements, and why those temporary arrangements usually entail an NDA and me *radically* toning down who I am, because there's no way women want that.

Women fantasize about the monster. But they don't really want him when he comes out to play.

Or, at least, no one did until Bianca.

Bianca, who entices him out of his cave. Who goads and antagonizes. Who seems to delight in the darkness as it pours out of the mouth of that rocky opening to consume her.

Bianca, who may very well be as fucked up as I am for some reason.

Well, not *as* fucked up. But at least we're playing in the same league.

"*Kratos.*"

Once again, I drag myself from the thoughts swirling in my mind.

"Sorry. What?"

Ares and I are sitting by the massive wall of windows in his gorgeous corner office at Thermopylae Holdings. Thermopylae, a nod to Ya-ya and her obsession with the Spartans, is our legitimate business venture. A hedge fund, to turn our dirty money into a LOT more money. Lots cleaner, too.

I never went to business school like Ares. But I'm a quick learner, and I've been absorbing this stuff by his side for years. But today, I'm distracted.

I'm thinking of that first kiss, and the ones that came after.

And how I want more.

It's sort of tough to pay attention to a goddamn P&L sheet when I'm trying to process the idea that I might be *far* more emotionally invested in my fake fiancée than I should be.

"Welcome back," Ares says dryly.

"You were saying…?"

My brother sighs, leaning back in his chair. "You want to talk about it?"

"About what?"

"Kratos. I do know a thing or two about marrying to stop a war."

I shake my head. "I'm fine," I shrug. "It is what it is."

Ares' brows furrow. "But I'm sorry you weren't given a choice. And that this was the way this shook out to avoid—"

"You don't have to apologize. This is what we do. What you give for family."

His mouth thins. "Look, I know you keep a lot that goes on inside that big head of yours from us…"

I smile wryly. "Nah, I'm an open book."

"And I'm the queen of fucking France. I'm not asking you to let me in, man. You have your reasons you don't want to, and that's cool. But I know you had it rougher than most of them realize when we were kids."

I say nothing, staring at the floor, my jaw clenched.

"Obviously I don't know the details, and again, you never have to tell me, although you know you always *can*. But I caught…glimpses." His brow furrows as he leans forward, steepling his hands. "I saw how brutal Atlas and Dad were to you. I saw the way Dad paraded you around to his buddies like some sort of heavyweight champ. Like a weapon. And—"

"Let's focus on the numbers and not the monsters under my bed, okay?"

Ares is silent for a moment. Then he reaches out and puts a hand on my knee. "I'm here for you, that's all."

"I know," I growl quietly.

He nods. "Good. Oh, before I forget." His brow furrows. "I got a weird call here at the office the other day."

"Oh?"

"Yeah, a Ms. Mircari's assistant called?"

I freeze.

I know now that *me* getting busted in that sting was deliberate. It's why Amaya or anyone else in the CIA never let my family know what happened and quieted all the paperwork.

She wants to use me. She wants me to spill secrets from my own family. And, apparently, now that it's clear that it'll be a cold day in hell before I ever do that, she's moved on to the Italians.

I've been ignoring her since she crashed the engagement party. So I know what her calling Ares is. This is a warning shot across the bow.

"Thanks," I grunt. "I'll call her back."

"Who is she?"

I shake my head. "Don't worry about it."

Ares eyes me. "*Don't worry about it* because I've been handling less of that stuff?"

It's true. With Ares running our family *and* Thermopylae, Hades, Deimos, and I have all taken on a lot more of our... less than legal business ventures, to keep Ares' hands clean.

"Or *don't worry about it* because something's fucked and you're trying to keep cool."

"Yes."

He scowls. "Which one, Kratos."

I glance at my watch. "I need to run, actually."

He gives me a look that says he's not even a little ready to drop this. But just as he opens his mouth, the door to his office swings open and Hades comes charging through, a black expression on his face.

"Fuck," Ares growls, rising. "What is it?"

Hades' mouth twists. "Hope neither of you had any bets going on when Davit was going to be back on his feet. That 'temporary liver thing' just killed him."

Shit.

"*Fuck,*" Ares swears. "FUCK!" He glances at me, then back to Hades. "Has Te Mallkuarit given any indication about—"

"Arian Kirakosian was officially made head of the organization about an hour ago."

Goddammit.

That's not good.

The phone on Ares' desk rings. When he answers, his face darkens as his secretary, Leigh, chirps something on the other end.

"I understand. Call him back, tell him we'll be right over."

He hangs up with a grim expression as he glances first at me, then Hades.

"Drazen Krylov would like to speak to us. Now."

———

HADES WHISTLES low when we step off the elevator into the entryway of Drazen's penthouse.

"God *damn*," he mutters, looking impressed as his eyes scan the pinnacle of opulent luxury surrounding us.

Not gonna lie, Ares and I have the same "holy shit" look on our faces as we gaze up at the enormous, vaulted ceilings and staggeringly huge walls of windows past the foyer that look out over Central Park.

Drazen doesn't live that far from the Drakos estate, actually. He's recently moved into the top of New York's newest ultra highrise on "billionaire's row", which looks out over all of Manhattan from near cloud level. As you might guess, there's a reason they call this billionaire's row: you've gotta have three damn commas in your net worth to even consider buying a unit here.

Drazen owns *three*, which he's had gutted and merged into what is almost certainly one of the top five most expensive residences in the city at this point.

When I say the Serbian-Russian motherfucker exploded onto the New York scene a year or so ago, I mean it.

"My friends," Drazen rumbles in his gruff but polished accented baritone. He appears from around the corner, clad in one of his usual custom dark gray suits that fits him perfectly. Yet, he always wears them with an element of disdain. It's like he knows it's part of the trappings he *has* to wear, but he hates the fact that in this world, he needs a well-cut suit to be taken seriously, rather than an AK-47.

"Please, come in."

There are a number of Krylov men in black suits standing around Drazen's gargantuan living area, which has double if not triple height windows overlooking the park from ninety stories up. But at the slightest dip of their boss' chin, they wordlessly file out.

"*Fuck me*," Hades mutters quietly, well out of earshot of our host. "How do we get that kind of discipline from our guys? That shit was surgical."

"Go fight an ethnic cleansing civil war in the Baltics," Ares mutters over his shoulder at us. "Most of Drazen's men were child soldiers with him during the Yugoslav Wars."

"Yeah, think I'll pass," Hades grunts back, making a face.

After his men have left, Drazen turns to us with a tight smile. He's objectively a handsome guy. But there's a bitterness to his looks, like there are scars hidden beneath the surface that still pain him.

"Please," he grunts, gesturing to the three huge, dark leather Chesterfield couches arranged near the windows. "Have a seat. May I offer you drinks?"

As a rule of thumb, if a Bratva *pahkan* offers you a drink, you take it. Doesn't matter if it's nine in the morning and you're in church.

The three of us nod as we sit. Drazen pours us all crystal tumblers of vodka and then strides back over.

"*Živeli*," he says, raising his glass.

Cheers.

We all drink and then set our glasses down on the table in the middle of the couches. Then Drazen takes a deep breath, settling back in his seat with his fingers tented in front of him.

"I have found New York extremely welcoming since moving here," he growls quietly. "In particular, your family has been very generous and fair in our business dealings. I want to thank you for that."

"And we appreciate the relationship, of course," Ares adds. "Especially with the West Side development".

Drazen's silence speaks volumes. My older brother smiles wryly.

"I'm guessing that's why we're here, isn't it."

The Serbian nods slowly.

"I'm afraid it is. You see, yours isn't the only family or organization that I've gone into business with since arriving in New York. As you know, I'm an investor in Club Venom, which puts me in bed...so to speak...with your fiancée's brother." He glances at me with a raised brow. "And by extension, the rest of The Commission. Additionally, I have...*business* with the Chernoff Bratva."

Fuck.

I clear my throat. "I'm guessing you heard about the dustup at my engagement party after you left."

Drazen nods again. "I doubt Mr. Chernoff is exactly pleased about his friend's nephew's broken face."

"He's lucky that's the only thing I broke," I growl quietly.

Drazen smiles slightly. "Again, I have no emotional tie to these people. *However*, money talks. And, at the end of the day, I'm a businessman."

"You have our word that nothing will be pursued against Grisha or any of Mr. Chernoff's interests," Ares says sternly.

"There's more." Drazen exhales thoughtfully. "Davit's passing and Arian's ascension to the throne is...troubling to me. Not just because Davit, may he rest in peace, raised a terror of a son. But because that son has the backing of a splinter group within Te Mallkuarit—one that would like to see the organization become much more...aggressive...in its methods of acquiring new territory and business."

God damn. I knew I didn't like Arian when I met him.

"So that's why I've invited you here," Drazen growls. "Out of respect to you, Ares," he says, nodding his chin. "I need you to know that none of this is personal. However, business is business, as I'm sure you'd agree. Right now, the Drakos family is...*entangled*, I suppose you could say...with two other business interests of mine, and one direct threat."

One of his eyebrows arches severely, a dark look spreading like smoke across his face.

"Should any of these entanglements escalate any further, I'm afraid I'll need to sever my business relationship with your family, including my investment in the West Side development."

Fuck. Me.

20

BIANCA

"BEEN a while since you were here, huh?"

I grin, glancing around Vito's dusty old office. He's right, I haven't set foot inside it in *years*. But it looks exactly the same.

It still smells like tobacco and the leather of the old Chesterfield couches in the corner. There's still the same globe bar-cart, the same crystal tumblers. Vito's desk—a massive wooden thing roughly the size and weight of a Cadillac—fills the middle of the room. The walls are festooned with the sexy glamor shots of the dancers who used to work here. And of course, the old "Lickety Splits" neon sign still hangs on the wall to the left of Vito's desk.

Vito never let me come here during business hours, obviously. But during the day, when quite possibly the best-named strip club in the history of strip clubs was closed, I'd come up here with him from time to time and just goof off.

I know it's cliched, and sounds like I'm biased. But Dad ran a different kind of strip club. He was never sleazy with the dancers and had a *strict* one-strike policy on any customers getting handsy. People used to joke that Vito treated "his girls" like they were his own daughters. But as he used to say, "They're *somebody's* daughters. And if mine were workin' in a joint like this, I'd want to know someone was keeping 'em safe."

Back then, a couple of the dancers were working to put themselves through school, and during the day, Vito would let them study up here in some of the smaller offices...for their nurse's license, or the Bar exam, or dental school.

Frequently, when I'd come in with Dad during the day and some of the girls were up here, they'd take a study break and give me makeovers, or have me show them my latest ballet moves. For a while, when I was like twelve, I got really into modern and hip hop dancing. This one woman, Candice, would show me her "sexy" moves, at least until Vito walked in one day and asked her politely to knock it the fuck off.

These days, the club on the first two floors is gone. Instead of stripper poles and VIP rooms, Dad's office now sits above a two Michelin star French restaurant and a tech startup. But up here, the vibe hasn't changed at all, and I love it.

"It's been a while, yeah," I smile, looking around. "I miss this place."

He chuckles. "I don't miss the headaches. Keeping the girls safe and the knuckleheads in line, dealing with the alcohol licensing board, the health inspectors, or...Jesus...the pearl-clutchers." He shrugs, looking around. "But there's a reason this old dump is still my office, even though I could have something overlooking Wall Street."

He grins at me, drumming his fingers on the edge of his desk excitedly.

"So, Bumblebee, cards on the table. I didn't ask you to stop by to go down memory lane and reminisce about when I was a shitty guardian bringing a kid to a titty bar."

I snort a laugh. "I distinctly remember never seeing a single titty, so don't worry. Nico, Carmy, and Dante, on the other hand…"

Vito groans, rolling his eyes. "Yeah, father of the year over here," he sighs. Then he grins at me again, and suddenly he's spryly jumping to his feet and stepping out from behind his desk. "C'mon. I want to show you something."

Curious, I follow Vito out of his main office and down the dusty hall. The big side room that we stop at used to be a changing room for the dancers. It's now pretty much empty, though one wall still has some old lockers bolted to it. The rest of the space is cluttered with boxes of old files and club fliers, and there's a huge old wardrobe against the far wall, locked with a padlock.

"Um…" I glance around the place skeptically.

Dad chuckles. "Gimme a sec. Gotta build the suspense." He clears his throat. "I heard you haven't found a wedding dress yet."

I groan, rolling my eyes. "Yes and no. I mean, Tempest, Naomi, and Milena found some *gorgeous* ones. But I'm not spending fifteen grand on a freaking dress."

Vito sighs. "Of course you're not. *I* am. I already told you it was on me, kiddo."

"Yeah, no." I shake my head. "I'm not letting anyone spend that much on something I'm going to wear once for a fake occasion."

There's *maybe* a bit more bitterness to the word "fake" than I intended. Vito doesn't seem to catch it, but still I turn away, glowering to myself.

It's *not* that I'm pining away wishing this marriage were a real one. Not at all. But as we get closer to "the big day", there seems to be more and more of a war of sorts going on inside my heart.

On the one hand, I know this isn't "real". I do like and enjoy the physical stuff Kratos and I have—the way he grabs me and kisses me possessively. The way he chases me and fucks me like it's a contact sport.

I mean, I *really* like that part. After the night two weeks ago when he took my virginity on the hard, grimy floor of the abandoned church with a knife to my throat—which was *insanely* hot—we've been back to replay that scene almost every night since.

I'm sore everywhere. I ache all over. My pussy has been swollen for like two weeks solid as I get used to taking Kratos' *enormous* size.

It's all worth it. *Very* worth it.

But as much as I want to say I fully understand that what we have between us is just sex, there's another part of me that...

I roll my eyes.

You're an idiot.

The other part wants more. Not more of the aggressiveness and the blisteringly hot sex—I mean, *yeah*, I want more of that, too—but more *from* him.

I know this wedding is about stopping mafia hostilities from turning the streets of New York into a war zone. I know we're not *actually* a couple.

But then, what are we? The easy answer would be friends with benefits or fuck-buddies, but it's not that, either.

It's like we *are* in a real relationship, but neither of us wants to admit it. Or maybe neither of us *can* admit it. Maybe it's just not in the cards for us.

I shouldn't be bothered by that.

But I am, more than I care to think. Because what I feel for the huge giant I'll be marrying soon is something I've never felt before. And sure, it could just be me confusing sex with something bigger. But I don't think so.

I *know* how I feel when I'm with him. I know how I miss him when I'm not. And I know it worries the hell out of me that I'm still calling whatever we are "fake".

"Well," Dad sighs. "If you *want* the expensive dress, it's yours. Done. I'll send one of my guys over right now to get it."

I grin at him.

"*But…*" He pulls a jangling keyring out of his pocket as he marches across the old dressing room to the padlocked wardrobe. "If you want another option…" He turns to smirk at me as he slips a key into the lock. "This might work, too. I've been keeping your mom's dress for you since the day you came to live with me."

The breath knocks out of me, a gasping, choking sensation wrapping around my throat and closing off my words. Half of me wants to sob as my heart wrenches. The other half *also* wants to cry, out of pure joy and love for this man.

"Are you…" Tears well in my eyes. "You're serious?"

Vito smiles at me. "Of course! Now, it could be dated as hell. I mean we're talking the 90s here. Not sure if poofy sleeves and bedazzling is your thing."

I choke out a laugh as I sniff back tears.

"And I haven't actually taken it out in years," Vito says as he unlocks the wardrobe. "But, I have a feeling she'd want you to wear—"

He jumps as I crash into him from behind, hugging him fiercely.

"*Thank you*," I blurt into him. "I love you, and thank you."

His arm wraps around me, patting my back. "Love you too, Bumblebee. Okie-dokie, let's check this thing out."

With a flourish, he flings open the double doors of the wardrobe. Instantly, both of our faces fall.

"*Son of a bitch!*" Vito chokes.

I blanch as stare into the dank, disgusting interior of the wardrobe, my heart sinking. The whole inside is black with mold, as are the four garment bags hanging on a rusty pole and a fifth slumped like a corpse on the floor. A dank, sour smell wafts out, making us cover our noses and step back quickly.

"*Fuck!*" Dad hisses, peering at the wardrobe.

I look too, and we notice it at the same time: the whole back of the wardrobe is rotted away. Behind it is a big gaping hole in the drywall of the room, with a wet, moldy pipe jutting out.

"Goddamn water leak!" Vito groans. He glances at me. Then he puts on a brave face and marches over to the wardrobe.

"No, Dad—"

"Hang on."

He yanks out one of the garment bags and carries it over to a table against the wall. He goes to open it, but the rusty zipper crumbles to dust as he does. When the bag finally opens, my heart drops when I see the moldy mess inside.

"Shit, kiddo…" Vito turns to me, stricken. "I'm so sorry…"

I use all my willpower not to cry. I know this meant as much to Vito as it did to me, and I'm not going to let him think this is breaking my heart. Even though it is.

"No, Dad," I smile, taking his hand and pulling him back as I shake my head. "It's fine. Really."

"I just…" He sighs. "I know you'd have looked gorgeous in it, that's all." He glares at the mess in the garment bag. "Now what."

"Well," I shrug. "There's always the fifteen grand one."

He snorts. "Do you like it?"

I don't *love* it. I wish with everything I have that I could wear my mother's own wedding dress instead. But it is what it is.

"I do, yeah," I smile, squeezing his hand.

Dad smacks the table. "Then that's settled. I'll send someone over now to scoop it up."

I throw my arms around him and hug him fiercely. Then I feel his arms tighten a little more, like he doesn't ever want to let go.

"I'm sorry for all of this, Bumblebee," he says softly.

I shake my head, still hugging him. "I did this, Dad."

"Yeah, but I promised you a long time ago—"

"Dad."

I pull back, smiling quietly into his eyes as I shake my head. "It's okay."

And it's not just "okay" because I'm going to put on a brave face and deal with this.

...It might just be because the idea of marrying Kratos doesn't sound so terrible anymore.

Not terrible at all, actually.

———

WE SKIP the usual bonus festivities of a wedding. There's no rehearsal dinner. No out-of-towners shindig. And as much as Milena yells, there's no bachelorette party, either.

And without those little steps along the way, it's a sudden thing when it hits me one night: I'm getting married the very next day.

In lieu of the bachelorette party—which I'm not sure my head or my nerves would have been in the right place for anyway—the night before the wedding, Milena, Naomi, and Tempest come over to my apartment to have dinner with me on my last night in the place.

Milena brings pizza from Lucali's, which is without question the best in New York. And Tempest grins as she reveals the three bottles of *insanely* old wine she swiped from my brother's personal cellar.

I show Tempest the wedding dress I finally settled on the other day. Part of me is still a little sad about not being able to wear my mother's dress, destroyed as it was. But everyone loves the one I picked out. It's fine.

We're just sitting down to eat at the kitchen island when there's a knock at the door. I slug back some wine before I walk over and open it. Matteo, one of my dad's men, greets me with a stiff nod, his bulky frame filling the doorway.

"Evening, Ms. Sartorre," he grunts. "You've got a visitor."

My brows fly up when he steps aside and I lay eyes on Callie, standing behind him with a huge garment bag in her arms.

"Hi," Kratos' sister smiles at me.

"Come in!" I nod to Matteo that it's okay, and he steps aside to let Callie into the apartment. She gives a little wave to the other girls when she spots them, and I wince. "I didn't have a bachelorette party, so…" My brows knit. "Shit, I'm an asshole. I should have invited you. Sorry."

"Please," she waves me off. "Don't worry about it. I'm just here playing delivery girl." She bites back a smile as she thrusts out her arms, presenting me with the garment bag. "Compliments of my big dumb brother."

I smile curiously as I take the bag. "Can I look?"

She winks. "I'd recommend it."

Over in the living room area, I drape the bag across the couch and unzip it. It takes me a second, but when I realize what I'm looking at, my breath catches. My eyes go wide as my hand flies to my mouth.

Impossible…

My head whips around to Callie. "*How?*" I whisper.

A week ago, when I saw this dress for the first time, it was all but destroyed, hanging in a water-damaged wardrobe at Vito's office, covered in mold and grime.

Now, my mother's wedding dress looks *stunning*.

It's not dated at all. No poofy 90s sleeves, no bedazzling anywhere. It's pure sophisticated elegance and beauty.

Silky and cream-colored, with thin, delicate straps over the shoulders, an open back that plunges to just above the base of the spine, and a sweetheart neckline. It falls in clean, silky lines down from the hips, reminding me of a 1920s jazz singer's dress, and an almost crepe-paper looking waterfall of silk lilies falls down the back of one shoulder.

"Holy shit, that's *gorgeous*," Milena breathes from over my shoulder. "What designer is that?"

"My dad," I whisper quietly. A small smile curls my lips as I look up at my friends. "I mean Dante's and my birth dad. He was a renowned tailor. Mostly menswear, but he made this for our mom for their wedding."

Naomi's hands clutch over her heart. "Oh my God, I want a guy like that."

I turn back to the gown, shaking my head. "Except..." I turn to look at Callie. "*How?*"

She grins. "Kratos. He got a hold of it from Vito and had some famous dress person..." Her brows furrow. "Veronica Beau-something?"

Milena's jaw drops. "*Véronique Beaumont?!*"

Callie points a finger at her. "That's the one."

"She's based in Paris."

"Yeah," Callie shrugs. "I guess he flew her out here the other day. Anyway, she fixed it up."

I blink in utter shock, turning to stare at my mother's gown.

"Okay, you gotta try that on, *asap*," Naomi blurts. "And make sure it fits. Because you're totally wearing that tomorrow."

Callie clears her throat. "Yeah, it, uh…" She grins. "It's gonna fit."

Somehow, I don't doubt it. Because something tells me that a man who flew a world-famous dress designer to New York from *Paris* in order to repair my mother's gown didn't exactly wing it on my sizes.

A smile creeps over my lips as a blush blooms on my cheeks.

He didn't have to do this. I never even mentioned the dress fiasco to him. I don't know if Kratos did this as a nice gesture, or if he truly knows how much it means to me. Either way, it's…unexpected.

And something tells me the goofy grin on my face right now is still going to be there tomorrow when I walk down the aisle toward him.

"*Thank you*," I whisper, pulling Callie into a hug. "Really. This…" I pull back, biting my lip. "This means a lot. Like, way more than he knows."

"Pretty sure he knows," she says quietly.

I grin. "Hey—you wanna stay?"

"I mean…I don't want to crash—"

"No crash! You and I haven't really had much time to get to know each other," I babble awkwardly. "And, I mean, we're going to be sisters…" I exhale. "And I don't really have a lot of friends."

Callie grins. "Same. I've got like five girlfriends, and I'm basically related by marriage to most of them." She bites her lip as she takes my hand and squeezes. "I'd actually love if we could be friends, too."

"Do you like wine and Lucali's?"

"Does the Pope work Sundays?"

MY HEART IS RACING, my pulse thundering in my ears as I step through the French doors and out into the manicured gardens. Yes, we're getting married at the Drakos estate. Not just because of the short notice in needing a venue. I mean, who *wouldn't* want to get married here?

The assembled crowd—one half from the Drakos side of things, the other from the Barones—turns and stands. Cameras flash. People whisper. My nerves are a fucking mess.

Then I rip my gaze forward and look at my fiancé.

Kratos' piercing blue eyes capture mine, and instantly, that whining, roaring, screaming anxiety in my head goes quiet.

Vito steps next to me, taking my arm. Momentarily, I pull my gaze away from Kratos to glance at him.

"Did you know?"

My dad smirks. "Hey, all I know is, one day that dress was a train wreck, and the next, some guy took it off my hands and did God-knows-what with it." He arches a brow, nodding toward the altar where Kratos is looking *obscenely* good in the sort of tuxedo a linebacker would wear to an ESPN awards ceremony. "And a little birdy told me that 'some guy' might just be the guy you're about to marry."

I chew on my bottom lip as it retreats between my teeth, my eyes locked with Kratos'.

"I want you to know how proud of you your mom and pop would be, Bumblebee," Vito says quietly. My eyes blur as I turn and hug him fiercely.

"*Thank you*," I whisper. "For everything. Always."

Then we're walking down the aisle, every step taking me closer to the man with the piercing blue eyes, and the inky black smoke swirling in his heart.

We stand face to face as the celebrant rattles off his lines. Kratos slips a ring onto my finger, and I do the same to his.

We say "I do".

And then...

The few times Kratos has kissed me, it's been the kiss of a man conquering a pair of lips. His kisses are savage and brutal. They devour me.

This time, it's different. His huge hand cups my face. His eyes lock with mine, a stormy kind of cloudy blue swirling in them. As he leans closer, the hand cupping my face slides into my hair as his other one slips to the small of my back, pulling me to him.

His lips crash to mine, decimating whatever resistance I had left. And this time, he's not demanding submission. He's not smashing down my defenses.

It's not a conquering.

It's a promise.

As the crowd stands and claps, and I lose myself in his kiss, I realize how very real this has become.

There's no question that the twisted darkness inside me has already met its match with the vicious blackness inside *him*.

But it's more than that.

There's a small chance I'm falling for the man I just married.

21

BIANCA

THE DAY AFTER THE WEDDING, I move into Kratos' brownstone in the East Village. I'm keeping my rental apartment and leaving most of my furniture there. But my clothes and personal belongings move with me to his place.

The second and third floors of the four-story building are definitely works-in-progress—livable, but clearly mid-renovation, which Kratos is apparently doing all himself.

Which is impressive. And honestly, kind of hot... But I digress.

The first floor is mostly done. It includes a huge living room, dining room, a gorgeous library, doors to what I can imagine will become a stunning back yard, and a truly *massive*, professional-grade kitchen.

That part of our tour gives me pause until I remember what Ya-ya said.

"I like to cook," he rumbles, shrugging his shoulders.

The fourth floor is almost entirely taken up with a sprawling master bedroom and ensuite bathroom, complete, I'm happy to note, with both a huge walk-in shower *and* a large white marble soaker tub.

When I step back out into the bedroom, my brow creases. There's a question that's been on my mind for a few days now, and I'm not quite sure how to ask it.

I mean, we're married.

We're physically...*intimate*, to say the least.

But...

I clear my throat and turn to him. "Where—"

"Here," he growls.

I blink. "You don't even know what I was going to ask."

He shrugs. "You were going to ask where you're sleeping. And the answer is here, in this bed," he says bluntly, tapping the foot of it.

My face heats. "Okay. And—"

"So am I." He looks at me, arching a brow. "Any other questions?"

"None," I croak out.

Not like I've literally ever *shared a bed with anyone, but here we are.*

A little while later, after I've unpacked a bit, I poke my head into the kitchen, where Kratos is chopping vegetables. I resist the urge to comment on how weirdly domestic this feels.

Not weird in a bad way at all. Just—different, considering that most of our interactions so far have been...*primal* in nature.

Dark, deviant, and fucked-up.

Not folding clothes into drawers or prepping mushrooms.

"Do you mind if I rinse off?"

He glances up at me, amusement on his face.

"It's your house."

"No, it's *your* house."

He sighs. "This isn't exactly a temporary arrangement, you know. It's not like you're crashing on my couch for a week."

Heat rushes up my neck.

"Right."

He shrugs. "*Mi casa es su casa.*"

He goes back to chopping, and my gaze wanders to the black t-shirt stretched over his thick biceps and filled by his massive shoulders. At the way the tattoo ink of a revolver on his forearm ripples as the tight, veined skin cords with his chopping motion.

Okay, domestic Kratos is seriously a turn-on.

I'm a second away from asking him if he wants to rinse off *with me*. But then I chicken out. It's something I've noticed as we've progressed to where we are now: in the church, in the dark, when he's wearing the mask and I'm his prey, I'm bold.

I ask him to fuck me. Beg him to hurt me or chase me.

But in the cold light of day, when it's just regular him and me, my nerves give out.

So instead I turn and head upstairs alone. In the master suite, I disrobe and pin up my hair as the tub fills with hot water and bubbles. When it's steaming and brimming with jasmine-scented suds, I step in, groaning as I sink into the heat.

My eyes close. A surreal, meditative calmness washes over me. I don't even realize I've started to nod off until I feel the water slosh around me. My eyes fly open, and the gasp locks in my throat as my gaze lands on Kratos.

…A very naked, very yummy looking Kratos as he steps into the tub opposite me and lowers his huge frame into it.

Embarrassment floods my face, but then I'm giggling as the displaced water splashes over the sides of the tub and onto the tiled floor.

"Overfilled it," he grunts.

"I…" I chew on my lip, my face burning hotly. "I wasn't expecting company."

He smirks. "No one expects the Spanish Inquisition."

"See, that's actually a misconception—"

"I know, babygirl."

My bottom lip retreats between my teeth again. I sink a little lower into the bubbles, enjoying the feel of the hot water teasing between my legs and rippling against my hardening nipples.

I should be in a panic right now.

Water in general is obviously a trigger. But it's not lost on me that for the very first time since...*that night*...I'm sitting in water alone with a man.

Relax.

It's not a hot tub.

There's no party.

You're fine.

Weirdly, it doesn't take the self-coaching I'd expected I'd need to put my mind at ease. When I look at him across the tub, I don't feel the anxiety or panic I assumed and expected I'd feel right now.

I don't overthink what that means. I just enjoy the fact I'm not having a panic attack right now.

Kratos exhales deeply as he sinks back against the tub. His massive arms drape over the sides as his eyes close. Meanwhile, I sit there trying to work out why the hell I'll eagerly say yes to being chased through the dark and fucked brutally, but don't have the courage to simply sit in my husband's lap in the bath.

"I don't think I've used this tub once since I installed it," he rumbles quietly in the stillness of the bathroom.

"What, like it's not part of your games?"

He opens his eyes, arching a brow at me. "My *games?*"

"You know," I shrug casually, trying to play it cool. "When you bring girls home."

Okay, yes. It's been occupying a fair amount of real estate in my head since I walked in here. I mean, he's not just ridiculously hot. And rich, *and* a member of a hugely powerful crime family. He also has to live in a gorgeous brownstone, in a quiet and super cool artsy neighborhood, that he's *fixing up himself?*

I mean, is there a girl equivalent to "shwing" from *Wayne's World?*

When he doesn't immediately respond, my mind goes into overdrive. Of course. I start imagining the *hordes* of girls from clubs and late-night bars that he charms over here, to show them the tub he's installed. Or his chef's kitchen, so he can cook them God-knows-what.

A piping hot batch of dropped panties, most likely.

I'm still simmering, my teeth gritted as I stare blankly at the wall, when he clears his throat.

"I'm, ah, not in the habit of bringing women to my home," he growls quietly.

My heart skips.

"When you say *not in the habit...*"

"You're the first woman I'm not related to who's been here," he grunts. When I glance back at him, there's a smug smirk on his face. "Happy?"

I shrug nonchalantly. Inside, I'm screaming like a freaking cheerleader and jumping up and down with pompoms.

"I mean, technically, we *are* related now."

"Well, there goes my erection."

I giggle loudly as he grins at me.

"Turn around."

I blush, feeling heat course through me.

"Why?"

Kratos' eyes pierce into mine.

"Just do it."

I suck on my lip.

"*Okay.*"

My skin tingles, and a needy throb begins to pulse in my core as I turn myself around, facing the wall. I can hear him moving behind me, and my imagination goes into X-rated overdrive because of course it does.

"What are you scheming at back—"

In one black, horrifying second, I'm plunged into sheer, drowning panic.

Water pours over my head, raking over the nerve endings in my skin like napalm claws. My vision goes dark, and my throat closes up like it's being squeezed. My lungs burn and my breath hitches as I spasm, my legs and arms jerking and flailing in random directions before suddenly, it's like I'm detonating.

In sheer terror, I explode up and stumble blindly out of the tub. My feet slip on the wet, sudsy floor, and I cry out as I go sprawling naked and shivering onto the tiles.

I struggle to get to my feet, kicking away from the tub and yanking a towel down from the rack behind me. Kratos' face caves in concern. He goes to lurch out of the tub.

"Stay there!" I scream, finally scrambling to my feet. I wrap the towel tight around myself, hunching as if to better hide my nakedness.

"Bianca—"

"I'm fine," I shudder, shaking as I turn to suck in a breath of air.

"Fuck. I was just going to wash your—"

"I said I'm *fine.*"

The bathroom goes still. With my back to him, my eyes squeeze shut.

I should tell him. I mean I *really* should, if only to make sure he doesn't think I'm a lunatic. But sharing that part of me with him is like working up the courage to crawl into his lap, or to ask him to join me in the tub in the first place.

In the absence of darkness, masks, and danger, apparently, I have no spine.

"Look, Bianca—"

"I'm going to go grab something to eat," I mumble over my shoulder as I fast-walk out of the bathroom. "Enjoy the tub."

SO MUCH FOR DOMESTIC BLISS.

A couple of hours later, we're like two strangers ignoring each other in the house. Kratos is on the second floor, pounding the shit out of something with a hammer. He's been there since my bathtub freakout.

I still don't have the courage to have *that* conversation with him. But I eventually at least work up the nerve to go up there to join him.

He looks to be framing a wall, pounding nails into pieces of two-by-four with a grim look on his face. He's in grubby jeans that fit him *way* too well, and a white t-shirt pulled tight over the broad muscles of his back.

When he takes a break and lays the hammer down, I walk up softly behind him. Kratos flinches a little when I wrap my arms around his middle from behind.

"*Fuck.*"

He spins around brusquely, half pushing me away from him as his brow furrows. I grin up into his face.

"Did I scare you?"

He's silent for a moment, his eyes stabbing down into mine.

"No."

He turns around again, seemingly ignoring the way I'm still hugging onto him as he reaches for his hammer again.

"Hey, one sec."

I stop his hand with mine on his arm. When he turns around again, I lick my lips as I look up into his eyes.

"I'm sorry," I say quietly. "I mean, before...the tub..."

He looks at me blankly.

"Okay."

Okay?

I shrug it away. I look up into his eyes, feeling my pulse race as I gather up my nerve, grip the front of his t-shirt, and attempt to pull him down as I stand up on tiptoes to kiss his mouth.

I don't make it.

Before I can kiss him, Kratos shakes his head and quietly pushes me back from him.

My brow furrows.

"Um, okay?"

He shrugs again, looking away.

"Look, I'm sorry about before," I venture. "You just startled me."

"No kidding."

My brows knit even deeper.

"Okay, did I do something wrong?"

He looks at me blankly, no emotion on his face, his eyes unblinking.

"No."

"Then what the fuck?"

I watch as his jaw grinds.

"Forget it, Bianca. It's fine. I'm sorry I startled you before."

He starts to turn away.

"Why'd you stop me from kissing you?"

He pauses, turning back to look at me. "Just forget it. Please."

"Kratos, it was just a kiss—"

"Maybe I don't want to."

"To *kiss me?*"

A lifted shoulder is his only reply. I purse my mouth.

"Wow, okay. My bad for looking for a little affection."

"I don't really do affection, now do I?"

"Guess not," I snap coldly, stepping back from him.

Kratos levels a withering gaze at me. "If that's going to be a problem for you, perhaps you should have thought twice before torching my car."

I bark a cold, brittle laugh. "Wow, we're still on that?"

"It is what it is."

"Married people kiss," I mutter.

"Well, we're not really a married couple, are we?"

I bristle, my eyes hardening on him. "I guess not. Actually," I snap coldly, "I guess we're not a real *couple* at all."

I whirl to storm away. Then I flinch when he roughly grabs my arm and spins me back around. I shiver when I come face to face with his wrath, his face darkened and angry.

"I don't *do* lovey-fucking-dovey, Bianca. I don't do snuggles, or affectionate kisses." His nostrils flare. "I don't do kisses at all, actually."

I roll my eyes. "Right, sorry, my mistake!" I spit. "You just like to chase girls around in the dark wearing a fucking mask and playing out rape fantasies with them!"

"You'd know."

I stiffen, glaring at him. "*What are we?*" I hiss. "An arrangement?"

"We're a peace treaty, Bianca."

"So," I seethe, "none of this matters? None of this means shit?"

He leans closer to me, his grip on my arm tightening.

"Do you enjoy it when I chase you?"

I swallow.

"When I catch you, and hurt you…" He looms over me, that ominous inky black power I always feel radiating off him in the church flexing around us. "When I *fuck you?*"

Kratos' hand suddenly teases across my stomach. I tremble, my breath sucking in as his fingers slip into the waist of my yoga pants before pushing lower. His hand delves under the lace of my panties, and I bite my lip as his thick finger pushes lower, dragging through my wet lips.

He chuckles darkly to himself.

"Your drippy, messy pussy says yes."

It should turn me on. Okay, it *does* turn me on. A lot. So much so that part of me wants to beg him to take me right here.

But still, it's not the same. And not just because we're not in the church and he's not wearing a mask.

All the other times we've played this game, it's on equal footing. Yes, I play the role of the submissive, and him the uber Dom. But we're coming to it with the same needs, wanting the same thing for the same reasons.

This time, he's doing it to win an argument. To "prove a point", or at the very least, to silence my dissent.

And that really, *really* rubs me the wrong way.

Somehow, summoning almost superhuman powers, I grab his wrist and shove his hand away, stepping back until it slips out of my panties.

Kratos looks half pissed and half amused as I adjust my yoga pants. Then I glare at him coldly.

"Is that all this is?" I choke. "Is that all we are? Just…sex?"

He gives me a hard stare. The seconds tick by as my nerves fray raw.

"That's all I have," he growls quietly. "Better get used to it."

I physically recoil, like he's just slapped me. Then I draw in a breath, collecting myself.

"I'm going for a walk."

Without another word, I turn, storming downstairs and out the front door.

Fuck you.

Anger, resentment, and humiliation boil inside me as I power walk through my new neighborhood. I almost want to scream, or break something, or maybe go get drunk. Instead, I find one of the many small little gardens that dot the Lower East Side and plant myself on a bench.

Breathe.

I exhale, trying to let go of the anger and anxiety. When I've settled down…well, a little…I get up again and go back to wandering the neighborhood to clear my head.

Eventually, I happen upon a super-cute bookstore-slash-cafe. And for the next two hours, that's where I hole up: nose in a Bastian Pierce book as I drain not one but *two* coconut milk chai lattes and polish off a big-ass chocolate chip cookie for lunch that Madame K. would definitely not approve of but fuck it.

Finally, I realize it's time to face the music. Or at least go home and sulk. I pay for my book, slip it into the front pocket of my hoodie, and head back to the brownstone.

I'm just about to open the little black iron gate and head up the walkway to the steps when the big front door opens.

I pause, puzzled when I hear a woman laugh and step outside, closing the door behind her. She turns, and I stiffen.

I've seen her before. At the engagement party. She was the "family friend" I walked in on talking very closely with Kratos.

Too closely.

Bitterness swells inside of me. Slowly, my eyes focus on her.

My chest tightens and my stomach drops.

She smirks at me as she finishes doing up the top few buttons on her blouse. Her brow cocks as she brings up a hand, smoothing down clearly messed-up hair.

A cold, stabbing sensation slices into my heart.

"Why hello again," the woman purrs, smiling with all the warmth of a blizzard.

She walks down the front steps of the brownstone, tucking her wild hair back into place. She gets closer, and my gaze slides to her mouth.

Her lipstick is smudged.

The blouse is still half untucked from her skirt.

Oh my God...

"I—"

"You're the little wifelet, yes," she drawls in a bored tone. "We didn't get a chance to speak properly before."

I feel sick as she extends a hand. I can't move. I just stare at it blankly before she laughs quietly and retracts it.

"Amaya, remember?" she says offhandedly. "Anyway, *so nice* to see you again."

Her hand comes up, and she giggles as she wipes her thumb across the smudge of lipstick right beneath her bottom lip.

"*Oopsie*," she smiles.

My stomach heaves.

"Now, word of warning." She turns, nodding her chin up at the house. "I know he's got a short recovery period. But he still might need a minute before you take your turn."

I physically gag, my face going white as my heart wrenches inside my chest.

Amaya grins. "*So nice* to see you again, Bianca. *Ciao.*"

I'm still numb as she pushes past me and walks on sky-high heels to a sleek black car parked at the curb. She gets in, revving the engine and turning to wave her fingers at me with a cruel smirk before she drives away.

I turn, and I *run*.

22

BIANCA

Music blares around me as the alcohol courses through my veins. The pounding pulse of the club beats in time with anarchy swirling in my heart as I close my eyes, toss my hair back, and throw my arms in the air, losing myself in the music.

Fuck. Him.

We've had one text exchange since I ran from the brownstone.

KRATOS

You've been gone a while.

ME

I'm going out with friends tonight. Don't wait up

KRATOS

Ok.

Ok?!?!

Rage explodes in my chest as I replay seeing that woman walking out of the brownstone—smudged lipstick, buttons undone on her blouse. "I just got fucked" sex hair.

The emotions that come surging out of me make me want to scream as loud as I can.

So I do.

Beside me, Naomi jolts, whirling as I throw my head back and shriek into the surging energy of the club. The music is loud enough that I doubt anyone else even hears it. But Naomi and Milena are close enough that both their heads snap to me.

"Are you sure you're okay?" Naomi yells into my ear.

"Peachy!" I scream back. "Just had to get out with my girls and *daaance*!"

My friends glance at each other, sharing a worried look.

"C'mon," I grab them both. "We need more drinks!"

I drag them both back through the crowd. At the bar, we maneuver to an open space, and I flag down the bartender.

"Three more shots!" I yell with a totally fake grin on my face. "Tequila!"

"Bianca." Milena puts her hand on my arm, a concerned look on her face. "What's going on? Seriously, you're—"

"No one's forcing you to hang out tonight."

She gives me a probing look. "Let's go somewhere where we can talk."

"Fine," I grumble. "But only if you do this shot with me."

She turns to Naomi for support. But our other friend is turned away, grinning and chatting away with some hot blonde guy. Milena turns back to me. "Fine. But after that, I get five minutes with you someplace quiet."

"Works for me," I shrug casually.

We elbow Naomi for her attention, the three of us taking our shots with grimaces. Naomi instantly turns back to her new friend as Milena grabs my arm and yanks me through the crowd. We head to the second floor of the neon-lit club, the music still pounding through our bodies. Then she tugs me outside to a roof deck.

It's warm out, but it's a lot cooler out here than in the swirling heat of the club. I shiver from a light breeze on my sweaty skin as I turn to face her.

"Well?"

She rolls her eyes at me. "It's me, B. You can drop the bullshit."

I shrug. "There's no bull—"

"Will you stop talking to me as if I *don't* know half a dozen girls who've had an arranged marriage? As if I don't get it?"

My lips purse.

"What happened, Bianca."

I shrug and glance away. "Nothing. It's fine."

"Did he hurt you?"

There's an uncharacteristic iciness to her tone that pulls my gaze back to her. I shake my head. "No, nothing like that."

"Because if he fucking did," she hisses, "I'll cut that fucking giant off at the knees."

I smile wryly. "Thank you, psycho. But he didn't..." My smile fades as I look away. The fury from earlier comes rushing back. "There was another girl," I snap. "Some other woman."

"Get the fuck out!" Milena breathes. "Seriously?"

I nod.

"How do you know?"

I bark out a cold laugh. "Because I *saw* her."

"Ew!" she blurts. "Like, you walked in on them!?"

"*No!*" My face twists bitterly.

So does my heart, as a million horrible, stabbing images of Kratos and Amaya start swirling through my head.

"No, I just..." I exhale heavily. Then I tell Milena about the I-guess-you-could-call-it argument that I had with Kratos, and then coming back afterward to find Amaya walking out like she'd just screwed him.

When I'm done, her jaw is hanging open and her face is livid.

"*Motherfucker!*" she chokes, shaking her head. "I mean, the fucking *gall!*" She angrily shoves her hair back from her face, looking away and gritting her teeth. Then she turns back, her brows thoughtful. "Wait...did you two..." She frowns. "Did you have any sort of talk about this?"

"About...what? Him fucking other women?" I spit. "We did *not.*"

"No, I mean..." Her mouth twists. "Look, I do know a bunch of girls who've had arranged mafia marriages, okay? Some of them turned out great, and it ends up they're head-over-heels for their arranged husband. Others, not so much. But most of them, regardless of how things are between them, have 'the talk' before they get hitched."

I frown. "What the fuck is *the talk*?"

Milena shrugs elegantly. "The 'are we exclusive' talk."

"*What?*"

"Think about it," she says. "You're forced to marry someone, usually someone you don't really know. You're supposed to spend your lives together so that one family can do business with another, or so that people don't go to war. Maybe you get lucky and they're hot, and you click with them. But maybe you don't. And anyone who says sex isn't a basic human need is lying. So…"

I stare at her. "You mean there are people who go into arranged marriages and then…"

"Give each other permission to fuck around because they're not into each other? Um, *yeah*."

I swallow the lump that's formed in my throat.

"So you and Kratos…."

I shake my head. "There wasn't ever a talk."

She nods, clearly unsatisfied.

"What?"

Milena makes a face. "Well, then you also never had a talk specifying that you're exclusive with each other, right?"

"We're fucking *married*," I hiss angrily, waving my ring finger in her face. "Call me old-fashioned, but I was pretty fucking sure that implied exclusivity."

"Not so much in our world, B," she says quietly, making a face. "I'm sorry, but…" she shrugs again. "That's our world."

I turn away, feeling sick as I shove my fingers through my hair. I suck in air, shaking with rage.

That *asshole*. That fucking ASSHOLE.

And I *hate* that it hurts this much. That it's not just that I feel duped, or lied to.

It's that I truly feel *cheated* on.

"But, I mean, given what you saw today…" Milena says gently. "I think it's fair to say you're free to do what you want too, right? I mean, *he* clearly is."

I turn to her, my mouth set. She makes a face.

"Sorry, girl," she mumbles. "Don't shoot the messenger."

"It's fine," I grumble, looking away.

"Hey, we're here, right?" she says brightly, trying to cheer me up. "Let's go dance. I'll even do another tequila shot with you."

My lips twist as I half smile at her. "I might hang out here another minute or two."

She nods and squeezes my arm. "You want company, or brooding solitude?"

"Brooding solitude sounds dandy right now."

She smiles comfortingly. "I'll be at the bar downstairs making sure Naomi doesn't make bad decisions. Come find us when you're ready, okay?"

When she's gone, I move to the edge of the rooftop patio, away from the other laughing club-goers. At the railing, I glare out over the city, my heart twisting as anger stabs through me.

I hate that I'm this mad. Hate that I never saw this coming.

But mostly, I hate that I caught feelings for a man who warned me a thousand different ways himself that he wasn't capable of reciprocating them.

Brutal fucking. Violence and sex. *That's* what Kratos and I have. That's what we share.

Nothing else.

Angrily, I yank out my phone out. I absently doom-scroll TikTok for a while, trying to clear my mind of lurid images involving Kratos and that woman fucking. When it doesn't work, I switch to Instagram. When that also fails to take my mind off things, suddenly, another thought crosses my mind.

I think it's fair to say you're free to do what you want too, right?

In a heartbeat, I'm opening the Club Venom site and logging in to my fake account.

It's not that I even want anyone else. And I hate that. I hate that even though he's apparently fine screwing some other woman, I still only want him.

I glare at my profile screen: not a single new match. No new messages. *Nothing.*

Pouting and feeling the heady effect of that last shot, my eyes slide up to the top of the screen.

Wait, what?

My gaze lands on a tiny little hyperlink under my profile name, and the profile picture I uploaded of my butt in yoga pants.

Reset profile options.

I frown and tap the little question mark next to it. A popup window opens on my phone:

Resetting profile options clears any cached data on your account. Warning: clicking this will entirely reset your match parameters, potentially giving you more matches than you may be looking for.

Sane me says to close the window, put the phone away, and go find my friends.

Tequila-drunk angry me taps the link.

Your match parameters have been reset.

Big deal. As if I'll get any new—

My phone dings. When I look at it, I freeze. A message I've seen before pops up.

Dear BrokenBee,

A match has been made for you with another Member. You have both been notified. Please use this link to initiate a private chat with your potential partner. Like at the Club itself, we encourage the use of anonymity, as well as open and honest communication. Both parties should discuss hard limits and safe words before meeting. Please enjoy your experience.

Holy shit.

My pulse jackrabbits as I stare at the message. Something twists uncomfortably in my chest, too. But I shove that feeling aside as horrible, toxic images of Kratos and *her* slither through my head.

Fuck you.

I click on the link. Instantly, a chat opens.

> **BLACKHEARTED1**
> I'm looking for tonight. You?

I swallow. My heart clenches.

No.

> **BROKENBEE**
> Yes

> **BLACKHEARTED1**
> Good. Then we can proceed.

I chew on my lip uneasily, remembering the first conversation I had with Kratos here. How dark, direct, and to the point he was. This person sounds similar, but there's something completely clinical in his response that throws me a little.

> **BROKENBEE**
> I'm married

I wrinkle my nose the second I hit send. Why did I tell him that? Probably guilt. Feeling that emotion only annoys me more.

Kratos doesn't deserve my guilt. Not when he's out cavalierly fucking other women. Not when he's responding to me saying don't wait up with "ok" and not checking in with a single text or call since then.

He's probably busy with some girl.

Angrily, the tequila burning in my system, I glare back at my phone screen.

> BLACKHEARTED1
>
> I don't really give a fuck if you are. Open, or angry

It takes a second before what he's asked clicks: am I married with an open relationship? Or am I married and pissed at my husband?

> BROKENBEE
>
> Angry. And available

> BLACKHEARTED1
>
> Your profile is fairly vague. What specifically are you looking for

I stare at the screen, pushing down the dull, twisting ache in my chest.

> BLACKHEARTED1
>
> If you have to think about it that long, perhaps we're done here

> BROKENBEE
>
> I don't have to think about it

I swallow.

> BROKENBEE
>
> I want you to chase me. Scare me. Hurt me

> BROKENBEE
>
> Fuck me

BLACKHEARTED1

I play rough, BrokenBee

BROKENBEE

Good

BLACKHEARTED1

Your safe word will be ORANGE. When are you available tonight

I close my eyes, my heart wrenching.

What the *fuck* am I doing?

I take a shaky breath and start to type "this was a mistake, sorry" to my new match. But then I switch to my texts, bring up the thread with Kratos, and text him.

ME

Are we exclusive

Only a few seconds later, he responds.

KRATOS

What?

ME

Like, monogamous

KRATOS

You're my fucking wife.

I shiver as I re-read that a few times, feeling the pulse of something hot in my core. But I refuse to allow myself to get pulled under his dark waves that blind me to the obvious. Not anymore.

ME

What does that mean to you

KRATOS

It means you're my wife.

ME

But does that MATTER to you

My mind flashes to Amaya walking out of the front door, probably still with the taste of his cum on her tongue. I swallow back bile as I focus on my phone.

ME

Are you even capable of that mattering to you?

There's a long pause. So long that I almost switch back to the Club Venom chat.

KRATOS

You found out who I was, and what I was and wasn't capable of, the day we met. I hope that answers your question.

I swallow as I type out a reply.

ME

And if it doesn't?

I wait. And I wait. Then I wait some more.

There's no reply. Or maybe in his mind he did already answer it.

My heart twists, my chest tight and constricted and my stomach dropping as I switch back to the Club Venom chat. I erase what I was about to send.

DARKHEARTED1

I don't like to be kept waiting

BROKENBEE

Now

BROKENBEE

I'm available right now

I don't want this. I don't want anyone else touching me.

But I *need* to feel something other than this searing hurt. I need whatever this stranger is offering to bury the ache in my chest, knowing that the one I really want doesn't give a shit, or simply can't.

I thought I could do it. I thought I'd be able to have this fake marriage, and just the physical, and be fine with it.

But that was before I fell for the darkness. For *his* darkness.

DARKHEARTED1

Be at this address in half an hour. And remember...I don't like to be kept waiting

He sends me an address not far away from the club.

BROKENBEE

Ok

DARKHEARTED1

Are you going to be a good little whore for me?

I flinch.

It sounds different coming from someone else. It feels dirty, and not in the good way.

BROKENBEE

Yes

DARKHEARTED1

Good

What the fuck am I doing? Shame and self-loathing wash over me as I head back inside and find my friends. I put on a happy face, telling Milena I appreciated her talk, and that I'm going to go home and curl up on the couch with Netflix. I smile brightly as I hug them both good night, then head outside to find a cab.

My heart knots as I slide into the back seat and drive off into the night.

23

BIANCA

THE TAXI PULLS UP in front of a luxurious building on Fifth Avenue.

There's no excitement burning in my veins as I pay and step out. No nervous, anxious desire.

There's only one man who stirs up those emotions in me.

And he's a lying, cheating asshole.

Okay, *maybe* scratch the "cheating" part, because we never had any sort of formal discussion about our "terms". But, I mean, call me old-fashioned: I sort of thought monogamy was *implied* when you got married to someone, barring any sort of other conversation.

Silly fucking me.

Regardless, here I am. God only knows why. A sour feeling curdles in my stomach as I approach the door to the building. But I pause just as the doorman bows and reaches for the front door. The hesitation has me turning to glance back at the taxi as it pulls away.

Just then, my phone dings.

Frowning, I pull it out of my bag. I swallow when I realize it's a message from my Venom account, and my teeth rake over my bottom lip as I open it.

DARKHEARTED1

When you're at the address, look for the black town car.

I hear a discreet honk behind me, and I whirl to see the black car waiting at the curb, apparently for me.

Woah, *what.*

BROKENBEE

I see it. I'm here

DARKHEARTED1

My driver will bring you to me

Okay, yeah, that does it. *That's* the smack of reality I need to shake me hard enough to snap out of whatever insanity I was just descending into.

I don't want this. I don't want some random guy, And I *really* don't want to play some sleight-of-hand bullshit involving multiple cars to unknown locations.

I close my eyes and exhale as I drop my head back.

BROKENBEE

I'm sorry, but I have to cancel for tonight

DARKHEARTED1

Are you joking?

BROKENBEE

No. I'm sorry to have wasted your time, but I can't do this

DARKHEARTED1

Because of your husband

I bark a bitter laugh aloud.

BROKENBEE

Yes, plus many other reasons. Sorry again

He's silent for a minute. Oh well. Hey, the app *is* anonymous.

DARKHEARTED1

I understand. No apology necessary. Listen, it's late. Why don't you let me offer you a ride home, or anywhere else you'd like. The town car is there anyway. It's at your disposal.

Wow. My husband might be a selfish asshole. But when a random internet stranger who was prepared to chase me and fuck me offers me a free ride home after I cancel on him, I guess that's a little bit of faith in humanity restored.

DARKHEARTED1

If it makes you more comfortable, you can have him drop you at a major intersection near your place rather than at your actual home.

Well, *shit*. And they say chivalry is dead.

I thank DarkHearted1 again and walk over to the car. The door is already open, so I slip in and close it. I say hi and give a little wave to the mustachioed driver with longish hair and sunglasses. He barely acknowledges me, just gives me a formal nod in the rearview mirror when I give him directions to the café around the corner from Kratos' brownstone.

I blow air out through my lips as the car pulls away from the curb.

Okay, there's a *small* chance I may have overreacted earlier. Yes, it was jarring to see that woman walk out looking like *that*, and basically telling me she'd just screwed him. But who knows? Maybe she's just some petty ex-girlfriend or someone he rejected being shitty now that he's married. Really, when I think about her again, she *did* look a lot older than him.

I groan as I drop my head back onto the headrest behind me. When the hell did I get like this? So trigger-happy with my emotions, and so impulsive, and so...*jealous*?

Of course, the answer is right there in front of me: it's probably when I realized whatever this thing is with Kratos was way more than just a twisted, fucked-up game.

When I realized it wasn't just that I wanted him to chase me. I wanted *him* to chase me.

As if on cue, my phone dings with a text.

KRATOS

Where are you?

ME

Are you home? I'm on my way

I'm in the middle of typing "I met that woman when she was leaving our place. Can we talk about that?" when my phone dies.

Goddammit.

"Sorry, hi," I lean forward to speak to the driver. "Do you have a charger up there? My phone died."

He nods and holds out his hand. I give my phone to him,

watching as he plugs it in to the USB cable up front. Then I sink back into the seat as we drive—

Wait.

"Excuse me, are you going uptown?"

When I glance out the window, I realize I'm right. I'm starting to recognize spots I know on the Upper West Side.

"Sorry, sir?" I say, concern lacing my voice. "I need to go *downtown*. I'm going to the *Lower* East Side?"

The driver doesn't respond. He takes a turn that leads us to an on-ramp to the West Side Highway, going north. Anxiety pools in my stomach as my pulse quickens.

"*Sir!*" I exclaim. "Sir, you're going the wrong way."

The driver still doesn't say a thing, and my nerves begin to shred.

"I'd like to get out now, please," I choke, fear creeping up my throat. "Right here is fine."

The car begins to accelerate.

"Let me out!" I yell. "Pull over! Right here! I want to get out!"

The doors lock.

"LET ME—!"

The partition between us rises, imprisoning me in the locked cell of the back of the town car as it accelerates even more.

"*LET ME OUT!*" I scream, pure panic and adrenaline exploding through my system. I yank off my seatbelt and lurch forward to the divider, pounding on it hard. "FUCK YOU!" I yell. "LET ME—"

"Sit down."

I jolt violently, gasping as a horrifyingly creepy, metallic, robotic voice rasps through a speaker.

"I—"

"I said sit the FUCK down."

"Fuck you!!!" I scream at the divider. I whirl back and start to pound on one of the side windows. Then I take off one of my heels and try and use that to smash it. I yelp when the shoe slips and my bare knuckles slam against the unyielding glass instead.

"Sit down." The robotic voice is tinny through the speaker. *"If I have to ask again, I'll fucking kill you."*

It feels like I've been slapped. All the fight goes out of me as my adrenaline is replaced by crippling, paralyzing fear.

"Please," I whisper, sinking back into my seat again. My arms wrap around myself protectively. "Where are you taking—"

"You'll see."

Suddenly, the windows start getting darker, like the tint is getting stronger. I turn to stare helplessly out the window as the highway outside fades to black.

———

I HAVE no idea how long we drive. Maybe an hour? But when the car stops, it's completely silent outside.

No city noise. No sounds of other cars, like we're at a gas station or a rest stop.

Nothing.

The driver's door opens, then shuts with a muffled *thunk*. Footsteps crunch on what sounds like dried leaves outside, coming to a stop right next to my door. The windows are still blacked out, and I can't see a thing.

My pulse thuds as I slowly back away from the door, my breath coming shallowly as I press myself into the far corner of the car, staring at the door, waiting for him to yank it open and rip me out.

The seconds tick by. Then minutes. Then what feel like several more. I swallow the lump in my throat, my breath still shaky and ragged as my eyes dart around the back seat of the town car.

"*Hello?*" I whisper quietly. I shudder, clearing my throat. "Hello?" I say again, louder this time, waiting for something. Anything. Even for my abductor to laugh at me, honestly. *Anything* to give me any idea of what's going on.

There's nothing.

I grab the door behind me to pull myself up from the little ball I've curled into. When I do, my fingers slip over the door handle, pulling it.

The door clicks and suddenly swings wide.

With a gasp, I half-fall, half-scramble out. I whirl, almost expecting the mustachioed driver to be waiting to lunge at me. When I don't see him, I scrape up all my courage and creep around to the other side of the car, to see if he's crouched down and waiting.

But no. I'm alone.

I shiver in the cool air, rubbing my arms and glancing around. My chest tightens as a cold, dangerous shiver drags a blade up my spine.

I'm alone *in the woods.*

There's not a single light. Not from a house, not from a streetlamp. *Nothing.* Shuddering, my eyes widen, trying to see into the darkness. I'm in a small clearing, the car parked at the end of a little, barely-paved road, a driveway to nowhere. There's nothing here—just a dead end, the clearing, and the vast, dark woods, looming and leering down at me.

Raw fear knots in my stomach. I whip around, my breath coming fast as my eyes stab into the shadowy, inky blackness. There's no sign of the driver, but then a thought hits me, and suddenly, I'm yanking the driver's side door open to see if the keys are…

No.

But what I *do* see chills me to the bone.

Laid across the driver's seat is a longish male wig, a glue-on fake mustache, dark sunglasses…

My eyes widen, a cold, eviscerating feeling stabbing into my gut.

And a black and white photo of me, walking out of the stage door of the Mercury Theater.

A snapping sound, maybe a stick breaking, sends my heart into my throat. I whirl as panic chemicals flood my system. My heart rate goes through the roof, my skin prickling to a million goosebumps as a wrenching shiver claws up my neck.

Another snap, from the woods at the other side of the clearing this time.

I start to pant, my breath shallow and disjointed. My pulse skips, and my skin turns clammy and cold.

What the fuck is this.

"H-hello?" I croak.

In the distance, an owl hoots. Something small rustles in a nearby tree.

A stick cracks violently behind me.

I whirl again, feeling my throat close as panic sets in. I whip around to stab my gaze into the front seat of the town car. With a cry that I swallow back, I lurch across the driver's seat and grab my phone, which is still plugged into the charger.

It's even *on*.

My hands shake as I snatch it out and scramble to unlock it.

Instantly, my hopes turn to ash in my hands.

There's no cell signal.

I shiver violently.

I'm alone.

The sound of a heavy step in the underbrush near the edge of the clearing has my body shaking horribly as I whirl.

Actually, you're not alone at all...

"Whoever you are," I yell, my voice cracking as I back against the side of the car. "You should know that my family is extremely dangerous. They're also wealthy, so—"

"I'm not interested in your fucking money."

Jesus H. Christ. The same metallic, robotically altered voice from the car rasps dementedly from the woods somewhere in front of me. My heart lurches as fear stabs in me. Even the fucking birds squawk and fly away as the monster speaks.

Not a fake monster with a pretend mask and an agreed-upon safe word.

A real one.

"I-I'm armed!" I stammer, my voice breaking. "I have a gun—"

"No you fucking don't."

My skin crawls as I cling to the side of the car, my nerves shattering as my chest heaves. I glance down at my phone, open to my last text exchange with Kratos.

KRATOS

Where are you?

ME

Are you home? I'm on my way

My mind races, trying to do the math. That was maybe an hour ago. By now, if I'm not home yet, or responding, maybe he's out looking for me?

A second after the thought crosses my mind, giving me hope, that same hope is dashed to the ground.

He won't be looking for you in the fucking woods an hour outside the city.

Not for days. Weeks, even.

Probably never.

"*I—*"

"*Let's play a game, little girl.*"

I shudder, trembling as the voice comes from the shadows all around me.

"W-what's the game?" I whisper.

"*It's called tag,*" the monster growls. "*And I'm IT.*"

It happens in a millisecond. He roars the last word through whatever is changing his voice, and as he does so, I hear the snapping of twigs and the crunching of underbrush as a shadow comes lurching out of the woods right in front of me.

Humans have an inherent fight or flight response to danger, from the days when we were living in caves trying not to be eaten. When a saber tooth tiger leaps at you, you have two options: stay put and fight for your life, or turn and run and take your chances.

In the second that the monster storms out of the shadows, I make my choice. I turn and fucking *run*.

I want to scream, but I'm incapable of making a sound as I bolt away from the car and the man chasing me. My heels fall off and I kick them away. I wince and cry out in pain as I slam through the underbrush of the forest at the edge of the clearing and crash into the blackness.

The clearing was almost pitch dark, with the moon behind the clouds. Here in the trees, it's like running through a black hole.

My pulse roars in my ears, and I keep my arms up in front of my face, flinching as they block the scrape and claw of branches that are trying to rip my face and snag my hair.

"Where are you, little girl…"

I choke back a scream when I hear him crashing through the brush behind me. I veer sharply to the right, pelting into the dark forest. I gasp, ducking at the very last minute to avoid running face-first into a low branch. It skins my elbow, though, and I cry out in pain.

"I can smell your fucking fear, little one."

I swallow another scream, zigging left to crash through the trees. Maybe there's *something* nearby. A rest stop, or a gas station. Even the road we took to get here. I mean, we're only an hour at most outside New York. It's not like we're in the middle of nowhere.

Hope catches fire inside me as I whirl to the left and push and claw my way through the trees and snarled branches.

"Shall I tell you what happens when I catch you?"

I almost scream. Fuck me, he's so close. *Way* closer than I thought he was, somewhere just to my right. I zig left, pushing myself, trying not to care about the underbrush slicing and ripping at my bare legs and the heavier branches arching to bash in my face.

"I'm going to fuck you till you bleed. I'm gonna hurt you, slut. I'm going to watch the light go out in your eyes as you choke on my fucking cock."

There are games, and there are nightmares. And I've tripped over my own impulsiveness right into the latter.

I shouldn't have run from the brownstone earlier. Shouldn't have gone out. Shouldn't have gone on the Venom site, and I *definitely* shouldn't have engaged with that demented stranger.

Because there's no question that's who's brought me here. Who's chasing me.

Who wants to hurt me, for real.

Panic surges through me as I crash down a small embankment and hide behind an uprooted tree. I pull out my phone, hoping against hope…

Oh my God.

I have one bar of service.

I can hear metallic snarling and the sound of crunching leaves and snapping twigs, like my attacker is getting closer.

I don't have much time. Or more than a prayer of a chance. But it's something. In the one millisecond I have, I text Kratos a map pin of my location. I wait, watching the send bar load tortuously slowly because of the almost no service.

But it goes through.

I jam my phone into my bag and force myself to get up. With a choked cry, I fling myself through the trees, running as fast as I can and trying to ignore the pain in my bare feet.

Praying that the break in the trees I think I can see ahead will open up to a road, or a house, or *anything*.

With a last gasp, I crash out of the woods and into a dark clearing.

Instantly, I go still and my heart drops.

I'm right back where I started.

"Too bad."

I scream as I whirl. The energy is draining from my aching muscles as I back away. Slowly, the branches move. A dark shadow emerges, stalking toward me.

The clouds begin to part, and a faint glow from the moon begins to bleed across the clearing. The man moves toward me, brimming with darkness and pure malice. He steps into the hazy, pseudo-light, and my throat seizes up as pure, stabbing fear cuts into me.

Jeans. Black boots. A black sweatshirt with the hood pulled up, and a mask. Not the one Kratos wears that I know and am addicted to. No, this one is almost pure black, with just two pale, grayish-white circles, one larger than the other, where the eyes should be.

The moonlight washes over his mask, and I choke on my fear.

Not circles. *Buttons.* The psycho has two mismatched buttons haphazardly sewn onto the all-black mask, leering at me as he stalks toward me.

A last jolt of fear gives me one final burst of energy. I whirl and run. The crunching, crashing sound of his heavy boots on the dry leaves behind me makes me scream. I can hear the metallic breathing rasping through his mask as he gets closer and closer, the sheer violence of him washing over my back like toxic radiation.

Suddenly, pain explodes across my scalp.

I cry out in agony as the monster grabs my hair in a fist and wrenches me around. I tip sideways, falling off balance as I slam into the side of the town car with a bruising thud.

Pain explodes through my hip and my ribs. Instantly, he's on me, snarling and growling like a beast. I choke on pure adrenaline and fear as he pins me to the car. I scream when I look up into his dark, uncaring, unflinching black mask. My hands flail and claw, smacking and scratching at his face. He snarls viciously and slaps me back, shoving me up against the side of the car.

I'm not going down without a fight.

My knee jerks up, catching him in the balls.

"*That was fucking foolish,*" the stranger snarls demonically.

I cry out as he roughly grabs my breasts, ripping my club dress down before brutally pinching a nipple and twisting, *hard*. I wince, sobbing out a choked cry before he lets go only to slap my bare nipple, sending a zap of pain and, horrifically, something electric through my core.

I flail at him, but his hand suddenly juts out, wrapping tight around my throat. He tweaks and slaps my other nipple, wrenching a sob from my lips.

Suddenly, my mind goes blank for half a second, and my thoughts go somewhere else.

To another chase, with another monster.

Say the word, babygirl, and this all ends.

"ORANGE"! I scream the word DarkHeart1 gave me before for a safe word, hoping to God this man is just too fucking nuts or too wrapped up in his own fantasy to realize that I *do not* want to do this.

But nothing happens.

"ORANGE!" I scream again as best I can with the hand around my throat. "ORANGE! ORANGE! ORA—"

The monster laughs roughly through the mask.

"How fucking adorable that you think I give a single fuck about your so-called safe word."

Oh God.

He spins me brutally and roughly shoves me down across the hood of the car. I scream as he pins my cheek to the still-warm metal, his fist in my hair. He grabs the back of my dress with his other hand, and pure fear and revulsion lance into me as he yanks it up, exposing my bare ass.

He slaps it, hard.

"Orange…" I sob. *"Orange—"*

He slaps my ass again. Then suddenly, he's cupping my pussy through my panties.

"Whose fucking pussy is this."

I scream, my chest hitching as the fear pierces my heart.

"I asked you a fucking question, slut," the voice snarls.

"Orange…"

I whimper as something lands on the hood of the car next to my face. My eyes focus, and I shudder when I realize he's taken off his mask and flung it there.

"Whose fucking pussy is this, babygirl."

The whole universe freezes. Gravity inverts. My entire reality flickers like a glitch in the matrix.

For a long second or two, I can't move. Talk. Even think. All I can do is try to process it all.

How it's possible.

The fear was *so fucking real—*

I cry out when Kratos' palm smacks my ass hard again and then roughly cups my pussy through my panties. He starts to rub me savagely, the friction making my clit raw as his fist tightens in my hair.

I'm soaking his fingers in a *nanosecond*.

It's as if the last hour of panicked fear thinking I was actually about to get raped and killed in the woods all hits me at the same time. But with him here, pulling me out of the nightmare and baptizing me in my fucked-up fantasy, it all gets turned into pure desire.

I don't just want him. I literally, physically *need him* right now.

I cry out as Kratos yanks my thong aside. He brutally rams two fingers into my soaking wet pussy, wrenching a cry from my throat as my back arches.

"I asked you a fucking question, slut," he snarls, yanking my hair tight. "*Whose fucking pussy is this!?*"

"YOURS!" I sob. "It's—!"

He pulls out his fingers and rams his huge cock in to the fucking hilt. The breath leaves my body in a rush, my hips bruising hard against the side of the car. My raw, brutalized nipples drag across the metal as he grabs my hip and starts to fuck me, violently.

Viciously.

Punishingly.

I scream, my toes curling against the dirt and my legs shaking as Kratos fucks the living shit out of me.

"I fucking *own* this slutty cunt, babygirl. This is *my* fucking pussy. SAY IT."

I sob as I claw at the hood of the car, drowning in the twisted pleasure he's wringing from my body.

"Yours!" I cry out. "All yours!"

"Mine and *only* mine," he snarls.

He slaps my ass one last time before he pulls out. I whimper as he flips me over without warning and shoves me up onto the hood. My thighs are slapped apart, and I gasp as he wraps his fingers around my throat and shoves me back across the hood, pinning me there as he lines his fat cock up with my eager, soaking wet hole.

My back arches violently off the hood as he rams into me. When I open my eyes, they lock with his in the stark shadows of the inky blackness and the pale moonlight.

There's no mask between us. No walls.

Just us.

His lips curl like one possessed as he fucks into me, the sloppy wet sounds filling the little clearing. His hand slides from my neck, slipping down to slap my breasts again and maul and brutalize my nipples in ways that have me gushing all over his cock. He slaps at my face, pulls my hair, and shoves his fingers into my mouth, watching me suck them greedily as he fucks me like a wild animal.

Staking his claim. Rutting into his mate. Making me his. Owning me.

Destroying me.

His thumb slides between my lips, thrusting in and out of my mouth as I moan and whimper.

"*There's* my greedy little whore," he snarls. "There's my good little *slut*."

His massive cock rams into me, pushing so deep it feels like he's in my throat. Like he's running me through. Like I might never walk properly again.

Worth it.

He keeps his thumb between my lips as his huge fingers splay out, cupping my jaw and wrapping around my slender neck. His pace gets harder, faster, rougher and more manic. My vision blurs at the edges, and I gasp as my eyes roll back and I open my mouth from around his thumb, screaming and screaming and screaming for the monster snarling above me, leering down into my face as he shoves me over the brink and into oblivion.

No. Not "the" monster.

My monster.

My beast.

My husband.

My love.

Fuckkk.

With a shudder and a wrenching cry, my core clenches tight

and spasms. My spine bends back into an arc as my hips rise, and when I explode for him, it's like being reborn.

Kratos yanks me up and crushes his lips to mine. He rams into me, holding his huge cock all the way inside of me as he comes over and over, spilling his hot cum deep within me as I crumble to dust around him, lost in his lips.

Lost in our sweetest madness.

24

KRATOS

They say rules were meant to be broken.

It would appear that the woman wrapped in my arms, her breath tickling across my chest, is that saying personified.

I may be the one that chases her. *I* might be the one that pins *her* to the ground, and savages her, and drags her with claws and snarling teeth over every line she's ever had.

But slowly, surely, in ways I honestly never saw coming, she's the one who's pulled me as well, far, *far* beyond lines I said I'd never cross. Shattered rules I set for myself that I've never broken up till now.

Given me "firsts" I swore I'd never have.

A first kiss. Being someone's first. Even the way we're tangled in each other's limbs right now across the back seat of the town car I borrowed from Ares.

Aftercare. Pillow talk. *Snuggling.*

These are things I've obliterated from my lexicon. Things I "don't do".

And yet, here I am. Here *we* are.

Maybe it's not that I don't do snuggling, just that I never had Bianca before.

I know she's awake. But her eyes are closed peacefully, her cheek against my bare chest and her small hand splayed across my abs. I watch the way my own large hand slides down the defined muscles of her bare dancer's back. The way my big fingers splay across her ass, cupping the whole cheek in one hand.

She's so fucking breakable. So *crushable*. And yet, I know I'd bleed my last ounce of strength in these arms shielding her from harm, rather than being the cause of it.

Her lips curl into a smile as I reach down and brush a lock of her hair back from her face.

Yes, I was furious when I watched via the hack on her phone as she "reset" her match parameters on the Venom site. In her case, it didn't do shit, because I'd already locked that function in her account on the back end. But seeing she had that intent made me see red.

The fact that she wanted another man. Another player to go toe to toe with in these games of ours.

I could have stopped it there. I could have found her at the club I knew she was at, dragged her into the bathroom, and reminded her *whose she is*.

But that's not really a reminder, it's a threat. And I don't want threats being what keeps this woman at my side. I don't want anything "keeping" her there at all.

I want her to simply *want* to be there.

So I played her game. I indulged in a role, because I wanted to see—*had* to see—if she'd truly seek someone else.

In the end, she didn't. She walked away. And not because she got cold feet.

It was because she realized I'm the only one she wants. And that's all I needed to see.

…But, I mean, I already had the car borrowed from Ares. And I'd bought the wig and fake mustache. And who am I to turn down a chance to feast on her screams as I chase her through the dark?

I still have questions, though. Something spooked her and pushed her away, and it sure as hell wasn't just me getting cold with her after she freaked out in the bath.

My teeth grit as I replay that scene, when Bianca threw up her walls, rebuking intimacy—intimacy that takes *a lot* for me to find within myself. Intimacy I haven't ever sought out with another person. It fucking hurt. Hence, my frostiness afterward.

"Who is she?"

I frown, pulled from my thoughts as my attention slides down to Bianca's face against my chest. Her eyes are open now, staring into the dim, cocooned warmth of the back seat as she strokes a finger over my ribs.

"Who's who—"

Her finger stills.

"That woman, Kratos. Just…tell me," she says quietly. "Tell me if you fucked—"

It hits me like a backhand to the face and makes me want to roar. It makes me want to break something.

Namely, Amaya's fucking neck.

"You saw her leaving the house."

Bianca says nothing. She doesn't have to. Because in an instant it all clicks into place, and I can see it right there on her face.

She ran into Amaya leaving the brownstone after the bitch stopped by unannounced to threaten me with prison time. I can only assume the miserable cunt did or said something to send Bianca running, because that's the kind of fucking ghoul she is.

That's why Bianca left. It's why she went out, and drank, and tried to find someone else on the Venom site.

Son of a bitch.

I suck in slow breaths, trying to calm the beast roaring inside of me. My arms squeeze around her a little tighter.

"Please," Bianca whispers, taking my silence the wrong way. "Put me out of my misery. If it's going to hurt, just do it fast instead of—"

"Her name is Amaya Mircari."

Bianca stiffens in my arms.

"And *no*," I hiss quietly. "I didn't fucking touch her."

Bianca exhales swiftly against my chest.

"I'm guessing she insinuated that she did?"

Bianca's lips purse tightly.

That's a yes.

I look away, my eyes stabbing viciously out the tinted window into the darkness of the forest.

"I'm going to tell you something I've never told anyone."

I can't tell her that Amaya is CIA. Not because it could mean trouble for me if the people in my world found out I was talking with the Feds...though it would.

I'm not worried about me. But I'm worried about *her*. Bianca's in this criminal world, too. If she knows about this, it could put her in danger. And I won't have that.

Bianca looks up at me, her eyes darting over my face like she's working up the courage to say something. Finally, she does.

"Do the two of you have a history?"

I nod.

"*Oh,*" she says quietly, her voice breaking a little as she looks away.

"It's not what you think."

"Kratos, it's none of my—"

"My father liked to parade me around when I was a kid, like I was some sort of gladiatorial hero. His champion. Even when I was young, I was big and tough, and he liked showing me off to his buddies and business associates, like an attack dog that he kept on a short leash."

I swallow, my jaw grinding.

"It worked, of course. I got dragged into mafia sit-downs way younger than I had any right to be. Dad thought it made him look tough to have me standing behind him, the whole room knowing I was only like ten and still so menacing."

Bianca's face collapses. She lowers her mouth, softly kissing my chest.

"As I got older, he pushed for me to do more than just stand behind him. I went to drops, stopped by the offices of people who owed him money, that sort of thing. I was a fucking twelve-year-old mafia enforcer...which is exactly what he wanted."

My eyes close. A razor drags over my heart.

She needs to know this. I'll keep Amaya's CIA connection from Bianca, but she needs to know what made me the way I am. *Why* I'm the way I am. If that sends her running, so be it...

I want her to know.

"I met Amaya when I was thirteen," I growl. "She worked for some influential people that my father wanted to curry favor with, and she had an 'interest' in me. They worked out a trade. He got in with the powerful people, and she got what she wanted from me."

Bianca's brows knit. "And what—"

Her face goes white as she visibly chokes.

"*Oh my fucking God...!*"

"I was thirteen," I say quietly. "She was thirty."

Bianca chokes on a sob, clinging to me as she presses her face tight to my chest. Her body hitches, her tears hot on my skin as she kisses my chest, my neck, my face.

My heart wrenches as my arms tighten around her. The razorblades of the past slash into me, slicing the skin and flaying me open. And yet, there's a balm right in front of me.

A soothing, healing touch.

A cure.

"It went on for years," I continue slowly. "It's pretty much why I picked a college in London."

"*Kratos…*"

"She…taught me things."

Bianca's face turns ashen. Her head shakes side to side, tears streaming down her cheeks. "Why are you telling—"

"Because I need you to know," I growl, cupping her face as my eyes stab into hers. "If you're going to stay—"

"*Of course I'm going to stay.*"

My eyes search hers. "Then you need to understand, Bianca. You need to know why I'm…" I look away. "What broke me."

Her soft touch lands on my cheek. Small, delicate fingers stroke my skin, pulling my gaze back into hers.

"You're not broken, Kratos," she whispers in the dark.

I shake my head. "Yes, I—"

"Just because you're made differently it doesn't mean you're broken. The scars you bear or the pain you've suffered don't either." Her eyes capture mine. "You're just put together different." Her mouth twists in a wry smile. "Like me."

My lips press softly to hers, kissing her deeply as my arms encircle her small body. When she hitches out a small cry, I pull away sharply with a furrowed brow.

"Babygirl..."

"I…" Her eyes are blurry with tears. She wipes them with the back of her hand, looking away. "I have to tell you something, too."

My jaw goes rigid as I stroke her hair back from her face. I slide a thick finger over her cheek, brushing away a teardrop.

"When you tried to wash my hair earlier…"

"Don't worry about—"

"No, it's…" Her eyes squeeze shut and she takes a heavy breath. "It's not that I didn't want you too. I'd *love* it if you washed my hair," she chokes. "It's just…"

I cup her face again, stroking her cheek with my thumb. Her hand wraps around mine, pulling me closer.

"When I was a sophomore in high school, I started going out with this guy, Tim Ciglione. He was a senior, and all the girls mooned over him. You know the type: rich, popular, captain of the lacrosse team. And smug about all of it."

Her mouth tightens. Her eyes go a little darker.

So do mine as my blood begins to simmer.

"His dad had this huge, luxury penthouse with a rooftop pool and hot tub and everything, so when Tim decided to throw a party when his dad was going to be out of town, it was *the* party to be at. We'd only gone on a few dates, but he told me he wanted the night to be special, and that he really wanted me to be there so he could show me off to all the cool, popular people he was friends with. So, I arrive at the party and he's instantly all over me. Smiling at me, laughing at all my dumb jokes, touching me…"

The beast inside me snarls.

"Giving me drinks. Soon, I was pretty drunk, and in the hot tub alone with him." She looks at me furtively. "We… We'd never done anything besides kissing, so that's what we were doing…just kissing."

Rage explodes in my chest, but I nod for her to continue. I know in my heart that I don't want to hear this, but just as I needed her to know about Amaya, she needs me to know about this.

If it goes where the acid in my blood thinks it's going, though, I know there's only one conclusion to this story: me, finding this Tim motherfucker, and putting him in the goddamn ground.

"Eventually, I told him I had to go home. But he started pushing for more. You know, wanting to put his hands under my bikini, that sort of thing."

I see pure red.

"I said no, so he started pressing *me* to touch *him*. He…"

She swallows, looking away.

"You don't have to tell me, babygirl."

"Yes, I do. I want to."

She takes a shaky breath.

"He pulled his dick out, grabbed my head, and tried to, like, *guide it* there."

Mother. *Fucker.*

He's a dead man. Fucking *dead.*

"When I said no, he pulled harder. When I tried to move away, he…" She grimaces. "He pushed my head underwater and tried to force his dick into my mouth."

She shudders in my arms. I shove aside my rage as I hold her tight, wrapping my arms around her as she cries softly into my chest.

She doesn't need my rage and vengeance right now. She just needs this.

Vengeance can, and *will*, come later.

"Ever since then, I can't do water over my head," she says in a brittle voice. She laughs coldly. "And I used to *love* swimming. I was even on the dive team, and I was *good*. Now?" Her lips twist. "You should see my bathing routine, it's fucking pathetic. I mean, I wash my hair bending over the bath—"

"It's not pathetic," I growl, taking her hand in mine. "It's survival. It's how we keep it together and cover the scars. Don't ever let anyone tell you otherwise."

Our eyes lock in the darkness. My fingers tangle in her hair, pulling her lips to mine.

I was wrong.

There's nothing breakable about her at *all*.

25

BIANCA

SOMETHING *AMAZING* FILTERS into my nose as I come downstairs after my bath. The clatter of metal against utensils, mixed with James Brown and the hiss of sautéing, drifts from the kitchen as I head down the hall. When I step in, my brows shoot up.

Woah.

Kratos mentioned this morning that he wanted to cook dinner for me.

"What, like a DATE?" dorky-ass me teased.

"Exactly," he'd murmured back.

Then he bent me over the bathroom vanity, spanked my ass until it was hot and sizzling, and fucked me hard, making me watch myself come in the mirror in front of us.

So, yeah. Somewhere in there, I didn't connect that "making us dinner tonight" really meant "cooking up a storm in the kitchen."

I stand in the doorway, feeling a little heat tease over my skin as I eye him.

Shit.

Some men make dressing up look hot as hell, Kratos included. Other guys look super sexy in workout clothes or playing sports.

Also Kratos included.

But I'm not sure I've ever really taken a second to watch a man cook or move around the kitchen with surgical precision. And now I'm wishing I had before. Because holy wow.

It's hot as *fuck.*

He's in black jeans and a white t-shirt, a small towel slung over his shoulder and a chef's apron tied around his waist, slung low on his hips. Behind him, various pans sizzle. The knife in his hand is a blur as he dices something with vicious efficiency on the kitchen island. And another hot little tingle teases through my core as I watch the blade glint and slice.

It probably shouldn't be this sexy to watch a man wielding a lethal blade. But maybe it's that I've got first-hand knowledge of *other* ways he's good at using a knife.

He pauses, his eyes snapping to mine like he's just realized I'm standing there. His gaze drags over me, and I shiver as the hungry glint ripples through them.

Okay, so, *maybe* that look is exactly the reason I chose this dress—a short, flirty, Latin-inspired thing, in black. The halter neck ties at the back, the hem is cut on a sharp angle, slicing diagonally up from mid-calf on one side almost all the way to my hip on the other. I don't need a bra under it. Coupled with the heels, I already feel *hot.*

But when he looks at me like he wants to devour me like this, I feel downright scorching.

"You like?" I grin, twirling a little.

Kratos says nothing. But his jaw grinds, his eyes flashing pure lust as he drinks me in.

"You said you were cooking Spanish tonight."

"And you certainly did bring the spice," he growls quietly.

I blush as I step into the kitchen. My teeth rake over my bottom lip as I survey the scene in front of me.

"You…seriously cook." I laugh, shocked at the array of dishes being prepped. "I mean, I knew you *cooked*, but…"

"You thought I was bad at it."

I giggle again. "*No*. I've just never had your cooking."

"Tonight, that changes."

I shiver as his hand slides over my hip, spinning me a little before he leans down to kiss me. When he pulls away, he turns to flip something sautéing on the stove that smells like shrimp. Then he reaches over to the speaker on the counter. He switches from James Brown to a sultry, Latin tango before he turns back to the stove again.

"I do love listening to James Brown when I cook," he murmurs over the sizzle on the stovetop. "But if we're doing a theme tonight…"

I grin, watching him flip, and turn, and dice. My hips begin to sway with the slow thud of the music. My eyes drift shut as I start to dance. I can sense his gaze on me.

My eyes fly open, and blush deeply when I see Kratos leaning against the counter, eying me with a dark, hungry look.

"*What?*" I blush, biting my lip.

"You," he growls.

"And here you thought ballet dancers could only pirouette in tutus?"

He grins. "Never once crossed my mind."

I flush as our eyes lock.

"You've never seen me dance before, have you?"

"Yes, I have."

I roll my eyes. "*When?*"

He lifts a shoulder. "All the time, actually."

My brow furrows. "No, you haven't—"

"I watch you dance almost every day."

Something tightens in my chest and my pulse beats a little quicker, a little hotter.

"*What?*"

He shrugs, turning back to the stove with his tongs. "You're very good."

My skin heats as I watch him scrape sliced steak from a cutting board and into a pan full of spices and onions.

"You…really watch me?"

"Yup," he says without hesitation, stirring the meat. "All the time."

My bottom lip retreats between my teeth. "What, like, from the shadows?"

"Bingo."

I simmer.

"*Stalker*," I tease.

Then I'm gasping as Kratos whirls. His hand grabs my hip, yanking me to his huge body as his gaze locks on mine.

"Now now, babygirl," he murmurs quietly. "Let's not pretend that the idea of me stalking you doesn't make you wet."

Fuck.

Heat throbs in my core. My skin is on fire as his fingers dig into the flesh of my hip. The heat of the kitchen melts over me as the tango music purrs sensually in my ears. Kratos' hips begin to sway. He drops the tongs onto the counter by the stove, putting both hands on my hips before one slides possessively to the small of my back.

Then we start to dance.

It's slow and teasing. Sensual and fierce. His eyes lock with mine, his strong hands gripping and twirling my body effort-lessly as we dance around the kitchen. I gasp when he backs me up hard against the fridge, leaning down close, ready to either kiss me or devour me. But before he even makes contact, he's pulling away and dancing us slowly around the kitchen again.

"You know how to tango?" I smile incredulously.

He smirks. "Apparently so."

"*How?*"

He shrugs dismissively. "I took lessons with Ya-ya a while back."

"You...learned to tango with your *grandmother*?"

"It was a birthday present, and she was really stoked about it," he grunts with a wry smile. "*Chill.*"

I giggle, then gasp as he spins me and pulls me into his arms.

"They really do think of you as such a good boy, don't they?"

His lips curl. "Indeed. Got 'em all fooled."

"You don't fool me," I breathe.

"*Good.* Now, please, let's not talk about my grandmother anymore."

I shiver as he spins us around, dipping me low and then bringing me back up again. His arm muscles ripple and bulge at the arms of his t-shirt, his veined forearms cording as he turns us once more.

Our bodies are pressed hotly together, facing each other, my nipples dragging electrically against his chest through his shirt and my dress. My thighs feel slick, and my pulse roars as we dance body-to-body to the sensual tango music.

Kratos' hands tighten around me even more. Our faces move closer together.

The fucking kitchen timer goes off.

I bite back a groan of sexual frustration as he pulls away with a smirk. "Dinner's ready."

THE BACK YARD isn't finished or fully landscaped yet. But it's gorgeous outside, and I seriously couldn't care less that all the bluestone pavers aren't down, or that not all the plants are in.

There's a small café table outside and two chairs. Add in food, wine, and *him?*

That's all I need.

Also, it turns out Kratos isn't just good at making cooking look sexy: he's also an insanely talented chef. We eat course after course of regional Spanish cuisine, from *gambas al ajillo*, *boquerones*, and *albondigas* to a a truly *delicious* steak and seafood paella, all paired with appropriate wines.

It might be the best date of my entire life.

It's dark out by the time we're done with dinner. And I'm laughing, full, and well past "buzzed" and into "drunk". Which is obviously, I decide, the perfect time to segue into tequila.

Straight from the bottle.

Kratos arches a quizzical brow at me as I come sauntering back out of the house into the yard carrying a bottle of añejo.

"Gonna be *that* kind of night, huh?"

"Uh-huh," I grin.

"Well, in that case…" He turns and cranks the volume on the outside speaker. Sultry tango music filters in to the back yard and I pull the cap off, my eyes fixed on Kratos' amused ones as I take a sip straight from the bottle.

I sidle over to him, passing him the tequila as my hips begin to sway to the music. Kratos' eyes stay on me as he takes a heavy sip, keeping the bottle in his hand. A soft, warm rain begins to sprinkle down. But it's still gorgeous out, I'm not ready to go in yet, and it's not heavy.

So I keep dancing, slowly swaying my hips and raising my arms as my fingers push through my hair.

"I want to watch you dance some more," he rumbles quietly.

I twist, glancing at him over my bare shoulder as my hips undulate.

"Yeah?"

There's something dangerous and primal in his gaze. A dark hunger that gets my blood pumping hot and my thighs clenching. I can feel my nipples pebble and tighten under the dress as my teeth rake over my lip.

"Yeah. Dance for me, babygirl."

An erotic, sultry heat pulses deep in me as I keep dancing and swaying my hips. My eyes close, my fingers shoving slowly through my hair before my hands glide down my body.

I know how to do almost any style of dance, and I know how to move my body. But this is a first. Maybe I've danced like this in a club full of other people. But I've never done it in front of someone.

Never done it in front of a man who's looking at me like he wants to lick me from the inside out and then swallow me whole.

I turn again, swaying my hips to the music as my eyes zone in on his. Kratos takes another pull of tequila, his gaze still roving hungrily over my body. I dance closer to him, reaching for the bottle, then gasp quietly when he roughly grabs my wrist and yanks me into his lap.

The rain begins to fall a little more heavily. But the drops are warm, and the feel of them teasing lightly over my skin and soaking my dress is a turn on. I take the tequila from his hand, taking a slow sip and whimpering softly when his mouth finds my neck.

His lips fasten on the soft skin there. I gasp sharply at the pierce of his teeth. I take another sip of tequila. This time, I don't swallow. I let it trickle out of my mouth, trailing down my chin to my neck. Kratos' growl rumbles against my jugular as he licks the tequila from my skin, his fingers tightening on my hips.

Suddenly, his hands are gliding up my back. He tugs the tie behind my neck, letting the top of my dress tumble down between us and my breasts spill free.

He growls quietly as he dips his head. His eyes lock with mine as he wraps his lips around one tight, pink, puckered nipple. I squeal as he bites down, viciously tugging and twisting the little bud between his teeth as I moan with desire. I take another sip, again letting the tequila dribble down my chin and onto my chest for him to lap up as my hips grind on his lap.

We're both panting as he suddenly slides his hands under my dress. I moan when I feel him yank his jeans open, and when I feel the huge thickness of his fat cock throbbing against my thigh, my breath catches.

His thick fingers yank my thong aside. He centers his swollen head at my eager, dripping wet lips. One hand wraps around my throat, the other gripping my hip. And in one thrust, he rams up, burying his cock inside my tight wetness in one brutal stroke.

"*Fuuuuck*," I groan, simmering with pleasure at the feel of him impaling me on his dick.

I don't think I'll ever get used to how big he is. But I love that. I love that it feels like he's sliding into me for the first time, every time.

I cry out as he lifts me up and yanks me back down, squeezing his fat dick into my swollen little pussy as my eyes roll back in bliss.

Maybe it's the masochist in me: the need for a little pain. For a little sour with the sweet.

The way I crave the Heaven and the Hell of him equally.

I just know I'll never not want this. I'll never want anything *but* this.

Kratos' hands are everywhere: squeezing around my throat, slapping my ass. Gripping my hips and mauling my breasts as his teeth rake down my jawline and my neck. My arms wrap tight around him, my hands gripping the back of his hair as I throw my head back, feeling the warm rain and the tequila heat wash over us both.

He rips his shirt off, and I shiver at the electric feel of my nipples dragging against his bare chest. His fingers dig into me as he grabs the bottle of tequila and takes a sip. Then he's kissing me hard, letting the añejo swirl and dance from his tongue to mine as I ride his big dick and bounce in his muscled lap.

The rain comes down harder. The sultry music surrounds us. The wet slipperiness of skin against skin and the slick squeeze of my pussy around his length drives us higher and higher as I squeal for more.

His finger drags down the cleft of my ass, pushing against my tight little back hole. My eyes flare, an erotic electricity coursing through my system as he teases me and slowly pushes his thick finger inside.

I grab him, kissing him hard and screaming into his mouth as I start to come undone, riding him for all I can. Kratos groans into my mouth, fucking up into me hard and ruthlessly, without mercy. His hand roughly pinches my nipple before sliding up to grip my throat tightly.

"*Good girl.*"

With another wail, I'm coming, and I'm coming *hard*. I can feel my entire body spasm and tighten, my pussy clenching and rippling up and down the thick length of him as he swells even bigger inside me. His hand roughly grips my chin, his thumb and forefinger pinching my lip and yanking my mouth to his as he kisses me deeply.

He groans into my lips as hot ropes of his cum spill deep inside me. I moan wildly and keep riding him, rolling my hips against him over and over until we both come apart.

We stay outside for so long I lose track of time. Just kissing as the rain comes down. Just holding each other as the world spins around us.

This is no longer a game of cat and mouse. It isn't a game of tag anymore, either.

This might be the most real thing I've ever felt in my life.

26

KRATOS

With a ten and a seven, hitting again is insanely risky. But I'm feeling a little reckless, and I'm in a fantastic mood. One, I can still taste Bianca's pussy on my tongue from when I pinned her to the floor earlier, before I went out. And two, I'm not *really* here to gamble tonight.

What I'm here for is a sure thing.

Situated beneath a dry cleaner's, a hipster bar, and a lingerie boutique, the Bratva-run Black Swan is one of New York's most exclusive, luxurious, and decidedly high-rollers-only underground casinos. I'm not much of a gambler myself. But I know that most of the people who come here to play cards, toss dice, or bet on sports or fights are all members of criminal organizations. The few that aren't but are crazy enough to want to play cards with gangsters for large sums of money are either, A: mafia-adjacent, or B: low-lifes and scumbags who've been barred from every legitimate casino in the New York area.

My target this evening falls squarely in category B. And knowing that he's here tonight is at least eighty percent the cause of the smile on my face.

…The other twenty being that despite not being much of a card player, I'm doing pretty great.

The dealer drops a card in front of me. Instantly, the whole table groans. Some of the players clap, and the Japanese Yakuza looking guy next to me nods his approval as he pats my arm.

I just hit the four of clubs on seventeen.

Twenty-one, baby.

I grin as the dealer pushes my sizable winnings toward me. But again, I'm not only smiling because of this.

I'm smiling because after two weeks of prying, hunting, and outright stalking, I've finally cornered my prey tonight.

Tim Ciglione, who now works for some douchebag hedge fund in the city, isn't just a scumbag piece of shit because he tried to force Bianca to blow him in a hot tub seven years ago. He's also the kind of scumbag with a gambling problem who gets barred from upstanding, mainstream casinos. That's why he's here, probably triple leveraging his own house or his grandmother's pension chasing the gambler's high.

Oh, and for extra fuckhead points, Tim also likes to slap his wife around when he's drunk—and *not* in a way she might like. He's also fucking his secretary.

Classy.

Anyway, he's about to have a very, *very* bad night. It's no accident I've chosen this table. From where I'm sitting, I can look across the room to see Tim balls-deep in losing his shirt at a high-stakes poker table. Even from here, I can smell the stench of desperation radiating off him, even with his back to me. His hair is fucked up from constantly running his fingers through it. He's ditched his jacket and his tie, his hand rubbing the back of his neck nervously.

With a smirk, I glance back down at my chips. I've got some time yet. It's when he's done at the table that I'll be making my move.

"Well," I smile, organizing my winnings into neat stacks. "Shall we play again?"

"I'm afraid the table's gone cold. My apologies to you all."

My ears perk up at the familiar voice. My eyes lift, my brow arching curiously.

The dealer has left. And in his place, looking right at me, sits a very stoic Lukas Komarov.

Around us, the other blackjack players shrug as they collect their chips and stand from the table. I clear my throat, sitting back in my chair with my arms folded over my chest.

"Lukas," I growl quietly with a nod at the man clad in a black suit with a black shirt, buttoned all the way up but without a tie.

He leans back in his chair, drumming his fingers on the table. "What are you doing in my casino, Kratos."

I arch a brow. "I was under the impression that this was Dima Novikov's casino."

"On paper, sure." His fingertips walk across the green baize of the card table. "So again, Kratos. What exactly are you doing here?"

"Blackjack, mainly. I hear it's the best odds for the player."

He looks the opposite of amused.

"Is that a problem, Lukas?"

"No," he murmurs. "But you don't gamble."

"You don't know that."

He smiles. "Actually, I do."

I could argue, but we're talking *Lukas* here. I might be good at stalking and hunting for prey or information. But Lukas Komarov is on another level.

"Because I like and respect you, let me make this clear for you, Kratos," he murmurs quietly, leaning forward. "Trust me when I say the usual mayhem you're looking for when you go out at night will not be found here. Drinks? Yes. Degenerate gamblers? Also yes. And I'm not gonna lie to you, you'll probably find fantastic cocaine and pretty much any other poison you might be partial to, if you ask the right people." His smile fades. "But my concern is that you're after your usual choice in vices, which matches my own. If you're looking for that here, you're wasting your time."

I shake my head. "I'm not looking for traffickers."

"What, then."

"I'm here to right a wrong."

"Personal?"

"You could say that. Someone hurt someone I care about." My pulse drums. "Someone I love."

Lukas' brow furrows. "And the nature of this wrong?"

"Sexual assault."

His face goes grim. *"Really,"* he growls.

I nod. "He likes to gamble, and he's in deep tonight..." I level a gaze across the table at Lukas. "And I'm *not* leaving without taking care of this. But I also didn't realize this was your place. So, for the trouble, I can pay—"

"I don't want your money, Kratos."

"Then I'll be in your debt for a favor."

He shakes his head. "Not that either."

Lukas rises from his seat, buttoning his black suit jacket. He walks around the table and drops a hand on my shoulder heavily as he leans close.

"Just try not to make a mess," he murmurs quietly. "Happy hunting, my friend."

Great minds think alike.

I stand from the table, pocketing my hefty winnings and stopping by the bar for a drink. I sip the whiskey slowly, eyeing the poker table across the room. Tim is spiraling, I can see it from here. He shoves his fingers through his greasy, thinning hair, looking nervous. The dealer flips the river, and I can almost hear Tim's stomach hitting the floor from here. He's just lost *more* money.

I wait until he stands on wobbly feet. He slams back his drink and turns to stagger toward the restroom.

My lips curl dangerously.

Go time.

Tim is in the middle of pissing into one of the urinals when I grab him. He squeals like a stuck pig, screaming and thrashing and getting pee all over himself as I yank him by the back of his collar across the bathroom floor.

I kick open the stall door, dragging him inside and punching him hard in the face. His nose breaks, and he screams and burbles in agony as blood gushes down over his mouth. Without so much as a word, I grab the scruff of his neck, yank him to the toilet, and shove his face down into it.

I wait there for a moment, cracking my neck and rolling my shoulders as I easily hold Tim's flailing, spasming body to the floor with his head in the toilet bowl. After about thirty seconds, I yank him out again, sputtering and choking and screaming as he blindly wipes bloodied, pink-tinged toilet water from his face.

"*Please!!*" he bleats. "Please! Tell him I'll pay! I swear to fuck I'll pay! I've got it, too!" he screams, clinging to my pants, begging on his knees. I scowl down at him and kick my leg, shaking him off like an annoying insect.

"This isn't about money, Tim."

He pales as I say his name.

"It's—it's not?"

"Nah."

I grab his neck and shove his face back into the toilet. This time, I drag it out a little longer, letting him truly feel the icy grip of death as the threat of drowning has him spasming and kicking.

He chokes and immediately vomits up toilet water when I drag him out again.

"Being held underwater *sucks*, doesn't it, Tim?"

He stares up at me with bleary, unfocused eyes. "W-what?"

He reels when I punch him in the mouth.

"Being grabbed, Tim," I hiss through clenched teeth. "And forced, against your will, underwater."

He blinks again, shaking. "I—I have no idea what you're talking—"

"Wrong answer."

The back of his head rattles the stall wall when I punch him again. His eyes bulge as I grab his throat and snarl down into his face.

"If you so much as *think* about telling me you're not sure *whose* head I'm talking about you holding underwater, I'll rip your goddamn throat out right here and now."

His face goes ashen as the penny drops.

"*P-please...*" he chokes, his voice quieter now, full of true fear. "Please, I never—"

"Never *what*, Tim? Gave a fuck whether she had any interest in sucking your pathetic excuse for a dick?" I snap, smirking at his shriveled "manhood" poking out of his fly.

He swallows violently, trembling as he looks up at me.

"Who...who is she to you?"

My wrath fills the bathroom as I leer down over him.

"*She's my wife.*"

"Oh God, please!" he squeals. "C'mon, man! *Please*!! I was a just a kid! You know? Just being stupid!"

"*Boys will be boys*, right, Tim?" I snarl. "Just *having a little fun* when you fucking shoved her head under the water?"

My hand clamps hard around his throat, squeezing until I see his eyes start from his head.

"*Please!*" he croaks. "Please! I have a wife!"

"You *hit* your wife, you piece of shit," I grunt. "*And* you're cheating on her. Try again."

His croak turns into a gurgle as I shove his face back down into the toilet bowl. When I pull him out, he sputters, choking and wiping water and blood out of his eyes.

"If I die, they'll go after *her* for the debt!"

Goddammit.

I exhale heavily.

Don't get involved. Don't get—

"Who will," I growl.

He swallows, his eyes darting around nervously.

"*Deep breath...*" I growl as I grab his hair.

"WAIT!"

My eyes narrow. "The Italians?"

A violent shake of his head.

"Not the Russians, surely…"

He smiles weakly, and I groan.

"You *dumb motherfucker*. You borrowed from the fucking *Bratva*?!"

He nods vigorously, looking ill.

"I'm guessing these fine gentlemen are all with you?" I mutter at Arian.

"You guess correctly. Let him go, Kratos."

"Yeah!" Grisha slurs, shoving at me. "Take your fuckin' hands off me!"

I don't mention that he was the one who suggested going another round. Instead, I just turn back to Arian, my hand still at Grisha's throat.

"I think you need and deserve a better class of friend, Arian."

"*Kratos...*" he warns.

With a grimace, I let the Russian shit-stain go. Ignoring his mutters and insults, I turn fully to Arian, my brow creasing.

"I didn't realize Te Mallkuarit did business with the Bratva."

Arian lifts a shoulder. "Who says we do?"

"Your questionable choice in poker buddies for the evening."

Arian just shrugs again, not confirming or denying a thing.

"So, *are you?*"

"Am I what, Kratos."

"Friends with the Russians."

"I'm friends with lots of people."

"How about this fucker's boss. Boris Chernoff."

Arian smiles thinly. "I didn't come to a casino tonight to be interrogated, Kratos."

I shake my head. "Not my intention. I was merely hoping you could help me tie off a loose end." I jam my hand into my pocket and pull out a dozen or so twenty-five-thousand-dollar chips before I pass them into the hands of a confused looking Arian. "This is to settle a debt Boris is owed by a certain Tim Ciglione. He has a wife. She's off the hook for anything after this."

Arian eyes me with a curious look. "Why not give this to Mr. Lenkov to pass along to his boss?"

"Because Mr. Lenkov is a fucking Muppet," I growl.

"*Fuck you!*"

"You're a guest here, Grisha," Arian glares past me, a warning note in his voice. "Control yourself." His eyes shift back to me, and he nods stiffly. "Consider it done."

"Thank you. I owe you." I clap his shoulder. "And again, my condolences on your father."

I'm turning to leave when suddenly, I hear the coughing hork of someone clearing phlegm from their throat.

Then something wet and disgusting hits the back of my head.

I go still and my shoulders stiffen before I slowly turn. Grisha is leering at me with a smug look on his drunk face.

Looks like I'm going to owe Lukas *two* favors by the end of tonight.

Arian groans, pinching the bridge of his nose. "*You dumb fuck*," he mutters quietly.

Grisha grins at him. "Wha?"

Arian's gaze drifts back to me. He sighs heavily, slipping the chips I gave him into his jacket pocket before he raises a finger.

"*Who.*"

His lips clamp shut.

"Tim, the next time you go in that toilet bowl, I'm fucking pissing in it at the same time. *Who.*"

If you knew me—the real me—you wouldn't necessarily think I had any weak points. But I do: innocent bystanders. People who have the misfortune of being around fuckheads like Tim.

I might be perfectly content flushing his face in the toilet until he drowns. But he's not wrong: if he croaks, the Russians will get the money he owes out of his wife, one way or another.

Tim squeals as I grab the back of his shirt and haul him, dripping toilet water, out of the stall and across the floor of the restroom. I slam him against the wall and let him crumple to the floor. Then I start to wash my hands.

"Chernoff!" he finally blubbers. "Boris Chernoff!"

I glare down at him.

You fucking idiot.

"Him and that fucking spooky witch of his!"

My brow furrows as I soap my hands. "Who's that?"

"*I* don't know!" he cries. "Chernoff's new attack dog. She's like his new consigliere, or whatever that is for the Bratva!"

I have no idea who he's talking about. But then, I don't pay that much attention to Bratva shit.

"How much do you owe Chernoff?"

He gulps weakly. "Three hundred grand."

I grit my teeth. I can't believe I'm about to spare this piece of shit's life for a measly three hundred grand. But I won't have his wife, whose only crime was saying "I do" to this walking choad, getting dragged into this.

"How much cash do you have on—"

Movement behind me pulls my attention up from the sink. In the mirror, I see Tim stumble to his feet, glance at me with terror in his eyes, and then lurch for the bathroom door. I roll my eyes as I turn.

"You're not seriously going to make a run for it, are—"

Tim's feet skid out, slipping on the toilet water. He gasps as he tips backward, a shocked expression on his dumb face as his world goes upside-down. With a choked bleat, he somehow does a half backflip before landing on the floor, head-first, with a sickening crunch sound.

The bathroom goes silent.

Fuck.

"Tim?"

I frown as I walk over, then crouch down to slap his face once or twice. "Tim."

Blood begins to form a puddle under his head. There's no *way* his neck is supposed to be at that angle. My fingers go to his jugular, and my jaw grinds.

Shit.

He's dead.

I exhale as I roll my shoulders and stand, staring down at him. Now, I'm not in any way shape or form *bent out of shape* about it. But it does look like I'm going to owe Lukas a favor after all.

I mean, he did ask me not to make a mess.

I'm on my way out of the Black Swan when someone catches my eye in one of the side poker rooms: Arian Kirakosian, sipping a glass of something, a grimace on his face.

Just leave, idiot.

I exhale with a groan.

In many respects—okay, in just about every respect—Bianca has been a one-thousand-percent net positive influence on my life. I'm noticing the goodness in the world. I sleep better at night. My...and my beast's...need for bloodshed and violence is certainly tempered.

Come to think of it, I don't think I've killed at all since she crashed into my life like a goddamn basket of daisies and kittens. Tim just now doesn't count. That's his fault for running like a fucking idiot.

But there's one side effect of overdosing on Bianca that's a pain in the ass: I've got this thing now where I *care*.

It's a habit I can't seem to shake these days, and it's a thorn in my fucking side. Every logical thought says to just walk the hell out of this casino right now. To leave well enough alone when it comes to Arian and the Albanians. And yet, even as I'm telling myself to walk the fuck away, go figure, my feet are carrying me into the room until I'm standing right in front of Arian.

The Bianca Effect, ladies and gentlemen, in all its chaotic glory.

Arian arches a brow as I stop in front of him.

"My condolences for your loss, Arian," I nod stiffly. "Your father was a good man."

He smiles wanly at me, but he nods back. "I appreciate that. He was short-sighted, maybe a little naive at times..." He shakes his head. "But thank you, Kratos." He clears his throat. "I, ah, didn't know you played cards."

"I don't," I rumble. "Just here tying up a loose end."

He smirks. "Should I be worried?"

"Not unless you need to piss anytime soon."

He gives me a curious look. Just then, someone shoves me in the back, hard.

"What the fuck is *he* doing here?" a voice slurs.

I turn. When my gaze lands on Grisha Lenkov, swaying on his feet with a drink in his hand and a snarl on his face, my eyes darken.

"You wanna go another round, you fuckin' *bitch*?" Grisha mumbles, breathing pure vodka in my face.

Goodness, that sounds like a *fantastic* idea.

Grisha's eyes go wide as I grab him by the throat and wind my other hand up to smash his face in on principle. Suddenly, someone grabs my arm.

"Mr. Lenkov is a *guest* of mine tonight, Kratos," Arian hisses, eyeing me coldly.

I'm about to make a sharp reply when I realize that just about every other guy in the room is looking at me with their hands hovering near their hips or the fronts of their jackets.

"I'm guessing these fine gentlemen are all with you?" I mutter at Arian.

"You guess correctly. Let him go, Kratos."

"Yeah!" Grisha slurs, shoving at me. "Take your fuckin' hands off me!"

I don't mention that he was the one who suggested going another round. Instead, I just turn back to Arian, my hand still at Grisha's throat.

"I think you need and deserve a better class of friend, Arian."

"*Kratos…*" he warns.

With a grimace, I let the Russian shit-stain go. Ignoring his mutters and insults, I turn fully to Arian, my brow creasing.

"I didn't realize Te Mallkuarit did business with the Bratva."

Arian lifts a shoulder. "Who says we do?"

"Your questionable choice in poker buddies for the evening."

Arian just shrugs again, not confirming or denying a thing.

"So, *are you?*"

"Am I what, Kratos."

"Friends with the Russians."

"I'm friends with lots of people."

"How about this fucker's boss. Boris Chernoff."

Arian smiles thinly. "I didn't come to a casino tonight to be interrogated, Kratos."

I shake my head. "Not my intention. I was merely hoping you could help me tie off a loose end." I jam my hand into my pocket and pull out a dozen or so twenty-five-thousand-dollar chips before I pass them into the hands of a confused looking Arian. "This is to settle a debt Boris is owed by a certain Tim Ciglione. He has a wife. She's off the hook for anything after this."

Arian eyes me with a curious look. "Why not give this to Mr. Lenkov to pass along to his boss?"

"Because Mr. Lenkov is a fucking Muppet," I growl.

"*Fuck you!*"

"You're a guest here, Grisha," Arian glares past me, a warning note in his voice. "Control yourself." His eyes shift back to me, and he nods stiffly. "Consider it done."

"Thank you. I owe you." I clap his shoulder. "And again, my condolences on your father."

I'm turning to leave when suddenly, I hear the coughing hork of someone clearing phlegm from their throat.

Then something wet and disgusting hits the back of my head.

I go still and my shoulders stiffen before I slowly turn. Grisha is leering at me with a smug look on his drunk face.

Looks like I'm going to owe Lukas *two* favors by the end of tonight.

Arian groans, pinching the bridge of his nose. "*You dumb fuck*," he mutters quietly.

Grisha grins at him. "Wha?"

Arian's gaze drifts back to me. He sighs heavily, slipping the chips I gave him into his jacket pocket before he raises a finger.

"You get one hit. *One.*"

The smug grin drops like a stone from Grisha's face. He whirls to Arian. "Wait, *what?!*"

I smile a shark-like grin as I roll my neck and turn to Grisha.

"Don't worry. I'll make it count."

———

BIANCA'S READING IN BED—*OUR* bed—when I get home. Wordlessly, I walk over to her as she puts the book down and grins at me.

"Hey, you—"

"Come with me."

She frowns curiously as I kiss her softly, then take her hand.

"Where—"

"Just come."

I usher her into the bathroom. I leave the lights off and light a couple of candles on the vanity, until the walls are glowing and flickering softly. Without a word, I start to fill the tub with warm water. I place a folded towel next to it, like she always does, before turning to her.

"Clothes off."

She smiles, an intrigued look on her face.

"This is new."

"What is?"

"You don't usually ask permission before my clothes come off."

I smile. "That's not what this is about. Just… Take them off."

She does. I watch hungrily, shamelessly devouring her body with my eyes. But again, that's not what this is.

At least, not yet.

"Kneel down."

She stiffens a little. "What—"

"I'm going to wash your hair."

Her lip disappears between her teeth. "Kratos…"

"Something in your past hurt you. It scared you, and scarred you, and took away what should be a simple pleasure." I stand and walk over to her, taking her hands in mine. "That thing doesn't exist anymore. It no longer has any power over you."

She probably knows me well enough by now to be able to read between the lines. She might even see it on my face, and guess what happened tonight. But she doesn't say anything, and it's not because she's scared of me, or the beast that lurks inside me.

Not anymore.

It's because she understands me. She knows what I am, and she *accepts* what I am. Entirely.

And maybe…just maybe…the darkness in her that mirrors my own is close enough to mine that she feels the same sense of elation knowing that the shadow from her past is gone.

Slowly, her eyes locked with mine, she nods her chin.

"*Okay*," she says in a small voice.

I lead her to the tub and squat down next to where she kneels on the towel and leans over the water. My fingers comb through her hair, pulling it forward and letting it touch the water. I use a cup to gently pour warm water over her long hair. Bianca stiffens a little at first, and her breath comes faster than normal.

But slowly, it turns peaceful. Slowly, her shoulders relax.

Her eyes close, and a small smile curls the corners of her lips.

I shampoo her hair for a long time, slowly, sudsing every lock ever so gently with my fingers. I rinse out the shampoo and then add conditioner, again taking the time to massage her scalp and run my fingers through her hair before I rinse that out too.

When we're done, her shoulders hitch a little. After I drape a towel around her, and then bundle her hair up in another one, she turns to me, a single tear beading in her eye as her lips pull into a smile.

Her hand reaches out, cupping my face.

"*I love you*," she whispers quietly in the stillness of the bathroom.

"I love you too."

27

KRATOS

"CREEP."

A smile spreads across my face. Twisting my head, I turn to let my eyes pierce the shadows. Bianca's in her leotard and tights, arms folded over her chest as she smirks at me.

"So. Busted," she grins.

"I never should have told you about me spying on you."

I've wondered how long it would take her to figure out where I watch her from at the theater. For a few weeks now, since I admitted to Bianca that I do it, I've watched from this very seat as she's tried to figure out where I'm hiding.

Doubting, I'm sure, if I even am.

But today, she's found me in my secret perch high up in one of the private boxes to the side of the stage, hidden within the curtains.

Down below, Madame Kuzmina barks orders, her ominous black shawl swishing. The array of ornate rings on her fingers glints in the stage lights as she brandishes a literal wooden switch—like they'd use for disciplining students in the 1800s—at the dancers.

Not that I'd ever have reason to, but I'm sure I'd never in a million years want to tangle with that woman. She's terrifying.

We're well hidden by the curtain as Bianca muffles her shriek with her hand as I yank her off her feet and into my lap. She breathes haltingly as her legs spread to either side of my thighs, the apex of her tights pulled snug against her pubic mound and pressing hard against my cock in my jeans.

"You know what I want to do right now?" she whispers, trembling as my mouth drags up her neck, biting her skin lightly.

"Is it what I want to do too?"

She moans a little. "You say first."

"Cut that sexy leotard and tights off of you with a blade, bite your nipples until you're writhing for me, and then fuck you over the railing of the box."

Bianca swallows, her eyes widening in the dim light as her breath hitches. Her nipples harden under her leotard, her face flushing darkly.

"Your turn," I murmur. She yelps and then bites her hand as I reach up to pinch one of those far-too-tempting nipples through the fabric, making it pebble even more.

"No, I like your idea," she whispers feverishly. "I was going to say something lame like kiss you."

"Not lame at all," I murmur as I grab a handful of her hair and crush my mouth to hers.

Fuck, I'll never tire of the way her breathy whimpers hum softly in her throat when I kiss her aggressively.

"Unfortunately, I'm going to get screamed at to come back to the stage in like sixty seconds," she sighs.

I smile. "I've got a work thing now anyway."

Her brow darkens a little.

"Just a meeting."

I haven't told Bianca every single detail of what my job entails. But, I mean, she grew up in the mafia. She understands how this works, and what I am, and how I use what I am for my family's benefit. Still, I know it worries her when I get called to go out someplace late and come back with bruised knuckles or blood on my shoes.

"Like a meeting-meeting, or the kind where I should have an ice pack ready for your hands?"

I grin as I cup her face and kiss her. "The only ice I'll need is for my drink. It's a sit-down thing. Gentlemanly. Civilized."

"*You?*" she scoffs. "Civilized and gentlemanly? I call bullshit."

I chuckle deeply as I kiss her again. "Careful. Or I'll show you how uncivilized I can be."

"Is that a promise?"

"You'll find out after dinner tonight at home."

She grins hungrily, her hips rocking as she slowly grinds herself into my lap.

"Deal."

"Careful," I murmur.

"Of?"

"Keeping that up, because I'll make even Madame Kuzmina wait until I'm done fucking you."

Her face blooms with heat, but she still gasps dramatically. "You wouldn't *dare* defy—"

"Understudies!" Madame K's cold, cigarette-tinged voice booms through the theater. "To the stage, NOW!"

"That woman is fucking *terrifying*," I mutter.

"She's really nice once you get to know her," Bianca ventures.

"Understudies!! RIGHT FUCKING NOW, LADIES AND GENTLEMEN!"

My brow arches skeptically. "Really."

Bianca giggles. "Actually? No." She sighs as she slides off my lap, pouting. "So, until dinner tonight."

"Tonight it is."

She beams as she leans down to kiss me again. "See you then. Love you."

"Love you too."

Well, shit. If my beast isn't curled up quietly in a corner of his cage.

Content.

"THANKS FOR COMING, KRATOS."

I nod as Arian ushers me into his study—I guess it's his late father's study—in the sprawling Upper West Side Gilded Age mansion which he now owns. I'm vaguely aware that Arian has a younger sister, but I'm unclear if she has much or anything to do with the family business. Regardless, she's at college right now at Knightsblood University.

"Good to see you again, Arian."

Honestly, I was wrong about him. Everything I'd heard about Davit's son was that he was an aggressive prick. When I first met him, when I stopped over here to chat with his dad before Bianca's and my engagement party, he seemed to live up to that hype.

But at the Black Swan the other night, he was calm, collected, and seemed to have his shit together—well, aside from hanging out with shits like Grisha Lenkov. And now again today, the man who greets me isn't the scowling, snarling prick who all but told me to go fuck myself when I came to see his father.

"I hope the aftermath of my...*disagreement* with your guest the other night didn't cause too much trouble for you."

He smirks. "Not really. Truth be told, I think Grisha was so drunk he might not have felt a punch even from you." He clears his throat. "Oh, and I passed on your message to Mr. Chernoff. The man who owed him seems to have skipped town. But Mr. Chernoff appreciated the debt being settled, however unorthodoxly. He considers the matter closed."

I nod. "I owe you."

His brow furrows a little before he shakes it off. "Don't worry about it. Can I offer you a drink?"

"Whatever you're having is perfect, thank you," I nod.

Arian pours us a couple of scotches, handing me a crystal tumbler before we both take seats on the couches by the windows. He takes a sip of his drink and then exhales slowly.

"I owe you an apology, Kratos."

My brow furrows. "For…?"

"My behavior, the first day we met, here in this office. I was…not myself."

I shake my head. "It's nothing, Arian. You had a lot to deal with. Your father was sick—"

"That's not entirely it. Though I appreciate the out." He takes another sip of his drink before his brow deepens slightly. "It was my idea to lend your family the crucifix, you know. And the reason I was so pissed off when it got blown to hell isn't because I give a shit about a bunch of old bones that my father's mysticism-junky advisors get hard for. It's because when it got fucked, I thought that was it for a potential alliance between your family and mine."

I nod. "Again, you have my sincere apologies—"

"*It isn't about the damn bones*, Kratos," he growls quietly. "This is about something bigger."

He scowls, knocking back the rest of his drink before setting the glass on the table between us. He steeples his hands as he leans back against the sofa, his foot over one knee.

"Were you aware that the Barone family had another party interested in their West Side development project, before inking a deal with your family?"

I shrug. "I would assume they had a few offers. Though, yes, I know during the later stages of negotiations, we were aware of one other aggressive interested party. But they dropped out when we radically upped our price."

Arian nods slowly. "You mean when Drazen Krylov became a silent partner in the deal, using his considerable assets to bump up the pot."

I eye Arian curiously. He quickly shakes his head.

"That isn't meant to be antagonistic. Just stating facts."

My head nods. "In that case, yes, Drazen became a silent partner in the project. I think it's fair to say we ended up paying more than expected. But it's still a solid investment, and I doubt we'd have clinched the deal at all without Drazen and his money." My brows knit "Where is this going, Arian?"

"What if I were to tell you that the party you were bidding against was *my* family."

I pause with my glass halfway to my lips.

Arian shakes his head again. "It's not what you're thinking. I wanted no part in any of that. Neither did my father, actually, but his hands were tied. You see, we *also* had a silent investment partner." His face darkens. "Or rather, a *not-so-silent* one. You asked me the other night if I was in business with Boris Chernoff."

The hairs go up on the back of my neck. "Arian..."

"Well." He spreads his arms, a bitter smile on his face. "Unfortunately, I am. Because I didn't just inherit my father's empire. I inherited his debts, and his *parasites*." Arian exhales. "How well do you know Drazen?"

I shake my head. "Not well. Just what most people know. All the usual bedtime stories to scare the kids."

His face is grim as he reaches over to the table next to him and grabs a stack of folders. Turning, he tosses them on the table between us.

"They're not bedtime stories."

Frowning, I pick up the first file. Inside, there's a bunch of grainy black and white photos of a guy in a suit, lounging on a yacht. The documents in the folder, official reports by the looks of them, are in Cyrillic.

"My Russian's pretty rusty," I mutter. I flip to the next page, and my frown deepens. "My Albanian's worse."

"Allow me to translate, then," Arian growls. "That's Serge Markarov, head of the Markarov Bratva based out of London." He grimaces. "Or rather, that *was* Serge Markarov, just like that *was* his yacht. Losing his life and his giant-ass boat on the same night wasn't the sum total of it, either. Actually, Serge was quite possibly on one of the worst streaks of shit luck in the history of the world in the two months before his death."

Arian starts to tick off his fingers.

"His father fell out a thirty-story window. All twelve of his shipping warehouses used for his illicit goods managed to catch fire, *on the same night*, and every single one of their fire suppression systems failed."

My brows arch. Arian keeps ticking his fingers.

"His uncle, who was terrified of open water, died in a scuba accident. His grandfather ate the business end of a shotgun. His mother's multiple affairs were exposed in a prominent British tabloid. *She* ended up stepping off a platform under an oncoming commuter train. Even his twenty-year-old nephew overdosed on a frankly superhuman amount of cocaine—and the kid was on a pre-Olympian track team. Body was a temple, never touched drugs in his life."

My jaw starts to grind.

"I'll give you the Cliff Notes version of the next couple of folders," Arian spits. "Savin Borisov, of the Borisov Bratva: hangs himself, leaving a note admitting his numerous affairs. But, hey, good news for the wife he left behind: none of the women he listed fucking *exist*. Too bad it didn't stop his widow from swallowing about a pound of sleeping pills the night of his funeral. Oh, and *his* warehouses must have had their fire suppression systems set up by the same dipshits, because all ten of his *also* failed the night they *all* caught on fire."

Fuck me.

"The Zaytsev Bratva: *pakhan* and entire empire wiped off the face of the Earth. Vlasov Bratva, same thing. Popov Bratva, take a guess." He smiles grimly. "Same fucking fate." Arian taps the table between us with a stiff finger. "Would you care to guess who the fuck they *all*, without fail, had secret meetings with, roughly a week before each of them died?"

My pulse thuds as I lean back in my seat, stroking my jaw.

"Krylov," I growl quietly.

Adrian nods. "Drazen fucking Krylov. Now, guess who just lost his cousin, who he was very close with, in a freak skiing accident? And who also just had three warehouses in Jersey go up in flames a few weeks ago?"

Oh, shit.

"And for the million-dollar prize, Kratos," Arian mutters, "guess who owned that West Side development project before times got tough and they were forced to sell it to Vito Barone, about thirty years ago?"

"You're fucking shitting me."

"The Chernoff family," Arian growls. "Boris Chernoff's grandfather poured everything he had into buying that property, when the Chernoff organization was nothing more than a bunch of street hustlers and bootleggers. Boris' mother was fucking *born* in that building. When I say Boris wanted to buy it back from Vito, I mean he was ready to open a vein if the Italians said that was what it would take. And then Drazen swans in and helps you and yours scoop up the whole thing."

Arian sits back in his chair, shaking his head.

"Let me guess, he's ready to pour some more money into a major remodel."

My jaw grinds. "Tentative plans involve razing the whole place to the ground first."

Arian snorts. "Yeah, I'll bet they do. And I'll bet he wants Chernoff to watch it happen before he buries him in the new foundation or something."

The Albanian across from me shakes his head slowly. "You and I aren't rivals, Kratos. We never have been." His eyes darken. "We're fucking *pawns*. This whole thing was Drazen Krylov waging a proxy war on Chernoff, and we were just his fucking foot soldiers."

Son of a bitch...

"Feels shitty, doesn't it," Arian mutters. "But fuck me, that Krylov. I mean that's some evil genius level shit, Kratos."

My fingers drum on the armrest. My nostrils flare as the wheels turn in my head. "Any idea what to do about it?"

Arian snorts again. "Like what? Walk away? From *Drazen?*" He whistles, shaking his head. "Your funeral, Kratos."

"What are you going to do about Chernoff?"

He smirks. "Well, the plan was *nothing*, and just wait for Krylov to cut off Chernoff's head or something. But while I wait for him to *do* that, Chernoff is fucking me over every way he can. Dad owed him a sizable debt—more than I have on hand. Boris has been milking me for a percentage of all my business, and the interest just keeps going up." He scowls. "He's even got his new attack bitch on my ass about it."

Something clicks in my head.

"What did you just say?"

Arian sighs. "I was saying the interest is fucking crushing—"

"No, after that."

This is the second time I've heard about Chernoff's new "attack dog", his new "consigliere". First from Tim, now from Arian.

"What, about his new number two, or whatever she is?"

"Yeah," I frown. "Who is she?"

"Scary, that's what," Arian growls darkly. "That woman means fucking business." His brows knit. "Arya, or something."

My jaw tightens. *"What?"*

"Or maybe Maya?"

Holy fucking shit.

Arian shudders. "Scary-looking cunt with a mean scar down the side of her neck, anyway."

My vision goes black for a second. My heart almost stops beating as a cold sensation twists in my gut.

"Amaya," I mutter through grit teeth.

Arian looks surprised. "Yeah, that's it. You know her?"

"We've met," I spit.

Arian exhales, nodding before he glances at his watch. His face darkens. "Fuck, I'm sorry, Kratos. I've got a meeting I need to get to."

Numbly, I stand and shake his hand in a daze.

"Look, I'm only telling you this because I'd like there to be no misunderstandings or bad blood between our families. I truly don't give a shit about the crucifix. All I want is to get out from under Chernoff's heel." His clears his throat. "And look, I'm not trying to push any agenda here. But since your family is doing business with the man who I expect might be cutting Boris' heart out in the near future..." He arches a brow significantly. "Perhaps you could put in a word with the Serbian to *move things along*."

A million thoughts are roaring through my head. My pulse jangles like shrapnel in my veins as I force a smile to my face and shake Arian's outstretched hand.

"I'm actually going to see him now."

Right the fuck now.

28

KRATOS

I'M ALREADY angry when I arrive at the front door. After I'm kept waiting there for fifteen minutes by Drazen's men, I'm fucking *pissed* by the time he finally deigns to greet me in his enormous penthouse.

The Serbian meets me in the foyer in one of his customary dark gray suits. He shakes my hand firmly. But when he sees the icy look on my face, his brow quirks up.

"Is this a friendly visit?" he growls in his deep baritone. "Or should I break out the dueling pistols. Because you look—"

"You're fucking playing us."

Drazen meditates on that for a second, stroking his chin before he turns.

"Why don't you come have a drink."

"This won't take long," I snap. "We can do it right here."

"Suit yourself," Drazen tosses over his shoulder. "*I'm* getting a drink."

Glaring daggers at his back, I follow him into his spacious, double height living room with its views of all of New York spread out ninety stories beneath us.

Drazen steps to the bar cart by the fireplace.

"You're sure you don't—"

"I don't need you to impress me, or glad-hand me, or placate me with expensive whiskey," I hiss. "That's not why I'm here."

Drazen nods, turning to pour himself a drink. "I've got shit whiskey, too, if that would make you more comfortable."

I seethe silently. "What would make me *more comfortable* is hearing from your own lips why you thought it was remotely okay to fuck with my family."

He turns back to eye me as he takes a sip.

"You mean my investment in your building."

"No, I mean you using us as pawns to fuck with *your* enemy."

He exhales. "Kratos, all I'm doing is helping your family buy a building. That's—"

"Bullshit," I snap. "You're having a pissing contest with Boris Chernoff."

Drazen's face darkens, his eyes flashing as they pierce into me.

"A *pissing contest?*" he chuckles quietly. His lips curl savagely in the corners. "No, Kratos. A pissing contest is bidding on the car your rival wants at auction, winning, and then demolishing that car just to be an asshole. A pissing contest is fucking that rival's woman. What I engage in, Kratos," he says coldly, his voice venomous, "isn't a *pissing contest*. It's guerrilla fucking warfare. And you haven't a single goddamn idea of my history with these people, or what goes on in my heart."

I bristle but stand my ground as he walks toward me and jabs a finger in my chest. "So back the *fuck* off."

"And if I don't?" I snarl.

He eyes me coolly. "Then maybe Ares and the rest of your family would be interested in hearing about your clandestine chats with CIA Agent Amaya Mircari. Who, as I'm sure you know by now, isn't working for the CIA anymore."

When I stiffen, he cocks his head, arching a cold brow.

"Don't mistake me for a blind man, Kratos. It could be fatal."

"Stay the fuck out of my and my family's lives, Drazen," I growl back.

"Gladly, if you rearrange your lives so as not to cross my goals."

My eyes lock with his. A second ticks by. Then, without another word, I turn and march out of the living room toward the door of his sprawling penthouse.

"Kratos?"

I stop at the door, turning my head partway around to catch his eye.

"You may be big, but I'm very close to your size. If you ever come into my home and threaten me again, I'll cut your fucking head off."

"Asshole!"

I let the final word of Ares' tirade sink in through the phone before I exhale.

"I should have checked in with you first."

"Oh, you fucking *think*?!" he hurls back. "Drazen is a fucking ally, dipshit!"

I scowl as I get out of the G-wagon, phone to my ear. "Maybe he's not an enemy, but do you still want to call him an ally after everything I've just told you?"

"What I want to do after everything you've just told me is have a fucking conversation!" he roars back. "All of us! Together! Not barge into his fucking home, guns blazing!"

I pinch the bridge of my nose tiredly as I walk around the corner to my brownstone. It's almost dinnertime, and after this shit-show of a day, all I want is to sit down with Bianca and eat.

Well, that's not entirely true. After *this* shitty a day, what I want is to abduct her from our home, drag her blindfolded and tied up to the old church, and then chase her through the dark before I fuck her until she can't walk for a week.

...Actually, that's what I might do when I get home in about seven seconds.

"Ares, I'm almost home. Let me call you back after—"

"Oh, fuck off," he snaps angrily. "I'll call *you* back, jackass."

He hangs up sharply.

Shit.

This will take some repairing. But I stand by what I did. Yeah, maybe Drazen's influence and money get that development built and our pockets lined. But I fucking *loathe* being someone else's pawn.

The front door to the brownstone swings shut behind me. I exhale the tension of the day, and slowly, a smile spreads over my face.

This place hasn't been my house for long. It also never felt like *home* until recently.

Until Bianca became a part of it.

My mind replays the feel of her sliding into my lap earlier as I turn to glance up the stairs.

"I'm home!" I call out. "Is it too cliche if I do Greek for din—"

My words stutter to a stop when my eyes land on the suitcase and backpack sitting at the bottom of the staircase.

"Bianca?"

My brows knit as I go to walk up the stairs.

"Bianca—"

"Is it true?"

My head whips around at the sound of her voice. Bianca's sitting in a chair in the living room, so still and quiet that I never even noticed her when I walked in. I frown as I move toward her.

"What's with the suitcases—"

"*Is. It. True.*"

Her voice is haggard and cold; soft, like it's being whispered from a mile away. She stands from her chair, her mouth a line and her hands clenched stiffly at her sides.

I shake my head as I move toward her. "I'm not sure—"

She flinches, backing away and keeping the coffee table between us.

"Were you trying to spy on my family?"

A single tear leaks down her cheeks, her eyes haunted and dark as she stares at me haggardly. I go still, my blood turning to ice.

Fuck. Amaya.

My jaw grinds. "Whatever that woman told you—"

"Don't lie to me, Kratos."

She's not screaming or throwing things. She's so quiet. Somehow, that makes it even worse.

"Bianca, listen to me," I growl. "I love you—"

"Please don't fucking say that right now," she says coldly, almost mechanically.

"That *bitch*," I snarl, "is full of shit."

"And I'm supposed to believe you?"

"Yes!"

"*Why.*"

"Because I'm your fucking *husband*!"

Her throat bobs as tears fill her eyes. Then she turns away, wiping at them with the back of her hand.

"Did she ask you to spy on my family in exchange for avoiding going to jail on gun charges?"

I remain silent.

"*Answer the fucking question*," she hisses, her voice quiet and cold.

"She asked me to, yes," I rumble darkly.

Bianca physically flinches, like I've struck her.

"But I didn't ever do it—"

"You also didn't ever *tell me* she asked you," Bianca spits. She's still not looking at me. Still looking away, her body rigid and her voice strained.

Silence chokes the room.

"Why is there a suitcase in the front hallway," I growl.

Bianca's throat bobs. "You know why."

Something vicious twists inside of me.

"Babygirl—"

"*No*," she chokes, her voice tight. "Don't call me that."

"Bianca—"

"This is done, Kratos."

The words hit me like so many bullets to the chest as she finally turns to look straight at me. Her eyes are red-rimmed, her expression stony.

"*We're* done."

No. "Excuse me?"

"As in over," she spits venomously. "Finished. I'm done with these ridiculous games we keep playing, and I'm done with *you*."

There's nothing behind her eyes. No anger, no pain. Just... blank emptiness.

"What the fuck is this," I whisper quietly.

A single tear trickling down her cheek is the only emotion she lets out.

"This is me growing a spine, Kratos. This is me taking control of my life." She stares right at me. "We're done. I'm leaving."

It feels like I've been punched in the throat. Or shot. I just stand there, stunned, as she storms past me to the front entryway. Suddenly, I snap.

"You're not going anywhere."

It's like a reflex. She flees, or tries to run, and I give chase. It's part of my nature I can't change. I whirl and grab her arm, tighter than I intended, a raw impulse not to let her go.

Bianca shivers, her eyes dropping to my hand gripping her forearm. She swallows, and the walls around her waver for a second. But then she sucks in air and the defenses go back up. Her eyes burn into me as she thrusts her chin up at me.

"Or what?" she says coldly. "You'll hurt me?"

The feeling of my heart breaking when she says it almost brings me to my knees.

"You know I wouldn't ever hurt you," I choke quietly. "Not like that."

Her arm yanks from my grip.

"*Kratos*," she whispers. "Apparently, I don't know who you are, what you're capable of, or the first thing about you."

She starts to back toward the front door.

"Bianca—"

"Stay right there," she chokes, her voice breaking a little but her face still stoic and cold, her emotions walled off.

"Baby—"

"I said *stay there*."

My brow furrows as I advance on her, my heart shattering as it races.

"I'm not letting you just walk out of here."

Her chest rises and falls slowly as her hands clench at her sides and her eyes fall shut.

When she opens them again and speaks, it's like ice hitting me in the face.

"*Vanish*."

My whole world shifts on its axis.

"*No*," I blurt, shaking my head as the room spins. "No, you—"

"*Vanish*."

"You don't get to use that fucking word! I love you!" I choke.

She flinches, like I've just struck her. Another tear trickles down her cheek.

"If you really love me," she says coldly, "you'll listen to me, and let me walk out that door."

Her eyes lock with mine. All the pain in the universe shatters behind them. Without another word, she turns and she walks out.

And my world crumbles.

29

KRATOS

I give her twelve hours.

For twelve hours, I allow her to be away from me. To ignore my calls and texts. To *not* be in our bed.

After that, I snap.

She's not getting away from me that easily. My monster won't let her. *I* won't let her.

Fuck the safe word. We're not playing a game anymore. This is real. This is for keeps.

She's not at her old apartment when I check. I slip a few hundred bucks to the doorman, and he confirms he hasn't seen her in weeks.

She *could* be at Vito's place, or with any of her brothers. But going to those places asking if they've seen her is going to raise questions I can't answer yet. Questions I don't have the time or patience to answer.

So I try the Mercury Opera House. But when I slip into my usual spot behind the curtains in the private box, my heart sinks. I see her friends, Naomi and Milena. I even spot the two bitches who left her in that alley that night.

No Bianca.

That's when my skin starts crawling with a nervous, dangerous energy.

Something's wrong if she's not here. I know how much dance means to her. I know from her own mouth that she's literally only ever taken *three days off* in eighteen years of ballet.

Even with everything that's just happened, she wouldn't not be here. Dance is her therapy.

Still, I wait until the bitter end, hoping for Bianca to stumble in late with an apology.

She never comes.

My nervous energy turns to full blown panic as I sit in the darkened box. The stage is empty now, but I'm still glaring down at it, as if I might finally see her pirouette onto the stage.

Eventually, I head down. I poke my head into the dressing room; by now, the other dancers have changed and left. I open a few of the lockers, until I know the one I've come to is hers.

It smells like her. The scent makes something in my chest tighten.

Inside, there's a picture of the two of us, from our wedding no less, tacked to the back wall. It'd be easy to roll my eyes at the memory of the utterly staged shot taken by the photographer no one asked Ya-ya to hire for the day. But when I pluck it out of her locker and look at it closely, a crooked smile spontaneously splits my lips.

"Kratos?"

Slowly, I turn. When I see who it is, my mouth twists angrily.

Alicia Houghton flashes me a weak smile from the doorway of the dressing room. "I know you don't like me," she says quietly, her hands twisting in front of her. "But I… I really need to tell you something."

My brow furrows as I nod. "Yes?"

"You know Grisha Lenkov…?"

"We've met," I growl.

She trembles. "Okay, so, he came over to my apartment last night. We're broken up, because he's a complete asshole. But he was drunk and making a scene, so I let him in so he wouldn't wake up the whole building."

She chews on her lip nervously.

"He was being a drunk douche, and trying to get me to sleep with him. Eventually, he got a call and stepped into my bathroom to take it. Except, he was drunk, and loud, so I heard…"

Her face pales as she looks up at me.

"He was bragging to someone about how he and 'the witch' had taken the 'Italian princess', and how they had her now."

Alarm bells start to ring inside my head.

"I…" she shudders. "I didn't know what he was talking about at the time. But when I didn't see Bianca today…"

Oh fuck.

She sucks on her lip, hugging herself and looking genuinely scared. "Kratos... I think Grisha might *have* Bianca. Like, maybe he took—"

She's not even done speaking before I'm shoving past her and bolting out the door. I slam open the theater door and race to my car. Just as I get to it, my phone rings with an unknown number.

My blood chills, my jaw setting as I answer it.

"Hello, Kratos."

The alarm bells in my head turn into an air raid siren when I hear Amaya's smug voice.

"I have something of yours," she purrs.

Red swims through my vision.

"I'm going to *kill you*," I hiss.

Amaya laughs coldly. "How about instead we make a trade."

My blood roars in my ears.

"You bring me Drazen Krylov, I give you your little plaything."

This woman's insane. "You want me to kidnap a *Bratva kingpin?*"

"Kidnap or invite, your choice," she spits. "But if you want little Bianca back in one piece, you'll bring Drazen, alive, to the West Side development building. Penthouse floor. *Tonight.*"

My teeth grind. "If you've touched a fucking hair on—"

"Come alone, Kratos. Just you and Drazen."

The line goes dead.

THEY SAY fortune favors the brave. Bullshit. What fortune *truly* favors is a man with nothing to lose, and the woman he loves being held in danger of her life.

Breaking into Drazen's building would be suicide. The doorman and concierge are both his men. More of his soldiers patrol every floor beneath his penthouse. And there's no way in hell I'm scaling all the way up to break in through a window *Mission Impossible* style.

There *is*, however, a helipad on the roof. And while trying to land your own chopper on it should *also* be suicide, given that he has yet more men patrolling the roof, that ends up being how I get in.

Thanks to Taylor.

I can't tell Ares what I'm doing. He'll either try to stop me or insist on getting involved, and I won't have any of my brothers getting hurt. But I *can* confide in my attorney and tell her that I'm in need of a Crown and Black helicopter.

Granted, she thinks she's helping me get a meeting with Drazen, not kidnap him. But Taylor comes through like a champ. She even has the pilot radio ahead to building security that one of their tenants is a client and has a "legal emergency" that needs dealing with.

Drazen's three guys on the roof never even know they've been played until they're already out cold and tied up in a corner.

The rest is easy.

Ish.

Down the maintenance staircase to the penthouse level. Take out two more guys in the hallway. Use one of their keycards to get inside Drazen's place.

Then wake the boogeyman himself up with a gun to his forehead.

"You should think *very* carefully about your next choices right now, Kratos," he growls quietly, his eyes on mine in the dimness of his bedroom. "*Very—*"

"You've been playing games with me and my family," I hiss.

"Kratos—"

"And even though I *hate* being a pawn," I growl, "that's not why I'm here right now." I lean closer. "I'm here because *your fucking games* have gotten *my fucking wife* kidnapped by Chernoff."

He doesn't blink.

"So, here's the deal," I spit. "You're going to fix this. Because *you're* the one who kicked the hornets nest. You're the one who poured gasoline on this fire."

I smile murder at Drazen.

"You're going to help me get her back."

Slowly, his mouth curls into a dark grin as he nods. "What exactly did you have in mind?"

30

BIANCA

"You know, if dance doesn't pan out, you'd make a *great* actor."

Rage, pain, and heartache sizzle like acid in me as I glare pure hate at the woman smirking down at me.

"Be mad if you want," Amaya shrugs. "It was meant as a compliment."

"*Fuck you*," I spit in reply.

She rolls her eyes. "Right back at ya, trust me. Seriously, you did well, Bianca." Her lips curl poisonously. "And look on the bright side: you saved his life."

My eyes close, as if to stop the pain from exploding though me.

It's the only reason I did what I did: to save him. To stop this psycho bitch from having him killed.

When the knock came at the front door yesterday, I jumped

up from the couch and ran to open it, assuming it was Kratos home early.

But instead of the man I love, I found myself face to face with Amaya, leveling a gun at my head, five men in full tactical gear with rifles standing behind her on the stoop.

Their brutal demands hit me so fast it sucked the very air from my lungs: pack a bag. Wait for Kratos to come home. Tell him it was over between us. I had ten minutes to convince him we were through and to walk out the front door *alone*, or Amaya's men, who'd be waiting by the windows with guns aimed, would kill Kratos on the spot.

I watched helplessly as she placed a hidden mic and camera in the living room. She explained with an acid smile that if I let on what was happening in any way, or tried to warn him or signal to him that he was in danger, they'd kill him right in front of me.

So I did the only thing I could think of that I knew would stop him from following me, as much as it broke my heart.

I used the nuclear option.

Vanish.

Even remembering the way I said it, and the haunted look in his eyes when he heard it, breaks my heart all over again.

Like I *broke* his *heart*.

Because that's what I saw in his face. I saw pain, and betrayal, and they almost broke me right there.

But if breaking his heart saved him, so be it. If my own broken heart is collateral damage, that's a price I'd pay a thousand times.

I shift in the chair I'm tied to, feeling the bite of the ropes binding my wrists behind me. We're in the old, mostly demolished executive suite on the top floor of the building Kratos' family recently acquired from my mine. The only light comes from the few construction bulbs, reflecting dimly off the bare metal frames of the walls and ceilings. The windows in the wall overlooking the Hudson River below have been removed in preparation of the complete teardown the Drakos family is planning, and a chilly wind whips through the gaping frames.

Amaya's phone goes off. She turns and walks away as she answers it brusquely.

The sound of a tongue clicking against teeth drags my attention across the cavernous space, where Grisha is leaning against the metal frame of a wall, leering at me.

"Yeah, great acting," he sneers. "Too bad all it did was buy that fucking husband of yours one more day of breathing."

I don't respond.

I did what I did before because all I could think of was sparing his life. Whatever they were going to do to me, whatever came next, as long as I knew I was stopping them from shooting Kratos in the back right there in the living room, I was fine with it.

And when they hauled me into the van and drove off into the night the second I stepped out of the brownstone with my suitcase, I swallowed my fear.

Because I knew he was safe.

But now I know I was so blinded by that immediate fear for him I couldn't see past the present, to what might come next.

Now I can.

Maybe Amaya's only real plan for me is to use me as a bargaining chip. I was in the room when she made the call telling Kratos to bring the Bratva *pakhan* Drazen Krylov here in exchange for me. Maybe it's all a trap, but I have to cling to some shred of hope.

When I look at Grisha, that hope shatters.

Amaya herself might genuinely just be looking to make an exchange. But there's something vicious in Grisha's eyes.

He's not here because he gives two shits about any Bratva politics going on here involving Drazen.

He's here because he wants to hurt Kratos. Maybe even kill him.

"Shame you're not in charge," I spit at him. "Just her little assistant."

Rage clouds his face as he storms across the room. I gasp, flinching, but there's no avoiding the back of his hand as it slaps my mouth, hard.

Grisha chuckles darkly as I wince, turning and spitting blood as my lip splits.

"You think I'm not in charge here?"

I swallow, glaring at him. "No one with half a brain would ever put you in charge, of anything" I hiss. "You're Boris Chernoff's errand boy. And now even his number two has you running around, taking orders from *her*."

Rage sparks in his eyes and I brace myself for another hit. But Grisha just smiles coldly, chuckling darkly.

"I know what you're doing, *shlyushka*," he growls. "Trying to bait me. Antagonize me." He grins. "It's not going to work. Not yet, at least. Not until that fucker gets here."

"*She* has business with him, though," I smile. "So does your boss. You can't—"

I choke on my breath as he surges into me, grabbing the nape of my neck tightly.

"Can't *what*, bitch," he snarls. "Touch him? Touch *you*?" His lips curl dangerously. "Let me make this clear. After the business has been concluded, and Mr. Chernoff and that bitch get Krylov, they're going to let me do whatever I want to your husband."

I shiver as he leans even closer.

"Whatever I want *to you*, too," he leers, his tone sickening.

"First, I'm going to break his legs, so he can't run away. Then I think I'll slice his eyelids off, so he can't close them." Grisha grins. "He's going to watch when I fuck you in every hole you have, like my own personal whore. When I invite my men to take their turns, too. Actually…"

I go cold as Grisha reaches for his fly. He smirks. "I'll tell you what. If you suck my dick right now, and you suck it good, maybe I'll be selfish later and not let my men have any fun. How about that? Just me using every one of your tight holes right in front of your little bitch of a husband." He grins. "Fuck, I can't wait to see him watching you on your knees, with my cock in your mouth."

"Grisha!" Amaya barks coldly from across the bare office. She snaps her fingers impatiently before turning back to her phone.

"*Go fetch*, boy," I hiss.

Grisha snarls at me, then obediently turns and starts to walk toward Amaya.

"He's going to kill you, you know."

The Russian stops and glances back at me.

"What?"

"Kratos. He's going to kill you," I say flatly, my voice even. "I don't mean figuratively. I mean he's literally going to kill you." My eyes turn cold. "He's going to break your teeth. Then he'll rip off your tiny balls, and stuff them down your throat through your ruined mouth."

Grisha's brow furrows.

"It'll be up to you if you want to choke on them or swallow them while he breaks every bone in your body before cutting out your heart. And you know how I know all this, Grisha?" I smile ruthlessly at him. "Because I'll be right there, telling him what to do next."

Grisha's face pales, looking green around the edges. A dark power in me surges.

Maybe Kratos' monster has rubbed off on me. Or maybe there's been a beast in me all along, and it's *him* that's taught me how to let it off its chain.

Suddenly, there's a commotion. Amaya starts snapping orders, and even Grisha pulls his shit together and starts barking at his men in Russian. I'm whipping my gaze around, trying to see what's happening, when Amaya strolls over, her eyes lancing into mine.

"Your boyfriend's here," she snaps coldly.

Hope surges in my chest.

"*Husband*," I hiss back.

She frowns.

"My *husband* is here." My lips curl. "You took so much from him," I say thoughtfully, shaking my head. "And yet you never got what you really wanted."

Her eyes narrow. "Careful, little girl."

"You're desperate enough for human contact that you had to abuse a *child* to get it, and you even deluded yourself into thinking it was...what?" I laugh coldly. "A relationship?! Did you think he felt anything for you besides fear and hatred? Did you seriously tell yourself you *loved* him? The *boy* you were abusing?"

Rage ignites in her face. Her eyes turn black, her lips curling.

"Is that what all this is about, you pathetic old hag?" I continue. "That I got from him what you never in a million years ever could? His love?"

Amaya blinks, her mouth opening and closing and her body swaying a little, like I've just hit her. I just smile.

"He loves me. And he fucking *hates* you—"

I cry out when her open palm connects sharply with my cheek.

"Ms. Mircari."

With a quiet snarl, she whirls away from me and to the guard who's just spoken.

"What?"

The man nods at the elevator, at the blinking lights signifying a rising car.

Amaya nods. "Get ready," she barks, her lips pulling into a cold, poisonous smile. "They're here."

The elevator dings. The doors open.

Then I see him, and my heart lurches.

He's wearing his mask.

Wordlessly, radiating a dark power, Kratos' huge frame lumbers out of the elevator. He's in black jeans and a black hoodie, wearing the mask I know all too well with the neon X's for eyes and the leering smile.

He turns and grabs something in the elevator. With a yank, he drags a man across the floor on his knees. He's wearing a dark gray suit, his hands bound behind his back. A black ski mask covers the man's face, its eyes and mouth sewn shut, blinding him. With a grunt, Kratos tosses the man to the floor in front of him.

The whole place is deathly quiet. You can see and feel the uneasiness of the guards as they glance at each other and then to the giant masked psychopath standing before them.

"My my, Kratos..."

Amaya strolls forward, her brow raised as she hefts the gun in her hand.

"Bit early for Halloween, isn't it?"

"I brought what you asked for."

Jesus fuck. He's using that same voice changer from before: the one that makes him sound like a demonic robot from hell.

Around me, everyone—the guards, Grisha and his men, even Amaya—stiffens a little, looking creeped the fuck out. Then Amaya recovers.

"You sure did," she purrs, eying Drazen as he kneels on the floor.

Kratos walks over behind the Serbian and roughly kicks him in the middle of the back, shoving him flat onto the ground.

"*You have what you wanted.*"

He turns and jabs a big finger right at me, making me shiver.

"*Now I want her.*"

Amaya half turns, nodding to two of her men. They lower their guns and walk over, grabbing Drazen under the arms and hauling him to the side of the room where they drop him back to the floor in a heap.

"You want *her*?" Amaya smiles, turning to me. My heart leaps into my throat as she raises her gun, waving it at me. "*Her*?"

Kratos doesn't react. He merely cocks his head to the side, that unnerving neon smile leering into Amaya's face.

"*Her*," he rasps in that creepy voice. "*Now*."

Movement catches my eye. My gaze snaps past Kratos to the four Chernoff men creeping up behind him with guns drawn.

"KRATOS!"

I scream, but not soon enough. Just as he starts to whip around, the men tackle him to the ground. Two of them roughly pin him to the ground on his knees as I cry out. The other two jam their gun barrels into his back.

"Get comfy, Kratos," Amaya sneers. She walks over to him and slowly slides the hunting knife out of the holster on his belt. A chill ripples down my back as she slowly turns to me, turning the blade in her hand thoughtfully. "I want you to watch what happens next."

She starts to walk toward me.

"Hold up," Grisha spits. "Mr. Chernoff and I had a deal."

"Really? What *deal* was that?" Amaya mutters.

Grisha grins salaciously. "I get to do what I want with the bitch."

Amaya rolls her eyes. "Well, that's…sad and pathetic. It's also not happening. She's *mine*."

She pushes past him, grinning darkly at me as she twirls the knife again. I shudder when she stops right in front of me and leans down close.

"You think you got something from him I never did?" she sneers quietly. "You think the little fucking games he plays with you are *love*?"

"I know abusing him sure the fuck wasn't," I spit.

She laughs uproariously. "A boy that age? Being given *what I gave him*?"

Bile rises in my stomach. Pure hatred and a brief, horrible twinge of jealousy rear up inside me. But mostly, what I feel is pain. Pain for the childhood that was torn from him. For the innocence she robbed him of.

Amaya chuckles quietly. "Oh, he loved me, you little cunt. I had him wrapped around my fing—"

Ballet is all about core strength. And I've been honing mine for eighteen fucking years. In one motion, I flex, lifting my body and the chair it's tied to about two inches up in the air before slamming back down.

The metal foot of the chair jams right into the open toe of Amaya's high heels.

She screams in agony, dropping the knife and collapsing to the ground. She clutches at her bleeding foot, howling in pain.

"That," she seethes, scrambling to her feet, "is going to fucking cost you!"

She snatches up the knife again. She lifts her arm, ready to plunge the blade into me.

"Not fucking yet!!!"

Her arm jerks to a violent stop as Grisha yanks it back.

"You're a fucking *tourist* in our organization, bitch," he snarls at Amaya. "Mr. Chernoff promised me I could use her as my fucking whore. And I'm not into necrophilia," he spits.

Amaya cocks her head to the side. "Necrophilia. Hmm. Funny, not my bag either. But you're still fucked."

Grisha's eyes bulge as a horrible gurgling sound burbles from his lips, together with red froth. His throat splits where Amaya just sliced it clean open, and a deluge of blood gushes out.

I choke out a scream as his eyes go dim and his body slumps to the ground.

Some of the guards start to aim their guns at Amaya. She stops them cold.

"I'll remind you all that I report directly to Mr. Chernoff!" she barks. "You'd do well to remember that!"

The men glance at each other. Guns are lowered.

Kratos laughs maniacally through his mask, the mechanical sound raising the hairs on everyone's neck.

"Is this your idea of leadership, Amaya?" he growls. *"Do you feel in control and in charge?"* He laughs again through the creepy vocoder. *"How pathetic."*

Rage clouds Amaya's face as she whirls on him.

"You think I'm not in control, Kratos?"

Without warning, she storms over to him. A scream rips from my mouth as she jams the edge of her knife right against his throat as the four men keep pinning him down.

"I'll show you what control is," she hisses, grabbing the top of his mask. "When I let her watch you *bleed*."

She yanks off the mask, and my jaw *drops* as Drazen Krylov smiles cruelly up at her.

"Surprise, *shlyushka*."

The lights go out. The guards roar and turn on gun-mounted flashlights. In the shadows, the man bound on the floor suddenly springs to his feet.

And his balaclava suddenly *glows*.

Two X's for eyes.

A leering, neon smile.

Two flashes of steel in his hands.

And then comes the carnage.

Gunfire explodes. Men's screams turn to wet, gasping gurgles. In the dim, flickering light, I see Drazen shake off the men pinning him. He whirls, savagely yanking a rifle out of one of the guards' hands and immediately using it to blow a hole through the man's head. I scream as he spins again, his face expressionless and cold as he cuts down half of the guards seemingly without any emotion at all.

Behind him, my neon-masked psychopath snarls and dips and dodges, cutting one man down, then another, and another.

I gasp sharply as I'm grabbed from behind. A blade cuts the ropes off me, and an arm wraps around my throat from behind. I choke, flailing and trying to scream as Amaya drags me away from the fray.

The neon mask turns to us. It tilts to the side and lets out a snarl of pure animalistic fury. Kratos charges across the carnage toward us, the knives in his hands glinting.

Suddenly, the cold metal of a gun barrel pushes against my temple. Instantly, Kratos stops. He reaches up and yanks off the mask, his face twisted with rage and worry as his eyes stab into me.

"Babygirl..." he says quietly.

I'm about to open my mouth when I feel cold air rippling up my legs. I glance behind me, and my heart lurches into my throat.

Amaya has us standing right by one of the glassless floor-to-ceiling window-frames overlooking the black river below. The sounds of traffic blare from outside. The lights of the city glitter like diamonds. Another gust of air ripples the construction plastic wrap covering some of the other window frames.

"Not another step, Kratos," she whispers.

Her arm trembles a little as she grips me tightly. Her other arm juts out, brandishing the gun at Kratos. But she's lost her advantage. Behind Kratos, all the Chernoff men lie on the ground, either dead or out cold. Drazen stands in the middle of them, looking nothing like the put-together, suit-wearing businessman I've met before, and everything like a blood-soaked monster.

"You lost, Amaya," Kratos growls quietly. "It's over. Let her go."

Amaya shakes her head, her fingers tightening around the gun.

"I—Kratos…"

I hear her swallow behind me as my eyes fix on my husband's.

"We…you and I…" she chokes. "We—"

"There never was a *we*, you miserable cunt," he snarls viciously. "We never *dated*," he hisses. "What you did to me was never a *relationship*."

"Kratos…" Her voice breaks.

"You stole my fucking childhood, you goddamned psycho," Kratos growls. "You raped a fucking child and convinced yourself you were in love." He shakes his head. "That wasn't love. I *didn't want that*. It was torture. I fucking *hated you* for it."

The breath leaves her body in a rush.

"And I still fucking do. So let her go. Because every second you keep me from *my wife*," he rasps, "*whom I love*, is another hour I'll drag out your suffering before I kill you."

"You… You *needed me*, Kratos!" she screams.

"Like I needed a hole in my head, you psycho bitch. *Let. Her. GO.*"

The room is silent and still. Amaya shakes as she keeps hold of me. Slowly, I watch her thumb draw back the hammer on her gun.

My eyes start from my head as her lips curl into a sneer.

"*No.*"

Everything goes into slow motion. I shriek as the gun goes off. The bullet explodes out and punches through the air just as Kratos lurches toward us. My scream sounds like it's underwater, a slow, drawn-out wail as the bullet slams into Kratos' chest. Blood explodes out of his back like a ketchup packet popping.

He doesn't stop. He doesn't slow. He just mouths the words "I love you" as his eyes lock on mine and he grabs me out of her arms and tosses me to safety.

My head snaps around. My breath leaves my body and my heart rips in two as Kratos slams into Amaya and the two of them topple backward.

Out the window, and into the night.

I scream so loud my ears pop, scrambling to my feet and bolting for the window. The silence is punctuated by a loud splash of water way down below. My fingers cling to the edges of the window frame, my eyes wide as I stare down into the inky blackness, waiting for him to surface.

And waiting.

He's not coming up.

Something changes in you when your love is ripped from you. Something snaps, and you forget yourself, all your demons, all your fears.

At least, I do. Because in an instant, ignoring whatever Drazen is yelling at me, I'm bolting to the window, leaping out into the night, and plummeting into the dark abyss below.

31

KRATOS

ALL I KNOW IS DARKNESS. Like a black snake, swallowing me whole. Like pure nothingness, its silence drowning out everything else.

Cold surrounds me, sucking me down. Pulling me deeper.

Thud.

Thud.

Thud.

Like the tick of a clock. Like grains of sand slipping through an hourglass. They're slowing. Time is slowing.

I'm slowing.

Thud.

Thud.

Thud.

No. It's not sand. It's my pulse. I can feel it growing weaker, slowing to a deadly pace as the cold inkiness surrounds me and pulls me deeper and deeper into the empty embrace of nothingness.

I want to tell her I love her. I want to tell her I'm sorry that I'm leaving so soon.

I want to tell her she's the best thing that's ever happened to me, and that I'm going to haunt the fuck out of her after my heart finally stops and the darkness swallows me up.

My vision clouds. The swirling shadows slow to a crawl as my limbs go numb.

This is it. Fuck, I wanted more time with her.

Suddenly, something's splitting the darkness.

A hand, reaching for me. I try to reach back, but I can't. All I can do is sink deeper, growing number.

Weaker.

Fading faster.

The hand thrusts deeper, gleaming, surrounded by a halo of light.

Save me, I want to whisper. *Pull me from the darkness. I fell in love with your light.*

But I can't.

It just all grows darker and colder.

And then—there's nothing at all.

32

BIANCA

UNDER THE STERILE fluorescent lights of the hospital hallway, Callie crashes into my arms. She clings to me, sobbing against my shoulder as I cry into hers. Through the tears, I'm dimly aware of others moving toward us: Ares, Hades, and Deimos. My brothers. Tempest.

Callie pulls away, and I collapse into Dante's embrace next, my tears staining his shirt as he holds me tightly.

Through the chaos and heartbreak exploding through my system, I hear the hushed murmurs of tense, serious words being spoken around me.

Fell twenty-five stories...

The bullet pierced his lung...

Sepsis...

That Amaya bitch is dead...

Drazen pulled them both out... Bianca wouldn't let go...

It comes back to me in flashes. I remember leaping out into space and feeling the yank of gravity. Not "facing" my fear of submersion, just simply not remembering I even had one as I dove under the water.

I remember reaching through the darkness for him, looking into his eyes as consciousness faded from them. Swimming deeper to grab him. Pulling with all my strength, lungs burning as I kicked toward the surface.

I remember Drazen screaming at me to take his hand. I remember refusing to let go of Kratos, and the Serbian kingpin diving in next to me to help pull Kratos' bulk out of the water.

She saved him...

I shudder as I sob into Dante's chest.

I don't know if I even did. Nobody does. Right now, Kratos is in emergency surgery with a specialist that just got airlifted here from Boston. When I grabbed a nurse ten minutes ago and asked what his chances were, she just pursed her lips and told me the important thing was to remember that I loved him.

I do.

And I'm not ready to lose him.

I can't.

The conversations around me go silent. Turning, my eyes land on Dimitra as she steps into the middle of us. With a sob, I pull away from my brother and rush to her. My arms wrap tightly around her, and I start to cry with more anguish and pain than I've ever felt before.

"*I'm sorry,*" I choke, clinging to her for dear life as the frail little old lady hugs me back firmly, being my rock. "*I'm so, so sorry—*"

"For what, *engoni?*" she says softly, stroking my hair. "Loving my grandson? *Saving* him?"

"I—" I choke back a sob. "I don't know if I did."

"*You did,*" she whispers fiercely. "Believe me, you—"

"Mrs. Drakos?"

Dimitra releases me and turns at the sound of a man's voice.

"Yes?"

His mouth twists awkwardly as he nods at me. "I, uh, I meant the other Mrs. Drakos."

My face pales. "*Yes?*" I croak.

The hallway goes silent.

The man clears his throat.

"Could we, uh… Could we talk privately?"

My heart wrenches and my legs threaten to give out. Just as I'm about to fall, Dimitra is there, grabbing my hand and gripping it firmly, pouring all her strength into me.

"Right here is fine," I choke.

The man's brow furrows. "I'm sorry, but hospital policy is for immediate fam—"

"We *are* his family," Ares growls.

"In this case, sir, immediate means spouse—"

The man gasps as Hades grabs him by the collar and slams him against the wall.

"*Is my brother going to live or die, you fuck?!*"

Wide-eyed and pale, the man looks at me. "Mr. Drakos is out of surgery and in recovery. He's going to be fine."

This time, as the hallway erupts into cheers, I do collapse to the ground. But the tears that fall down my face aren't tears of sadness.

They're tears of pure joy.

Gratitude.

Relief.

And *love*.

EPILOGUE

KRATOS

I WAS eight when I stole for the first time. It was a Snickers bar, from the gift shop of some ritzy hotel on the other side of Central Park.

I'm no Oliver Twist or Aladdin. This wasn't stealing to eat and survive, or anything noble and poetic like that. I mean for fuck's sake, I could *see* the damn hotel from *the grounds* of my family estate towering over Central Park South.

Even at that age, I knew how my family made money. I knew what we were, and what I'd probably become. I remember rationalizing the theft by telling myself the hotel charging two grand a night for a room didn't need the Snickers bar. Especially when they were trying to sell the fucking thing for *nine goddamn dollars*.

I mean, fuck right off with that shit.

Dimitra caught me, because of course she did. I gave her the same rationalization I'd given myself. It made her smile, but she still made me bring the Snickers bar back and apologize to the gift shop clerk who probably didn't give a shit anyway.

But there was a lesson for me in that, courtesy of Ya-ya. And it was that even if we're a family of criminals, and even though I'd probably grow up to steal more shit, it was important to remember that every action has a reaction.

Every theft, no matter what you're taking, has a victim. So if you're going to steal, make sure the victim deserves it.

Okay, probably not common grandmotherly words of wisdom, but I took them to heart. Since then, I've stolen a lot of shit: TVs, jewelry, sneakers—Hades and I stole a *fuckton* of Nikes when we were younger—cars, and more. But I always made sure that when I stole, I stole from someone who probably deserved to get their shit yoinked.

In this case, I'd say Death almost certainly deserves to get fucked over now and then, wouldn't you?

I've never stolen my own life back from Death's icy grip before. But then, I've never had a partner in crime to *assist* me in that before.

I'm glad I did, when it came down to it.

Because there's something else I stole: her heart. And I don't care who finds out, or has a problem with it.

I'm never giving it back. Ever.

It's sunny out when I leave Mt. Sinai two weeks after my fall into the Hudson. I got a punctured lung from the bullet, plus a fun little variety pack of a broken arm, four cracked ribs, split head, broken nose, lacerated spleen, punctured kidney, and bruises like someone went at me with a grudge and a baseball bat from the fall itself.

But I'm alive.

And I've got Bianca by my side.

...Grumbling for me to get back in the goddamn wheelchair.

"They give it to you for a reason!" she mutters.

"Yeah, to milk sympathy from your friends and family," I grin.

She rolls her eyes. "You *did* just fall off a fucking building, you know."

"So did you."

She gives me a withering look. "I *dove* off. There's a difference."

"Diving's just falling with style."

She giggles, biting her lip as she looks up into my bruised face.

"Fine," she sighs. "But if you're not going to sit in the wheelchair, at least humor me and sit in *that*."

I frown. "In what?"

She holds up a key fob and pushes the button. A car beeps.

"That."

Curious, I turn.

Holy. Shit.

My jaw drops a little, my eyes wide as I stare at the gleaming black 1980 Defender 110. It even has the Euro specs with the steering wheel on the right hand side.

Stunned, I turn back to her. "*What?*"

She grins. "Don't thank me. Thank Hades. He flew in some sort of Land Rover experts from the UK, and he's spent the last two weeks straight with the three of them rebuilding it."

I gape at her. "*This* is the one you blew up? That was in, like, fragments."

She blushes, rolling her eyes. "Yyyeah. But seriously, do *not* thank me—"

"Too bad." She giggles as I grab her, ignoring the pain in… well, everywhere…as I lean down and kiss her fiercely. "I'm going to anyway."

"Yeah, well," she shrugs casually. "I guess I *did* save your life."

"My hero," I murmur, pulling her into my arms. "How can I ever repay you?"

"You could…." She frowns thoughtfully. "Marry me? Again? For real?"

"Done and done. What else?"

She grins. "Take me back to our church, chase me around, and fuck me within an inch of my life?"

"Depends," I growl.

She rolls her eyes. "*On?*"

Bianca gasps quietly as I pull her into my arms. My lips brush her ear, and she jolts as I bite down hard on the soft skin of her neck.

"On if you're going to be a good little slut for me."

She whimpers. "*Always.*"

"In that case, yes. Anything else?"

She nods, her face flushed as her eyes lock on mine. "Yeah. Maybe you could…love me forever?"

"*Deal,*" I murmur, and my lips find hers.

. . .

The Venomous Gods series will continue with Drazen's story in *Monstrous Urges*.

Haven't gotten enough of Kratos and Bianca?
Get their extra scene here, or type this link into your browser: http://Bookhip.com/MNHCJHB

This isn't an epilogue or continuation to *Corrupted Heart*. But this extra hot "follow-up" story is guaranteed to keep the spice going.

ALSO BY JAGGER COLE

Venomous Gods:

Toxic Love

Devious Vow

Poisonous Kiss

Corrupted Heart

Monstrous Urges

Dark Hearts:

Deviant Hearts

Vicious Hearts

Sinful Hearts

Twisted Hearts

Stolen Hearts

Reckless Hearts

Kings & Villains:

Dark Kingdom

Burned Cinder (Cinder Duet #1)

Empire of Ash (Cinder Duet #2)

The Hunter King (Hunted Duet # 1)

The Hunted Queen (Hunted Duet #2)

Prince of Hate

Savage Heirs:

Savage Heir

Dark Prince

Brutal King

Forbidden Crown

Broken God

Defiant Queen

Bratva's Claim:

Paying The Bratva's Debt

The Bratva's Stolen Bride

Hunted By The Bratva Beast

His Captive Bratva Princess

Owned By The Bratva King

The Bratva's Locked Up Love

The Scaliami Crime Family:

The Hitman's Obsession

The Boss's Temptation

The Bodyguard's Weakness

Power:

Tyrant

Outlaw

Warlord

Standalones:

Broken Lines

Bosshole

Grumpaholic

Stalker of Mine

ABOUT THE AUTHOR

A reader first and foremost, Jagger Cole cut his romance writing teeth penning various steamy fan-fiction stories years ago. After deciding to hang up his writing boots, Jagger worked in advertising pretending to be Don Draper. It worked enough to convince a woman way out of his league to marry him, though, which is a total win.

Now, Dad to two little princesses and King to a Queen, Jagger is thrilled to be back at the keyboard.

When not writing or reading romance books, he can be found woodworking, enjoying good whiskey, and grilling outside - rain or shine.

You can find all of his books at
www.jaggercolewrites.com

f X ⊙